THE BLACK REAPER

COLLINS CHILLERS

· THE · BLACK ·
· REAPER ·

TALES OF TERROR BY
BERNARD CAPES

Edited, with an Introduction, by
HUGH LAMB

HarperCollins*Publishers*

HarperCollins*Publishers*
1 London Bridge Street
London SE1 9GF
www.harpercollins.co.uk

This edition 2017

First published in Great Britain
by Equation 1989

Foreword © Ian Burns 2017
Selection, introduction and notes © Hugh Lamb 2017

A catalogue record for this book
is available from the British Library

ISBN 978-0-00-824907-6

Typeset by Palimpsest Book Production Ltd, Falkirk, Stirlingshire

Printed and bound in the UK by CPI Group (UK) Ltd, Croydon, CR0 4YY

MIX
Paper from
responsible sources
FSC™ C007454

This book is produced from independently certified FSC™ paper
to ensure responsible forest management.

For more information visit: www.harpercollins.co.uk/green

CONTENTS

Foreword by Ian Burns   ix
Introduction by Hugh Lamb   xiii

The Black Reaper   3
The Vanishing House   14
The Thing in the Forest   20
The Accursed Cordonnier   23
The Shadow-Dance   56
William Tyrwhitt's 'Copy'   60
A Queer Cicerone   74
A Gallows-bird   82
The Sword of Corporal Lacoste   106
The Glass Ball   131
Poor Lucy Rivers   135
The Apothecary's Revenge   150
The Green Bottle   154
The Closed Door   168
The Dark Compartment   178
The Marble Hands   182
The Moon Stricken   185
The Queer Picture   209
Dark Dignum   213
The Mask   222

The Strength of the Rope 241
The White Hare 253
An Eddy on the Floor 256

Acknowledgements 295
Bibliography 297

To my good friends,
Steve Jones and Randy Broecker,
and happy times at the Shakespeare.

FOREWORD

These words are the culmination (so far, at least!) of a series of events which, together, tell a story that would have appealed hugely to Bernard Capes. It is a story of coincidences and timing, and the odd ounce or nanogram of good luck – all essential tools for an author. We could add, for the spookily-minded, a dash of the metaphysical to properly set the scene.

What made me go on to the Internet? Well, nothing other than ego: I wanted to see whether a book I'd written a few years ago could be purchased today. Without even a hint of surprise, it wasn't listed anywhere; so I proceeded, with little confidence, to look up my grandfather 'Bernard Capes'. And, lo! (I'm not sure why we use this expression, when we mean the exact opposite) there he was! Bernard E. Capes, *At a Winter's Fire*, 1969 – seventy years after it was first published. Why on earth would someone reissue a comprehensively-forgotten (I thought) author, and then not in his own country?

The journey had begun!

I then wrote, for the Amazon Books site, a brief piece about my grandfather which – lo! again – drew a response from John in Connecticut, who'd come across a single phrase in *Bloody Murder* by Julian Symons: '. . . Bernard Capes's neglected *tour de force The Skeleton Key*'.

Shortly after, I received an e-mail from Bruce in New York, who'd come across another Capes book that I didn't know of, and – yet another lo! – he sent me a photocopy of the introduction to the original 1989 edition of *The Black Reaper*, another book I hadn't heard of. It was a collection of short stories, and the editor was identified only as 'Hugh Lamb, Sutton, Surrey, England'.

This wasn't much to go on, but Lamb's words (I almost said 'tales') told me so much that I didn't know about my grandfather that I simply had to write to him. Indeed, until I read Hugh's introduction, which filled in many gaps, all I knew about my grandfather was that my mother had adored him, that he had quite a sense of humour, that he died in a 'flu epidemic twenty years before I was born, and that his work was peppered with peerless similes.

Would my letter reach Hugh Lamb? Would he still be alive? And would he reply?

Yes, my letter *was* delivered. Bless Royal Mail!

Yes, he was still alive. Bless . . . well someone!

And yes, he *did* reply. Bless Hugh!

In his introduction, Hugh talks about my grandfather's contrarian angel, and the bad luck he must have experienced, which led me somewhat to consider the parallels in our lives (his and mine). I've been fortunately deprived on the bad luck front and over-supplied on the good. However, bad luck is relative. To win second prize in a $30,000 competition at age forty-three, and first prize a year later, is luck of a kind that I would quite happily contribute half of my pension to receive! (From an Australian perspective, as well, being unable to breed rabbits would, to us, have been nearly as valuable as the Gold Rushes.)

The portrait of my grandfather that has been built up ought to give heart to other authors engaged in the eternal struggle to get published. Not many can say that they started at an age when many would have given up, and then actually had work published at an average rate of two books a year over a twenty-year period; and in fields ranging from poetry (two volumes) and history to detective stories, mysteries, romances, and – in numerous magazines – inventive tales of ghosts and other things which, deliciously, still go bump in the night.

Hugh speculates that Bernard probably had to bear his share of literary snobbery, but he might have had a bit of his own. His daughter (my mother) said that he made some disparaging remarks about authors of detective or crime stories – 'Anyone could write that sort of stuff' kind of thing – and was obviously called out by his publishers, William Collins. In something akin to petard and hoist, the result was *The Skeleton Key*, now recognised as the first original crime novel issued by that legendary publishing house.

My 1990s search for my name on the Internet – even before Google! – now brings up fourteen books, including *Four Hander: Paths to Murder*, which was directly inspired by HarperCollins re-issuing *The Mystery of the Skeleton Key* in 2015 and now *The Black Reaper*. Being the fourth generation in our family to have been published, it appears to me that there's something in this gene thing. Or maybe it's due to a clammy, twisting English Channel mist rolling its indefatigable, irresistible way through unsuspecting generations of veins across the Seven Seas and over more than a few black-cragged threatening mountain ranges . . .

And so, thanks to the Internet, some un-met friends in the States, two highly professional libraries (Sutton, England; Mercantile, New York), several happy coincidences, impeccable timing, Hugh Lamb, the oft-maligned postal service, several tons of good luck, and – above all – the spirits who inhabit those worlds so often visited by Bernard Capes, I commend to your reading this new edition of some of the work of my grandfather, (very) late of Winchester, England. I hope the old stories entertain you, and whip the odd tingle up your spine, more than a supernatural century since they were written. He would be amused.

Ian Burns
Melbourne
July 2017

INTRODUCTION

Literary fame seems almost like a lottery; ghost story writers in particular seem to pick losing tickets more than any other kind of author. It is an interesting exercise to ponder why certain authors and their works in this vein, just as well equipped to stand the test of time as their contemporaries, fall into speedy obscurity, while others stay in the public eye. The Victorian era is a fine example of this – for every tale of terror that has survived in print today, there are a hundred languishing in undeserved obscurity.

Bernard Capes is a case in point. During his writing career, he published forty-one books, contributed to all the leading Victorian magazines, and left behind some of the most imaginative tales of terror of his era – yet within ten years of his death, he had slipped down the familiar slope into total neglect. Until the early 1980s, Capes seldom appeared in reference works in this (or any other) field of literature, and even histories of Victorian writers published in his lifetime give him scant mention. He was overlooked by every anthologist in this genre from his death in 1918 right up until 1978: sixty years of lingering in the dark while many of his contemporaries were brought back to light.

I would place Capes among the most imaginative writers of his day. He turned out plot after plot worthy of the recognition accorded to such contemporaries as Stevenson, Haggard, and Conan Doyle, all of whom are still in print today. I hope this selection of his stories will help put Capes in his deserved position with the leading talents of Victorian fantasy.

Bernard Edward Joseph Capes was born in London on 30 August 1854, a nephew of John Moore Capes, a prominent figure in the Oxford Movement. He was educated at Beaumont College and brought up as a Catholic. His elder sister, Harriet Capes (1849–1936), was to become a noted translator and writer of children's books, publishing a dozen or more up to 1932.

As we will see, a very awkward angel perched on Capes's shoulder all his life, and made its presence felt at an early stage of his career. He was meant to go into the army; but somehow there was an almighty bureaucratic tangle, and his intended commission was not granted due to some mistake about the age he should have been when presenting himself for examination. There is no record as to why he did not pursue the matter further but the army career came to nothing.

Capes's awkward angel then accompanied him on the long string of ventures that he made into the world at large. After the army fiasco, he started work in a tea-broker's office. It must have been dreadfully dull – the tea business in the 1870s was not the most exciting field of human activity, and the young Capes must have endured it in silence until, after a few years, he packed it in and went to study art at the Slade School. What he did about an art career is not recorded; but we do know that in 1888 he went to work for the publishers Eglington and Co., and succeeded Clement Scott as editor of the journal *The Theatre*.

At this point in his career, he made his first attempts at novel writing, publishing two under the pseudonym 'Bevis Cane': *The Haunted Tower* (1888) and *The Missing Man* (1889), the latter being issued by Eglington. Presumably neither novel won him success, as 'Bevis Cane' never appeared again; and what was generally thought to have been his first novel –

under his own name – did not appear for another eight years.

Capes must have thought he had found his niche at last; this foray into writing was to spark off his final (and successful) career. But the angel was not finished yet. Eglington and Co. went out of business in 1892, and Capes must have been really stuck for an occupation to follow his editorship of *The Theatre*, for he is next discovered making an unsuccessful attempt at, of all things, rabbit farming. There is a dreadful black humour in the thought of a man who cannot successfully breed rabbits.

At long last, however, Capes, aged forty-three, found his true vocation. In 1897 he entered a competition for new authors organised by the *Chicago Record*. Capes came second with his novel *The Mill of Silence*, published in Chicago that year by Rand, McNally.

Obviously heartened by this turn of events, Capes entered the competition in 1898 when the *Chicago Record* repeated it. This time he hit the jackpot. His entry, *The Lake of Wine* – a long, sometimes quite macabre tale of a fabulous ruby bearing the title of the book – won the competition. It was published by Heinemann the same year, and Capes was a writer from then on.

And write he did. Out flooded short stories, articles, newspaper editorials, reviews, and novels. He published a further two in 1898 (including the book bearing one of the most unappetising titles of all time: *The Adventures of the Comte de la Muette During the Reign of Terror*). All through the early 1900s, with a four-book bulge in 1910, and right up through the First World War, Capes knocked out a couple of books every year.

Each novel took three months to write, working six hours a day, and Capes would take a month's holiday after finishing the book. He also played the piano and made games for his children. Another great interest was painting and illustrating.

When I met Ian Burns and Helen Capes in October 2002, they honoured me by showing me (and letting me hold!) a precious family heirloom – the only copy of Bernard's *The Book Of The Beasts*. Subtitled 'Being certain animals which through their own perversity or ill temper have become extinct', the book had been hand-made by Capes, written and illustrated with his own watercolours, for his children. It was fascinating. No wonder Renalt said of his father in 1982: 'Bernard was the nicest, kindest man I have ever known, and never had anything nasty to say about anybody at all.'

He wrote mainly novels, but every so often he issued a book of his stories collected from their various magazine appearances. The list of magazines he contributed to is impressive, and includes *Blackwood's, Cassell's, Cornhill, The Idler, Illustrated London News, Lippincott's, Macmillan's, Pall Mall* and *Pearson's*: a roll of honour of the finest magazines of the era.

In 1889, Bernard Capes married Rosalie Amos (1865–1949) and they moved from Streatham to Winchester, where he spent the rest of his life. Rosalie appears to have been some-thing of a domestic tyrant, handling the finances and running the household (vigorously, so it seems). Bernard must have been quite happy to concentrate on his writing. They had three children: Gareth (1893–1921), Nerine (1897–1967), and Renalt (1905–1983). Gareth had an army career (perhaps to make up for the one his father never had), while Renalt Capes (1905–1983) became, like his father, a writer late in life. He published three books in the late 1940s, including studies on Lord Nelson and Alexandre Dumas. He also wrote short stories, one of which was filmed as *Dual Alibi* (1946) with Herbert Lom. Nerine married Graham Burns and had an eventful time in the Second World War; Graham was later to be the last European killed in the Malayan emergency in 1952. Their son, Ian Burns, lives in Australia and carries on the Capes's writing tradition, as the author of the children's book *Scratcher* (1987) and many more since.

Bernard was very popular in Winchester and Renalt

recalled one incident which indicates why. He remembered the First Army, the 'contemptible little army' according to the Kaiser, on its way from Winchester to Southampton, there to go to France, at the beginning of the first world war. The soldiers marched past Bernard's house (for three days) and he set up tables outside, with coffee, sandwiches and cigarettes for the troops.

Even during his period of literary success, Bernard Capes's angel was never far away. With a new novel on the stocks (*The Skeleton Key*, published posthumously), Capes was struck down by the influenza epidemic which swept Europe at the end of the First World War. A short illness was followed by heart failure, and he died in Winchester on 1 November 1918. He was sixty-four, and had had only twenty years at writing. Capes's luck, as always, ran out at the wrong time.

Rosalie organised a plaque for him in Winchester Cathedral, among the likes of Izaak Walton and Jane Austen. It can still be seen, next to the entrance to the crypt.

He had earned enough of a reputation to merit an obituary in *The Times* on 4 November 1918. It called him a 'busy writer, and always a readable one . . . as he grew older, his style mellowed, for gifted as he was he took some time to find himself'; then added, in typically sniffy fashion, 'Nor were his *The Fabulists*, a collection of eerie tales, unworthy of him.' This fastidious approach to tales of terror is very familiar, even now; Capes probably had to bear his share of literary snobbery in his lifetime. Ghost stories are always treated as a poor relation by literary thinkers, although heaven knows why – they are one of the longest surviving branches of literature.

Capes received a less snooty obituary from *The New Witness*, which called him 'one of our most brilliant contributors'. It said of him that 'He had a very real genius for the supernatural, his ghost stories are among the best in the language. He had an eerie gift for touching on the very quick of horror and never spoilt a supernatural situation by the suggestion of materialism.'

Capes had also earned the enthusiasm of G.K. Chesterton, who wrote an introduction for Capes's posthumous *The Skeleton Key* (a fine detective novel). Chesterton said of Capes; 'It may seem a paradox to say that he was insufficiently appreciated because he did popular things well. But it is true to say that he always gave a touch of distinction to a detective story or a tale of adventure; and so gave it where it was not valued, because it was not expected.' Chesterton obviously knew about the sniffy tones of the day as well. He praised Capes's 'technical liberality of writing a penny-dreadful so as to make it worth a pound. In his short stories . . . he did indeed permit himself to be poetic in a more direct and serious fashion.' And it is those stories which concern us now.

Capes's imagination soared. He imagined the moon being the repository of lost souls ('The Moon Stricken'); the soul of a dead glassblower trapped in a bottle and released to terrorise a foolish investigator ('The Green Bottle'); a smuggler brought down by the man whose death he caused twenty years earlier ('Dark Dignum'); a werewolf priest in a grisly variation of 'Little Red Riding Hood' ('The Thing in the Forest'); a prison cell haunted by a dead man who makes the dust swirl constantly ('An Eddy on the Floor'); a suicide returning to teach his ne'er-do-well nephew a grisly lesson ('The Closed Door'); and a wicked ancestor who steps down from his portrait to give visitors a guided tour ('A Queer Cicerone'). He ranged from Napoleonic terrors to haunted typewriters; from marble hands which come to life to plague-stricken villagers haunted by a scythe-wielding ghost; from werewolves to the Wandering Jew. Bernard Capes rang the changes on tales of terror like very few writers of his day. It makes his neglect all the more surprising.

Of the tales in this book, nearly all appeared first in magazine form and were then collected into various books of short stories as Capes published them. Those from *The Fabulists* need some explanation. The shorter stories first appeared in *The New Witness*, and were tales told by four young men who decide to journey from village to village telling stories to earn their keep. They merely narrate the tales, without necessarily appearing in them; but the stories all bear the marks of a camp-fire yarn. As for the others, they stand up superbly on their own. Capes could hit the mark better than most.

We must never forget the sardonic angel on Capes's shoulder. When I reprinted a couple of these stories in *Tales from a Gas-Lit Graveyard* in 1979, I sent a copy of the volume to Robert Aickman, one of our foremost ghost story writers (his grandfather, Richard Marsh, was in the book as well). Aickman wrote back, commenting on the stories, and said this of Capes: 'His stories reveal the author's desperate frustration, an all too familiar property of the trade. He also uses words in a curious way at many places; as if he were writing under the influence of drink, as perhaps he was, when one considers his basic attitude.'

Intrigued by Aickman's insight (I had not told him of Capes's long record of failure), I asked him to elaborate for the benefit of this book when it finally appeared. His reply deserves reprinting:

Consider the opening paragraph and second paragraph in 'The Green Bottle'. When Capes describes himself as 'happening to be grinding his literary barrel organ – always adaptable to the popular need', this is not character drawing but an expression of rueful awareness that the words are largely true. Similarly, the contempt expressed for Sewell is partly self contempt and partly contempt for the awful people one has to mix with in the awful trade of popular authorship. Thus again with the first paragraph of 'An Eddy on the Floor'; these words do not even pretend to be in character. They are

Capes speaking. No man who sees himself as even reasonably content or fulfilled writes like this. The entire atmosphere is saturated with disappointment, disillusionment, and despair. None of this means that Capes's stories are without good qualities. Still less does it mean that Capes was necessarily justified in his apparent estimate of his powers and deserts. Least of all does it mean that you have to accept a word I say on the subject.

Anyone who knew Robert Aickman would accept his word on this like a shot. Aickman did his fair share of research into ghost stories and knew his authors well.

If you examine Capes's tales, you won't find any conventional heroes or conventional happy endings. His protagonists wander into situations or are obliged to take action almost by default, while suffering humanity gets short shrift as well. He also seems to reserve harsh fates for gentlemen of the press – consider 'The Green Bottle', 'An Eddy on the Floor', or 'William Tyrwhitt's "Copy"'. Capes hardly needed to populate the moon with lost souls – he sends them wandering blindly through the pages of his stories down here on earth.

Perhaps it is his basic pessimism that gives Capes's stories their undoubted power. Few authors from the time conjured up such dark canvasses as he paints in 'A Gallows-bird' or 'The Sword of Corporal Lacoste'. However, this dark vision never seemed to extend to his novels, which are often lighter, less grim, historical follies. *The Pot of Basil* (1913), for instance, is an airy, whimsical piece about eighteenth century court life in Italy – a long way from the grinding horror of 'A Gallows-bird'. And the lovers in *The Story of Fifine* (1914) are in a world far removed from the blossoming courtship we see outlined in 'The Accursed Cordonnier'.

Capes soon passed into the neglect so common in this field. After *The Skeleton Key* was published in 1919, nothing more appeared in Britain until a couple of re-issues in 1928 and 1929 – and then that was it. His neglect over the years is strange indeed, especially when other authors from the same era are reprinted mercilessly.

I hope that this new edition of *The Black Reaper* will bring Bernard Capes back into the eye of the ghost story enthusiast, and a wider public. He deserves reprinting and a second chance. We must hope that his usual bad luck died with him.

Hugh Lamb
Sutton, Surrey
February 2017

THE BLACK REAPER

THE BLACK REAPER

*Taken from the Q— Register of Local Events,
as Compiled from Authentic Narratives*

Now I am to tell you of a thing that befell in the year 1665
of the Great Plague, when the hearts of certain amongst men,
grown callous in wickedness upon that rebound from an
inhuman austerity, were opened to the vision of a terror that
moved and spoke not in the silent places of the fields.
Forasmuch as, however, in the recovery from delirium a
patient may marvel over the incredulity of neighbours who
refuse to give credence to the presentments that have been
ipso facto to him, so, the nation being sound again, and its
constitution hale, I expect little but a laugh for my piety in
relating of the following incident; which, nevertheless, is as
essential true as that he who shall look through the knot-
hole in the plank of a coffin shall acquire the evil eye.

For, indeed, in those days of a wild fear and confusion,
when every condition that maketh for reason was set wandering
by a devious path, and all men sitting as in a theatre of death
looked to see the curtain rise upon God knows what horrors,
it was vouchsafed to many to witness sights and sounds beyond
the compass of Nature, and that as if the devil and his minions
had profited by the anarchy to slip unobserved into the world.
And I know that this is so, for all the insolence of a recovered
scepticism; and, as to the unseen, we are like one that traverseth

the dark with a lanthorn, himself the skipper of a little moving blot of light, but a positive mark for any secret foe without the circumference of its radiance.

Be that as it may, and whether it was our particular ill-fortune, or, as some asserted, our particular wickedness, that made of our village an inviting back-door of entrance to the Prince of Darkness, I know not; but so it is that disease and contagion are ever inclined to penetrate by way of flaws or humours where the veil of the flesh is already perforated, as a kite circleth round its quarry, looking for the weak place to strike: and, without doubt, in that land of corruption we were a very foul blot indeed.

How this came about it were idle to speculate; yet no man shall have the hardihood to affirm that it was otherwise. Nor do I seek to extenuate myself, who was in truth no better than my neighbours in most that made us a community of drunkards and forswearers both lewd and abominable. For in that village a depravity that was like madness had come to possess the heads of the people, and no man durst take his stand on honesty or even common decency, for fear he should be set upon by his comrades and drummed out of his government on a pint pot. Yet for myself I will say was one only redeeming quality, and that was the pure love I bore to my solitary orphaned child, the little Margery.

Now, our vicar – a patient and God-fearing man, for all his predial tithes were impropriated by his lord, that was an absentee and a sheriff in London – did little to stem that current of lewdness that had set in strong with the Restoration. And this was from no lack of virtue in himself, but rather from a natural invertebracy, as one may say, and an order of mind that, yet being no order, is made the sport of any sophister with a wit for paragram. Thus it always is that mere example is of little avail without precept – of which, however, it is an important condition – and that the successful directors of men be not those who go to the van and lead, unconscious of the gibes and mockery in their rear, but such rather as drive the mob before them with a smiting hand and no infirmity of purpose. So, if a certain affection for our pastor dwelt in our hearts, no tittle of respect was there to leaven it and justify his high office before Him that consigned the trust; and ever deeper and deeper we sank in the slough of corruption, until was brought about this pass – that naught but some scourging despotism of the Church should acquit us of the fate of Sodom. That such, at the eleventh hour, was vouchsafed us of God's mercy, it is my purpose to show; and, doubtless, this offering of a loop-hole was to account by reason of the devil's having debarked his reserves, as it were, in our port; and so quartering upon us a soldiery that we were, at no invitation of our own, to maintain, stood us a certain extenuation.

It was late in the order of things before in our village so much as a rumour of the plague reached us. Newspapers were not in those days, and reports, being by word of mouth, travelled slowly, and were often spent bullets by the time they fell amongst us. Yet, by May, some gossip there was of the distemper having gotten a hold in certain quarters of London and increasing, and this alarmed our people, though it made no abatement of their profligacy. But presently the reports coming thicker, with confirmation of the terror and panic that was enlarging on all sides, we must take measures for our safety; though into June and July, when the pestilence was raging, none infected had come our way, and that from our remote and isolated position. Yet it needs but fear for the crown to that wickedness that is self-indulgence; and forasmuch as this fear fattens like a toadstool on the decomposition it springs from, it grew with us to the proportions that we were set to kill or destroy any that should approach us from the stricken districts.

And then suddenly there appeared in our midst *he* that was appointed to be our scourge and our cautery.

Whence he came, or how, no man of us could say. Only one day we were a community of roysterers and scoffers, impious and abominable, and the next he was amongst us smiting and thundering.

Some would have it that he was an old collegiate of our vicar's, but at last one of those wandering Dissenters that found never as now the times opportune to their teachings – a theory to which our minister's treatment of the stranger gave colour. For from the moment of his appearance he took the reins of government, as it were, appropriating the pulpit and launching his bolts therefrom, with the full consent and encouragement of the other. There were those, again, who were resolved that his commission was from a high place, whither news of our infamy had reached, and that we had best give him a respectful hearing, lest we should run a chance of having our hearing stopped altogether. A few were convinced he was no man at all, but rather a fiend sent to thresh us with the scourge of our own contriving, that we might be tender, like steak, for the cooking; and yet other few regarded him with terror, as an actual figure or embodiment of the distemper.

But, generally, after the first surprise, the feeling of resentment at his intrusion woke and gained ground, and we were much put about that he should have thus assumed the pastorship without invitation, quartering with our vicar, who kept himself aloof and was little seen, and seeking to drive us by terror, and amazement, and a great menace of retribution. For, in truth, this was not the method to which we were wont, and it both angered and disturbed us.

This feeling would have enlarged the sooner, perhaps, were it not for a certain restraining influence possessed of the newcomer, which neighboured him with darkness and mystery. For he was above the common tall, and ever appeared in public with a slouched hat, that concealed all the upper part of his face and showed little otherwise but the dense black beard that dropped upon his breast like a shadow.

Now with August came a fresh burst of panic, how the desolation increased and the land was overrun with swarms of infected persons seeking an asylum from the city; and our anger rose high against the stranger, who yet dwelt with us and encouraged the distemper of our minds by furious denunciations of our guilt.

Thus far, for all the corruption of our hearts, we had maintained the practice of church-going, thinking, maybe, poor fools! to hoodwink the Almighty with a show of reverence; but now, as by a common consent, we neglected the observances and loitered of a Sabbath in the fields, and thither at the last the strange man pursued us and ended the matter.

For so it fell that at the time of the harvest's ripening a goodish body of us males was gathered one Sunday for coolness about the neighbourhood of the dripping well, whose waters were a tradition, for they had long gone dry. This well was situate in a sort of cave or deep scoop at the foot of a cliff of limestone, to which the cultivated ground that led up to it fell somewhat. High above, the cliff broke away into a wide stretch of pasture land, but the face of the rock itself was all patched with bramble and little starved birch trees clutching for foothold; and in like manner the excavation beneath was half-stifled and gloomed over with undergrowth, so that it looked a place very dismal and uninviting, save in the ardour of the dog-days.

Within, where had been the basin, was a great shattered hole going down to unknown depths; and this no man had thought to explore, for a mystery held about the spot that was doubtless the foster-child of ignorance.

But to the front of the well and of the cliff stretched a noble field of corn, and this field was of an uncommon shape, being, roughly, a vast circle and a little one joined by a neck and in suggestion not unlike an hour-glass; and into the crop thereof, which was of goodly weight and condition, were the first sickles to be put on the morrow.

Now as we stood or lay around, idly discussing of the news, and congratulating ourselves that we were for once quit of our incubus, to us along the meadow path, his shadow jumping on the corn, came the very subject of our gossip.

He strode up, looking neither to right nor left, and with the first word that fell, low and damnatory, from his lips, we knew that the moment had come when, whether for good or evil, he intended to cast us from him and acquit himself of further responsibility in our direction.

'Behold!' he cried, pausing over against us, 'I go from among ye! Behold, ye that have not obeyed nor inclined your ear, but have walked everyone in the imagination of his evil heart! Saith the Lord, "I will bring evil upon them, which they shall not be able to escape; and though they shall cry unto Me, I will not hearken unto them."'

His voice rang out, and a dark silence fell among us. It was pregnant, but with little of humility. We had had enough of this interloper and his abuse. Then, like Jeremiah, he went to prophesy:

'I read ye, men of Anathoth, and the murder in your hearts. Ye that have worshipped the shameful thing and burned incense to Baal – shall I cringe that ye devise against me, or not rather pray to the Lord of Hosts, "Let me see Thy vengeance on them"? And he answereth, "I will bring evil upon the men of Anathoth, even the year of their visitation."'

Now, though I was no participator in that direful thing that followed, I stood by, nor interfered, and so must share the blame. For there were men risen all about, and their faces lowering, and it seemed that it would go hard with the stranger were he not more particular.

But he moved forward, with a stately and commanding gesture, and stood with his back to the well-scoop and threatened us and spoke.

'Lo!' he shrieked, 'your hour is upon you! Ye shall be mowed down like ripe corn, and the shadow of your name shall be swept from the earth! The glass of your iniquity is turned, and when its sand is run through, not a man of ye shall be!'

He raised his arm aloft, and in a moment he was overborne. Even then, as all say, none got sight of his face; but he fought with lowered head, and his black beard flapped like a wounded crow. But suddenly a boy-child ran forward of the bystanders, crying and screaming—

'Hurt him not! They are hurting him – oh, me! oh, me!'

And from the sweat and struggle came his voice, gasping, 'I spare the little children!'

Then only I know of the surge and the crash towards the well-mouth, of an instant cessation of motion, and immediately of men toiling hither and thither with boulders and huge blocks, which they piled over the rent, and so sealed it with a cromlech of stone.

That, in the heat of rage and of terror, we had gone further than we had at first designed, our gloom and our silence on the morrow attested. True we were quit of our incubus, but on such terms as not even the severity of the times could excuse. For the man had but chastised us to our improvement; and to destroy the scourge is not to condone the offence. For myself, as I bore up the little Margery to my shoulder on my way to the reaping, I felt the burden of guilt so great as that I found myself muttering of an apology to the Lord that I durst put myself into touch with innocence. 'But the walk would fatigue her otherwise,' I murmured; and, when we were come to the field, I took and carried her into the upper or little meadow, out of reach of the scythes, and placed her to sleep amongst the corn, and so left her with a groan.

But when I was come anew to my comrades, who stood at the lower extremity of the field – and this was the bottom of the hour-glass, so to speak – I was aware of a stir amongst them, and, advancing closer, that they were all intent upon the neighbourhood of the field I had left, staring like distraught creatures, and holding well together, as if in a panic. Therefore, following the direction of their eyes, and of one that pointed with rigid finger, I turned me about, and looked whence I had come; and my heart went with a somersault, and in a moment I was all sick and dazed.

For I saw, at the upper curve of the meadow, where the well lay in gloom, that a man had sprung out of the earth, as it seemed, and was started reaping; and the face of this man was all in shadow, from which his beard ran out and down like a stream of gall.

He reaped swiftly and steadily, swinging like a pendulum; but, though the sheaves fell to him right and left, no swish of the scythe came to us, nor any sound but the beating of our own hearts.

Now, from the first moment of my looking, no doubt was in my lost soul but that this was him we had destroyed come back to verify his prophecy in ministering to the vengeance of the Lord of Hosts; and at the thought a deep groan rent my bosom, and was echoed by those about me. But scarcely was it issued when a second terror smote me as that I near reeled. Margery – my babe! put to sleep there in the path of the Black Reaper!

At that, though they called to me, I sprang forward like a madman, and running along the meadow, through the neck of the glass, reached the little thing, and stooped and snatched her into my arms. She was sound and unfrighted, as I felt with a burst of thankfulness; but, looking about me, as I turned again to fly, I had near dropped in my tracks for the sickness and horror I experienced in the nearer neighbourhood of the apparition. For, though it never raised its head, or changed the steady swing of its shoulders, I knew that it was aware of and was *reaping at me*. Now, I tell you, it was ten yards away, yet the point of the scythe came gliding upon me silently, like a snake, through the stalks, and at that I screamed out and ran for my life.

I escaped, sweating with terror; but when I was sped back to the men, there was all the village collected, and our vicar to the front, praying from a throat that rattled like a dead leaf in a draught. I know not what he said, for the low cries of the women filled the air; but his face was white as a smock, and his fingers writhed in one another like a knot of worms.

'The plague is upon us!' they wailed. 'We shall be mowed down like ripe corn!'

And even as they shrieked the Black Reaper paused, and,

putting away his scythe, stooped and gathered up a sheaf in his arms and stood it on end. And, with the very act, a man – one that had been forward in yesterday's business – fell down amongst us yelling and foaming; and he rent his breast in his frenzy, revealing the purple blot thereon, and he passed blaspheming. And the reaper stooped and stooped again, and with every sheaf he gathered together one of us fell stricken and rolled in his agony, while the rest stood by palsied.

But, when at length all that was cut was accounted for, and a dozen of us were gone each to his judgment, and he had taken up his scythe to reap anew, a wild fury woke in the breasts of some of the more abandoned and reckless amongst us.

'It is not to be tolerated!' they cried. 'Let us at once fire the corn and burn this sorcerer!'

And with that, some five or six of them, emboldened by despair, ran up into the little field, and, separating, had out each his flint and fired the crop in his own place, and retreated to the narrow part for safety.

Now the reaper rested on his scythe, as if unexpectedly acquitted of a part of his labour; but the corn flamed up in these five or six directions, and was consumed in each to the compass of a single sheaf: whereat the fire died away. And with its dying the faces of those that had ventured went black as coal; and they flung up their arms, screaming, and fell prone where they stood, and were hidden from our view.

Then, indeed, despair seized upon all of us that survived, and we made no doubt but that we were to be exterminated and wiped from the earth for our sins, as were the men of Anathoth. And for an hour the Black Reaper mowed and trussed, till he had cut all from the little upper field and was approached to the neck of juncture with the lower and larger. And before us that remained, and who were drawn back amongst the trees, weeping and praying, a fifth of our comrades lay foul, and dead, and sweltering, and all blotched over with the dreadful mark of the pestilence.

Now, as I say, the reaper was nearing the neck of juncture; and so we knew that if he should once pass into the great field towards us and continue his mowing, not one of us should be left to give earnest of our repentance.

Then, as it seemed, our vicar came to a resolution, moving forward with a face all wrapt and entranced; and he strode up the meadow path and approached the apparition, and stretched out his arms to it entreating. And we saw the other pause, awaiting him; and, as he came near, put forth his hand, and so, gently, on the good old head. But as we looked, catching at our breaths with a little pathos of hope, the priestly face was thrown back radiant, and the figure of him that would give his life for us sank amongst the yet standing corn and disappeared from our sight.

So at last we yielded ourselves fully to our despair; for if our pastor should find no mercy, what possibility of it could be for us!

It was in this moment of an uttermost grief and horror, when each stood apart from his neighbour, fearing the contamination of his presence, that there was vouchsafed to me, of God's pity, a wild and sudden inspiration. Still to my neck fastened the little Margery – not frighted, it seemed, but mazed – and other babes there were in plenty, that clung to their mothers' skirts and peeped out, wondering at the strange show.

I ran to the front and shrieked: 'The children! the children! He will not touch the little children! Bring them and set them in his path!' And so crying I sped to the neck of the meadow, and loosened the soft arms from my throat, and put the little one down within the corn.

Now at once the women saw what I would be at, and full a score of them snatched up their babes and followed me. And here we were reckless for ourselves; but we knelt the innocents in one close line across the neck of land, so that the Black Reaper should not find space between any of them to swing his scythe. And having done this, we fell back with our hearts bubbling in our breasts, and we stood panting and watched.

He had paused over that one full sheaf of his reaping; but now, with the sound of the women's running, he seized his weapon again and set to upon the narrow belt of corn that yet separated him from the children. But presently, coming out upon the tender array, his scythe stopped and trailed in his hand, and for a full minute he stood like a figure of stone. Then thrice he walked slowly backwards and forwards along the line, seeking for an interval whereby he might pass; and the children laughed at him like silver bells, showing no fear, and perchance meeting that of love in his eyes that was hidden from us.

Then of a sudden he came to before the midmost of the line, and, while we drew our breath like dying souls, stooped and snapped his blade across his knee, and, holding the two parts in his hand, turned and strode back into the shadow of the dripping well. There arrived, he paused once more, and, twisting him about, waved his hand once to us and vanished into the blackness. But there were those who affirmed that in that instant of his turning, his face was revealed, and that it was a face radiant and beautiful as an angel's.

Such is the history of the wild judgment that befell us, and by grace of the little children was foregone; and such was the stranger whose name no man ever heard tell, but whom many have since sought to identify with that spirit of the pestilence that entered into men's hearts and confounded them, so that they saw visions and were afterwards confused in their memories.

But this I may say, that when at last our courage would fetch us to that little field of death, we found it to be all blackened and blasted, so as nothing would take root there then or ever since; and it was as if, after all the golden sand of the hour-glass was run away and the lives of the most impious with it, the destroyer saw fit to stay his hand for sake of the babes that he had pronounced innocent, and for such as were spared to witness to His judgment. And this I do here, with a heart as contrite as if it were the morrow of the visitation, the which with me it ever has remained.

THE VANISHING HOUSE

'My grandfather,' said the banjo, 'drank "dog's-nose", my father drank "dog's-nose", and I drink "dog's-nose". If that ain't heredity, there's no virtue in the board schools.'

'Ah!' said the piccolo, 'you're always a-boasting of your science. And so, I suppose, your son'll drink "dog's-nose", too?'

'No,' retorted the banjo, with a rumbling laugh, like wind in the bung-hole of an empty cask; 'for I ain't got none. The family ends with me; which is a pity, for I'm a full-stop to be proud on.'

He was an enormous, tun-bellied person – a mere mound of expressionless flesh, whose size alone was an investment that paid a perpetual dividend of laughter. When, as with the rest of his company, his face was blackened, it looked like a specimen coal on a pedestal in a museum.

There was Christmas company in the Good Intent, and the sanded tap-room, with its trestle tables and sprigs of holly stuck under sooty beams, reeked with smoke and the steam of hot gin and water.

'How much could you put down of a night, Jack?' said a little grinning man by the door.

'Why,' said the banjo, 'enough to lay the dustiest ghost as ever walked.'

'*Could* you, now?' said the little man.

'Ah!' said the banjo, chuckling. 'There's nothing like settin'

one sperit to lay another; and there I could give you proof
number two of heredity.'

'What! Don't you go for to say you ever see'd a ghost?'

'Haven't I? What are you whisperin' about, you blushful
chap there by the winder?'

'I was only remarkin', sir, 'twere snawin' like the devil!'

'*Is* it? Then the devil has been misjudged these eighteen
hundred and ninety odd years.'

'But *did* you ever see a ghost?' said the little grinning man,
pursuing his subject.

'No, I didn't, sir,' mimicked the banjo, 'saving in coffee
grounds. But my grandfather in *his* cups see'd one; which
brings us to number three in the matter of heredity.'

'Give us the story, Jack,' said the 'bones', whose agued
shins were extemporising a rattle on their own account before
the fire.

'Well, I don't mind,' said the fat man. 'It's seasonable; and
I'm seasonable, like the blessed plum-pudden, I am; and the
more burnt brandy you set about me, the richer and headier
I'll go down.'

'You'd be a jolly old pudden to digest,' said the piccolo.

'You blow your aggrawation into your pipe and sealing-wax
the stops,' said his friend.

He drew critically at his 'churchwarden' a moment or so,
leaned forward, emptied his glass into his capacious recep-
tacles, and, giving his stomach a shift, as if to accommodate
it to its new burden, proceeded as follows:

'Music and malt is my nat'ral inheritance. My grandfather
blew his "dog's-nose", and drank his clarinet like a artist; and
my father—'

'What did you say your grandfather did?' asked the piccolo.

'He played the clarinet.'

'You said he blew his "dog's-nose".'

'Don't be an ass, Fred!' said the banjo, aggrieved. 'How
the blazes could a man blow his dog's nose, unless he muzzled
it with a handkercher, and then twisted its tail? He played

the clarinet, I say; and my father played the musical glasses, which was a form of harmony pertiklerly genial to him. Amongst us we've piped out a good long century – ah! we have, for all I look sich a babby bursting on sops and spoon meat.'

'What!' said the little man by the door. 'You don't include them cockt hatses in your experience?'

'My grandfather wore 'em, sir. He wore a play-actin' coat, too, and buckles to his shoes, when he'd got any; and he and a friend or two made a permanency of "waits" (only they called 'em according to the season), and got their profit goin' from house to house, principally in the country, and discoursin' music at the low rate of whatever they could get for it.'

'Ain't you comin' to the ghost, Jack?' said the little man hungrily.

'All in course, sir. Well, gentlemen, it was hard times pretty often with my grandfather and his friends, as you may suppose; and never so much as when they had to trudge it across country, with the nor'-easter buzzin' in their teeth and the snow piled on their cockt hats like lemon sponge on entry dishes. The rewards, I've heard him say – for he lived to be ninety, nevertheless – was poor compensation for the drifts, and the influenza, and the broken chilblains; but now and again they'd get a fair skinful of liquor from a jolly squire, as 'd set 'em up like boggarts mended wi' new broomsticks.'

'Ho-haw!' broke in a hurdle-maker in a corner; and then, regretting the publicity of his merriment, put his fingers bashfully to his stubble lips.

'Now,' said the banjo, 'it's of a pertikler night and a pertikler skinful that I'm a-going to tell you; and that night fell dark, and that skinful were took a hundred years ago this December, as I'm a Jack-pudden!'

He paused for a moment for effect, before he went on:

'They were down in the sou'-west country, which they little knew; and were anighing Winchester city, or should 'a' been. But they got muzzed on the ungodly downs, and before they guessed, they was off the track. My good hat! there they was, as lost in the snow as three nut-shells a-sinkin' into a hasty pudden. Well, they wandered round; pretty confident at first, but getting madder and madder as every sense of their bearings slipped from them. And the bitter cold took their vitals, so they saw nothing but a great winding sheet stretched abroad for to wrap their dead carcasses in.

'At last my grandfather he stopt and pulled hisself together with an awful face, and says he: "We're Christmas pie for the carrying-on crows if we don't prove ourselves human. Let's fetch our pipes and blow our trouble into 'em." So they stood together, like as if they were before a house, and they played "Kate of Aberdare" mighty dismal and flat, for their fingers froze to the keys.

'Now, I tell you, they hadn't climbed over the first stave, when there come a skirl of wind and spindrift of snow as almost took them off their feet; and, on the going down of it, Jem Sloke, as played the hautboy, dropped the reed from his mouth, and called out, "Sakes alive! if we fools ain't been standin' outside a gentleman's gate all the time, and not knowin' it!"

'You might 'a' knocked the three of 'em down wi' a barley straw, as they stared and stared, and then fell into a low, enjoyin' laugh. For they was standin' not six fut from a tall iron gate in a stone wall, and behind these was a great house showin' out dim, with the winders all lighted up.

'"Lord!" chuckled my grandfather, "to think o' the tricks o' this vagarious country! But, as we're here, we'll go on and give 'em a taste of our quality."

'They put new heart into the next movement, as you may guess; and they hadn't fair started on it, when the door of the house swung open, and down the shaft of light that shot out as far as the gate there come a smiling young gal, with a tray of glasses in her hands.

'Now she come to the bars; and she took and put a glass

through, not sayin' nothin', but invitin' someone to drink with a silent laugh.

'Did anyone take that glass? Of course he did, you'll be thinkin'; and you'll be thinkin' wrong. Not a man of the three moved. They was struck like as stone, and their lips was gone the colour of sloe berries. Not a man took the glass. For why? The moment the gal presented it, each saw the face of a thing lookin' out of the winder over the porch, and the face was hidjus beyond words, and the shadder of it, with the light behind, stretched out and reached to the gal, and made her hidjus, too.

'At last my grandfather give a groan and put out his hand; and, as he did it, the face went, and the gal was beautiful to see agen.

'"Death and the devil!" said he. "It's one or both, either way; and I prefer 'em hot to cold!"

'He drank off half the glass, smacked his lips, and stood staring a moment.

'"Dear, dear!" said the gal, in a voice like falling water, "you've drunk blood, sir!"

'My grandfather gave a yell, slapped the rest of the liquor in the faces of his friends, and threw the cup agen the bars. It broke with a noise like thunder, and at that he up'd with his hands and fell full length into the snow.'

There was a pause. The little man by the door was twisting nervously in his chair.

'He came to – of course, he came to?' said he at length.

'He come to,' said the banjo solemnly, 'in the bitter break of dawn; that is, he come to as much of hisself as he ever was after. He give a squiggle and lifted his head; and there was he and his friends a-lyin' on the snow of the high downs.'

'And the house and the gal?'

'Narry a sign of either, sir, but just the sky and the white stretch; and one other thing.'

'And what was that?'

'A stain of red sunk in where the cup had spilt.'

There was a second pause, and the banjo blew into the bowl of his pipe.

'They cleared out of that neighbourhood double quick, you'll bet,' said he. 'But my grandfather was never the same man agen. His face took purple, while his friends' only remained splashed with red, same as birth marks; and, I tell you, if ever he ventur'd upon "Kate of Aberdare", his cheeks swelled up to the reed of his clarinet, like as a blue plum on a stalk. And forty years after, he died of what they call solution of blood to the brain.'

'And you can't have better proof than that,' said the little man.

'That's what *I* say,' said the banjo. 'Next player, gentlemen, please.'

THE THING IN THE FOREST

Into the snow-locked forests of Upper Hungary steal wolves in winter; but there is a footfall worse than theirs to knock upon the heart of the lonely traveller.

One December evening Elspet, the young, newly wedded wife of the woodman Stefan, came hurrying over the lower slopes of the White Mountains from the town where she had been all day marketing. She carried a basket with provisions on her arm; her plump cheeks were like a couple of cold apples; her breath spoke short, but more from nervousness than exhaustion. It was nearing dusk, and she was glad to see the little lonely church in the hollow below, the hub, as it were, of many radiating paths through the trees, one of which was the road to her own warm cottage yet a half-mile away.

She paused a moment at the foot of the slope, undecided about entering the little chill, silent building and making her plea for protection to the great battered stone image of Our Lady of Succour which stood within by the confessional box; but the stillness and the growing darkness decided her, and she went on. A spark of fire glowing through the presbytery window seemed to repel rather than attract her, and she was glad when the convolutions of the path hid it from her sight. Being new to the district, she had seen very little of Father Ruhl as yet, and somehow the penetrating knowledge and burning eyes of the pastor made her feel uncomfortable.

The soft drift, the lane of tall, motionless pines, stretched on in a quiet like death. Somewhere the sun, like a dead fire, had fallen into opalescent embers faintly luminous: they were enough only to touch the shadows with a ghastlier pallor. It was so still that the light crunch in the snow of the girl's own footfalls trod on her heart like a desecration.

Suddenly there was something near her that had not been before. It had come like a shadow, without more sound or warning. It was here – there – behind her. She turned, in mortal panic, and saw a wolf. With a strangled cry and trembling limbs she strove to hurry on her way; and always she knew, though there was no whisper of pursuit, that the gliding shadow followed in her wake. Desperate in her terror, she stopped once more and faced it.

A wolf! – was it a wolf? O who could doubt it! Yet the wild expression in those famished eyes, so lost, so pitiful, so mingled of insatiable hunger and human need! Condemned, for its unspeakable sins, to take this form with sunset, and so howl and snuffle about the doors of men until the blessed day released it. A werewolf – not a wolf.

That terrific realisation of the truth smote the girl as with a knife out of darkness: for an instant she came near fainting. And then a low moan broke into her heart and flooded it with pity. So lost, so infinitely hopeless. And so pitiful – yes, in spite of all, so pitiful. It had sinned, beyond any sinning that her innocence knew or her experience could gauge; but she was a woman, very blest, very happy, in her store of comforts and her surety of love. She knew that it was forbidden to succour these damned and nameless outcasts, to help or sympathise with them in any way. But—

There was good store of meat in her basket, and who need ever know or tell? With shaking hands she found and threw a sop to the desolate brute – then, turning, sped upon her way.

But at home her secret sin stood up before her, and, interposing between her husband and herself, threw its shadow upon both their faces. What had she dared – what done? By her own act forfeited her birthright of innocence; by her own act placed herself in the power of the evil to which she had ministered. All that night she lay in shame and horror, and all the next day, until Stefan had come about his dinner and gone again, she moved in a dumb agony. Then, driven unendurably by the memory of his troubled, bewildered face, as twilight threatened she put on her cloak and went down to the little church in the hollow to confess her sin.

'Mother, forgive, and save me,' she whispered, as she passed the statue.

After ringing the bell for the confessor, she had not knelt long at the confessional box in the dim chapel, cold and empty as a waiting vault, when the chancel rail clicked, and the footsteps of Father Ruhl were heard rustling over the stones. He came, he took his seat behind the grating; and, with many sighs and falterings, Elspet avowed her guilt. And as, with bowed head, she ended, a strange sound answered her – it was like a little laugh, and yet not so much like a laugh as a snarl. With a shock as of death she raised her face. It was Father Ruhl who sat there – and yet it was not Father Ruhl. In that time of twilight his face was already changing, narrowing, becoming wolfish – the eyes rounded and the jaw slavered. She gasped, and shrunk back; and at that, barking and snapping at the grating, with a wicked look he dropped – and she heard him coming. Sheer horror lent her wings. With a scream she sprang to her feet and fled. Her cloak caught in something – there was a wrench and crash and, like a flood, oblivion overswept her.

It was the old deaf and near senile sacristan who found them lying there, the woman unhurt but insensible, the priest crushed out of life by the fall of the ancient statue, long tottering to its collapse. She recovered, for her part: for his, no one knows where he lies buried. But there were dark stories of a baying pack that night, and of an empty, blood-stained pavement when they came to seek for the body.

THE ACCURSED CORDONNIER

I

*Poor Chrymelus, I remember, arose from the diversion of
a card-table, and dropped into the dwellings of darkness.*

Hervey

It must be confessed that Amos Rose was considerably out of
his element in the smoking-room off Portland Place. All the
hour he remained there he was conscious of a vague rising
nausea, due not in the least to the visible atmosphere – to
which, indeed, he himself contributed languorously from a
crackling spilliken of South American tobacco rolled in a maize
leaf and strongly tinctured with opium – but to the almost
brutal post-prandial facundity of its occupants.

Rose was patently a degenerate. Nature, in scheduling his
characteristics, had pruned all superlatives. The rude armour
of the flesh, under which the spiritual, like a hide-bound
chrysalis, should develop secret and self-contained, was
perished in his case, as it were, to a semi-opaque suit, through
which his soul gazed dimly and fearfully on its monstrous
arbitrary surroundings. Not the mantle of the poet, philosopher, or artist fallen upon such, can still its shiverings, or give
the comfort that Nature denies.

Yet he was a little bit of each – poet, philosopher, and artist;
a nerveless and self-deprecatory stalker of ideals, in the pursuit

of which he would wear patent leather shoes and all the apologetic graces. The grandson of a 'three-bottle' JP, who had upheld the dignity of the State constitution while abusing his own in the best spirit of squirearchy; the son of a petulant dyspeptic, who alternated seizures of long moroseness with fits of abject moral helplessness, Amos found his inheritance in the reversion of a dissipated constitution, and an imagination as sensitive as an exposed nerve. Before he was thirty he was a neurasthenic so practised, as to have learned a sense of luxury in the very consciousness of his own suffering. It was a negative evolution from the instinct of self-protection – self-protection, as designed in this case, against the attacks of the unspeakable. Another evolution, only less negative, was of a certain desperate pugnacity, that derived from a sense of the inhuman injustice conveyed in the fact that temperamental debility not only debarred him from that bold and healthy expression of self that it was his nature to wish, but made him actually appear to act in contradiction to his own really sweet and sound predilections.

So he sat (in the present instance, listening and revolting) in a travesty of resignation between the stools of submission and defiance.

The neurotic youth of today renews no ante-existent type. You will look in vain for a face like Amos's amongst the busts of the recovered past. The same weakness of outline you may point to – the sheep-like features falling to a blunt prow; the lax jaw and pinched temples – but not to that which expresses a consciousness that combative effort in a world of fruitless results is a lost desire.

Superficially, the figure in the smoking-room was that of a long, weedy young man – hairless as to his face; scalped with a fine lank fleece of neutral tint; pale-eyed, and slave to a bored and languid expression, over which he had little control, though it frequently misrepresented his mood. He was dressed scrupulously, though not obtrusively, in the mode, and was smoking a pungent cigarette with an air that seemed balanced between a genuine effort at self abstraction and a fear of giving offence by a too pronounced show of it. In this state, flying bubbles of conversation broke upon him as he sat a little apart and alone.

'Johnny, here's Callander preaching a divine egotism.'

'Is he? Tell him to beg a lock of the Henbery's hair. Ain't she the dog that bit him?'

'Once bit, twice shy.'

'Rot! – In the case of a woman? I'm covered with their scars.'

'What,' thought Rose, 'induced me to accept an invitation to this person's house?'

'A divine egotism, eh? It jumps with the dear Sarah's humour. The beggar is an imitative beggar.'

'Let the beggar speak for himself. He's in earnest. Haven't we been bred on the principle of self-sacrifice, till we've come to think a man's self is his uncleanest possession?'

'There's no thinking about it. We've long been alarmed on your account, I can assure you.'

'Oh! I'm no saint.'

'Not you. *Your* ecstasies are all of the flesh.'

'Don't be gross. I—'

'Oh! take a whisky and seltzer.'

'If I could escape without exciting observation,' thought Rose.

Lady Sarah Henbery was his hostess, and the inspired projector of a new scheme of existence (that was, in effect, the repudiation of any scheme) that had become quite the 'thing'. She had found life an arbitrary design – a coil of days (like fancy pebbles, dull or sparkling) set in the form of a main spring, and each gem responsible to the design. Then she had said, 'Today shall not follow yesterday or precede tomorrow'; and she had taken her pebbles from their setting and mixed them higgledy-piggledy, and so was in the way to wear or spend one or the other as caprice moved her. And she became without design and responsibility, and was thus able to indulge a natural bent towards capriciousness to the extent that – having a face for each and every form of social hypocrisy and licence – she was presently hardly to be put out of countenance by the extremest expression of either.

It followed that her reunions were popular with worldlings of a certain order.

By-and-by Amos saw his opportunity, and slipped out into a cold and foggy night.

II

De savoir votr' grand age,
Nous serions curieux;
A voir votre visage,
Vous paraissez fort vieux;
Vous avez bien cent ans,
Vous montrez bien autant?

A stranger, tall, closely wrapped and buttoned to the chin, had issued from the house at the same moment, and now followed in Rose's footsteps as he hurried away over the frozen pavement.

Suddenly this individual overtook and accosted him. 'Pardon,' he said. 'This fog baffles. We have been fellow-guests, it seems. You are walking? May I be your companion? You look a little lost yourself.'

He spoke in a rather high, mellow voice – too frank for irony.

At another time Rose might have met such a request with some slightly agitated temporising. Now, fevered with disgust of his late company, the astringency of nerve that came to him at odd moments, in the exaltation of which he felt himself ordinarily manly and human, braced him to an attitude at once modest and collected.

'I shall be quite happy,' he said. 'Only, don't blame me if you find you are entertaining a fool unawares.'

'You were out of your element, and are piqued. I saw you there, but wasn't introduced.'

'The loss is mine. I didn't observe you – yes, I did!'

He shot the last words out hurriedly – as they came within the radiance of a street lamp – and his pace lessened a moment with a little bewildered jerk.

He had noticed this person, indeed – his presence and his manner. They had arrested his languid review of the frivolous forces about him. He had seen a figure, strange and lofty, pass from group to group; exchange with one a word or two, with another a grave smile; move on and listen; move on and speak; always statelily restless; never anything but an incongruous apparition in a company of which every individual was eager to assert and expound the doctrines of self.

This man had been of curious expression, too – so curious that Amos remembered to have marvelled at the little comment his presence seemed to excite. His face was absolutely hairless – as, to all evidence, was his head, upon which he wore a brown silk handkerchief loosely rolled and knotted. The features were presumably of a Jewish type – though their entire lack of accent in the form of beard or eyebrow made identification difficult – and were minutely covered, like delicate cracklin, with a network of flattened wrinkles. Ludicrous though the description, the lofty individuality of the man so surmounted all disadvantages of appearance as to overawe frivolous criticism. Partly, also, the full transparent olive of his complexion, and the pools of purple shadow in which his eyes seemed to swim like blots of resin, neutralised the superficial barrenness of his face. Forcibly, he impelled the conviction that here was one who ruled his own being arbitrarily through entire fearlessness of death.

'You saw me?' he said, noticing with a smile his companion's involuntary hesitation. 'Then let us consider the introduction made, without further words. We will even

expand to the familiarity of old acquaintanceship, if you like
to fall in with the momentary humour.'

'I can see,' said Rose, 'that years are nothing to you.'

'No more than this gold piece, which I fling into the night.
They are made and lost and made again.'

'You have knowledge and the gift of tongues.'

The young man spoke bewildered, but with a strange warm
feeling of confidence flushing up through his habitual reserve.
He had no thought why, nor did he choose his words or
inquire of himself their source of inspiration.

'I have these,' said the stranger. 'The first is my excuse for
addressing you.'

'You are going to ask me something.'

'What attraction—'

'Drew me to Lady Sarah's house? I am young, rich, presumably a desirable *parti*. Also, I am neurotic, and without the
nerve to resist.'

'Yet you knew your taste would take alarm – as it did.'

'I have an acute sense of delicacy. Naturally I am prejudiced
in favour of virtue.'

'Then – excuse me – why put yours to a demoralising test?'

'I am not my own master. Any formless apprehension – any
shadowy fear enslaves my will. I go to many places from the
simple dread of being called upon to explain my reasons for
refusing. For the same cause I may appear to acquiesce in
indecencies my soul abhors; to give countenance to opinions
innately distasteful to me. I am a quite colourless personality.'

'Without force or object in life?'

'Life, I think, I live for its isolated moments – the first half-
dozen pulls at a cigarette, for instance, after a generous meal.'

'You take the view, then—'

'Pardon me. I take no views. I am not strong enough to
take anything – not even myself – seriously.'

'Yet you know that the trail of such volitionary ineptitude
reaches backwards under and beyond the closed door you
once issued from?'

'Do I? I know at least that the ineptitude intensifies with every step of constitutional decadence. It may be that I am wearing down to the nerve of life. How shall I find that? diseased? Then it is no happiness to me to think it imperishable.'

'Young man, do you believe in a creative divinity?'

'Yes.'

'And believe without resentment?'

'I think God hands over to His apprentices the moulding of vessels that don't interest Him.'

The stranger twitched himself erect.

'I beg you not to be profane,' he said.

'I am not,' said Rose. 'I don't know why I confide in you, or what concern I have to know. I can only say my instincts, through bewildering mental suffering, remain religious. You take me out of myself and judge me unfairly on the result.'

'Stay. You argue that a perishing of the bodily veil reveals the soul. Then the outlook of the latter should be the cleaner.'

'It gazes through a blind of corruption. It was never designed to stand naked in the world's market-places.'

'And whose the fault that it does?'

'I don't know. I only feel that I am utterly lonely and helpless.'

The stranger laughed scornfully.

'You can feel no sympathy with my state?' said Rose.

'Not a grain. To be conscious of a soul, yet to remain a craven under the temporal tyranny of the flesh; fearful of revolting, though the least imaginative flight of the spirit carries it at once beyond any bodily influence! Oh, sir! Fortune favours the brave.'

'She favours the fortunate,' said the young man, with a melancholy smile. 'Like a banker, she charges a commission on small accounts. At trifling deposits she turns up her nose. If you would escape her tax, you must keep a fine large balance at her house.'

'I dislike parables,' said the stranger drily.

'Then, here is a fact in illustration. I have an acquaintance, an impoverished author, who anchored his ark of hope on Mount Olympus twenty years ago. During all that time he has never ceased to send forth his doves; only to have them return empty beaked with persistent regularity. Three days ago the olive branch – a mere sprouting twig – came home. For the first time a magazine – an indifferent one – accepted a story of his and offered him a pound for it. He acquiesced; and the same night was returned to him from an important American firm an understamped MS, on which he had to pay excess postage, half a crown. That was Fortune's commission.'

'Bully the jade, and she will love you.'

'Your wisdom has not learned to confute that barbarism?'

The stranger glanced at his companion with some expression of dislike.

'The sex figures in your ideals, I see,' said he. 'Believe my long experience that its mere animal fools constitute its only excuse for existing – though' (he added under his breath) 'even they annoy one by their monogamous prejudices.'

'I won't hear that with patience,' said Rose. 'Each sex in its degree. Each is wearifully peevish over the hateful rivalry between mind and matter; but the male only has the advantage of distractions.'

'This,' said the stranger softly, as if to himself, 'is the woeful proof, indeed, of decadence. Man waives his prerogative of lordship over the irreclaimable savagery of earth. He has warmed his temperate house of clay to be a hot-house to his imagination, till the very walls are frail and eaten with fever.'

'Christ spoke of no spiritual division between the sexes.'

There followed a brief silence. Preoccupied, the two moved slowly through the fog, that was dashed ever and anon with cloudy blooms of lamplight.

'I wish to ask you,' said the stranger at length, 'in what has the teaching of Christ proved otherwise than so impotent to reform mankind, as to make one sceptical as to the divinity of the teacher?'

'Why, what is your age?' asked Rose in a tone of surprise.

'I am a hundred tonight.'

The astounded young man jumped in his walk.

'A hundred!' he exclaimed. 'And you cannot answer that question yourself?'

'I asked you to answer it. But never mind. I see faith in you like a garden of everlastings – as it should be – as of course it should be. Yet disbelievers point to inconsistencies. There was a reviling Jew, for instance, to whom Christ is reported to have shown resentment quite incompatible with His teaching.'

'Whom do you mean?'

'Cartaphilus; who was said to be condemned to perpetual wandering.'

'A legend,' cried Amos scornfully. 'Bracket it with Nero's fiddling and the hymning of Memnon.'

A second silence fell. They seemed to move in a dead and stagnant world. Presently said the stranger suddenly—

'I am quite lost; and so, I suppose, are you?'

'I haven't an idea where we are.'

'It is two o'clock. There isn't a soul or a mark to guide us. We had best part, and each seek his own way.'

He stopped and held out his hand.

'Two pieces of advice I should like to give you before we separate. Fall in love and take plenty of exercise.'

'Must we part?' said Amos. 'Frankly, I don't think I like you. That sounds strange and discourteous after my ingenuous confidences. But you exhale an odd atmosphere of witchery; and your scorn braces me like a tonic. The pupils of your eyes, when I got a glimpse of them, looked like the heads of little black devils peeping out of windows. But you can't touch my soul on the raw when my nerves are quiescent; and then I would strike any man that called me coward.'

The stranger uttered a quick, chirping laugh, like the sound of a stone on ice.

'What do you propose?' he said.

'I have an idea you are not so lost as you pretend. If we are anywhere near shelter that you know, take me in and I will be a good listener. It is one of my negative virtues.'

'I don't know that any addition to my last good counsel would not be an anti-climax.'

He stood musing and rubbing his hairless chin.

'Exercise – certainly. It is the golden demephitizer of the mind. I am seldom off my feet.'

'You walk much – and alone?'

'Not always alone. Periodically I am accompanied by one or another. At this time I have a companion who has tramped with me for some nine months.'

Again he pondered apart. The darkness and the fog hid his face, but he spoke his thoughts aloud.

'What matter if it does come about? Tomorrow I have the world – the mother of many daughters. And to redeem this soul – a dog of a Christian – a friend at Court!'

He turned quickly to the young man.

'Come!' he said. 'It shall be as you wish.'

'Do you know where we are?'

'We are at the entrance to Wardour Street.'

He gave a gesture of impatience, whipped a hand at his companion's sleeve, and once more they trod down the icy echoes, going onwards.

The narrow lane reverberated to their footsteps; the drooping fog swayed sluggishly; the dead blank windows and high-shouldered doors frowned in stubborn progression and vanished behind them.

The stranger stopped in a moment where a screen of iron bars protected a shop front. From behind them shot leaden glints from old clasped bookcovers, hanging tongues of Toledo steel, croziers rich in nielli – innumerable and antique curios gathered from the lumber-rooms of history

A door to one side he opened with a latch-key. A pillar of light, seeming to smoke as the fog obscured it, was formed of the aperture.

Obeying a gesture, Rose set foot on the threshold. As he was entering, he found himself unable to forbear a thrill of effrontery.

'Tell me,' said he. 'It was not only to point a moral that you flung away that coin?'

The stranger, going before, grinned back sourly over his shoulder.

'Not only,' he said. 'It was a bad one.'

III

> . . . *La Belle Dame sans merci*
> *Hath thee in thrall!*

All down the dimly luminous passage that led from the door straight into the heart of the building, Amos was aware, as he followed his companion over the densely piled carpet, of the floating sweet scent of amber-seed. Still his own latter exaltation of nerve burned with a steady radiance. He seemed to himself bewitched – translated; a consciousness apart from yesterday; its material fibres responsive to the least or utmost shock of adventure. As he trod in the other's footsteps, he marvelled that so lavish a display of force, so elastic a gait, could be in a centenarian.

'Are you ever tired?' he whispered curiously.

'Never. Sometimes I long for weariness as other men desire rest.'

As the stranger spoke, he pulled aside a curtain of stately black velvet, and softly opening a door in a recess, beckoned the young man into the room beyond.

He saw a chamber, broad and low, designed, in its every rich stain of picture and slumberous hanging, to appeal to the sensuous. And here the scent was thick and motionless. Costly marqueterie; Palissy candlesticks reflected in half-concealed mirrors framed in embossed silver; antique Nankin vases brimming with potpourri; in one corner a suit of Milanese armour, fluted, *damasquinée*, by Felippo Negroli; in another a tripod table of porphyry, spectrally repeating in its polished surface the opal hues of a vessel of old Venetian glass half-filled with some topaz-coloured liqueur – such and many more tokens of a luxurious aestheticism wrought in the observer an immediate sense of pleasurable enervation. He noticed, with a swaying thrill of delight, that his feet were on a padded rug of Astrakhan – one of many, disposed eccentrically about the yellow tessellated-marble floor; and he noticed that the sole light in the chamber came from an iridescent globed lamp, fed with some fragrant oil, that hung near an alcove traversed by a veil of dark violet silk.

The door behind him swung gently to: his eyes half-closed in a dreamy surrender of will: the voice of the stranger speaking to him sounded far away as the cry of some lost unhappiness.

'Welcome!' it said only.

Amos broke through his trance with a cry.

'What does it mean – all this? We step out of the fog, and here – I think it is the guest-parlour of Hell!'

'You flatter me,' said the stranger, smiling. 'Its rarest antiquity goes no further back, I think, than the eighth century. The skeleton of the place is Jacobite and comparatively modern.'

'But you – the shop!'

'Contains a little of the fruit of my wanderings.'

'You are a dealer?'

'A casual collector only. If through a representative I work my accumulations of costly lumber to a profit – say thousands per cent – it is only because utility is the first principle of Art. As to myself, here I but pitch my tent – periodically, and at long intervals.'

'An unsupervised agent must find it a lucrative post.'

'Come – there shows a little knowledge of human nature. For the first time I applaud you. But the appointment is conditional on many things. At the moment the berth is vacant. Would you like it?'

'My (paradoxically) Christian name was bestowed in compliment to a godfather, sir. I am no Jew. I have already enough to know the curse of having more.'

'I have no idea how you are called. I spoke jestingly, of course; but your answer quenches the flicker of respect I felt for you. As a matter of fact, the other's successor is not only nominated, but is actually present in this room.'

'Indeed? You propose to fill the post yourself?'

'Not by any means. The mere suggestion is an insult to one who can trace his descent backwards at least two thousand years.'

'Yes, indeed. I meant no disparagement, but—'

'I tell you, sir,' interrupted the stranger irritably, 'my visits are periodic. I could not live in a town. I could not settle anywhere. I must always be moving. A prolonged constitutional – that is my theory of health.'

'You are always on your feet – at your age—'

'I am a hundred tonight – But – mark you – *I have eaten of the Tree of Life.*'

As the stranger uttered these words, he seized Rose by the wrist in a soft, firm grasp. His captive, staring at him amazed, gave out a little involuntary shriek.

'Hadn't I better leave? There is something – nameless – I don't know; but I should never have come in here. Let me go!'

The other, heedless, half-pulled the troubled and bewildered young man across the room, and drew him to within a foot of the curtain closing the alcove.

'Here,' he said quietly, 'is my fellow-traveller of the last nine months, fast, I believe, in sleep – unless your jarring outcry has broken it.'

Rose struggled feebly.

'Not anything shameful,' he whimpered – 'I have a dread of your manifestations.'

For answer, the other put out a hand, and swiftly and silently withdrew the curtain. A deepish recess was revealed, into which the soft glow of the lamp penetrated like moonlight. It fell in the first instance upon a couch littered with pale, uncertain shadows, and upon a crucifix that hung upon the wall within.

In the throb of his emotions, it was something of a relief to Amos to see his companion, releasing his hold of him, clasp his hands and bow his head reverently to this pathetic symbol. The cross on which the Christ hung was of ebony a foot high; the figure itself was chryselephantine and purely exquisite as a work of art.

'It is early seventeenth century,' said the stranger suddenly, after a moment of devout silence, seeing the other's eyes absorbed in contemplation. 'It is by Duquesnoy.' (Then, behind the back of his hand) 'The rogue couldn't forget his bacchanals even here.'

'It is a Christ of infidels,' said Amos, with repugnance. He was adding involuntarily (his *savoir faire* seemed suddenly to have deserted him) – 'But fit for an unbelieving—' when his host took him up with fury—

'Dog of a Gentile! – if you dare to call me Jew!'

The dismayed start of the young man at this outburst blinded him to its paradoxical absurdity. He fell back with his heart thumping. The eyes of the stranger flickered, but in an instant he had recovered his urbanity.

'Look!' he whispered impatiently. 'The Calvary is not alone in the alcove.'

Mechanically Rose's glance shifted to the couch; and in that moment shame and apprehension and the sickness of being were precipitated in him as in golden flakes of rapture.

Something, that in the instant of revelation had seemed part only of the soft tinted shadows, resolved itself into a presentment of loveliness so pure, and so pathetic in its innocent self-surrender to the passionate tyranny of his gaze, that the manhood in him was abashed in the very flood of its exaltation. He put a hand to his face before he looked a second time, to discipline his dazzled eyes. They were turned only upon his soul, and found it a reflected glory. Had the vision passed? His eyes, in a panic, leaped for it once more.

Yes, it was there – dreaming upon its silken pillow; a grotesque carved dragon in ivory looking down, from a corner of the fluted couch, upon its supernal beauty – a face that, at a glance, could fill the vague desire of a suffering, lonely heart – spirit informing matter with all the flush and essence of some flower of the lost garden of Eden.

And this expressed in the form of one simple slumbering girl; in its drifted heap of hair, bronze as copper-beech leaves in spring; in the very pulsing of its half-hidden bosom, and in its happy morning lips, like Psyche's, night-parted by Love and so remaining entranced.

A long light robe, sulphur-coloured, clung to the sleeper from low throat to ankle; bands of narrow nolana-blue ribbon crossed her breast and were brought together in a loose cincture about her waist; her white, smooth feet were sandalled; one arm was curved beneath her lustrous head; the other lay relaxed and drooping. Chrysoberyls, the sea-virgins of stones, sparkled in her hair and lay in the bosom of her gown like dewdrops in an evening primrose.

The gazer turned with a deep sigh, and then a sputter of fury—

'Why do you show me this? You cruel beast, was not my life barren enough before?'

'Can it ever be so henceforward? Look again.'

'Does the devil enter? Something roars in me! Have you no fear that I shall kill you?'

'None. I cannot die.'

Amos broke into a mocking, fierce laugh. Then, his blood shooting in his veins, he seized the sleeper roughly by her hand.

'Wake!' he cried, 'and end it!'

With a sigh she lifted her head. Drowsiness and startled

wonderment struggled in her eyes; but in a moment they caught the vision of the stranger standing aside, and smiled and softened. She held out her long, white arms to him.

'You have come, dear love,' she said, in a happy, low voice, 'and I was not awake to greet you.'

Rose fell on his knees.

'Oh, God in Heaven!' he cried, 'bear witness that this is monstrous and unnatural! Let me die rather than see it.'

The stranger moved forward.

'Do honour, Adnah, to this our guest; and minister to him of thy pleasure.'

The white arms dropped. The girl's face was turned, and her eyes, solemn and witch-like, looked into Amos's. He saw them, their irises golden-brown shot with little spars of blue; and the soul in his own seemed to rush towards them and to recoil, baffled and sobbing.

Could she have understood? He thought he saw a faint smile, a gentle shake of the head, as she slid from the couch and her sandals tapped on the marble floor.

She stooped and took him by the hand.

'Rise, I pray you,' she said, 'and I will be your handmaiden.'

She led him unresisting to a chair, and bade him sweetly to be seated. She took from him his hat and overcoat, and brought him rare wine in a cup of crystal.

'My lord will drink,' she murmured, 'and forget all but the night and Adnah.'

'You I can never forget,' said the young man, in a broken voice.

As he drank, half-choking, the girl turned to the other, who still stood apart, silent and watchful.

'Was this wise?' she breathed. 'To summon a witness on this night of all – was this wise, beloved?'

Amos dashed the cup on the floor. The red liquid stained the marble like blood.

'No, no!' he shrieked, springing to his feet. 'Not that! It cannot be!'

In an ecstasy of passion he flung his arms about the girl, and crushed all her warm loveliness against his breast. She remained quite passive – unstartled even. Only she turned her head and whispered: 'Is this thy will?'

Amos fell back, drooping, as if he had received a blow.

'Be merciful and kill me,' he muttered. 'I – even I can feel at last the nobility of death.'

Then the voice of the stranger broke, lofty and passionless.

'Tell him what you see in me.'

She answered, low and without pause, like one repeating a cherished lesson—

'I see – I have seen it for the nine months I have wandered with you – the supreme triumph of the living will. I see that this triumph, of its very essence, could not be unless you had surmounted the tyranny of any, the least, gross desire. I see that it is incompatible with sin; with offence given to oneself or others; that passion cannot live in its serene atmosphere; that it illustrates the enchantment of the flesh by the intellect; that it is happiness for evermore redeemed.'

'How do you feel this?'

'I see it reflected in myself – I, the poor visionary you took from the Northern Island. Week by week I have known it sweetening and refining in my nature. None can taste the bliss of happiness that has not you for master – none can teach it save you, whose composure is unshadowed by any terror of death.'

'And love that is passion, Adnah?'

'I hear it spoken as in a dream. It is a wicked whisper from far away. You, the lord of time and of tongues, I worship – you, only you, who are my God.'

'Hush! But the man of Nazareth?'

'Ah! His name is an echo. What divine egotism taught He?'

Where lately had Amos heard this phrase? His memory of all things real seemed suspended.

'He was a man, and He died,' said Adnah simply.

The stranger threw back his head, with an odd expression

of triumph; and almost in the same moment abased it to the crucifix on the wall.

Amos stood breathing quickly, his ears drinking in every accent of the low musical voice. Now, as she paused, he moved forward a hurried step, and addressed himself to the shadowy figure by the couch—

'Who are you, in the name of the Christ you mock and adore in a breath, that has wrought this miracle of high worship in a breathing woman?'

'I am he that has eaten of the Tree of Life.'

'Oh, forego your fables! I am not a child.'

'It could not of its nature perish' (the voice went on evenly, ignoring the interruption). 'It breathes its immortal fragrance in no transplanted garden, invisible to sinful eyes, as some suppose. When the curse fell, the angel of the flaming sword bore it to the central desert; and the garden withered, for its soul was withdrawn. Now, in the heart of the waste place that is called Tiah-Bani-Israïl, it waits in its loveliness the coming of the Son of God.'

'He has come and passed.'

It might have been an imperceptible shrug of the shoulders that twitched the tall figure by the couch. If so, it converted the gesture into a bow of reverence.

'Is He not to be revealed again in His glory? But there, set as in the crater of a mountain of sand, and inaccessible to mortal footstep, stands unperishing the glory of the earth. And its fragrance is drawn up to heaven, as through a wide chimney; and from its branches hangs the undying fruit, lustrous and opalescent; and in each shining globe the world and its starry system are reflected in miniature, moving westwards; but at night they glow, a cluster of tender moons.'

'And whence came *your* power to scale that which is inaccessible?'

'From Death, that, still denying me immortality, is unable to encompass my destruction.'

The young man burst into a harsh and grating laugh.

'Here is some inconsistency!' he cried, 'By your own showing you were not immortal till you ate of the fruit!'

Could it be that this simple deductive snip cut the thread of coherence? A scowl appeared to contract the lofty brow for an instant. The next, a gay chirrup intervened, like a little spark struck from the cloud.

'The pounding logic of the steam engine!' cried the stranger, coming forward at last with an open smile. 'But we pace in an altitude refined above sensuous comprehension. Perhaps before long you will see and believe. In the meantime let us be men and women enjoying the warm gifts of Fortune!'

IV

Nous pensions comme un songe
Le récit de vos maux;
Nous traitions de mensonge
Tous vos plus grands travaux!

In that one night of an unreality that seemed either an enchanted dream or a wilfully fantastic travesty of conventions, Amos alternated between fits of delirious self-surrender and a rage of resignation, from which now and again he would awake to flourish an angry little bodkin of irony.

Now, at this stage, it appeared a matter for passive acquiescence that he should be one of a trio seated at a bronze table, that might have been recovered from Herculaneum, playing three-handed cribbage with a pack of fifteenth-century cards – limned, perhaps, by some Franceso Bachiacca – and an ivory board inlaid with gold and mother-of-pearl. To one side a smaller 'occasional' table held the wine, to which the young man resorted at the least invitation from Adnah.

In this connection (of cards), it would fitfully perturb him to find that he who had renounced sin with mortality, had not only a proneness to avail himself of every oversight on the part of his adversaries, but frequently to peg-up more holes than his hand entitled him to. Moreover, at such times, when the culprit's attention was drawn to this by his guest – at first gently; later, with a little scorn – he justified his action on the assumption that it was an essential interest of all games to attempt abuse of the confidence of one's antagonist, whose skill in checkmating any movement of this nature was in right ratio with his capacity as a player; and finally he rose, the sole winner of a sum respectable enough to allow him some ingenuous expression of satisfaction.

Thereafter conversation ensued; and it must be remarked that nothing was further from Rose's mind than to apologise for his long intrusion and make a decent exit. Indeed, there seemed some thrill of vague expectation in the air, to the realisation of which his presence sought to contribute; and already – so rapidly grows the assurance of love – his heart claimed some protective right over the pure, beautiful creature at his feet.

For there, at a gesture from the other, had Adnah seated herself, leaning her elbow, quite innocently and simply, on the young man's knee.

The sweet strong Moldavian wine buzzed in his head; love and sorrow and intense yearning went with flow and shock through his veins. At one moment elated by the thought that, whatever his understanding of the ethical sympathy existing between these two, their connection was, by their own acknowledgement, platonic; at another, cruelly conscious of the icy crevasse that must gape between so perfectly proportioned an organism and his own atrabilarious personality, he dreaded to avail himself of a situation that was at once an invitation and a trust; and ended by subsiding, with characteristic lameness, into mere conversational commonplace.

'You must have got over a great deal of ground,' said he to his host, 'on that constitutional hobby horse of yours?'

'A great deal of ground.'

'In all weathers?'

'In all weathers; at all times; in every country.'

'How do you manage – pardon my inquisitiveness – the little necessities of dress and boots and such things?'

'Adnah,' said the stranger, 'go fetch my walking suit and show it to our guest.'

The girl rose, went silently from the room, and returned in a moment with a single garment, which she laid in Rose's hands.

He examined it curiously. It was a marvel of sartorial tact and ingenuity; so fashioned that it would have appeared scarcely a solecism on taste in any age. Built in one piece to resemble many, and of the most particularly chosen material, it was contrived and ventilated for any exigencies of weather and of climate, and could be doffed or assumed at the shortest notice. About it were cunningly distributed a number of strong pockets or purses for the reception of diverse articles, from a comb to a sandwich-box; and the position of these was so calculated as not to interfere with the symmetry of the whole.

'It is indeed an excellent piece of work,' said Amos, with considerable appreciation; for he held no contempt for the art which sometimes alone seemed to justify his right of existence.

'Your praise is deserved,' said the stranger, smiling, 'seeing that it was contrived for me by one whose portrait, by Giambattista Moroni, now hangs in your National Gallery.'

'I have heard of it, I think. Is the fellow still in business?'

'The tailor or the artist? The first died bankrupt in prison – about the year 1560, it must have been. It was fortunate for me, inasmuch as I acquired the garment for nothing, the man disappearing before I had settled his claim.'

Rose's jaw dropped. He looked at the beautiful face reclining against him. It expressed no doubt, no surprise, no least sense of the ludicrous.

'Oh, my God!' he muttered, and ploughed his forehead with his hands. Then he looked up again with a pallid grin.

'I see,' he said. 'You play upon my fancied credulity. And how did the garment serve you in the central desert?'

'I had it not then, by many centuries. No garment would avail against the wicked Samiel – the poisonous wind that is the breath of the eternal dead sand. Who faces that feels, pace by pace, his body wither and stiffen. His clothes crackle like paper, and so fall to fragments. From his eyeballs the moist vision flakes and flies in powder. His tongue shrinks into his throat, as though fire had writhed and consumed it to a little scarlet spur. His furrowed skin peels like the cerements of an ancient mummy. He falls, breaking in his fall – there is a puff of acrid dust, dissipated in a moment – and he is gone.'

'And this you met unscathed?'

'Yes; for it was preordained that Death should hunt, but never overtake me – that I might testify to the truth of the first Scriptures.'

Even as he spoke, Rose sprang to his feet with a gesture of uncontrollable repulsion; and in the same instant was aware of a horrible change that was taking place in the features of the man before him.

V

Trahentibus autem Judaeis Jesum extra praetorium cum venisset ad ostium, Cartaphilus praetorii ostiarius et Pontii Pilati, cum per ostium exiret Jesus, pepulit Eum pugno contemptibiliter post tergum, et irridens dixit, 'Vade, Jesu citius, vade, quid moraris?' Et Jesus severo vultu et oculo respiciens in eum, dixit: 'Ego, vado, et expectabis donec veniam!' Itaque juxta verbum Domini expectat adhuc Cartaphilus ille, qui tempore Dominicae passionis – erat quasi triginta annorum, et semper cum usque ad centum attigerit aetatem redeuntium annorum redit redivivus ad illum aetatis statum, quo fuit anno quand passus est Dominus.

Matthew of Paris, *Historia Major*

The girl – from whose cheek Rose, in his rough rising, had seemed to brush the bloom, so keenly had its colour deepened – sank from the stool upon her knees, her hands pressed to her bosom, her lungs working quickly under the pressure of some powerful excitement.

'It comes, beloved!' she said, in a voice half-terror, half-ecstasy.

'It comes, Adnah,' the stranger echoed, struggling – 'this periodic self-renewal – this sloughing of the veil of flesh that I warned you of.'

His soul seemed to pant grey from his lips; his face was bloodless and like stone; the devils in his eyes were awake and busy as maggots in a wound. Amos knew him now for wickedness personified and immortal, and fell upon his knees beside the girl and seized one of her hands in both his.

'Look!' he shrieked. 'Can you believe in him longer? believe that any code or system of his can profit you in the end?'

She made no resistance, but her eyes still dwelt on the contorted face with an expression of divine pity.

'Oh, thou sufferest!' she breathed; 'but thy reward is near!'

'Adnah!' wailed the young man, in a heartbroken voice. 'Turn from him to me! Take refuge in my love. Oh, it is natural, I swear. It asks nothing of you but to accept the gift – to renew yourself in it, if you will; to deny it, if you will, and chain it for your slave. Only to save you and die for you, Adnah!'

He felt the hand in his shudder slightly; but no least knowledge of him did she otherwise evince.

He clasped her convulsively, released her, mumbled her slack white fingers with his lips. He might have addressed the dead.

In the midst, the figure before them swayed with a rising throe – turned – staggered across to the couch, and cast itself down before the crucifix on the wall.

'Jesu, Son of God,' it implored, through a hurry of piercing groans, 'forbear Thy hand: Christ, register my atonement! My punishment – eternal – and oh, my mortal feet already weary to death! Jesu, spare me! Thy justice, Lawgiver – let it not be vindictive, oh, in Thy sacred name! lest men proclaim it for a baser thing than theirs. For a fault of ignorance – for a word of scorn where all reviled, would *they* have singled *one* out, have made him, most wretched, the scapegoat of the ages? Ah, most holy, forgive me! In mine agony I know not what I say. A moment ago I could have pronounced it something seeming less than divine that Thou couldst so have stultified with a curse Thy supreme hour of self-sacrifice – a moment ago, when the rising madness prevailed. Now, sane once more – Nazarene, oh, Nazarene! not only retribution for my deserts, but pity for my suffering – Nazarene, that Thy slanderers, the men of little schisms, be refuted, hearing me, the very witness to Thy mercy, testify how the justice of the Lord triumphs supreme through that His superhuman prerogative – that they may not say, He can destroy, even as we; but can He redeem? The sacrifice – the yearling lamb; – it awaits Thee, Master, the proof of my abjectness and my sincerity. I, more curst than Abraham, lift my eyes to Heaven, the terror in my heart, the knife in my hand. Jesu – Jesu!'

He cried and grovelled. His words were frenzied, his abasement fulsome to look upon. Yet it was impressed upon one of the listeners, with a great horror, how unspeakable blasphemy breathed between the lines of the prayer – the blasphemy of secret disbelief in the Power it invoked, and sought, with its tongue in its cheek, to conciliate.

Bitter indignation in the face of nameless outrage transfigured Rose at this moment into something nobler than himself. He feared, but he upheld his manhood. Conscious that the monstrous situation was none of his choosing, he had no thought to evade its consequences so long as the unquestioning credulity of his co-witness seemed to call for his protection. Nerveless, sensitive natures, such as his, not infrequently give the lie to themselves by accesses of an altruism that is little less than self-effacement.

'This is all bad,' he struggled to articulate. 'You are hipped by some devilish cantrip. Oh, come – come! – in Christ's name I dare to implore you – and learn the truth of love!'

As he spoke, he saw that the apparition was on its feet again – that it had returned, and was standing, its face ghastly and inhuman, with one hand leaned upon the marble table.

'Adnah!' it cried, in a strained and hollow voice. 'The moment for which I prepared you approaches. Even now I labour. I had thought to take up the thread on the further side; but it is ordained otherwise, and we must part.'

'Part!' The word burst from her in a sigh of lost amazement.

'The holocaust, Adnah!' he groaned – 'the holocaust with which every seventieth year my expiation must be punctuated! This time the cross is on thy breast, beloved; and tomorrow – oh! thou must be content to tread on lowlier altitudes than those I have striven to guide thee by.'

'I cannot – I cannot, I should die in the mists. Oh, heart of my heart, forsake me not!'

'Adnah – my selma, my beautiful – to propitiate—'

'Whom? Thou hast eaten of the Tree, and art a God!'

'Hush!' He glanced round with an awed visage at the dim hanging Calvary; then went on in a harsher tone, 'It is enough – it must be.' (His shifting face, addressed to Rose, was convulsed into an expression of bitter scorn). 'I command thee, go with him. The sacrifice – oh, my heart, the sacrifice! And I cry to Jehovah, and He makes no sign; and into thy sweet breast the knife must enter.'

Amos sprang to his feet with a loud cry.

'I take no gift from you. I will win or lose her by right of manhood!'

The girl's face was white with despair.

'I do not understand,' she cried in a piteous voice.

'Nor I,' said the young man, and he took a threatening step forward. 'We have no part in this – this lady and I. Man or devil you may be; but—'

'Neither!'

The stranger, as he uttered the word, drew himself erect with a tortured smile. The action seemed to kilt the skin of his face into hideous plaits.

'I am Cartaphilus,' he said, 'who denied the Nazarene shelter.'

'The *Wandering Jew*!'

The name of the old strange legend broke involuntarily from Rose's lips.

'Now you know him!' he shrieked then. 'Adnah, I am here! Come to me!'

Tears were running down the girl's cheeks. She lifted her hands with an impassioned gesture; then covered her face with them.

But Cartaphilus, penetrating the veil with eyes no longer human, cried suddenly, so that the room vibrated with his voice, 'Bismillah! Wilt thou dare the Son of Heaven, questioning if His sentence upon the Jew – to renew, with his every hundredth year, his manhood's prime – was not rather a forestalling through His infinite penetration, of the consequences of that Jew's finding and eating of the Tree of Life? Is it Cartaphilus first, or Christ?'

The girl flung herself forward, crushing her bosom upon the marble floor, and lay blindly groping with her hands.

'He was a God and vindictive!' she moaned. 'He was a man and He died. The cross – the cross!'

The lost cry pierced Rose's breast like a knife. Sorrow, rage, and love inflamed his passion to madness. With one bound he met and grappled with the stranger.

He had no thought of the resistance he should encounter. In a moment the Jew, despite his age and seizure, had him broken and powerless. The fury of blood blazed down upon him from the unearthly eyes.

'Beast! that I might tear you! But the Nameless is your refuge. You must be chained – you must be chained. Come!'

Half-dragging, half-bearing, he forced his captive across the room to the corner where the flask of topaz liquid stood.

'Sleep!' he shrieked, and caught up the glass vessel and dashed it down upon Rose's mouth.

The blow was a stunning one. A jagged splinter tore the victim's lip and brought a gush of blood; the yellow fluid drowned his eyes and suffocated his throat. Struggling to hold his faculties, a startled shock passed through him, and he dropped insensible on the floor.

VI

'Wandering stars, to whom is reserved the blackness of darkness for ever.'

Where had he read these words before? Now he saw them as scrolled in lightning upon a dead sheet of night.

There was a sound of feet going on and on.

Light soaked into the gloom, faster – faster; and he saw—

The figure of a man moved endlessly forward by town and pasture and the waste places of the world. But though he, the dreamer, longed to outstrip and stay the figure and look searchingly in its face, he could not, following, close upon the intervening space; and its back was ever towards him.

And always as the figure passed by populous places, there rose long murmurs of blasphemy to either side, and bestial cries: 'We are weary! the farce is played out! He reveals Himself not, nor ever will! Lead us – lead us, against Heaven, against hell; against any other, or against ourselves! The cancer of life spreads, and we cannot enjoy nor can we think cleanly. The sins of the fathers have accumulated to one vast mound of putrefaction. Lead us, and we follow!'

And, uttering these cries, swarms of hideous half-human shapes would emerge from holes and corners and rotting burrows, and stumble a little way with the figure, cursing and jangling, and so drop behind, one by one, like glutted flies shaken from a horse.

And the dreamer saw in him, who went ever on before,

the sole existent type of a lost racial glory, a marvellous survival, a prince over monstrosities; and he knew him to have reached, through long ages of evil introspection, a terrible belief in his own self-acquired immortality and lordship over all abased peoples that must die and pass; and the seed of his blasphemy he sowed broadcast in triumph as he went; and the ravenous horrors of the earth ran forth in broods and devoured it like birds, and trod one another underfoot in their gluttony.

And he came to a vast desolate plain, and took his stand upon a barren drift of sand; and the face the dreamer longed and feared to see was yet turned from him.

And the figure cried in a voice that grated down the winds of space: 'Lo! I am he that cannot die! Lo! I am he that has eaten of the Tree of Life; who am the Lord of Time and of the races of the earth that shall flock to my standard!'

And again: 'Lo! I am he that God was impotent to destroy because I had eaten of the fruit! He cannot control that which He hath created. He hath builded His temple upon His impotence, and it shall fall and crush Him. The children of His misrule cry out against Him. There is no God but Antichrist!'

Then from all sides came hurrying across the plain vast multitudes of the degenerate children of men, naked and unsightly; and they leaped and mouthed about the figure on the hillock, like hounds baying a dead fox held aloft; and from their swollen throats came one cry:

'There is no God but Antichrist!'

And thereat the figure turned about – and it was Cartaphilus the Jew.

VII

There is no death! What seems so is transition.

Uttering an incoherent cry, Rose came to himself with a shock of agony and staggered to his feet. In the act he traversed no neutral ground of insentient purposelessness. He caught the thread of being where he had dropped it – grasped it with an awful and sublime resolve that admitted no least thought of self-interest.

If his senses were for the moment amazed at their surroundings – the silence, the perfumed languor, the beauty and voluptuousness of the room – his soul, notwithstanding, stood intent, unfaltering – waiting merely the physical capacity for action.

The fragments of the broken vessel were scattered at his feet; the blood of his wound had hardened upon his face. He took a dizzy step forward, and another. The girl lay as he had seen her cast herself down – breathing, he could see; her hair in disorder; her hands clenched together in terror or misery beyond words.

Where was the other?

Suddenly his vision cleared. He saw that the silken curtains of the alcove were closed.

A poniard in a jewelled sheath lay, with other costly trifles, on a settle hard by. He seized and, drawing it, cast the scabbard clattering on the floor. His hands would have done; but this would work quicker.

Exhaling a quick sigh of satisfaction, he went forward with a noiseless rush and tore apart the curtains.

Yes – he was there – the Jew – the breathing enormity, stretched silent and motionless. The shadow of the young man's lifted arm ran across his white shirt front like a bar sinister.

To rid the world of something monstrous and abnormal – that was all Rose's purpose and desire. He leaned over to strike. The face, stiff and waxen as a corpse's, looked up into his with a calm impenetrable smile – looked up, for all its eyes were closed. And this was a horrible thing, that, though the features remained fixed in that one inexorable expression, something beneath them seemed alive and moving – something that clouded or revealed them as when a sheet of paper glowing in the fire wavers between ashes and flame. Almost he could have thought that the soul, detached from its envelope, struggled to burst its way to the light.

An instant he dashed his left palm across his eyes; then shrieking, 'Let the fruit avail you now!' drove the steel deep into its neck with a snarl.

In the act, for all his frenzy, he had a horror of the spurting blood that he knew must foul his hand obscenely, and sprinkle his face, perhaps, as when a finger half-plugs a flowing water-tap.

None came! The fearful white wound seemed to suck at the steel, making a puckered mouth of derision.

A thin sound, like the whinny of a dog, issued from Rose's lips. He pulled out the blade – it came with a crackling noise, as if it had been drawn through parchment.

Incredulous – mad – in an ecstasy of horror, he stabbed again and again. He might as fruitfully have struck at water. The slashed and gaping wounds closed up so soon as he withdrew the steel, leaving not a scar.

With a scream he dashed the unstained weapon on the floor and sprang back into the room. He stumbled and almost fell over the prostrate figure of the girl.

A strength as of delirium stung and prickled in his arms. He stooped and forcibly raised her – held her against his breast – addressed her in a hurried passion of entreaty.

'In the name of God, come with me! In the name of God, divorce yourself from this horror! He is the abnormal! – the deathless – the Antichrist!'

Her lids were closed; but she listened.

'Adnah, you have given me myself. My reason cannot endure the gift alone. Have mercy and be pitiful, and share the burden!'

At last she turned on him her swimming gaze.

'Oh! I am numbed and lost! What would you do with me?'

With a sob of triumph he wrapped his arms hard about her, and sought her lips with his. In the very moment of their meeting, she drew herself away, and stood panting and gazing with wide eyes over his shoulder. He turned.

A young man of elegant appearance was standing by the table where *he* had lately leaned.

In the face of the newcomer the animal and the fanatic were mingled, characteristics inseparable in pseudo-revelation.

He was unmistakably a Jew, of the finest primitive type – such as might have existed in preneurotic days. His complexion was of a smooth golden russet; his nose and lips were cut rather in the lines of sensuous cynicism; the look in his polished brown eyes was of defiant self-confidence, capable of the extremes of devotion or of obstinacy. Short curling black hair covered his scalp, and his moustache and small crisp beard were of the same hue.

'Thanks, stranger,' he said, in a somewhat nasal but musical voice. 'Your attack – a little cowardly, perhaps, for all its provocation – has served to release me before my time. Thanks – thanks indeed!'

Amos sent a sick and groping glance towards the alcove. The curtain was pulled back – the couch was empty. His vision returning, caught sight of Adnah still standing motionless.

'No, no!' he screeched in a suffocated voice, and clasped his hands convulsively.

There was an adoring expression in her wet eyes that grew and grew. In another moment she had thrown herself at the stranger's feet.

'Master,' she cried, in a rich and swooning voice: 'O Lord and Master – as blind love foreshadowed thee in these long months!'

He smiled down upon her.

'A tender welcome on the threshold,' he said softly, 'that I had almost renounced. The young spirit is weak to confirm the self-sacrifice of the old. But this ardent modern, Adnah, who, it seems, has slipped his opportunity?'

Passionately clasping the hands of the young Jew, she turned her face reluctant.

'He has blood on him,' she whispered. 'His lip is swollen like a schoolboy's with fighting. He is not a man, sane, self-reliant and glorious – like you, O my heart!'

The Jew gave a high, loud laugh, which he checked in mid-career.

'Sir,' he said derisively, 'we will wish you a very pleasant good-morning.'

How – under what pressure or by what process of self-effacement – he reached the street, Amos could never remember. His first sense of reality was in the stinging cold, which made him feel, by reaction, preposterously human.

It was perhaps six o'clock of a February morning, and the fog had thinned considerably, giving place to a wan and livid glow that was but half-measure of dawn.

He found himself going down the ringing pavement that was talcous with a sooty skin of ice, a single engrossing resolve hammering time in his brain to his footsteps.

The artificial glamour was all past and gone – beaten and frozen out of him. The rest was to do – his plain duty as a Christian, as a citizen – above all, as a gentleman. He was, unhypnotised, a law-abiding young man, with a hatred of notoriety and a detestation of the abnormal. Unquestionably his forebears had made a huge muddle of his inheritance.

About a quarter to seven he walked (rather unsteadily) into Vine Street Police Station and accosted the inspector on duty.

'I want to lay an information.'

The officer scrutinised him, professionally, from the under side, and took up a pen.

'What's the charge?'

'Administering a narcotic, attempted murder, abduction, profanity, trading under false pretences, wandering at large – great heavens! what isn't it?'

'Perhaps you'll say. Name of accused?'

'Cartaphilus.'

'Any other?'

'The Wandering Jew.'

The Inspector laid down his pen and leaned forward, bridging his finger-tips under his chin.

'If you take my advice,' he said, 'you'll go and have a Turkish bath.'

The young man grasped and frowned.

'You won't take my information?'

'Not in that form. Come again by-and-by.'

Amos walked straight out of the building and retraced his steps to Wardour Street.

'I'll watch for his coming out,' he thought, 'and have him arrested, on one charge only, by the constable on the beat. Where's the place?'

Twice he walked the length of the street and back, with dull increasing amazement. The sunlight had edged its way into the fog by this time, and every door and window stood out sleek and self-evident. But amongst them all was none that corresponded to the door or window of his adventure.

He hung about till day was bright in the air, and until it occurred to him that his woeful and bloodstained appearance was beginning to excite unflattering comment. At that he trudged for the third time the entire length to and fro, and so coming out into Oxford Street stood on the edge of the pavement, as though it were the brink of Cocytus.

'Well, she called me a boy,' he muttered; 'what does it matter?'

He hailed an early hansom and jumped in.

THE SHADOW-DANCE

'Yes, it was a rum start,' said the modish young man.

He was a modern version of the crutch and toothpick genus, a derivative from the 'Gaiety boy' of the Nellie Farren epoch, very spotless, very superior, very – fundamentally and combatively – simple. I don't know how he had found his way into Carleon's rooms and our company, but Carleon had a liking for odd characters. He was a collector, as it were, of human pottery, and to the collector, as we know, primitive examples are of especial interest.

The bait in this instance, I think, had been Bridge, which, since some formal 'Ducdame' must serve for calling fools into a circle, was our common pretext for assembling for an orgy of talk. We had played, however, for insignificant stakes and, on the whole, irreverently as regarded the sanctity of the game; and the young man was palpably bored. He thought us, without question, outsiders, and not altogether good form; and it was even a relief to him when the desultory play languished, and conversation became general in its place.

Somebody – I don't remember on what provocation – had referred to the now historic affair of the Hungarian Ballet, which, the rage in London for a season, had voluntarily closed its own career a week before the date advertised for its termination; and the modish young man, it appeared, was the only one of us all who had happened to be present in the theatre on the occasion of the final performance. He told us so; and added that 'it was a rum start'.

'The abrupt finish was due, of course,' said Carleon, bending forward, hectic, bright-eyed, and hugging himself, as was his wont, 'to Kaunitz's death. She was the bright particular "draw". It would have been nothing without her. Besides, there was the tragedy. What was the "rum start"? Tell us.'

'The way it ended that night,' said the young man. He was a little abashed by the sudden concentration of interest on himself; but carried it off with *sang-froid*. Only a slight flush of pink on his youthful cheek, as he flicked the ash from his cigarette with the delicate little finger of the hand that held it, confessed to a certain uneasy self-consciousness.

'I have heard something about it,' said Carleon. 'Give us your version.'

'I'm no hand at describing things,' responded the young man, committed and at bay; 'never wrote a line of description in my life, nor wanted to. It was the *Shadow-Dance*, you know – the last thing on the programme. I dare say some of you have seen Kaunitz in it.'

One or two of us had. It was incomparably the most beautiful, the most mystic, idyll achieved by even that superlative dancer; a fantasia of moonlight, supported by an ethereal, only half-revealed, shimmer of attendant sylphids.

'Yes,' said Carleon eagerly.

'Well, you know,' said the young man, 'there is a sort of dance first, in and out of the shadows, a mysterious, gossamery kind of business, with nobody made out exactly, and the moon slowly rising behind the trees. And then, suddenly, the moon reaches a gap in the branches, and – and it's full moon, don't you know, a regular white blaze of it, and all the shapes have vanished; only you sort of guess them, get a hint of their arms and faces hiding behind the leaves and under the shrubs and things. And that was the time when Kaunitz ought to have come on.'

'Didn't she come on?'

'Not at first; not when she ought to. There was a devil of a pause, and you could see something was wrong. And after a bit there was a sort of rustle in the house, and people began to cough; and the music slipped round to the beginning again; and they danced it all over a second time, until it came to the full moonlight – and there she was this time all right – how, I don't know, for I hadn't seen her enter.'

'How did she dance – when she *did* appear?'

The young man blew the ash from his cigarette. 'Oh, I don't know!' he said.

'You must know. Wasn't it something quite out of the common? You called it a rum start, you remember.'

'Well, if you insist upon it, it was – the most extraordinary thing I ever witnessed – more like what they describe the Pepper's Ghost business than anything else I can think. She was here, there, anywhere; seemingly independent of what d'ye call – gravitation, you know; she seemed to jump and hang in the air before she came down. And there was another thing. The idea was to dance to her own shadow, you see – follow it, run away from it, flirt with it – and it was the business of the moon, or the limelight man, to keep the shadow going.'

'Well?'

'Well, there was no shadow – not a sign of one.'

'That may have been the limelight man's fault.'

'Very likely; but I don't think so. There was something odd about it all; and most in the way she went.'

'How was that?'

'Why, she just gave a spring, and was gone.'

Carleon sank back, with a sigh as if of repletion, and sat softly cracking his fingers together.

'Didn't you notice anything strange about the house, the audience?' he said – 'people crying out; girls crouching and hiding their faces, for instance?'

'Perhaps, now I think of it,' answered the modish youth.

'I noticed, anyhow, that the curtain came down with a bang, and that there seemed a sort of general flurry and stampede of things, both behind it and on our side.'

'Well, as to that, it is a fact, though you may not know it, that after that night the company absolutely refused to complete its engagement on any terms.'

'I dare say. They had lost Kaunitz.'

'To be sure they had. She was already lying dead in her dressing-room when the *Shadow-Dance* began.'

'Not when it began?'

'So, anyhow, it was whispered.'

'Oh I say,' said the young man, looking rather white; 'I'm not going to believe that, you know.'

WILLIAM TYRWHITT'S 'COPY'

This is the story of William Tyrwhitt, who went to King's Cobb for rest and change, and, with the latter, at least, was so far accommodated as for a time to get beyond himself and into regions foreign to his experiences or his desires. And for this condition of his I hold myself something responsible, inasmuch as it was my inquisitiveness was the means of inducing him to an exploration, of which the result, with its measure of weirdness, was for him alone. But, it seems, I was appointed an agent of the unexplainable without my knowledge, and it was simply my misfortune to find my first unwitting commission in the selling of a friend.

I was for a few days, about the end of a particular July, lodged in that little old seaboard town of Dorset that is called King's Cobb. Thither there came to me one morning a letter from William Tyrwhitt, the polemical journalist (a queer fish, like the cuttle, with an ink-bag for the confusion of enemies), complaining that he was fagged and used up, and desiring me to say that nowhere could complete rest be obtained as in King's Cobb.

I wrote and assured him on this point. The town, I said, lay wrapped in the hills as in blankets, its head only, winking a sleepy eye, projecting from the top of the broad, steep gully in which it was stretched at ease. Thither few came to the droning coast; and such as did, looked up at the High Street baking in the sun, and, thinking of Jacob's ladder, composed them to slumber upon the sand and left the climbing to the angels. Here, I said, the air and the sea were so still that one could hear the oysters snoring in their beds; and the little frizzle of surf on the beach was like to the sound to dreaming ears of bacon frying in the kitchens of the blest.

William Tyrwhitt came, and I met him at the station, six or seven miles away. He was all strained and springless, like a broken child's toy – 'not like that William who, with lance in rest, shot through the lists in Fleet Street'. A disputative galley-puller could have triumphed over him morally; a child physically.

The drive in the inn brake, by undulating roads and scented valleys, shamed his cheek to a little flush of self-assertion.

'I will sleep under the vines,' he said, 'and the grapes shall drop into my mouth.'

'Beware,' I answered, 'lest in King's Cobb your repose should be everlasting. The air of that hamlet has matured like old port in the bin of its hills, till to drink of it is to swoon.'

We alighted at the crown of the High Street, purposing to descend on foot the remaining distance to the shore.

'Behold,' I exclaimed, 'how the gulls float in the shimmer, like ashes tossed aloft by the white draught of a fire! Behold these ancient buildings nodding to the everlasting lullaby of the bay waters! The cliffs are black with the heat apoplexy; the lobster is drawn scarlet to the surface. You shall be like an addled egg put into an incubator.'

'So,' he said, 'I shall rest and not hatch. The very thought is like sweet oil on a burn.'

He stayed with me a week, and his body waxed wondrous round and rosy, while his eye acquired a foolish and vacant expression. So it was with me. We rolled together, by shore and by road of this sluggard place, like spent billiard balls; and if by chance we cannoned, we swerved sleepily apart, until, perhaps, one would fall into a pocket of the sand, and the other bring up against a cushion of sea-wall.

Yet, for all its enervating atmosphere, King's Cobb has its fine traditions of a sturdy independence, and a slashing history withal; and its aspect is as picturesque as that of an opera bouffe fishing-harbour. Then, too, its High Street, as well as its meandering rivulets of low streets, is rich in buildings, venerable and antique.

We took an irresponsible, smiling pleasure in noting these advantages – particularly after lunch; and sometimes, where an old house was empty, we would go over it, and stare at beams and chimney-pieces and hear the haunted tale of its fortunes, with a faint half-memory in our breasts of that one-time bugbear we had known as 'copy'. But though more than once a flaccid instinct would move us to have out our pencils, we would only end by bunging our foolish mouths with them, as if they were cigarettes, and then vaguely wondering at them for that, being pencils, they would not draw.

By then we were so sinewless and demoralised that we could hear in the distant strains of the European Concert nothing but an orchestra of sweet sounds, and would have given ourselves away in any situation with a pound of tea. Therefore, perhaps, it was well for us that, a peremptory summons to town reaching me after seven days of comradeship with William, I must make shift to collect my faculties with my effects, and return to the more bracing climate of Fleet Street.

And here, you will note, begins the story of William Tyrwhitt, who would linger yet a few days in that hanging garden of the south coast, and who would pull himself together and collect matter for 'copy'.

He found a very good subject that first evening of his solitude.

I was to leave in the afternoon, and the morning we spent in aimlessly rambling about the town. Towards mid-day, a slight shower drove us to shelter under the green verandah of a house, standing up from the lower fall of the High Street, that we had often observed in our wanderings. This house

– or rather houses, for it was a block of two – was very tall and odd-looking, being all built of clean squares of a whitish granite; and the double porch in the middle base – led up to by side-going steps behind thin iron railings – roofed with green-painted zinc. In some of the windows were jalousies, but the general aspect of the exterior was gaunt and rigid; and the whole block bore a dismal, deserted look, as if it had not been lived in for years.

Now we had taken refuge in the porch of that half that lay uppermost on the slope; and here we noticed that, at a late date, the building was seemingly in process of repair, painters pots and brushes lying on a window-sill, and a pair of steps showing within through the glass.

'They have gone to dinner,' said I. 'Supposing we seize the opportunity to explore?'

We pushed at the door; it yielded. We entered, shut ourselves in, and paused to the sound of our own footsteps echoing and laughing from corners and high places. On the ground floor were two or three good-sized rooms with modern grates, but cornices, chimney-pieces, embrasures finely Jacobean. There were innumerable under-stair and over-head cupboards, too, and pantries, and closets, and passages going off darkly into the unknown.

We clomb the stairway – to the first floor – to the second. Here was all pure Jacobean; but the walls were crumbling, the paper peeling, the windows dim and foul with dirt.

I have never known a place with such echoes. They shook from a footstep like nuts rattling out of a bag; a mouse behind the skirting led a whole camp-following of them; to ask a question was, as in that other House, to awaken the derisive shouts of an Opposition. Yet, in the intervals of silence, there fell a deadliness of quiet that was quite appalling by force of contrast.

'Let us go down,' I said. 'I am feeling creepy.'

'Pooh!' said William Tyrwhitt; 'I could take up my abode here with a feather bed.'

We descended, nevertheless. Arrived at the ground floor, 'I am going to the back,' said William.

I followed him – a little reluctantly, I confess. Gloom and shadow had fallen upon the town, and this old deserted hulk of an abode was ghostly to a degree. There was no film of dust on its every shelf or sill that did not seem to me to bear the impress of some phantom finger feeling its way along. A glint of stealthy eyes would look from dark uncertain corners; a thin evil vapour appear to rise through the cracks of the boards from the unvisited cellars in the basement.

And here, too, we came suddenly upon an eccentricity of out-building that wrought upon our souls with wonder. For, penetrating to the rear through what might have been a cloak-closet or butler's pantry, we found a supplementary wing, or rather tail of rooms, loosely knocked together, to proceed from the back, forming a sort of skilling to the main building. These rooms led direct into one another, and, consisting of little more than timber and plaster, were in a woeful state of dilapidation. Everywhere the laths grinned through torn gaps in the ceilings and walls; everywhere the latter were blotched and mildewed with damp, and the floor-boards rotting in their tracks. Fallen mortar, rusty tins, yellow teeth of glass, whitened soot – all the decay and rubbish of a generation of neglect littered the place and filled it with an acrid odour. From one of the rooms we looked forth through a little discoloured window upon a patch of forlorn weedy garden, where the very cats glowered in a depression that no surfeit of mice could assuage.

We went on, our nervous feet apologetic to the grit they crunched; and, when we were come to near the end of this dreary annexe, turned off to the left into a short gloom of passage that led to a closed door.

Pushing this open, we found a drop of some half-dozen steps, and, going gingerly down these, stopped with a common exclamation of surprise on our lips.

Perhaps our wonder was justified, for we were in the stern cabin of an ancient West Indiaman.

Some twenty feet long by twelve wide – there it all was, from the deck transoms above, to the side lockers and great curved window, sloping outwards to the floor and glazed with little panes in galleries, that filled the whole end of the room. Thereout we looked, over the degraded garden, to the lower quarters of the town – as if, indeed, we were perched high up on waves – and even to a segment of the broad bay that swept by them.

But the room itself! What phantasy of old seadog or master-mariner had conceived it? What palsied spirit, condemned to rust in inactivity, had found solace in this burlesque of shipcraft? To renew the past in such a fixture, to work oneself up to the old glow of flight and action, and then, while one stamped and rocked maniacally, to feel the refusal of so much as a timber to respond to one's fervour of animation! It was a grotesque picture.

Now, this cherished chamber had shared the fate of the rest. The paint and gilding were all cracked and blistered away; much of the glass of the stem-frame was gone or hung loose in its sashes; the elaborately carved lockers mouldered on the walls.

These were but dummies when we came to examine them – mere slabs attached to the brickwork, and decaying with it.

'There should be a case-bottle and rummers in one, at least,' said William Tyrwhitt.

'There are, sir, at your service,' said a voice behind us.

We started and turned.

It had been such a little strained voice that it was with something like astonishment I looked upon the speaker. Whence he had issued I could not guess; but there he stood behind us, nodding and smiling – a squab, thick-set old fellow with a great bald head, and, for all the hair on his face, a tuft like a teasel sprouting from his under lip.

He was in his shirt-sleeves, without coat or vest; and I noticed that his dirty lawn was oddly plaited in front, and that about his ample paunch was buckled a broad belt of leather. Greased hip-boots encased his lower limbs, and the heels of these were drawn together as he bowed.

William Tyrwhitt – a master of nervous English – muttered 'Great Scott!' under his breath.

'Permit me,' said the stranger – and he held out to us a tin pannikin (produced from Heaven knows where) that swam with fragrance.

I shook my head. William Tyrwhitt, that fated man, did otherwise. He accepted the vessel and drained it.

'It smacks of all Castille,' he said, handing it back with a sigh of ecstasy. 'Who the devil are you, sir?'

The stranger gave a little crow.

'Peregrine Iron, sir, at your service – Captain Peregrine Iron, of the *Raven* sloop amongst others. You are very welcome to the run of my poor abode.'

'Yours?' I murmured in confusion. 'We owe you a thousand apologies.'

'Not at all,' he said, addressing all his courtesy to William. Me, since my rejection of his beaker, he took pains to ignore.

'Not at all,' he said. 'Your intrusion was quite natural under the circumstances. I take a pleasure in being your cicerone. This cabin' (he waved his hand pompously) '—a fancy of mine, sir, a fancy of mine. The actual material of the latest of my commands brought hither and adapted to the exigencies of shore life. It enables me to live eternally in the past – a most satisfying illusion. Come tonight and have a pipe and a glass with me.'

I thought William Tyrwhitt mad.

'I will come, by all means,' he said.

The stranger bowed us out of the room.

'That is right,' he exclaimed. 'You will find me here. Goodbye for the present.'

As we plunged like dazed men into the street, now grown sunny, I turned on my friend.

'William,' I said, 'did you happen to look back as we left the cabin?'

'No.'

'I did.'

'Well?'

'There was no stranger there at all. The place was empty.'

'Well?'

'You will not go tonight?'

'You bet I do.'

I shrugged my shoulders. We walked on a little way in silence. Suddenly my companion turned on me, a most truculent expression on his face.

'For an independent thinker,' he said, 'you are rather a pusillanimous jackass. A man of your convictions to shy at a shadow! Fie, sir, fie! What if the room *were* empty? The place was full enough of traps to permit of Captain Iron's immediate withdrawal.'

Much may be expressed in a sniff. I sniffed.

That afternoon I went back to town, and left the offensive William to his fate.

It found him at once.

The very day following that of my retreat, I was polishing phrases by gaslight in the dull sitting-room of my lodgings in the Lambeth Road, when he staggered in upon me. His face was like a sheep's, white and vacant; his hands had caught a trick of groping blindly along the backs of chairs.

'You have obtained your "copy"?' I said.

I made him out to murmur 'yes' in a shaking under-voice. He was so patently nervous that I put him in a chair and poured him out a wine-glassful of London brandy. This generally is a powerful emetic, but it had no more effect upon him than water. Then I was about to lower the gas, to save his eyes, but he stopped me with a thin shriek.

'Light, light!' he whispered. 'It cannot be too light for me!'

'Now, William Tyrwhitt,' I said, by-and-by, watchful of him, and marking a faint effusion of colour soak to his cheek, 'you would not accept my warning, and you were extremely rude to me. Therefore you have had an experience—'

'An awful one,' he murmured.

'An awful one, no doubt; and to obtain surcease of the haunting memory of it, you must confide its processes to me. But, first, I must put it to you, which is the more pusillanimous – to refuse to submit one's manliness to the tyranny of the unlawful, or, to rush into situations you have not the nerve to adapt yourself to?'

'I could not foresee, I could not foresee.'

'Neither could I. And that was my very reason for declining the invitation. Now proceed.'

It was long before he could. But presently he essayed, and gathered voice with the advance of his narrative, and even unconsciously threw it into something the form of 'copy'. And here it is as he murmured it, but with a gasp for every full-stop.

'I confess I was so far moved by the tone of your protest as, after your departure, to make some cautious inquiries about the house we had visited. I could discover nothing to satisfy my curiosity. It was known to have been untenanted for a great number of years; but as to who was the landlord, whether Captain Iron or another, no one could inform me; and the agent for the property was of the adjacent town where you met me. I was not fortunate, indeed, in finding that anyone even knew of the oddly appointed room; but considering that, owing to the time the house had remained vacant, the existence of this eccentricity could be a tradition only with some casual few, my failure did not strike me as being at all bodeful. On the contrary, it only whetted my desire to investigate further in person, and penetrate to the heart of a very captivating little mystery. But probably, I thought, it is quite simple of solution, and the fact of the repairers and the landlord being in evidence at one time, a natural coincidence.

'I dined well, and sallied forth about nine o'clock. It was a night pregnant with possibilities. The lower strata of air were calm, but overhead the wind went down the sea with a noise of baggage-wagons, and there was an ominous hurrying and gathering together of forces under the bellying standards of the clouds.

'As I went up the steps of the lonely building, the High Street seemed to turn all its staring eyes of lamps in my direction. "What a droll fellow!" they appeared to be saying; "and how will he look when he reissues?"

'"There ain't nubbudy in that house," croaked a small boy, who had paused below, squinting up at me.

'"How do you know?" said I. "Move on, my little man."

'He went; and at once it occurred to me that, as no notice was taken of my repeated knockings, I might as well try the handle. I did, found the door unlatched, as it had been in the morning, pushed it open, entered, and swung it to behind me.

'I found myself in the most profound darkness – that darkness, if I may use the paradox, of a peopled desolation that men of but little nerve or resolution find insupportable. To me, trained to a serenity of stoicism, it could make no demoralising appeal. I had out my matchbox, opened it at leisure, and, while the whole vaulting blackness seemed to tick and rustle with secret movement, took a half-dozen vestas into my hand, struck one alight, and, by its dim radiance, made my way through the building by the passages we had penetrated in the morning. If at all I shrank or perspired on my spectral journey, I swear I was not conscious of doing so.

'I came to the door of the cabin. All was black and silent.

'"Ah!" I thought, "the rogue has played me false."

'Not to subscribe to an uncertainty, I pushed at the door, saw only swimming dead vacancy before me, and tripping at the instant on the sill, stumbled crashing into the room below and slid my length on the floor.

'Now, I must tell you, it was here my heart gave its first somersault. I had fallen, as I say, into a black vault of emptiness; yet, as I rose, bruised and dazed, to my feet, there was the cabin all alight from a great lanthorn that swung from the ceiling, and our friend of the morning seated at a table, with a case-bottle of rum and glasses before him.

'I stared incredulous. Yes, there could be no doubt it was he, and pretty flushed with drink, too, by his appearance.

'"Incandescent light in a West Indiaman!" I muttered; for not otherwise could I account for the sudden illumination. "What the deuce!"

'"Belay that!" he growled. He seemed to observe me for the first time.

'"A handsome manner of boarding a craft you've got, sir," said he, glooming at me.

'I was hastening to apologise, but he stopped me coarsely.

'"Oh, curse the long jaw of him! Fill your cheek with that, you Barbary ape, and wag your tail if you can, but burn your tongue."

'He pointed to the case-bottle with a forefinger that was like a dirty parsnip. What induced me to swallow the insult, and even some of the pungent liquor of his rude offering? The itch for "copy" was, no doubt, at the bottom of it.

'I sat down opposite my host, filled and drained a bumper. The fire ran to my brain, so that the whole room seemed to pitch and courtesy.

'"This is an odd fancy of yours," I said.

'"What is?" said he.

'"This," I answered, waving my hand around – "this freak of turning a back room into a cabin."

'He stared at me, and then burst into a malevolent laugh.

'"Back room, by thunder!" said he. "Why, of course – just a step into the garden where the roses and the buttercupses be a-growing."

'Now I pricked my ears.

'"Has the night turned foul?" I muttered. "What a noise the rain makes beating on the window!"

'"It's like to be a foul one for you, at least," said he. "But, as for the rain, it's blazing moonlight."

'I turned to the broad casement in astonishment. My God! what did I see? Oh, my friend, my friend! will you believe me? By the melancholy glow that spread therethrough I saw that the whole room was rising and sinking in rhythmical motion; that the lights of King's Cobb had disappeared, and that in their place was revealed a world of pale and tossing water, the pursuing waves of which leapt and clutched at the glass with innocuous fingers.

'I started to my feet, mad in an instant.

'"Look, look!" I shrieked. "They follow us – they struggle to get at you, you bloody murderer!"

'They came rising on the crests of the billows; they hurried fast in our wake, tumbling and swaying, their stretched, drowned faces now lifted to the moonlight, now over-washed in the long trenches of water. They were rolled against the galleries of glass, on which their hair slapped like ribbons of seaweed – a score of ghastly white corpses, with strained black eyes and pointed stiff elbows crookt up in vain for air.

'I was mad, but I knew it all now. This was no house, but the good, ill-fated vessel *Rayo*, once bound for Jamaica, but on the voyage fallen into the hands of the bloody buccaneer, Paul Hardman, and her crew made to walk the plank, and most of her passengers. I knew that the dark scoundrel had boarded and mastered her, and – having first fired and sunk his own sloop – had steered her straight for the Cuban coast, making disposition of what remained of the passengers on the way, and I knew that my great-grandfather had been one of these doomed survivors, and that he had been shot and murdered under orders of the ruffian that now sat before me. All this, as retailed by one who sailed for a season under Hardman to save his skin, is matter of old private history; and of common report was it that the monster buccaneer, after years of successful trading in the ship he had stolen, went into secret and prosperous retirement under an assumed name, and was never heard of more on the high seas. But,

it seemed, it was for the great-grandson of one of his victims
to play yet a sympathetic part in the grey old tragedy.

'How did this come to me in a moment – or, rather, what
was that dream buzzing in my brain of "proof" and "copy"
and all the tame stagnation of a long delirium of order? I
had nothing in common with the latter. In some telepathic
way – influenced by these past-dated surroundings – dropped
into the very den of this Procrustes of the seas, I was there
to re-enact the fearful scene that had found its climax in the
brain of my ancestor.

'I rushed to the window, thence back to within a yard of
the glowering buccaneer, before whom I stood, with tost
arms, wild and menacing.

'"They follow you!" I screamed. "Passive, relentless, and
deadly, they follow in your wake and will not be denied. The
strong, the helpless, the coarse and the beautiful – all you
have killed and mutilated in your wanton devilry – they are
on your heels like a pack of spectre-hounds, and sooner or
later they will have you in their cold arms and hale you
down to the secret places of terror. Look at Beston, who
leads, with a fearful smile on his mouth! Look at that pale
girl you tortured, whose hair writhes and lengthens – a swarm
of snakes nosing the hull for some open port-hole to enter
by! Dog and devil, you are betrayed by your own hideous
cruelty!"

'He rose and struck at me blindly; staggered, and found
his filthy voice in a shriek of rage.

'"Jorinder! make hell of the galley-fire! heat some irons
red and fetch out a bucket of pitch. We'll learn this dandy
galloot his manners!"

'Wrought to the snapping-point of desperation, I sprang
at and closed with him; and we went down on the floor
together with a heavy crash. I was weaponless, but I would
choke and strangle him with my hands. I had him under,
my fingers crookt in his throat. His eyeballs slipped forward,
like banana ends squeezed from their skins; he could not

speak or cry, but he put up one feeble hand and flapped it aimlessly. At that, in the midst of my fury, I glanced above me, and saw a press of dim faces crowding a dusk hatch; and from them a shadowy arm came through, pointing a weapon; and all my soul reeled sick, and I only longed to be left time to destroy the venomous horror beneath me before I passed.

'It was not to be. Something, a physical sensation like the jerk of a hiccup, shook my frame; and immediately the waters of being seemed to burst their dam and flow out peaceably into a valley of rest.'

William Tyrwhitt paused, and 'Well?' said I.

'You see me here,' he said. 'I woke this morning, and found myself lying on the floor of that shattered and battered closet, and a starved demon of a cat licking up something from the boards. When I drove her away, there was a patch there like ancient dried blood.'

'And how about your head?'

'My head? Why, the bullet seemed stuck in it between the temples; and there I am afraid it is still.'

'Just so. Now, William Tyrwhitt, you must take a Turkish bath and some cooling salts, and then come and tell me all about it again.'

'Ah! you don't believe me, I see. I never supposed you would. Good-night!'

But when he was gone, I sat ruminating.

'That Captain Iron,' I thought, 'walked over the great rent in the floor without falling through. Well, well!'

A QUEER CICERONE

I had paid my sixpence at the little informal 'box-office,' and received in exchange my printed permit to visit the Castle. It was one of those lordly 'show places' whose owners take a plain business view of the attractions at their disposal, while ostensibly exploiting them on behalf of this or that charity. How the exclusive spirits of eld, represented on their walls in the numerous pictured forms they once inhabited, regard this converting of their pride and panoply to practical ends, is a matter for their descendants to judge; but no doubt the most of them owed, and still owe, a debt to humanity, any liquidation of which in terms of charity would be enough to reconcile them to the indignity of being regarded like waxworks. For my part, I am free to confess that, did I see any profit in an ancestor, I should apply it unequivocally to the charity that begins at home.

I discovered, when I entered, quite a little party waiting to be personally conducted round the rooms. Obviously trippers of the most commonplace type (and what was I better?), they stood herded together in a sort of gelid ante-chamber, pending the arrival of the housekeeper who was to act as cicerone. A hovering menial, in the nature of a commissionaire, had just disappeared in quest of the errant lady, and for the moment we were left unshepherded.

Assuming the nonchalant air of a chance visitor of distinction to whom palaces were familiar, I casually, while

sauntering aloof from it, took the measure of my company.
It was not in the least unusual or interesting. It comprised a
couple of rather sickly 'gents' of the haberdashery type; two
flat ladies in pince-nez, patently in search of culture and
instruction; a huge German tourist, all bush and spectacles,
with a mighty sandwich-box slung over his shoulder, and a
voice of guttural ferocity; an ample but diffident matron,
accompanied by a small youth in clumping boots and a new
ready-made Norfolk suit a size too large for him, and, finally,
a pair of tittering hobble-skirted young ladies, of the class
that parades pavements arm-in-arm. All whispered in their
separate groups, each suspicious of the other, but with voices
universally hushed to the sacred solemnity of the occasion.
Only the German showed a disposition to truculent neigh-
bourliness, proffering some advances to the hobble-skirted
damsels, which were first haughtily, and then gigglingly,
ignored. Whereat the flat ladies, though intellectually addicted
to his race, showed their sense of his unflattering preference
by turning their backs on him.

The room in which we were delayed was the first of a
suite, and very chill and melancholy in its few appointments.
There were some arms, I remember, on the walls, and a
sprinkling of antlers – of all mural decorations the most
petrifyingly depressing. They offered no scope to my assumption of critical ease, and – conscious of an inquisition, a little
derisive, I thought, in its quality, on the part of the company
– I was gravitating towards the general group, when we were
all galvanised into animation by hearing the sound of a light,
quick footfall approaching us from the direction of the room
we were about to traverse. It tripped on, awakening innumerable small echoes in its advance, and suddenly materialised
before us in the form of a very elegant gentleman, of young
middle-age and distinguished appearance.

'Permit me,' he said, halting, hand on heart, with an
inimitable bow. 'I make it my pleasure to represent for the
nonce the admirable but unctuous Mrs Somerset, our valued

housekeeper, who is unfortunately indisposed for the moment.'

I could flatter myself at least that my manner had so far impressed the party as to cause it to constitute me by mute agreement its spokesman. I accepted, as they all looked towards me, the compliment for what it implied, though with a certain stiffness which was due as much to surprise as to embarrassment. For surely courtesy, in the person of this distinguished stranger, was taking a course as unusual as the clothes he inhabited were strange. They consisted of a dark blue, swallow-tailed coat, with a high velvet collar and brass buttons, a voluminous stock, a buff waistcoat, and mouse-coloured tights, having a bunch of seals pendent from their fob and ending in smart pumps. His hair, ample and dusty golden, was brushed high from his forehead in a sort of ordered mane; the face underneath was an ironically hand-some one, but so startlingly pale that the blue eyes fixed in it suggested nothing so much as the 'antique jewels set in Parian marble stone' of a once famous poem. He bowed again, and to me, accepting the general verdict.

'It is most good of you,' I said. 'Of course, if we had known, if we had had any idea—'

He interrupted me, I thought, with a little impatience:

'Not at all. It is, as I informed you, a pleasure – a rare opportunity. I fancy I may promise you a fuller approximation to the truth, regarding certain of our family traditions, than you would ever be likely to attain through the lips of the meritorious but diplomatic Somerset.'

He turned, inviting us, with an incomparable gesture, into the next room. He was certainly an anachronism, a marvel; yet I was willing to admit to myself that eccentrics, sartorial and otherwise, were not confined to the inner circle of society. As to the others, I perceived that they were self-defensively prepared to accept this oddity as part of the mysterious ritual appertaining to the sacred obscurities of the life patrician.

'The first two rooms,' said our guide, halting us on the

threshold, 'are, as you will perceive, appropriated to family portraits. The little furniture that remains is inconsiderable and baroque. It is what survives from the time of the fourth marquis. We observe his portrait here' (he signified a canvas on the wall, representing a dull, arrogant-looking old gentleman in an embroidered coat and a bob-wig), 'and can readily associate with it the tasteless ostentation which characterised his reign. He was really what we should call now a complete aristocratic bounder.'

His tone suggested a mixture of flippancy and malice, which was none the less emphatic because his voice was a peculiarly soft and secret one. Somehow, hearing it, I thought of slanders sniggered from behind a covering hand. The young ladies tittered, as if a little shamefaced and uneasy, drawing his attention to them. He was obviously attracted at once. Their smart modernity, piquant in its way, proved a charm to him that he made no pretence of discounting. He addressed himself instantly to the two:

'Sacred truth, ladies, upon my honour. He was a "throwback", as we say of dogs. The mark of the prosperous cheesemonger was all over him.'

'Ach!' said the German, vibratingly asserting himself, 'a dror-back? Vot is dart?'

'A Teutonic reaction,' said the stranger, taking the speaker's measure insolently, with his chin a little lifted, and his eyes narrowed; 'or rather a recrudescence of barbarism in a race or line that has emerged from it. Your countrymen, from what I hear, should afford many illustrations of the process.'

The flat ladies exchanged a little scornful laugh, which they repeated less disguisedly as the German responded: 'I do not ondorrstand.'

The common little boy, holding to his mother's skirts, urged her on to the next picture, a full-length portrait of a grim Elizabethan warrior in armour.

'Look at his long sword, mother!' he whispered.

'*He* didn't wear corsets – not much,' said one of the

haberdashery youths facetiously, in an audible voice to the other; and the nearest spinster, with a sidelong stare of indignation at him, edged away.

'A crusader?' said the second flat lady, as if putting it to herself. 'I wonder, now.'

The stranger smiled ironically to the hobble-skirts, one of whom was emboldened to ask him:

'Was he one of the family, sir?'

'By Heraldry out of Wardour Street,' answered our guide. 'Very dark horses, both of them.' And then he added, going a few steps: 'You do us too much honour, sweet charmer – positively you do.' He tapped the portrait of a ponderous patrician: 'The first marquis,' he said, 'created in 1784 out of nothing. The King represented the Almighty in that stupendous achievement. God save the King!'

'Let's go, mother,' whispered the small common boy, pressing suddenly against the ample skirts. 'I don't like it.'

'Hush, 'Enery dear,' she returned, in a whispered panic. 'There ain't nothing to be afraid of.'

'Wasn't there none of you before that, sir?' asked the second haberdashery youth.

The stranger sniggered. 'I'll let you all into a little secret,' he said confidently. 'The antiquity of the family, despite our ingenious Mrs Somerset, is mere hocus-pocus. The first marquis's grandfather was a Huntingdonshire dairy-farmer, who amassed a considerable fortune over cheeses. He came to London, speculated in South Sea stock, and sold out at top prices just before the crash. We don't like it talked about, you know; but it was his grandson who was the real founder of the house. He was in the Newcastle administration of '57, and was ennobled for the owlish part he took in opposing the reconquest of India under Clive. And, after that, the more fat-headed he became, the higher they foisted him to get him out of the way. Fact, I assure you. Our crest should be by rights a Stilton rampant, our arms a cheese-scoop, silver on a trencher powdered mites, and our motto, in your own admirable vernacular, "Ain't I the cheese!"'

The young ladies tittered, sharing a little protesting wriggle between him. Then one urged the other, who responded *sotto voce*: 'Ask him yourself, stupid.'

'Charmed,' said the stranger. 'Those roguish lips have only to command.'

'We only wanted to know,' said number two blushfully, 'which is the wicked lord – don't push so, Dolly!'

'Ah!' The stranger showed his teeth in a stiffly creased smile, and shook a long forefinger remonstrantly at the speaker. 'You have been studying that outrageous guide-book, I perceive. What is the passage – eh? "Reputed to have been painted by a mysterious travelling artist of sinister appearance, who, being invited in one night to play with his lordship, subsequently liquidated the debt he incurred by painting his host's portrait."'

He turned on his heel and pointed into the next room. Full in our view opposite the door appeared a glazed frame, but black and empty in seeming – an effect I supposed to be due to the refraction of light upon its surface.

'A most calumniated individual,' he protested, wheeling round again. 'There is his place; we shall come to it presently; but only, I regret, to find it vacant. A matter of restoration, you see, and much to be deplored at the moment. I should have liked to challenge your verdict, face to face with him. These libels die hard – and when given the authority of a guide-book! Take my word for it, he was a most estimable creature, morally worth dozens of the sanctimonious humbugs glorified in the Somerset hagiology. Pah! I am weary, I tell you, of hearing their false virtues extolled. But wait a minute, and you shall learn. The "wicked lord," young misses? And so he is the flattered siderite of your regard. Well, it is well to be sought by such eyes on any count; but I think his would win your leniency. Only excess of love proved his undoing; and I am sure you would not consider that a crime.'

We were all struck a little dumb, I think, by this outburst. The two girls had linked together again, both silent and somewhat white; the gaunt spinsters, rigid and upright, exchanged petrified glances; the fat woman was mopping her face, a tremulous sigh fluttering the hem of her handkerchief; the two young shopmen dwelt slack-jawed; even the German tourist, glaring through his spectacles, shook a little in his breathing, as if a sudden asthma had caught him. But our host, as though unconscious of the effect he had produced, motioned us on smilingly; and so, mechanically obeying, we paused at the next canvas – the uncompleted full-length of a beautiful young woman with haunting eyes.

'The Lady Betty,' he said, 'as she sat for "Innocence" to Schleimhitz. The portrait was only finished, as you see, as far as the waist. He was a slow worker, and not good at drapery.'

The German cleared his throat, and pushing his way past the flat ladies (I thought for the moment one was near furiously hooking at him with her umbrella), glanced with an air of amorous appropriation at the hobble-skirts, and spoke:

'Schleimhitz wass fery goot at drapery. There wass a reason berhaps—'

'Ah – tut – tut!' exclaimed the stranger, with a little hurried smile; and led us on.

'Portrait,' he said, 'by Gainsborough, of a boy – unidentified. There was a story of his having been mislaid by his father, the second marquis, on the occasion of that gentleman's first marriage, and never discovered again.'

'Poor little chap,' murmured one of the hobble-skirts. 'I wonder what became of him? Isn't he pretty?'

'An ancestress,' said our cicerone, at the next canvas, 'who married an actor. He played first gentleman on the stage, and first cad off it. I believe he broke her heart – or her spirit; I forget which. She kept them both in one decanter.' He sniggered round at the two girls. 'No, 'pon honour,' he said, 'I vow to the truth of it. You must trust me above Mrs Somerset.

'A collateral branch this,' he said, passing on. 'He buried three wives, who lie and whisper together in the family vault. He himself was buried, by his own direction, at sea. They say the coffin hissed as it touched the water.'

The little common boy suddenly began to cry loudly. 'I'm frightened, mother!' he wailed. 'Take me away.'

The stranger, bending to look for him, made as if to claw through the group. I saw a most diabolical expression on his face.

'Ah!' he said, 'I'll have you yet!'

The child screamed violently, and beat in frantic terror against his mother. I interposed, an odd damp on my forehead.

'Look here,' I said; 'leave the boy alone, will you?'

They were all backing, startled and scared, when there came a hurried, loud step into the room from behind us, and we turned in a panic huddle. It was the commissionaire, very flustered and irate.

'Now, then, you know,' he said, 'you'd no right to take it upon yourselves to go round like this unattended.'

'Pardon me,' I said, resuming my charge of spokesman; 'we did nothing of the sort. This gentleman offered himself to escort us.'

I turned, as did all the others, and my voice died in my throat. There was no gentleman at all – the room was empty. As I stood stupidly staring, I was conscious of the voice of the commissionaire, aggrieved, expostulatory, but with a curious note of distress in it:

'What gentleman? There's nobody has the right but Mrs Somerset, and she's ill – she's had a stroke. We've just found her in her room, with a face like the horrors on her.'

Suddenly one of the women shrieked hysterically: 'O look! He's there! O come away!'

And, as she screamed, I saw. The empty picture frame in the next room was empty no longer. It was filled by the form of him, handsome and smiling, he who had just been conducting us round the walls.

A GALLOWS-BIRD

In February of the year 1809, when the French were sat down before Saragossa – then enduring its second and more terrific siege within a period of six months – it came to the knowledge of the Duc d'Abrantes, at that time the General commanding, that his army, though undoubtedly the salt of the earth, was yet so little sufficient to itself in the matter of seasoning, that it was reduced to the necessity of flavouring its soup with the saltpetre out of its own cartridges. In this emergency, d'Abrantes sent for a certain Ducos, captain on the staff of General Berthier, but at present attached to a siege train before the doomed town, and asked him if he knew whence, if anywhere in the vicinity, it might be possible to make good the deficiency.

Now this Eugene Ducos was a very progressive evolution of the times, hatched by the rising sun, emerged stinging and splendid from the exotic quagmires of the past. A facile linguist, by temperament and early training an artist, he had flown naturally to the field of battle as to that field most fertile of daring new effects, whose surprises called for record rather than analysis. It was for him to collect the impressions which, later, duller wits should classify. And, in the meantime, here he was at twenty a captain of renown, and always a creature of the most unflagging resourcefulness.

'You were with Lefebvre-Desnouettes in Aragon last year?' demanded Junot.

'I was, General; both before the siege and during it.'

'You heard mention of salt mines in this neighbourhood?'

'There were rumours of them, sir – amongst the hills of Ulebo; but it was never our need to verify the rumours.'

'Take a company, now, and run them to earth. I will give you a week.'

'Pardon me, General; I need no company but my own, which is ever the safest colleague.'

Junot glared demoniacally. He was already verging on the madness which was presently to destroy him.

'The devil!' he shouted. 'You shall answer for that assurance! Go alone, sir, since you are so obliging, and find salt; and at your peril be killed before reporting the result to me. Bones of God! is every skipjack with a shoulder-knot to better my commands?'

Ducos saluted, and wheeled impassive. He knew that in a few days Marshal Lannes was to supplant this maniac.

Up and away amongst the intricate ridges of the mountains, where the half-unravelled knots of the Pyrenees flow down in threads, or clustered threads, which are combed by-and-by into the plains south of Saragossa, a dusky young goatherd loitered among the chestnut trees on a hot afternoon. This boy's beauty was of a supernal order. His elastic young cheeks glowed with colour; his eyebrows were resolute bows; his lips, like a pretty phrase of love, were set between dimples like inverted commas. And, as he stood, he coquetted like Dinorah to his own shadow, *chassé* to it, spoke to it, upbraiding or caressing, as it answered to his movements on the ground before him—

'Ah, pretty one! ah, shameless! Art thou the shadow of the girl that Eugenio loved? Fie, fie! thou wouldst betray this poor Anita – mock the round limbs and little feet that will not look their part. Yet, betray her to her love returning, and Anita will fall and kiss thee on her knees – kiss the very shadow of Eugenio's love. Ah, little shadow! take wings and fly to him, who promised quickly to return. Say I am good but sad, awaiting him; say that Anita suffers, but is patient. He will remember then, and come. No shadow of disguise shall blind him to his love. Go, go, before I repent and hold thee, jealous that mine own shadow should run before to find his lips.'

She stooped, and, with a fantastic gesture, threw her soul upon the winds; then rose, and leaned against a tree, and began to sing, and sigh and murmur softly:

'At the gate of heaven are sold brogues
For the little bare-footed angel rogues—'

'Ah, little dear mother! it is the seventh month, and the sign is still delayed. No baby, no lover. Alack! why should he return to me, who am a barren olive! The husbandman asks a guerdon for his care. Give me my little doll, Santissima, or I will be naughty and drink holy water: give me the shrill wee voice, which pierces to the father's heart, when even passion loiters. Ah, come to me, Eugenio, my Eugenio!'

She raised her head quickly on the word, and her heart leaped. It was to hear the sound of a footstep, on the stones far below, coming up the mountainside. She looked to her shirt and jacket. Ragged as they were, undeveloped as was the figure within them, she had been so jealous a housewife that there was not in all so much as an eyelet hole to attract a peeping Tom. Now, leaving her goats amongst the scattered boulders of the open, she backed into the groves, precautionally, but a little reluctant, because in her heart she was curious.

The footsteps came on toilfully, and presently the man who was responsible for them hove into sight. He wore the dress of an English officer, save for the shepherd's felt hat on his head; but his scarlet jacket was knotted loosely by the sleeves about his throat, in order to the disposition of a sling which held his left arm crookt in a bloody swathe. He levered himself up with a broken spear-shaft; but he was otherwise weaponless. A pistol, in Ducos's creed, was the argument of a fool. He carried *his* ammunition in his brains.

Having reached a little plateau, irregular with rocks shed from the cliff above, he sat down within the shadow of a grove of chestnut and carob trees, and sighed, and wiped his brow, and nodded to all around and below him.

'Yes, and yes, and of a truth,' thought he: 'here is the country of my knowledge. And yonder, deep and far amongst its myrtles and mulberries, crawls the Ebro; and to my right, a browner clod amongst the furrows of the valleys, heaves up the ruined monastery of San Ildefonso, which Daguenet sacked, the radical; whilst I occupied (ah, the week of sweet *malvoisie* and sweeter passion!) the little inn at the junction of the Pampeluna and Saragossa roads. And what has become of Anita of the inn? Alack! if my little *fille de joie* were but here to serve me now!'

The goatherd slipped round the shoulder of a rock and stood before him, breathing hard. Her black curls were, for all the world, bandaged, as it might be, with a yellow napkin (though they were more in the way to give than take wounds), and crowned rakishly with a dusky sombrero. She wore a kind of gaskins on her legs, loose, so as to reveal the bare knees and a little over; and across her shoulders was slung a sunburnt shawl, which depended in a bib against her chest.

Now the one stood looking down and the other up, their visions magnetically meeting and blending, till the eyes of the goatherd were delivered of very stars of rapture.

Was this a spirit, thought Ducos, summoned of his hot and necessitous desire? But the other had no such misgiving. All in a moment she had fallen on her brown knees before him, and was pitifully kissing his bandaged arm, while she strove to moan and murmur out the while her ecstasy of gratitude.

'Nariguita!' he murmured, rallying as if from a dream; 'Nariguita!'

She laughed and sobbed.

'Ah, the dear little happy name from thy lips! A thousand times will I repeat it to myself, but never as thou wouldst say it. And now! Yes, Nariguita, Eugenio – thine own "little nose" – thy child, thy baby, who never doubted that this day would come – O darling of my soul, that it would come!' – (she clung to him, and hid her face) – 'Eugenio! though the blossom of our love delays its fruitage!'

He smiled, recovered from his first astonishment. Ministers of coincidence! In all the fantastic convolutions of war, the merry, the *danse macabre*, should not love's reunions have a place? It was nothing out of that context that here was he chanced again, and timely, upon that same sweet instrument which he had once played on and done with, and thrown aside, careless of its direction. Now he had but to stoop and reclaim it, and the discarded strings, it seemed, were ready as heretofore to answer to his touch with any melody he listed.

He caressed her with real delight. She was something more than lovable. He made himself a very Judas to her lips.

'Anita, my little Anita!' he began glowingly; but she took him up with a fevered eagerness, answering the question of his eyes.

'So long ago, ah Dios! And thou wert gone; and the birds were silent; and under the heavy sky my father called me to him. He held a last letter of thine, which had missed my hands for his. Love, sick at our parting, had betrayed us. O, the letter! how I swooned to be denied it! He was for killing me, a traitor. Well, I could not help but be. But Tia Joachina had pity on me, and dressed me as you see, and smuggled me to the hills, that I might at least have a chance to live without suffering wrong. And, behold! the heavens smiled upon me, knowing my love; and Señor Cangrejo took me to herd his goats. For seven months – for seven long, faithful months; until the sweetest of my heart's flock should return to pasture in my bosom. And now he has come, my lamb, my prince, even as he promised. He has come, drawing me to him over the hills, following the lark's song of his love as it dropped to earth far forward of his steps. Eugenio! O, ecstasy! Thou hast dared this for my sake?'

'Child,' answered the admirable Ducos, 'I should have dared only in breaking my word. *Un honnête homme n'a que sa parole*. That is the single motto for a poor captain, Nariguita. And who is this Señor Cangrejo?'

Some terror, offspring of his question, set her clinging to him once more.

'What dost thou here?' she cried, with immediate inconsistency – 'a lamb among the wolves! Eugenio!'

'Eh!' – he took her up, with an air of bewilderment. 'I am Sir Zhones, the English *capitaine*, though it lose me your favour, mamselle. What! Damn it, I say!'

She fell away, staring at him; then in a moment gathered, and leapt to him again between tears and laughter.

'But this?' she asked, her eyes glistening; and she touched the bandage.

'Ah! that,' he answered. 'Why, I was wounded, and taken prisoner by the French, you understand? Also, I escaped from my captors. It comes, blood and splint and all, from the smashed arm of a *sabreur*, who, indeed, had no longer need of it.'

'For the love of Christ!' she cried in a panic. 'Come away into the trees, where none will observe us!'

'Bah! I have no fear, I,' said Ducos. But he rose, nevertheless, with a smile, and, catching up the goatherd, bore her into the shadows. There, sitting by her side, he assured her, the rogue, of the impatience with which he had anticipated, of the eagerness with which he had run to realise this longed-for moment. The escapade had only been rendered possible, he said truthfully, by the opportune demand for salt. Doubtless she would help him, for love's sake, to justify the venture to his General?

But, at that, she stared at him, troubled, and her lip began to quiver.

'Ah, God!' she cried; 'then it was not I in the first place! Go thy ways, love; but for pity's heart-sake let me weep a little. Yes, yes, there is salt in the mountains, that I know, and where the caves lie. But there are also Cangrejo – whom you French ruined and made a madman – and a hundred like him, wild-cats hidden amongst the leaves. And there, too, are the homeless friars of St Ildefonso; and, dear body of Christ! the tribunal of terror, the junta of women, who are the worst of all – lynx-eyed demons.'

He smiled indulgently. Her terror amused him.

'Well, well,' he said; 'well, well. And what, then, is this junta?'

'It is a scourge,' she whispered, shivering, 'for traitors and for spies. It gathers nightly, at sunset, in the dip yonder, and there waters with blood its cross of death. This very evening, Cangrejo tells me—'

She broke off, cuddled closer to her companion, and clasping her hands and shrugging up her shoulders to him, went on awfully—

'Eugenio, there was a wagon-load of piastres coming secretly for Saragossa by the Tolosa road. It was badly convoyed. One of your generals got scent of it. The guard had time to hide their treasure and disperse, but him whom they thought had betrayed them the tribunal of women claimed, and tonight—'

'Well, he will receive his wages. And where is the treasure concealed?'

'Ah! that I do not know.'

Ducos got to his feet, and stretched and yawned.

'I have a fancy to see this meeting-place of the tribunal. Wilt thou lead me to it, Nariguita?'

'Mother of God, thou art mad!'

'Then I must go alone, like a madman.'

'Eugenio, it is cursing and accurst. None will so much as

look into it by day; and, at dusk, only when franked by the holy church.'

'So greatly the better. Adios, Nariguita!'

It took them half an hour, descending cautiously, and availing themselves of every possible shelter of bush and rock, to reach a strangely formed amphitheatre set stark and shallow amongst the higher swales of the valley, but so over-hung with scrub of myrtle and wild pomegranate as to be only distinguishable, and that scarcely, from above. A ragged track, mounting from the lower levels into this hollow, tailed off, and was attenuated into a point where it took a curve of the rocks at a distance below.

As Ducos, approaching the rim, pressed through the thicket, a toss of black crows went up from the mouth ahead of him, like cinders of paper spouted from a chimney. He looked over. The brushwood ceased at the edge of a consid-erable pit, roughly circular in shape, whose sides, of bare sloping sand, met and flattened at the bottom into an extended platform. Thence arose a triangular gibbet, a very rack in a devil's larder, all about which a hoard of little pitchy bird scullions were busy with the joints. Holy mother, how they squabbled, and flapped at one another with their sleeves, it seemed! The two carcasses which hung there appeared, for all their heavy pendulosity, to reel and rock with laughter, nudging one another in eyeless merriment.

Ducos mentally calculated the distance to the gallows below from any available coign of concealment.

'One could not hide close enough to hear anything,' he murmured, shaking his head in aggravation; 'and this junta of ladies – it will probably talk. What if it were to discuss that very question of the piastres? Nariguita, will you go and be my little reporter at the ceremony?'

Anita, crouching in the brush behind him, whispered terri-fied: 'It is impossible. They admit none but priests and women.'

'And are not you a woman, most beautiful?'

'God forbid!' she said. 'I am the little goatherd Ambrosio.'

He stood some moments, frowning. A scheme, daring and characteristic, was beginning to take shape in his brain.

'What is that clump of rags by the gallows?' he asked, without looking round.

'It is not rags; it is rope, Eugenio.'

He thought again.

'And when do they come to hang this rascal?' he said.

'It is always at dusk. O, dear mother!' she whimpered, for the young man had suddenly slipped between the branches, and was going swiftly and softly down the pit-side.

Already the basin of sand was filled with the shadows from the hills. Ducos approached the gibbet. The last of the birds remaining arose and dispersed, quarrelling with nothing so much as the sunlight which they encountered above.

'It is an abominable task,' said the aide-de-camp, looking up at the dangling bodies; 'but – for the Emperor – always for the Emperor! That fellow, now, in the domino – it would make us appear of one build. And as for complexion, why, he at least would have no eyes for the travesty, Mon Dieu! I believe it is a Providence.'

There was a ladder leaned against the third and empty beam. He put it into position for the cloaked figure, and ran up it. The rope was hitched to a hook in the crosspiece. He must clasp and lever up his burden by main strength before he could slacken and detach the cord. Then, with an exclamation of relief, he let the body drop upon the sand beneath. He descended the ladder in excitement.

'Anita!' he called.

She had followed, and was at hand. She trembled, and was as pale as death.

'Help me,' he panted – 'with this – into the bush.'

He had lifted *his* end by the shoulders.

'What devil possesses you? I cannot,' she sobbed; 'I shall die.'

'Ah, Nariguita! for my sake! There is no danger if thou art brave and expeditious.'

Between them they tugged and trailed their load into the dense undergrowth skirting the open track, and there let it plunge and sink. Ducos removed the domino from the body, rolling and hauling at that irreverently. Then he saw how the wretch had been pinioned, wrists and ankles, beneath.

Carrying the cloak, he hastened back to the gallows. There he cautiously selected from the surplus stock of cord a length of some twelve feet, at either end of which he formed a loop. So, mounting the ladder, over the hook he hitched this cord by one end, and then, swinging himself clear, slid down the rope until he could pass both his feet into the lower hank.

'*Voila*!' said he. 'Come up and tie me to the other with some little pieces round the waist and knees and neck.'

She obeyed, weeping. Her love and her duty were to this wonder of manhood, however dreadful his counsel. Presently, trussed to his liking, he bade her fetch the brigand's cloak and button it over all.

'Now,' said he, 'one last sacramental kiss; and, so descending and placing the ladder and all as before, thou shalt take standing-room in the pit for this veritable dance of death.'

A moment – and he was hanging there, to all appearance a corpse. The short rope at his neck had been so disposed and knotted – the collar of the domino serving – as to make him look, indeed, as if he strained at the tether's end. He had dragged his long hair over his eyes; his head lolled to one side; his tongue protruded. For the rest, the cloak hid all, even to his feet.

The goatherd snivelled.

'Ah, holy saints, he is dead!'

The head came erect, grinning.

'Eugenio!' she cried; 'O, my God! Thou wilt be discovered – thou wilt slip and strangle! Ah, the crows – body of my body, the crows!'

'Imbecile! have I not my hands? See, I kiss one to thee. Now the sun sinks, and my ghostly vigil will be short. Pray heaven only they alight not on that in the bush. Nariguita, little heroine, this is my last word. Go hide thyself in the bushes above, and watch what a Frenchman, the most sensitive of mortals, will suffer to serve his Emperor.'

It was an era, indeed, of sublime lusts and barbaric virtues, when men must mount upon stepping-stones, not of their dead selves, but of their slaughtered enemies, to higher things. Anita, like Ducos, was a child of her generation. To her mind the heroic purpose of this deed overpowered its pungency. She kissed her lover's feet; secured the safe disposition of the cloak about them; then turned and fled into hiding.

At dusk, with the sound of footsteps coming up the pass, the crows dispersed. Eugene, for all his self-sufficiency, had sweated over their persistence. A single more gluttonous swoop might at any moment, in blinding him, have laid him open to a general attack before help could reach him from the eyrie whence unwearying love watched his every movement. Now, common instance of the providence which waits on daring, the sudden lift and scatter of the swarm left his hearing sensible to the tinkling of a bridle, which came rhythmical from the track below. Immediately he fell, with all his soul, into the pose of death.

The cadence of the steely warning so little altered, the footsteps stole in so muffled and so deadly, that, peering presently through slit eyelids for the advent of the troop, it twitched his strung nerves to see a sinister congress already drawn soundless about the gibbet on which he hung. Perhaps for the first time in this stagnant atmosphere he realised the peril he had invited. But still the gambler's providence befriended him.

They were all women but two – the victim, a sullen, whiskered Yanguesian, strapped cuttingly to a mule, and a paunchy shovel-hatted Carmelite, who hugged a crucifix between his roomy sleeves.

Ducos had heard of these banded *vengeresses*. Now, he was Frenchman enough to appreciate in full the significance of their attitude, as they clustered beneath him in the dusk, a veiled and voiceless huddle of phantoms. 'How,' he thought, peeping through the dropped curtain of his hair, 'will the adorables do it?' He had an hysterical inclination to laugh, and at that moment the monk, with a sudden decision to action, brushed against him and set him slowly twirling until his face was averted from the show.

Immediately thereon – as he interpreted sounds – the mule was led under the gallows. He heard the ladder placed in position, heard a strenuous shuffling as of concentrated movement. What he failed to hear (at present) was any cry or protest from the victim. The beam above creaked, a bridle tinkled, a lighter drop of hoofs receded. A pregnant pause ensued, broken only by a slight noise, like rustling or vibrating – and then, in an instant, by a voice, chuckling, hateful – the voice of the priest.

'What! to hang there without a word, Carlos? Wouldst thou go, and never ask what is become of that very treasure thou soldst thy soul to betray? The devil has rounded on thee, Carlos; for after all it is thou that art lost, and not the treasure. That is all put away – shout it in the ears of thy neighbours up there – it is all put away, Carlos, safe in the salt mines of the Little Hump. Cry it to the whole world now. Thou mayst if thou canst. In the salt mines of the Little Hump. Dost hear? Ah, then, we must make thee answer.'

With his words, the pit was all at once in shrill hubbub, noise indescribable and dreadful, the shrieking of harpies bidden to their prey. It rose demoniac – a very Walpurgis.

'No, no,' thought Ducos, gulping under his collar. He was almost unnerved for the moment. 'It is unlawful – they have no right to!'

He was twisting again, for all his mad will to prevent it. He would not look, and yet he looked. The monk, possessed, was thrashing the torn and twitching rubbish with his crucifix. The others, their fingers busy with the bodkins they had plucked from their mantillas, had retreated for the moment to a little distance.

Suddenly the Carmelite, as if in an uncontrollable frenzy, dropped his weapon, and scuttling to the mule, where it stood near at hand, tore a great horse pistol from its holster among the trappings, and pointed it at the insensible body.

'Scum of all devils!' he bellowed. 'In fire descend to fire that lasts eternal!'

He pulled the trigger. There was a flash and shattering explosion. A blazing hornet stung Ducos in the leg. He may have started and shrieked. Any cry or motion of his must have passed unnoticed in the screaming panic evoked of the crash. He clung on with his hands and dared to raise his head. The mouth of the pass was dusk with flying skirts. Upon the sands beneath him, the body of the priest, a shape-less bulk, was slowly subsiding and settling, one fat fist of it yet gripping the stock of a pistol which, overgorged, had burst as it was discharged.

The reek of the little tragedy had hardly dissipated before Ducos found himself. The sentiment of revolt, deriving from his helpless position, had been indeed but momentary. To feel his own accessibility to torture, painted torture to him as an inhuman lust. With the means to resist, or escape, at will, he might have sat long in ambush watching it; even condoning it as an extravagant posture of art.

With a heart full of such exultation over the success of his trick that for the moment he forgot the pain of his wound, he hurriedly unpicked the knots of the shorter cords about him, and, jumping to the ground, waited until the shadow of a little depressed figure came slinking across the sand towards him.

'Eugenio!' it whispered; 'what has happened? O! art thou hurt?'

She ran into his arms, sobbing.

'I am hurt,' said Ducos. 'Quick, child! unstrap this from my arm and bind it about my calf. Didst hear? But it was magnificent! Two birds with a single stone. The piastres in pickle for us. Didst see, moreover? Holy Emperor! it was laughable. I would sacrifice a decoration to be witness of the meeting of those two overhead. It should be the Yanguesian for my money, for he has at least his teeth left. Look how he shows them, bursting with rage! Quick, quick, quick! we must be up and away, before any of those others think of returning.'

'And if one should,' she said, 'and mark the empty beam?'

'What does it matter, nevertheless! I must be off tonight, after thou hast answered me one single question.'

'Off? Eugenio! O! not without me?'

'God, little girl! In this race I must not be hampered by so much as a thought. But I will return for thee – never fear.'

He still sat in his domino. She knelt at his feet, stanching the flow from the wound the pistol had made in his leg. At his words she looked up breathlessly into his face; then away, to hide her swimming eyes. In the act she slunk down, making herself small in the sand.

'Eugenio! My God! we are watched!'

He turned about quickly.

'Whence?'

'From the mouth of the pass,' she whispered.

'I can see nothing,' he said. 'Hurry, nevertheless! What a time thou art! There, it is enough of thy bungling fingers. Help me to my feet and out of this place. Come!' he ended, angrily.

He had an ado to climb the easy slope. By the time they were entered amongst the rocks and bushes above, it was black dusk.

'Whither wouldst thou, dearest?' whispered the goatherd.

He had known well enough a moment ago – to some point, in fact, whence she could indicate to him the direction of the Little Hump, where the treasure lay; afterwards, to the very hill-top where some hours earlier they had forgathered. But he would not or could not explain this. Some monstrous blight of gloom had seized his brain at a swoop.

He thought it must be one of the crows, and he stumbled along, raving in his heart. If she offered to help him now, he would tear his arm furiously from her touch. She wondered, poor stricken thing, haunting him with tragic eyes. Then at last her misery and desolation found voice—

'What have I done? I will not ask again to go with thee, if that is it. It was only one little foolish cry of terror, most dear – that they should suspect, and seize, and torture me. But, indeed, should they do it, thou canst trust me to be silent.'

He stopped, swaying, and regarded her demoniacally. His face was a livid and malignant blot in the thickening dusk. To torture her? What torture could equal his at this moment? She sought merely to move him by an affectation of self-renunciation. That, of course, called at once for extreme punishment. He must bite and strangle her to death.

He moved noiselessly upon her. She stood spell-bound before him. All at once something seemed to strike him on the head, and, without uttering a sound, he fell forward into the bush.

Ducos opened his eyes to the vision of so preternaturally melancholy a face, that he was shaken with weak laughter over the whimsicality of his own imagination. But, in a very little, unwont to dreaming as he was, the realisation that he was looking upon no apparition, but a grotesque of fact, silenced and absorbed him.

Presently he was moved to examine his circumstances. He was lying on a heap of grass mats in a tiny house built of boards. Above him was a square of leaf-embroidered sky cut out of a cane roof; to his left, his eyes, focusing with a queer stiffness, looked through an open doorway down precipices of swimming cloud. That was because he lay in an eyrie on the hillside. And then at once, into his white field of vision, floated the dismal long face, surmounted by an ancient cocked-hat, slouched and buttonless, and issuing like an august Aunt Sally's from the neck of a cloak as black and dropping as a pall.

The figure crossed the opening outside, and wheeled, with the wind in its wings. In the act, its eyes, staring and protuberant, fixed themselves on those of the Frenchman. Immediately, with a little stately gesture expressive of relief and welcome, it entered the hut.

'By the mercy of God!' exclaimed the stranger in his own tongue.

Then he added in English: 'The Inglese recovers to himself?'

Ducos smiled, nodding his head; then answered confidently, feeling his way: 'A little, sir, I tank you. Thees along night. Ah! it appear all one pain.'

The other nodded solemnly in his turn—

'A long night indeed, in which the sunksink tree very time.'

'Comment!' broke out the aide-de-camp hoarsely, and instantly realised his mistake.

'Ah! devil take the French!' said he explanatorily. 'I been in their camp so long that to catch their lingo. But I spik l'Espagnol, señor. It shall be good to us to converse there.'

The other bowed impenetrably. His habit of a profound and melancholy aloofness might have served for mask to any temper of mind but that which, in real fact, it environed – a reason, that is to say, more lost than bedevilled under the long tyranny of oppression.

'I have been ill, I am to understand?' said Ducos, on his guard.

'For three days and nights, señor. My goatherd came to tell me how a wounded English officer was lying on the hills. Between us we conveyed you hither.'

'*Ah, Dios*! I remember. I had endeavoured to carry muskets into Saragossa by the river. I was hit in the leg; I was captured; I escaped. For two days I wandered, señor, famished and desperate. At last in these mountains I fell as by a stroke from heaven.'

'It was the foul blood clot, señor. It balked your circulation. There was the brazen splinter in the wound, which I removed, and God restored you. What fangs are theirs, these reptiles! In a few days you will be well.'

'Thanks to what ministering angel?'

'I am known as Don Manoel di Cangrejo, señor, the most shattered, as he was once the most prosperous of men. May God curse the French! May God' (his wild, mournful face twitched with strong emotion) 'reward and bless these brave allies of a people more wronged than any the world has yet known!'

'Noble Englishman,' said he by and by, 'thou hast nothing at present but to lie here and accept the grateful devotion of a heart to which none but the inhuman denies humanity.'

Ducos looked his thanks.

'If I might rest here a little,' he said; 'if I might be spared—'

The other bowed, with a grave understanding.

'None save ourselves, and the winds and trees, señor. I will nurse thee as if thou wert mine own child.'

He was as good as his word. Ducos, pluming himself on his perspicacity, accepting the inevitable with philosophy, lent himself during the interval, while feigning a prolonged weakness, to recovery. That was his, to all practical purposes, within a couple of days, during which time he never set eyes on Anita, but only on Anita's master. Don Manoel would often come and sit by his bed of mats; would even sometimes retail to him, as to a trusted ally, scraps of local information. Thus was he posted, to his immense gratification, in the topical after-history of his own exploit at the gallows.

'It is said,' whispered Cangrejo awfully, 'that one of the dead, resenting so vile a neighbour, impressed a goatherd into his service, and, being assisted from the beam, walked away. Truly it is an age of portents.'

On the third morning, coming early with his bowl of goat's milk and his offering of fruits, he must apologise, with a sweet and lofty courtesy, for the necessity he was under of absenting himself all day.

'There is trouble,' he said – 'as when is there not? I am

called to secret council, señor. But the boy Ambrosio has my orders to be ever at hand shouldst thou need him.'

Ducos's heart leapt. But he was careful to deprecate this generous attention, and to cry *Adios*! with the most perfect assumption of composure.

He was lying on his elbow by and by, eagerly listening, when the doorway was blocked by a shadow. The next instant Anita had sprung to and was kneeling beside him.

'Heart of my heart, have I done well? Thou art sound and whole? O, speak to me, speak to me, that I may hear thy voice and gather its forgiveness!'

For what? She was sobbing and fondling him in a very lust of entreaty.

'Thou hast done well,' he said. 'So, we were seen indeed, Anita?'

'Yes,' she wept, holding his face to her bosom. 'And, O! I agonise for thee to be up and away, Eugenio, for I fear.'

'Hush! I am strong. Help me to my legs, child. So! Now, come with me outside, and point out, if thou canst, where lies the Little Hump.'

She was his devoted crutch at once. They stood in the sunlight, looking down upon the hills which fell from beneath their feet – a world of tossed and petrified rapids. At their backs, on a shallow plateau under eaves of rock, Cangrejo's eyrie clung to the mountain-side.

'There,' said the goatherd, indicating with her finger, 'that mound above the valley – that little hill, fat-necked like a great mushroom, which sprouts from its basin among the trees?'

'Wait! mine eyes are dazzled.'

'Ah, poor sick eyes! Look, then! Dost thou not see the white worm of the Pampeluna road – below yonder, looping through the bushes?'

'I see it – yes, yes.'

'Now, follow upwards from the big coil, where the pine tree leans to the south, seeming a ladder between road and mound.'

'Stay – I have it.'

'Behold the Little Hump, the salt mine of St Ildefonso, and once, they say, an island in the midst of a lake, which burst its banks and poured forth and was gone. And now thou knowest, Eugenio?'

He did not answer. He was intently fixing in his memory the position of the hill. She waited on his mood, not daring to risk his anger a second time, with a pathetic anxiety. Presently he heaved out a sigh, and turned on her, smiling.

'It is well,' he said. 'Now conduct me to the spot where we met three days ago.'

It was surprisingly near at hand. A labyrinthine descent – by way of aloe-homed rocks, with sandy bents and tufts of harsh juniper between – of a hundred yards or so, and they were on the stony plateau which he remembered. There, to one side, was the coppice of chestnuts and locust trees. To the other, the road by which he had climbed went down with a run – such as he himself was on thorns to emulate into the valleys trending to Saragossa. His eyes gleamed. He seated himself down on a boulder, controlling his impatience only by a violent effort.

'Anita,' he said, drilling out his speech with slow emphasis, 'thou must leave me here alone awhile. I would think – I would think and plan, my heart. Go, wait on thy goats above, and I will return to thee presently.'

She sighed, and crept away obedient. O, forlorn, most forlorn soul of love, which, counting mistrust treason, knows itself a traitor! Yet Anita obeyed, and with no thought to eavesdrop, because she was in love with loyalty.

The moment he was well convinced of her retreat, Ducos got to his legs with an immense sigh of relief. Love, he thought, could be presuming, could be obtuse, could be positively a bore. It all turned upon the context of the moment; and the present was quick with desires other than for endearments. For it must be related that the young captain, having manoeuvred matters to this accommodating pass, was designing nothing less than an instant return, on the wings of transport, to the blockading camp, whence he proposed returning, with a suitable force and all possible dispatch, to seize and empty of its varied treasures the salt mine of St Ildefonso.

'Pouf!' he muttered to himself in a sort of ecstatic aggravation; 'this accursed delay! But the piastres are there still – I have Cangrejo's word for it.'

He turned once, before addressing himself to flight, to refocus in his memory the position of the mound, which still from here was plainly visible. In the act he pricked his ears, for there was a sound of footsteps rising up the mountain path. He dodged behind a boulder. The footsteps came on – approached him – paused – so long that he was induced at last to peep for the reason. At once his eyes encountered other eyes awaiting him. He laughed, and left his refuge. The newcomer was a typical Spanish Romany – slouching, filthy, with a bandage over one eye.

'God be with thee, Caballero!' said the Frenchman defiantly.

To his astonishment, the other broke into a little scream of laughter, and flung himself towards him.

'Judge thou, now,' said he, 'which is the more wide-awake adventurer and the better actor!'

'My God!' cried Ducos; 'it is de la Platière!'

'Hush!' whispered the mendicant. 'Are we private? Ah, bah! Junot should have sent me in the first instance.'

'I have been hurt, thou rogue. Our duel of wits is yet postponed. In good time hast thou arrived. This simplifies matters. Thou shalt return, and I remain. Hist! come away, and I will tell thee all.'

Half an hour later, de la Platière – having already, for his part, mentally absorbed the details of a certain position – swung rapidly, with a topical song on his lips, down the path he had ascended earlier. The sound of his footfalls receded and died out. The hill regathered itself to silence. Ducos, on terms with destiny and at peace with all the world, sat for hours in the shadow of the trees.

Perhaps he was not yet Judas enough to return to Anita, awaiting him in Cangrejo's eyrie. But at length, towards evening, fearing his long absence might arouse suspicion or uneasiness, he arose and climbed the hill. When he reached the cabin, he found it empty and silent. He loitered about, wondering and watchful. Not a soul came near him. He dozed; he awoke; he ate a few olives and some bread; he dozed again. When he opened his eyes for the second time, the shadows of the peaks were slanting to the east. He got to his feet, shivering a little. This utter silence and desertion discomforted him. Where was the girl? God! was it possible after all that she had betrayed him? He might have questioned his own heart as to that; only, as luck would have it, it was such a tiresomely deaf organ. So, let him think. De la Platière, with his men (as calculated), would be posted in the Pampeluna road, round the spur of the hill below, an hour after sunset – that was to say, at fifteen minutes to six. No doubt by then the alarm would have gone abroad. But no great resistance to a strong force was to be apprehended. In the meantime – well, in the meantime, until the moment came for him to descend under cover of dark and assume the leadership, he must possess his soul in patience.

The sun went down. Night flowing into the valleys seemed to expel a moan of wind; then all dropped quiet again. Darkness fell swift and sudden like a curtain, but no Anita appeared, putting it aside, and Ducos was perplexed. He did not like this bodiless, shadowless subscription to his scheming. It troubled him to have no one to talk to – and deceive. He was depressed.

By and by he pulled off, turned inside-out and resumed his scarlet jacket, which he had taken the provisional precaution to have lined with a sombre material. As he slipped in his arms, he started and looked eagerly into the lower vortices of dusk. In the very direction to which his thoughts were engaged, a little glow-worm light was burning steadily from the thickets. What did it signify – Spaniards or French, ambush or investment? Allowing – as between himself on the height and de la Platière on the road below – for the apparent discrepancy in the time of sunset, it was yet appreciably before the appointed hour. Nevertheless, this that he saw made the risk of an immediate descent necessary.

Bringing all his wits, his resolution, his local knowledge to one instant focus, he started, going down at once swiftly and with caution. The hills rose above him like smoke as he dropped; the black ravines were lifted to his feet. Sometimes for scores of paces he would lose sight altogether of the eye of light; then, as he turned some shoulder of rock, it would strike him in the face with its nearer radiance, so that he had to pause and readjust his vision to the new perspective. Still, over crabbed ridges and by dip of thorny gulches he descended steadily, until the mound of the Little Hump, like a gigantic thatched kraal, loomed oddly upon him through the dark.

And, lo! the beacon that had led him down unerring was a great lantern hung under the sagging branch of a chestnut tree at the foot of the mound – a lantern, the lurid nucleus of a little coil of tragedy.

A cluster of rocks neighboured the clearing about the tree. To these Ducos padded his last paces with a catlike stealth – crouching, hardly breathing; and now from that coign of peril he stared down.

A throng of armed guerrillas, one a little forward of the rest, was gathered about a couple more of their kidney, who, right under the lantern, held the goatherd Anita on her knees in a nailing grip. To one side, very phantoms of desolation, stood Cangrejo and another. The faces of all, densely shadowed in part by the rims of their sombreros, looked as if masked; their mouths, corpse-like, showed a splint of teeth; their ink-black whiskers hummocked on their shoulders.

So, in the moment of Ducos's alighting on it, was the group postured – silent, motionless, as if poised on the turn of some full tide of passion. And then, in an instant, a voice boomed up to him.

'Confess!' it cried, vibrating: 'him thou wert seen with at the gallows; him whom thou foisted, O! unspeakable, thou devil's doxy! on the unsuspecting Cangrejo; him, thy Frankish gallant and spy' (the voice guttered, and then, rising, leapt to flame) – 'what hast thou done with him? where hidden? Speak quickly and with truth, if, traitor though thou be, thou wouldst be spared the traitor's *estrapade*.'

'Alguazil, I cannot say. Have mercy on me!'

Ducos could hardly recognise the child in those agonised tones.

The inquisitor, with an oath, half-wheeled.

'Pignatelli, father of this accursed – if by her duty thou canst prevail?'

A figure – agitated, cadaverous, as sublimely dehumanised as Brutus – stepped from Cangrejo's side and tossed one gnarled arm aloft.

'No child of mine, alguazil!' it proclaimed in a shrill, strung cry. 'Let her reap as she hath sown, alguazil!'

Cangrejo leapt, and flung himself upon his knees by the girl.

'Tell Don Manoel, chiquita. God! little boy, that being a girl (ah, naughty!) is half-absolved. Tell him, tell him – ah, there – now, now, now! He, thy lover, was in the cabin. I left him prostrate, scarce able to move. When the council comes to seek him, he is gone. Away, sayst thou? Ah, child, but I must know better! It could not be far. Say where – give him up – let him show himself only, chiquita, and the good alguazil will spare thee. Such a traitor, ah, Dios! And yet I have loved, too.'

He sobbed, and clawed her uncouthly. Ducos, in his eyrie, laughed to himself, and applauded softly, making little cymbals of his thumbnails.

'But he will not move her,' he thought – and, on the thought, started; for from his high perch his eye had suddenly caught, he was sure of it, the sleeking of a French bayonet in the road below.

'Master!' cried Anita, in a heart-breaking voice; 'he is gone – they cannot take him. O, don't let them hurt me!'

The alguazil made a sign. Cangrejo, gobbling and resisting, was dragged away. There was a little ugly, silent scuffle about the girl; and, in a moment, the group fell apart to watch her being hauled up to the branch by her thumbs.

Ducos looked on greedily.

'How long before she sets to screaming?' he thought, 'so that I may escape under cover of it.'

So long, that he grew intolerably restless – wild, furious. He could have cursed her for her endurance.

But presently it came, moaning up all the scale of suffering. And, at that, slinking like a rat through its run, he went down swiftly towards the road – to meet de la Platière and his men already silently breaking cover from it.

And, on the same instant, the Spaniards saw them.

'*Peste*!' whispered de la Platière. 'We could have them all at one volley but for that!'

Between the French force, ensconced behind the rocks whither Ducos had led them, and the Spaniards who, completely taken by surprise, had clustered foolishly in a body under the lantern, hung the body of Anita, its torture suspended for the moment because its poor wits were out.

'How, my friend!' exclaimed Ducos. 'But for what?'

'The girl, that is all.'

'She will feel nothing. No doubt she is half-dead already. A moment, and it will be too late.'

'Nevertheless, I will not,' said de la Platière.

Ducos stamped ragingly.

'Give the word to me. She must stand her chance. For the Emperor!' he choked – then shrieked out, 'Fire!'

The explosion crashed among the hills, and echoed off.

A dark mass, which writhed and settled beyond the lantern shine, seemed to excite a little convulsion of merriment in the swinging body. That twitched and shook a moment; then relaxed, and hung motionless.

THE SWORD OF
CORPORAL LACOSTE

*'Tis many a wise Man's hap, while he is
providing against one Danger, to fall into another:
And for his very Providence to turn his Destruction.'*

Corporal Lacoste – cuirassier in the following of Murat, the
Rupert of an Imperial army – had had a long dream, chiefly
of a roaring thunder of surf bursting upon jagged rocks. And,
as the storm of water thrashed the very pinnacles that toppled
into mist, he had seen the ribs of cliff laid bare and bleeding
– as it were the laceration of a living land that he looked on.
Then, *'Corne et tonnerre!'* he had seemed to cry to himself,
'the very world is torn by some inhuman power, and flows
to the sea in rivers of purple!' and he heard the bells of the
ocean receding innumerably, choke at their moorings, muffled
and congested with the floating scum of carnage that no wind
might ruffle and only God's fire cleanse.

Now, in a moment, he saw that what he had taken for
land was in truth a great cliff built up of human bodies – a
vast reserve of human force accumulated by, and for the use
of, a single dominant will. And this cliff was washed by the
waves of an ocean of blood, to which its life contributed in
a thousand spouting rivulets. And it was compact of limitless
pain; and the cry of torture never ceased within it. And
suddenly the dreamer – as in the way of dreams – felt himself

to be a constituent agony of that he gazed upon – a pulp of suffering self-contained, yet partaking of the wretchedness of all.

Suddenly there was a faint stir and pushing here and there into the mound, a quiet soft heaving such as a mole makes; and whenever this ceased a moment, a shriek, thin as a needle, pierced the very nerve of the mass. And, with horror indescribable, the dreamer felt the approach of the thing, testing and feeling at one point or another, until it reached and entered his breast. 'Hideous and unnameable!' he would have screamed, but clenched his teeth upon the cry; for lo! it was but a little familiar hand, plump and white, that groped within his ribs, seeking to find and snap the tendons that held his heart in place.

Then he found voice, and whispered in his extremity, 'Spare me, my Emperor!' But the hand neither shook nor hurried, severing his chords of being one by one, until it could lift the heart from its socket and fling it into the waves that leapt like wolves beneath. And, at the instant of the lifting, it was as if a tooth of flame were thrust into him and withdrawn; and thereafter he fell cold – colder, waxing blithe and painless, until he was moved to laugh to himself with a secret ecstasy of applause.

'A good soldier has no heart. Of a truth, *le p'tit caporal* must now as always have his way. And he has done it so deftly that I scarce feel a wound.'

The very association of the word seemed to open his eyes morally and physically. Immediately he was conscious of a slit of blinding daylight; of the grip upon some exposed parts of his body of a frost sharp enough to hold him by the legs like a mantrap. Yet, save for these partial seizures, he appeared to be reclining under a blanket so suffocatingly thick that he could not account for his certain conviction that the heat was slowly retiring from it.

All in a moment he had comprehended, and was struggling to relieve himself of his incubus. It rolled from him as he

emerged from under it. It fell ridiculously into the caricature
of a dead dragoon. Corporal Lacoste knew the thing for a
mess-sergeant of his late acquaintance. He nodded to the
body as he sat himself down in the snow.

'Thou never servedst a comrade so well before, sergeant,'
said he; and, indeed, he would surely have died of the frost
in his wound had not this unconscious trooper given him
the heat of his own vitality.

'But, what made the man delay his going till the sun rose?'
thought Corporal Lacoste.

He looked again, and started.

The dragoon's throat had been pierced by a sword-thrust.
A thread of vermilion yet crawled from it down his swarthy
neck, like the awkward tracing by a schoolboy of a river on
a map.

Corporal Lacoste screwed his eyes, intuitively and obliquely,
to get glimpse of his own right shoulder. There was a sensation of wet numbness thereabouts. Something had pricked
him pretty deeply – possibly the point of the very murderous
weapon that had finished off the dragoon.

'It was when I dreamt of the tooth of flame,' thought
Corporal Lacoste. 'There have been vampires here amongst
the wounded.'

It hardly troubled him, this familiar experience. Those of
Murat's hated *beaux sabreurs* who fell alive and had the misfortune to be left for dead, must always run the risk of
mutilation. It was enough for him that the blow that had
prostrated him had failed of its deadliness; that his senseless
condition had not been made by the frost everlasting; that
he owed his salvation to the accidental superimposition of a
wounded dragoon.

He took his dazed head between his hands, and indulged
a little retrospect of the events that had preceded his downfall, as he dwelt upon the scene before him.

That was marvellous enough to a Gascon. He crouched in
the bed of a precipitous defile that joined higher and lower

terraces of the Amstetten forest. Beneath him, the gully went down with a rush of trampled snow, in the swirl of which dead horses and men and the wreck of accoutrements, half-buried in a foam of white, seemed the very freebooty of a frost-stricken waterfall. It was a strange picture of furious motion held in suspension – the more wonderful for its framing. For all the trees, great and small, that over-stooped the lip and sprouted from the sides of the pass, were hung with monstrous lustres of ice, up which millions of little reflected suns travelled like beads of champagne rising in specimen-glasses.

Of the stunning effectiveness of these icicles, as a species of natural artillery, Corporal Lacoste had had a recent demonstration. His mind now was slowly electrotyping, in the midst of a clearing obscurity, certain images impressed upon it during the moments antecedent to his collapse. He recalled the weird long ride through forest vaults so roofed with snow that the world had seemed one vast tent propped by countless poles. He recalled how here and there a sluice of sunlight pouring through a rift overhead had reminded him of that strange Roman Pantheon that he had once seen when serving in the military suite of M. Barthollet, the appraiser of works of art to the Directory. He recalled how, jingling blithely in his saddle in the wake of his swashbuckler general, with all the glory of the late capitulation of Ulm tingling in his careless heart, he had started to the sudden shout, the recoiling shock of ambush; and had seen and heard the outlet of this very glen, down which Murat and his advance-guard were riding, clank to the wheel of an Austrian regiment, that shut upon it like a gate of steel. He remembered the thunderous rush that succeeded – the charge of the *beaux sabreurs* down the defile – the crash, the retreat, the rally; and again he saw the young artillery officer – some *cadet inconnu* – gallop his two pieces into position, and, at the critical moment, discharge his buzzing canisters of grape into the welter of the enemy.

Corne et tonnerre! what a clearing of the pass! It had been like cleaning a pipe-stem with a fizz of gunpowder. But, at the same time, a catastrophe quite unexpected had resulted. For the explosion had brought down a very avalanche of snow and icicles from the weighted branches a hundred feet above; and these terrific bolts, bursting as it were in a cloud of smoke, had salvoed on helmet and breastplate of friend and foe alike, with a sound like the clanging of enormous cymbals, and had hurled horses and men in one shouting ruin to the ground.

And it was precisely at this point that Corporal Lacoste's perceptions had been severed, and so left for the night as clean-ended as a pack of straw in a chaff-cutter.

But destiny – his particular Atropos – was now to turn at the knife again – for a time.

'To be floored by an icicle!' he muttered, twirling his fierce moustache. '*Corne et tonnerre*! it is after all a weapon unknown to courage and passion. This Queen of the snow is a barbarous fighter. Yet all night she kisses the wounds of her victims that they may not bleed. She woos to her embraces by the twin snares of hurt and pity. It is an amiable artifice, not unfamiliar to the experience of us that ply the sword. Whom a woman strikes she loves. My faith – but she was a chill bed-fellow, nevertheless!'

He was feeling now very sick. His wounds, opening to his returned vitality, were beginning to run afresh. He rose and looked about for his helmet. It lay, a mere crushed tin kettle, under the dead dragoon. But his sword was flung aside uninjured, and this he recovered and slipped back into its scabbard.

'It retires with a hiss. *Mon Dieu*, what a poisonous snake!' he said; and then he took off his neckcloth and fastened it about his battered head.

It was while he was thus engaged that his vision, wandering afield, rested on a figure that moved at the far end of the glen. This figure – that seemed to be the only thing living in all the length of the pass – had an odd appearance to the dim eyes of the corporal. It was squat, and of fantastic garb and gesture; and to his weak exalted perceptives it presented itself as a gnome, crept, like a hound from the womb of sin, out of some icy dark crypt of the forest. Now and again it would stoop; now and again fling a goblin dance, and then all of a sudden it seemed to catch sight of the tall shape standing high in the lift of the defile, and stopped motionless and shaded its forehead with horizontal palm.

Now, in a moment it appeared to set an extinguisher on its head, literally, as if subduing an unholy flame; and immediately it came up the glen with a quick elastic step, the cone standing back at a rakish angle.

The creature drew near.

'Much cry and little wool!' muttered Corporal Lacoste, with a rallying twinge of self-contempt; for the thing had resolved itself into nothing more formidable than a little fat monk in a cowl; and '*Bénédicité, mon père,*' he added, as a concession to a certain traditional superstition that yet affected him.

'My cap is already doffed, or I would pull it off to your reverence,' he said, leavening his grace with a pinch of mockery. 'But – *corne et tonnerre*! I am forgetting. You will only converse in your own detestable tongue.'

'I know a little French,' said the monk promptly.

'It is well,' cried the soldier, but without surprise; for, indeed, he could not comprehend how one could speak any other language from choice.

'And what was my father doing down there?' he asked. 'And why did he dance?'

The monk had steady little brown eyes, of the shape and fulness of a rabbit's. His face was round, ruddy, and extremely dirty; his chin peaked and under-hung; his stomach shaped like a case-bottle, but a hogshead in capacity. He had on a hooded cassock, the original black of which had paid a fine interest of coppery blotches to the investors of *trinkgeld* in that hallowed paunch; and he was altogether a very typical example, it must be admitted, of a filthy little Bavarian priest.

'I looked,' he said – 'yes, I looked for one or two yet in the state to receive the *viaticum*.'

'And that was a good thought, *mon pére*; but the frost-demon had an earlier and a better. Still, it does not explain why you danced.'

The monk kept each of his hands thrust up the wide sleeve of the opposite arm. He seemed to hug himself over some nameless jest – the physical condition of what was thus concealed, perhaps. But he was more ostentatious of his teeth, the under-row of which broke up his conscious smile into unlovely intervals, and were like little dilapidated gravestones to the memory of deceased appetites.

'I danced because the cold bit my feet,' he said.

'Oh!' said Corporal Lacoste. 'And is not the cold, like the sunlight, a dispensation of Providence?'

'Of Providence, assuredly – yes, of Providence.'

The soldier smacked his chest, consequentially but feebly.

'Behold a Providence, then, that favours its recreant children at the expense of its ministers! That which is your chastisement hath been my salvation. So it rebukes the arrogance of priestcraft, and demonstrates it more an honour to be a soldier than a monk.'

The stranger lifted his elbows and embraced himself, drawing in his breath.

'Sometimes,' he said, suddenly giggling and voluble, 'it sanctifies, we understand, the double gift. The Bishop of Beauvais, he was soldier and divine: the Archbishop of Canterbury also. It is good to be either in its season – very good to be both. To know to put one you slay on the road to heaven, eh?'

'If there is time. But, *mon père*, do you always stop to show him the way?'

He took the monk invitingly by a sleeve, and led him to the dead dragoon.

'He is passed before I come,' said the *curé*.

'It is all a question of tenses,' said the corporal. 'Come or came: which is it? And who killed him, my father?'

'How – do you say?'

'Why, dead men do not bleed if you stick them through the neck.'

'Doubtless that is so.'

'And he hath lain on me all night like a toast; yet I wake to find him with the fresh blood running.'

'It must be, then, that the sun-warmth broke anew his wound that the frost had closed.'

'*Corne et tonnerre*! It was a fine lance of sunwarmth to go clean through his neck and into my shoulder.'

The priest rolled his eyes, so as to show little parings of white at their edges. His fingers seemed to twitch within the sleeves. Suddenly he burst out, sputtering—

'You damned devil, if you think that I, a servant of God, killed this man!'

Corporal Lacoste was inexpressibly shocked – as much to hear this snake of profanity hiss from an anointed vessel, as to find that he had been understood to suggest a charge so execrable. At the same time his instincts as a soldier were hard set to discount a truism.

'I ask only for information,' he cried, dismayed. 'A dead man struck does not bleed. If you are priest only, there may be those of the flock abroad who would give their pastor an opportunity to exercise his office.'

The monk mumbled to himself like an angry layman.

'Those and those! But it is you that empty the land – that desolate the hearths – that convert the innocuous hind into a beast of desperation!'

He was gesticulating violently with his shoulders.

'They crashed down the defile!' he yelled, wheeling himself about: 'they carried all before them with atrocious glee – the hopes, the happiness, the innocent life of the poor jocund foresters. Follow, you, down the glen! Track the storm by its

litter! Go, rejoin your comrades of blood, that the measure
of your iniquity may be theirs.'

Corporal Lacoste stood amazed.

'My father,' he said, 'the rebuke may be just; but the long
night and many leagues by now stretch between me and
mine. And I am a wounded and famished man.'

Perhaps he was discreetly humble in his realisation of the
fact that he was abandoned alone to the perils of a hostile
country.

'*Confiteor Deo omnipotenti,*' he began to murmur, jogging a
drowsy memory. He bowed his head and struck his dinted
breastplate, his expression studiously set to the very formula
of deprecation.

The rabbit eyes seemed all pupil in their searching watch-
fulness of him.

'God forbid!' said the priest at last, 'that I deny succour to
the worst of His erring sons. But what is this courage that,
in its aggregate, roars down the world, and, disintegrated,
cries for help, abasing itself before the least of its would-be
victims?'

His tone and speech, to the common hearing, were sufficiently fraught with a sarcastic bitterness. But, in moments
of excitement, he would relapse into his native Low German,
the barbarous gutturals of which, shouldering their way
amongst the crisp bowing idioms of the more courtly tongue,
would confound the intelligibility they sought to emphasise.
Therefore Corporal Lacoste – whose hearing, indeed, was at
the moment a diffuse faculty – took no umbrage of the affront,
and recognised only that the priest – as he pushed by him
to pass on his way – was pattering *aves* innumerable in expiation of his late verbal transgression.

At what number he ceased, having squared his account
with Heaven, it did not appear; and in the meanwhile he
was going with his dancing step up the glen, having first
signed to the wounded soldier to follow him.

Before Corporal Lacoste's eyes the goblin figure rose from

terrace to terrace of the pass, mounting to the chill black portico, as it were, of the forest above. Reaching this, it turned, beckoned, and faced about – and immediately darkness took it at a gulp.

Instinctive mockery, some old-worn rags of reverence, contempt and trepidation were all confused in the soldier's mind with an ever-present consciousness of suffering. His skull – as he reeled in pursuit of the gnomish thing by endless corridors of trunks, stark and silent, above which the roof, like slabs of stone, let in slits and blotches of piercing light – seemed to sway to the roll of a shifting cargo of quicksilver, his legs to move independent of any will to control them. But through all he never lost sight of the fact that he was a *beau sabreur*. His sword, flapping against his thigh, was a link long enough to connect any apparent discrepancies in mind or matter. He longed very ardently, nevertheless, for a period to be put to his pain and fatigue.

Still the priest went on before, flitting and hopping like some ungainly lob of the underworld, by glades of thronging gloom as voiceless and sightless as the streets of an excavated city. Once or twice only he turned about sharply as he sped.

'It pleases you,' he would demand, 'to know how your comrades left you without thought or care where you fell?'

'*Mon père*,' the cuirassier would cry, answering, 'it pleases me in that my abandonment means their success. Pity is, in truth, a flower; but one cannot stop to pick flowers during a pursuit.'

Again, to emphasise a final enquiry, the monk had fallen back a little.

'What is this Emperor, then, to you?'

'He is my god!' Corporal Lacoste answered promptly.

'Be the measure of his mercy thy judgment,' had been the reply; and thereat they had come into a sudden mist of twilight, that broadened and increased until it broke into the blinding glare of day beating upon a little house set in the flat of a snowy clearing.

Corporal Lacoste started, hung fire, and dropped his hand to his sword-hilt.

'A tavern!' he exclaimed.

The priest wheeled round and faced him, his head cocked derisively in the shadow of his cowl.

'And what better house of rest and entertainment to a brave *chasseur* of the Emperor?' said he.

'But the people, my father! It is to lead a blind man into a nest of hornets!'

'Truly, if you fear the stings of beauty. There is no peril other than that.'

The frost was in the trooper's blood, and sickness in his brain.

'Lead on!' he cried. 'A gallant soldier dreads neither man nor devil.'

They went forward to the house. It was a mean enough little shanty, sloughing piecemeal its skin of rough-cast. From the thatched lean-to of the porch, that went up to the broken shingles of the roof above, a pole, with a withered fardel of heather tied to its end, stuck out like an ironical finger-post to signify to the convivial wanderer any direction but that immediately behind it.

Nevertheless, the two men passed under, walking straight into a ramshackle kitchen, where only the figure of a solitary wench moved in a world of disorder.

She was busying herself desultorily near a great open hearth, above which projected a wedge-shaped chimney-hood of battered plaster, with an iron chain and hook pendulous from its sooty maw. A crazy wooden partition cut the room at a third of its length; and over this appeared the top of a ladder, on whose highest rung a squatting hen reposed. Some steaming dishcloths drooped from a line; parings and foul greasy scraps littered the corners into which they had been kicked; and the brick floor was everywhere sodden, as from the precipitated atmosphere of much unsqueamish revelry.

'Wilma, *mein mädchen*,' said the priest softly.

The girl glanced round and up, as she stooped. The gallant corporal's heart seemed to fill to so great an extent as to ease the throbbing of his wounds. This composed, this actually stolid-looking jade in her stone-grey petticoat and striped corset and degraded slippers – *Corne et tonnerre*! she was a very Hebe, a wall-peach, a china-rose of prettiness. One might wish to cull her face at its slender neck like a flower, and put it in a vase of fragrant water to watch the blue eyes bud and open.

'Here,' said Corporal Lacoste, 'I may divest myself of all fear save that this love is plighted to another.'

The girl expressed no surprise, no concern, very little interest. Indeed, she did not understand a word that he spoke. But the priest interpreted.

'He would swear his heart to you at the outset. He is a wounded enemy that had not the courage to enter until I assured him that you were alone. Now he would willingly value his life at the price of your favour. Wilt thou minister to him, Wilma?'

'Ask him,' said the girl, in a low dull voice, 'why the peril lies here when all our manhood is flown to Vienna?'

The soldier stood smiling, and desperately catching himself from an inclination to faint.

'But it is right, is it not, Wilma,' continued the priest, without heeding her answer, 'to forgive our enemies, though they come like the wolves at night into a peaceful fold, wantonly harrying and destroying? "*Et dimitte nobis debita nostra.*" Yet we must trespass to be forgiven; and heaven loves a repentant sinner, Wilma.'

'Where is my father?' said the girl (they seemed to talk at cross-purposes). 'Hast thou left him down there?'

'I saw him watching us from ambush. Be assured he will follow soon.'

The girl turned away.

'The stranger, like any other,' she said coldly, 'can share, for the paying, in whatever he and his devil-comrades have left us;' and with that she went to feel her drying dishcloths.

The priest turned upon the Corporal.

'It is the custom in our Bavarian inns,' said he, 'for the guest to bring his own food. Wine, you will understand, is another matter.'

'*S'il ne tient qu'à ça*!' cried Corporal Lacoste jovially. 'I have meat in my haversack and louis-d'ors in my pouch. We will make a feast, my father!'

He was so direfully in need of stimulant that he would do nothing till he had drunk.

'Here!' he shouted arrogantly, conscious of the hesitation of the other; and he fetched out and clapped upon a plank-table hard by a fistful of jangling pieces.

'Put them away,' said the priest, his eyes quite rigid in their sockets. 'My profession is one of faith.'

He profited by demonstration, however, to give an entirely generous order. Wilma attended to it with the cold tranquillity that seemed to characterise all her actions. She was like a beautiful cataleptic.

The hole in Corporal Lacoste's head served as no vent, apparently, to the heady Steinwein. The core of heat it represented appeared rather to aggravate the potency of the fumes. He reddened, he sang, he rattled; by the time he had put down his share of the first bottle he was clamorous with good-fellowship and braggadocio.

'Oh, *mon Dieu Jésus*!' he cried; 'to accuse us of stripping you when, in this chance corner, I find such wine and such beauty!'

The monk was no coy toss-pot. He pledged the other glass for glass, till his heated face glared forward of its cowl like a great opening nasturtium bud. He showed, moreover, a tendency to coarseness and violence of speech that effectively counter-buffed the soldier's insolence.

Corporal Lacoste's veins were flushed to their remotest channels. They made up in fever what they had lost in measure. Once he suddenly leapt to his feet.

'To pluck the fruit that will not fall!' he shouted – and staggered away from the table.

In a moment the priest had risen and thrown himself upon him. He was little and under-weighted; but he held the cuirassier in a clutch as crippling as that of a 'scavenger's daughter'.

'You go to insult the maid!' he shrieked. 'My God, I will tear your heart out!'

Corporal Lacoste vainly struggled, shaken with crapulous laughter.

'But for dessert to the feast!' he protested: 'my lips only to the warm side of the peach!'

The part profile of Wilma, seated knitting against the farther lintel of a rough opening in the partition, seemed unruffled by the least interest or apprehension. It did not even turn towards the wrestling men. At the instant, as it happened, that these came to the floor, the priest uppermost, the house-door was flung open, and a man ran into the room.

'Hold his hands from his neck, my father!' cried this newcomer, in a small biting voice; and, flicking a thin knife from his sleeve, he dropped quickly upon his knees at the head of the labouring soldier and raised his arm.

The monk uttered a stifled oath.

'Down, down!' he cried in fury, as if to a dog. 'Don't you see the girl?'

The man leapt to his feet, springing straight from his soles backwards with an odd nimble movement. There he stood watching the soldier – his eyes as sharp as flint-stones – as the latter, released by the monk, scrambled upright, staggering.

The trooper, the instant he felt himself free, swept his blade from its sheath.

'The sword of Corporal Lacoste!' he shouted, the wild tipsy Gascon. 'Is there a wolf here will set his tooth against that?'

The word might have been haphazard – or vinously inspired. For, indeed, the face and attitude of the man opposite him were curiously wolfish in character – the temples wide, the forehead sweeping downwards and forth into a pinched snout, the projecting under-jaw spiked with savage teeth and hung with tangs of brindled hair. If, for the rest, the creature was phenomenally small and lithe and active for a Bavarian peasant, still it was a peasant patently and clothed as such, from its close-bodied homespun tunic belted by a crimson sash, and its rusty cloak buckled under the right arm, to its cap of mangy fur from which a flock of coarse hair fell upon its shoulders.

'The sword of Corporal Lacoste!' howled the soldier again, and spun his weapon so that it whistled, making an arc of light.

The stranger stood rigidly set, the hilt of his long lancet clutched against his shoulder, his head thrust forward like a pointing hound's. There could be no least doubt as to which would prove the deadlier adversary.

Now, as they stood a moment, watchful of each other, the apple in the peasant's throat flickered of a sudden; and immediately a rising moan, a very strange little ululation, began to make itself audible, and the man lifted his chin, as if to give some voice in him freer passage. At once the priest, in an ecstasy of haste, flung himself between the two.

'On the threshold of the Church!' he screamed; 'and the girl looking on!'

For the first time, indeed, Wilma was alert.

The peasant relaxed from his rigid pose. Corporal Lacoste saw the man's tongue, curling like a red leaf, pass over and across his upper lip. The movement gave him a little thrilling shock, as if of terror.

'What am I to do, my father?' asked the creature.

The priest pushed back his cowl and passed a trembling hand across his forehead.

'The cards,' he muttered confusedly, affecting an impossible laugh. 'Let us reconcile all over a bout at ombre.'

He suddenly bethought himself, and repeated his proposal

in French. The soldier threw his sword into the air, recovered it by the hilt, and returned it to its sheath.

'At bottle or pasteboard!' he cried: '*c'la m'est égal* – I am a match for the devil!'

He seemed, at least, a match for these commoner spirits. Luck stood at his shoulder, as was befitting when a *beau sabreur* of Murat staked against a clown and a Friar-Rush.

The three played and drank and wrangled up to midday of the blessed bright morn. Not a soul came in to disturb them. The neighbourhood, it appeared, was depopulated by conscription – stunned by fear. Only the girl moved staidly in the background of the reeking kitchen, quite silent over her simple duties, even when from time to time she brought a fresh bottle to the table and came under fire of the reckless trooper's badinage.

The play waxed fast and furious. Oaths and execrations, flying from fecund lips, seemed to swarm obscenely under the very rafters overhead. The monk, educated perhaps to the rich vocabulary of anathema, was peculiarly apt at fulminating expletive. He bawled and he cursed from the conscious standpoint of privilege. He never damned but to hell, or failed to translate his most consuming maledictions for the soldier's benefit.

Now it chanced that once during the morning Corporal Lacoste, happening to glance up as Wilma fetched an empty jug from their midst in order to the replenishing of it, saw the girl's strange eyes fixed upon him in a curious stare. She looked away immediately; but he rose, took the jug from her with a '*permettez-moi, mam'selle,*' and followed her to the rear of the premises.

The lip of the dog-man lifted. The priest caught his hand in a warning clinch.

'Between Angelus and Angelus, Wolfzahn,' he muttered.

'What does he with the girl, then, my father?'

'What does he? The wine consumes his nerve. He is a man of gingerbread. Let him be.'

'How came we to miss him down there? Between Angelus and Angelus, say'st thou? So! I will whet my tooth. But beware, my father! the dark in these days is an early guest. How came we to miss him – him and his fat gold pieces?'

'Hush! *Der Herr Jesus* recompenses otherwise the agents of His vengeance. Little Wolfzahn, the gold shall pay for masses to his soul – his, and the others. Not here, before the girl! The devil, I think, has commerce with her nowadays. Often I see him peep from the windows of her eyes. Between Angelus and Angelus: one snap of thy tooth – and there are twenty fresh indulgences to quit thee of thy purgatory.'

'But, here, in the forest! Ah, *mein Vater*! when will thy indulgences quit me of this in the forest?' The strange creature gave a sort of sob, a bay, and buried his face in his hands.

In the meanwhile Corporal Lacoste followed Wilma to the cellar. She neither invited nor repulsed him. She went down a flight of humid steps, through a square aperture in the floor, into a little musty cavern, the walls of which seemed all eyes. These were the 'kicks' of bottles whose long snouts were thrust into wooden racks. Elsewhere a cask or two lolled on its belly, its tap run into purple like a drowsy drunken nose; and the tracks of snails went all over the ceiling.

The girl struck light from a flint, kindled a greasy dip, and, holding it in her hand, turned suddenly round on her escort. The soldier, in whose brain a wanton fever flared, swayed himself steady, endeavouring to return her gaze.

'Ludwig!' she whispered hurriedly – 'my Ludwig that went with Wimpffen's dragoons to defend the pass – my Ludwigchen that would have taken me out of hell. When I caught thy face against the light, *ach, mein Gott*! I could have cried in pain. Thou art so like him.'

She held the candle nearer the fuddled stupid eyes. Her own glittered to them like sparks through a curtain of smoke. She drew back with a quick hopeless movement.

'But I forget,' she murmured. 'Thou canst not understand – nor would, nor would, though we spoke in one language.'

She filled the jug, and went hastily past him. Then, at a thought, she turned, with her foot on the first step, and spoke back into his very ear, '*Hüten Sie sich vor dem Wehrwolf!*'

'Wilma!' howled her father from above.

Corporal Lacoste reeled back to his cards, with an obfuscated impression that something of moment had been spoken to him. His soul, pregnantly engaged in hatching wind-eggs, squatted in a little private dark-house of cunning, from which it looked forth as full of self-importance as a monkey in a cage.

Now, again, play being resumed, the fetid air of the kitchen blattered with oaths. It was as if, approaching a dunghill, the returned gambler had disturbed a settled cloud of flies.

Howl, and uproar, and the jangle of unbridled tongues! A knife was drawn; the soldier staggered to his feet, and his chair crashed on the floor. At the moment a timepiece tinkled out midday from some attic above. The priest flung up his arm and yelled, 'Angelus, Angelus, ye swine of the Gadarenes!'

He fell upon his knees. '*Angelus Domini nuntiavit Mariæ,*' he began to gabble.

'*Et concepit de Spiritu Sancto,*' responded the peasant, who, at the word, had pulled from his breast a little leaden image of St Christopher carrying a baby Christ, and prostrated himself before it.

But as to Corporal Lacoste, it was for him to drop upon the floor and asleep simultaneously.

Something – it might have been a savagely restrained kick – aroused the slumbering man. He started up, sitting, and beat away a red-hot film of cobwebs that seemed to stretch and flicker before his eyes. Slowly at first, then by sickening leaps, consciousness returned to him. He looked vacantly from point to point of the frowsy kitchen. Wilma sat knitting as though she had never moved; the dog-like peasant crouched on the hearth, his red eyes glinting back the ember-glow; and whenever he yawned a little singing whine issued from his throat. The priest, his hands as heretofore vanished up the meeting cuffs of his cassock, his cowl pulled forward over his eyes, stood a yard withdrawn from and looking down upon him. At the sound of the first word between them the creature before the fire flashed alert.

'The noon draws on,' said the monk. 'If you wish to track your comrades in safety you must be out of the forest by dusk.'

The trooper got to his feet. He was steady enough on them now. It was his head that seemed to roll and totter.

'I have delayed too long already,' he cried peevishly. 'What does the sword of Corporal Lacoste in this ignoble den? To death or victory, my father – if I but knew the way!'

The monk whistled to the man on the hearth.

'Up!' he cried; 'he would have us show him the way – to victory or death. The issue is his.'

He turned to the soldier.

'It is the will of God that shall be wrought at the hands of His agents.'

'Meaning thyself, my father?'

'Surely, and Wolfzahn here. Arise, and we will put thee on the road.'

'Thou wear'st His livery, at least. *Corne et tonnerre*! it is true a priest must not be judged out of his own mouth. To refute the devil one must speak the devil's tongue. And, after all, thy face rounds as jovial as an English rennet.'

'Hasten!' cried the peasant from the door, to which he had run. 'I can hear far off the dusk striking amongst the trees like a woodreeve.'

'A moment, Wolfzahn!' exclaimed the priest. 'One parting dram of brandy for a lock to the stomach!'

As Corporal Lacoste took his *petit-verre* from Wilma, he was troubled by a desperately elusive thought of some confidence that had passed between him and her. Then he remembered that they had no word in common. It could not be. As for any temptation to gallantry, the nausea following debauch had robbed him of all inclination to it.

But glancing back once, when he had swaggered from the house into the shuddering chillness of the snow without, it startled him to see, as he thought, the white face of the girl pressed against the lattice. The sight, the shadow, gave him a momentary thrill of uneasiness – something like a strange swerve of the heart that was surely inexplicable in a *sabreur* of the great army.

After the turn of noon a sombreness of cloud had usurped the happy throne of morning. The forest had fallen into deathly silence. The trees were ranked stiffly, each seeming to edge into each in terror of some nameless oppression. From the hollows came trooping grey spectres of mist that climbed the branches to overlook the travellers, or peered stealthily from behind enormous trunks. Not a voice, not a sound but the squeaking crunch of the wayfarers' feet as they trod the beds of snow that had silted through the openings in the roof above, broke the vast quiet.

This was a matter of concern to the swashbuckler corporal, who rose many times from the deep waters of his dejection to clutch at some straw of comfort in the shape of a monosyllabic utterance by one or other of his guides. It was of no use. The straw would sink with him, leaving him again submerged.

Suddenly light grew upon them – light wan and grudging, but still a beacon of hope. At the same moment their ears were aware of a long quarrelling moan – a diffuse liquid snarl uttered and echoed from a score of points on the ground below them on their left. The peasant, who led, sprang at the instant behind a tree, from the covert of which he looked forth and down into a narrow sloping defile – that very riven pass in which the wounded soldier had spent the night.

The priest stood stricken, petrified, where he had halted at the top of the glen, in a wedge of white slanting mist. The wondering trooper hurried to join him.

'*Mon Dieu Jésus*!' cried the latter, dumfounded; 'is it that way we must go?'

The gorge was dotted with wolves – ravenous, unclean.

Wherever a shapeless bulge of cloth, a hooped flank of man or charger projected, there a bloody snout burrowed and tore, spattering the white with red.

Corporal Lacoste drew and whirled aloft his sabre.

'Forward, comrades!' he shouted. 'It is the sword of Corporal Lacoste!'

He was a man again – a *beau sabreur* of the wild Murat in face of immediate danger. He ran down into the glen alone and slashed at the first brute he reached. It fled screeching, a near-severed ear flapping against its jaw as it galloped.

He paused a moment, turned, and beckoned to the two above him. They were drawn together, and the priest, it appeared, was frantically beating back the other from descending.

'*Canaille*!' hissed Corporal Lacoste between his teeth, and he faced about once more to his business of aggression.

The alarm was gone abroad. The beasts, converging from their isolated positions, were forming into a compact body.

To the tactician, the moment of rally offers as full opportunity for assault as the moment of retreat. Either is the twilight of disorder. Corporal Lacoste snatched a flung cloak from the ground, wrapped it about his left arm, and with a screaming '*huéc*!' charged down upon the foe.

At the very outset the wings of the dastard troop folded back before the furious onrush, leaving the formation a wedge. The point of this the soldier crumpled up, thrusting and threshing. His blade flung aloft a spray of crimson; the whole hotchpotch of writhing shapes seemed to boil into hideous jangle; he shrieked again and again as he drove his way into it. Then in a moment the pass was won. The pack, recoiling upon its rear to escape the swingeing flail, fell into demoralisation, showed its panic tail, and went off in a wind of uproar down the glen.

The instant they were vanished, the monk and his companion descended from their coign of 'reserve'. The soldier held out his dripping weapon mutely, and with a stare of scorn.

'It is, in truth, a blade worthy of the arm that wields it,' cried the priest cringingly. His voice shook. He kept glancing furtively at the peasant by his side. This man's eyes had a strange glare in them, and his mouth was dribbling.

Corporal Lacoste cleansed his sword scrupulously on the cloak he had appropriated.

'Dishonouring blood,' he said, 'for the imbruing of a noble weapon! But – *corne et tonnerre*! – a king must take tribute of chief and villain alike. At least, now, the stain is wiped away.'

He ran the sword back into its scabbard with a clank.

'*En avant*!' he cried disdainfully, and swaggered off down the defile.

Perhaps for a mile they proceeded in this order, the *beau sabreur* indulging his fancy with a priest and peasant for lackeys. Now and again he would turn and cry 'Which way?' – but, for the rest, he condescended to no familiarity with cravens.

By-and-by the dead air tightened, the trees thinning so as to make but a ragged canopy of the snow overhead. Then the toiling monk quavered out a 'halt!' to him that strode in front.

'Monsieur,' he panted, 'it necessitates that we part at the cross-tracks.'

'How, then!' exclaimed Corporal Lacoste, facing about.

The two men advanced. The peasant passed the trooper a half-dozen paces, and wheeled round softly. They were all by then come into a little open dell, drowsy with snow, into which the fog drooped from above, like smoke in the downdraught of a chimney. Not a twig of all the laden bushes stirred. The very heart of nature, frozen and constricted, had ceased of its audible beating.

The priest pulled his cowl farther over his eyes.

'My God, the cold!' he muttered. Then he appeared to shudder himself into fury.

'Have we not brought you far enough? Thither goes the road to St Pölten and Wien. *Mein Gott*, the assurance, the assurance—!'

He leapt back. The point of the wolf's tooth had almost pricked him as it shot through Corporal Lacoste's throat.

'*Stehen sie auf!* ah, you devil!' he sobbed, as the dog-man threw himself upon the quivering tumbled body, snarling and quarrelling with the knife that would not be withdrawn.

Suddenly a terrible lust overtook the onlooker. He tore the trooper's sword from its sheath and slashed at the senseless face till the blade streamed.

'The blood of a wolf!' he screeched – 'of a ravisher and despoiler! Unbuckle me the scabbard. It shall stay here – the red shall stay, and mingle presently, for all his boasting, with that of the beasts to which he was kin!'

For long the winged flakes had fallen, the huddled labyrinths of the forest been dense as with the myriad settling of ghost-moths. Here, indeed, was the spinning-mill of Fate, drawing steadily, relentlessly, from the loaded distaff of the clouds, working an impenetrable warp for the snaring of forfeited lives. Lost, gasping, and horror-stricken, the monk stumbled aimlessly onward, the trooper's sheathed sword clasped convulsively – half unconsciously – under his arm, the trooper's gold clinking in his mendicant pouch. He beat his way anywhither among the glimmering trunks, and the terror of hell was in his soul.

For, not a hundred paces of their return journey had the murderers traversed, when the blinding hood of the snow-wraith shut upon the shameful scene – upon all the woodlands of Amstetten, blotting out the voiceless passes, obscuring and confusing the familiar avenues of retreat. Too well then these men realised, out of their knowledge of it, the menace of the dumb eclipse – of the trackless silence that no instinct might interpret. But the fulness of dismay was for one only of the two.

In a minute they were astray; at the end of an hour, two hours, they were still ice-bound wanderers – white spectres of the living death. And so at last the natural dusk, weaving weft into warp of darkness, had crept upon them; and a greater fear, long-foreshadowed, had knocked at the priest's heart – a sickening thud to every step he took. Then his eyes, straining in the inhuman blackness, would seek frantically to resolve the character of that that pattered at his side; and he had jibbed as he walked, daring neither to question nor to touch.

Suddenly an attenuated whimper, that swelled to a piercing yaup, had sounded at his very ear, and something had leapt from his neighbourhood and gone scurrying into the darkness.

Then he knew that what he had dreaded had befallen, and the utter ecstasy of horror entered into and possessed his soul.

Now, all in a moment, he broke from the thronged terrorism of trees into a little ghastly glen. A bursting sigh, compound of a dozen clashing emotions, issued from his lungs. He could faintly see here once more; and he knew himself to have happened upon that very pass wherein he had been busy in the morning imbruing his hands, by wolfish proxy, in the blood of the wounded.

But he had not climbed a score of yards up the slope in a whirl of flakes, when a guttural sound, that seemed to come from almost under his feet, shocked him to a pause. He stood, forcibly striving to constrict his heart lest the thud of it knocking on his ribs should betray him. For the wolves were in the glen again. His every nerve jumped to the consciousness of their neighbourhood.

The swinish sound went on. Suddenly the ticking wheel of Life touched off its alarum. Wrought to the topping pitch of endurance, he gave way, uttering scream after scream in a mere paralysis of fright. The whole glen seemed to howl in echo: there came a snarling rush.

Who had shouted it? – 'The sword of Corporal Lacoste!' The cry, he could have sworn, clanged in his frantic ears. It rallied him to recollection of what he held in his hand. The sword! At least, in his despair, he could endeavour to do with it as he had seen done.

A score of rabid snouts budded through the gloom before him. He clutched at the hilt. Some latent memory, perhaps, of the stinging thrash of the weapon it looked upon kept the pack at bay a moment. But clutch and tear as the priest might, the blade would not come forth. The lust of hatred that had sheathed it, wet with the life of its victim, had recoiled upon itself. Corporal Lacoste still claimed his sword – claimed it by testimony of his blood, that had dried upon it, gluing it within its scabbard.

A low laugh issued from the thick of the pack – an unearthly bark confusedly blended of the utterance of beast and man. It was as if some one brute, intelligent above its fellows, had realised the humour of the situation.

A grey snout, grinning and slavering from a single long tooth, came nozzling itself through the herd.

The priest screamed and fell upon his knees.

THE GLASS BALL

It happened in the winter of 1881 (said my friend). You remember that winter? It began to freeze hard early in November, and the frost never fairly broke until the second or third week in March. I had come up to town by the South-Western Railway, travelling through a white and wind-less country; and the cold was stupefying. I lay most of the way in a sort of torpor, gelid from toe to brain, and only just sensible of the still and silent flow of things outside the window. A desolate day, with hardly a human shape aboard to emphasise its loneliness. I don't know if I slept at all. I was alone in my compartment, and in a sort of mental stupor, as I say. And then suddenly I was awake and staring. It was snowing outside, and something had spoken to me – or tried to speak. There was an impression in my brain as of a little, black, leaning figure, infinitely small as if infinitely distant – a mere oblique accent on the sheeted immensity of things – of a staggered white face, of a loud, subconscious voice. And here, without and within, were only void and running silence. I shook, as one shakes escaping by a hair's-breadth the insidious clutch of a nightmare. It had been a nightmare, I supposed, of the kind that discovers a minute rent in the veil over the unseen, synchronously with some malefic horror on the further side. And, as always, the rent had been closed, only just timely for me. Such dreams are momentarily demor-alising: oddly enough the fear of this one dwelt with me for days. I could not shake off its memory, in the tremor of which was mingled, nevertheless, a strange emotion like pity. Imagine some lone survivor in the Arctic wastes uttering instinctively, as he sinks to his death, that call for human aid which none, even the most daring, may forego at the last. For some nameless reason that image, or its like, hung constantly in my mind, until presently it wrought in me an only half-reluctant desire to have my dream again. What, I thought, if that dreadful approaching face seen through the rent had been addressed to me not in malignity, but in an agony of supplication?

That was a morbid fancy, resolutely to be dismissed. A few strenuous days in London promised to see the last of it. Christmas was near, and with it an engagement to a family of young relatives, who would certainly expect seasonable presents. I prepared for the sacrifice.

It was then that the name of John Trent swam suddenly into my field of mental vision, and with a click, stood focused there. Who was John Trent? I knew no more than that he was a lost gentleman, whose whereabouts his family, or lawyers, or natural representatives were daily seeking through advertisement in the papers and police-stations. It was only one case like fifty others, and there was no known reason why it should suddenly absorb my attention. Yet quite unaccountably it did. Each morning I turned for first news to that reiterated paragraph in the agony column offering money for whatsoever information as to the movements of the vanished John Trent. He had last been seen, it appeared, on the afternoon of my journey to London (perhaps it was that slight coincidence which attracted me), when he had left his lodgings at Winchfield for a walk; and thereafter he had been seen no more. Some later particulars gave his age as forty, his disposition as solitary, his temper as peculiar and inclined to rashness. He had been something wont, in the past, to self-obliterations, it seemed; yet hardly after this senseless fashion. And there the tale of him ended.

One afternoon I walked down to the Lowther Arcade, then drearily existent, to effect my purchases. It was all a long medley of toys and fancy stuff from which to select; but I chose with an eye to meetness and economy, even down to the baby, on whose behalf I had the inspiration to buy a glass snowing-ball. You know the sort? I hadn't seen one since I was a child myself, and I was delighted. There is a man inside, with a little wintry landscape, and a Swiss châlet, and when you turn the ball upside down and round again, thick snow is falling. That is the rule, but I observed at once that the specimen I received from the superior young lady was an exception to the rule. It had inside it only the solitary figure of a man, and the man was skating. Yes, he skated actually, moving in little swoops and circles over a sheet of ice which seemed to dissect the ball; and as he skated the snow fell.

I stood staring stupidly and, as I stared, the man went through the ice and disappeared.

'That's different from the others,' I said loudly to the girl. I suppose my tone startled her; I'm sure it startled me. 'Is it?' she said. 'I don't think so.' And no more it was. When I looked again at the thing in my hand, there were the peasant and the châlet, and the little landscape, all correct and all motionless in their places.

I didn't buy the ball, but something else; and from the Arcade I went straight to the nearest police-station where, among the posted bills, figured that relating to the disappearance of John Trent. 'I think,' I said to the inspector, 'I can tell you where he is. He is under the ice in Fleet pond.'

And so he was; and thence they dragged him when the bitter frost came to an end. The little oblique accent on the whirling white sheet half seen, half dreamt, by me, the mortal expression, the loud cry – they had all represented the fate of John Trent skating, like a madman, solitary and unsuspected, on that vast plane of ice beside the track. He had gone insanely to his doom, on that stark, inhuman day, without a word to, and unseen by, a solitary soul save myself, and by me only in that exchange of sub-conscious recognitions which obliterates intervening space. To mine alone, in all that running, close-shut train, had his been able to appeal – yet with what purpose from such a man?

I think I know. He had a young child – one – legitimately and wholly dependent on him. Until they could produce certain evidence that he, John Trent, was dead and not merely disappeared, that child would be a beggar. And that was why he had wanted his fate to be definitely known – why, to my still deficient understanding, he had turned its little inmates out of their glass snowing-house, and had taken their place.

POOR LUCY RIVERS

The following story was told to a friend – with leave, conditionally, to make it public – by a well-known physician who died last year.

I was in Paul's typewriting exchange (says the professional narrator), seeing about some circulars I required, when a young lady came in bearing a box, the weight of which seemed to tax her strength severely. She was a very personable young woman, though looking ill, I fancied – in short, with those diathetic symptoms which point to a condition of hysteria. The manager, who had been engaged elsewhere, making towards me at the moment, I intimated to him that he should attend to the newcomer first. He turned to her.

'Now, madam?' said he.

'I bought this machine second-hand of you last week,' she began, after a little hesitation. He admitted his memory of the fact. 'I want to know,' she said, 'if you'll change it for another.'

'Is there anything wrong with it, then?' he asked.

'Yes,' she said; 'No!' she said; 'Everything!' she said, in a crescendo of spasms, looking as if she were about to cry. The manager shrugged his shoulders.

'Very reprehensible of us,' said he; 'and hardly our way. It is not customary; but, of course – if it doesn't suit – to give satisfaction—' he cleared his throat.

'I don't want to be unfair,' said the young woman. 'It doesn't suit *me*. It might another person.'

He had lifted, while speaking, its case off the typewriter, and now, placing the machine on a desk, inserted a sheet or two of paper, and ran his fingers deftly over the keys.

'Really, madam,' said he, removing and examining the slip, 'I can detect nothing wrong.'

'I said – perhaps – only as regards myself.'

She was hanging her head, and spoke very low.

'But!' said he, and stopped – and could only add the emphasis of another deprecatory shrug.

'Will you do me the favour, madam, to try it in my presence?'

'No,' she murmured; 'please don't ask me. I'd really rather not.' Again the suggestion of strain – of suffering.

'At least,' said he, 'oblige me by looking at this.'

He held before her the few lines he had typed. She had averted her head during the minute he had been at work; and it was now with evident reluctance, and some force put upon herself, that she acquiesced. But the moment she raised her eyes, her face brightened with a distinct expression of relief.

'Yes,' she said; 'I know there's nothing wrong with it. I'm sure it's all my fault. But – but, if you don't mind. So much depends on it.'

Well, the girl was pretty; the manager was human. There were a dozen young women, of a more or less pert type, at work in the front office. I dare say he had qualified in the illogic of feminine moods. At any rate, the visitor walked off in a little with a machine presumably another than that she had brought.

'Professional?' I asked, to the manager's resigned smile addressed to me.

'So to speak,' said he. 'She's one of the "augment her income" class. I fancy it's little enough without. She's done an occasional job for us. We've got her card somewhere.'

'Can you find it?'

He could find it, though he was evidently surprised at the request – scarce reasonably, I think, seeing how he himself had just given me an instance of that male inclination to the attractive, which is so calculated to impress women in general with the injustice of our claims to impartiality.

With the piece of pasteboard in my hand, I walked off then and there to commission 'Miss Phillida Gray' with the job I had intended for Paul's. Psychologically, I suppose, the case interested me. Here was a young person who seemed, for no *practical* reason, to have quarrelled with her unexceptionable means to a livelihood.

It raised more than one question; the incompleteness of woman as a wage earner, so long as she was emancipated from all but her fancifulness; the possibility of the spontaneous generation of soul – the *divina particula aurae* – in man-made mechanisms, in the construction of which their makers had invested their whole of mental capital. Frankenstein loathed the abortion of his genius. Who shall say that the soul of the inventor may not speak antipathetically, through the instrument which records it, to that soul's natural antagonist? Locomotives have moods, as any engine-driver will tell you; and any shaver, that his razor, after maltreating in some fit of perversity one side of his face, will repent, and caress the other as gently as any sucking-dove.

I laughed at this point of my reflections. Had Miss Gray's typewriter, embodying the soul of a blasphemer, taken to swearing at her?

It was a bitterly cold day. Snow, which had fallen heavily in November, was yet lying compact and unthawed in January. One had the novel experience in London of passing between piled ramparts of it. Traffic for some two months had been at a discount; and walking, for one of my years, was still so perilous a business that I was long in getting to Miss Gray's door.

She lived West Kensington way, in a 'converted flat', whose

title, like that of a familiar type of Christian exhibited on platforms, did not convince of anything but a sort of paying opportunism. That is to say, at the cost of some internal match-boarding, roughly fitted and stained, an unlettable private residence, of the estimated yearly rental of forty pounds, had been divided into two 'sets' at thirty-five apiece – whereby fashion, let us hope, profited as greatly as the landlord.

Miss Gray inhabited the upper section, the door to which was opened by a little cockney drab, very smutty, and smelling of gas stoves.

'Yes, she was in.' (For all her burden, 'Phillida', with her young limbs, had outstripped me.) 'Would I please to walk up?'

It was the dismallest room I was shown into – really the most unattractive setting for the personable little body I had seen. She was not there at the moment, so that I could take stock without rudeness. The one curtainless window stared, under a lid of fog, at the factory-like rear of houses in the next street. Within was scarce an evidence of dainty feminine occupation. It was all an illustration of the empty larder and the wolf at the door. How long would the bolt withstand him? The very walls, it seemed, had been stripped for sops to his ravening – stripped so nervously, so hurriedly, that ribbons of paper had been flayed here and there from the plaster. The ceiling was falling; the common grate cold; there was a rag of old carpet on the floor – a dreary, deadly place! The typewriter – the new one – laid upon a little table placed ready for its use, was, in its varnished case, the one promi-nent object, quite healthy by contrast. How would the wolf moan and scratch to hear it desperately busy, with click and clang, building up its paper rampart against his besieging!

I had fallen of a sudden so depressed, into a spirit of such premonitory haunting, that for a moment I almost thought I could hear the brute of my own fancy snuffling outside. Surely there was something breathing, rustling near me – something—

I grunted, shook myself, and walked to the mantelpiece. There was nothing to remark on it but a copy of some verses on a sheet of notepaper; but the printed address at the top, and the signature at the foot of this, immediately caught my attention. I trust, under the circumstances (there was a coincidence here), that it was not dishonest, but I took out my glasses, and read those verses – or, to be strictly accurate, the gallant opening quatrain – with laudable coolness. But inasmuch as the matter of the second and third stanzas, which I had an opportunity of perusing later, bears upon one aspect of my story, I may as well quote the whole poem here for what it is worth.

> Phyllis, I cannot woo in rhyme,
>   As courtlier gallants woo,
> With utterances sweet as thyme
>   And melting as the dew.
>
> An arm to serve; true eyes to see;
>   Honour surpassing love;
> These, for all song, my vouchers be,
>   Dear love, so thou'lt them prove.
>
> Bid me – and though the rhyming art
>   I may not thee contrive—
> I'll print upon thy lips, sweetheart,
>   A poem that shall live.

It may have been derivative; it seemed to me, when I came to read the complete copy, passable. At the first, even, I was certainly conscious of a thrill of secret gratification. But, as I said, I had mastered no more than the first four lines, when a rustle at the door informed me that I was detected.

She started, I could see, as I turned round. I was not at the trouble of apologising for my inquisitiveness.

'Yes,' I said; 'I saw you at Paul's Exchange, got your address, and came on here. I want some circulars typed. No doubt you will undertake the job?'

I examined her narrowly while I spoke. It was obviously a case of neurasthenia – the tendril shooting in the sunless vault. But she had more spirit than I calculated on. She just walked across to the empty fireplace, collared those verses, and put them into her pocket. I rather admired her for it.

'Yes, with pleasure,' she said, sweetening the rebuke with a blush, and stultifying it by affecting to look on the mantelpiece for a card, which eventually she produced from another place. 'These are my terms.'

'Thank you,' I replied. 'What do you say to a contra account – you to do my work, and I to set my professional attendance against it? I am a doctor.'

She looked at me mute and amazed.

'But there is nothing the matter with me,' she murmured, and broke into a nervous smile.

'O, I beg your pardon!' I said. 'Then it was only your instrument which was out of sorts?'

Her face fell at once.

'You heard me – of course,' she said. 'Yes, I – it was out of sorts, as you say. One gets fancies, perhaps, living alone, and typing – typing.'

I thought of the discordant clack going on hour by hour – the dead words of others made brassily vociferous, until one's own individuality would become emerged in the infernal harmonies.

'And so,' I said, 'like the dog's master in the fable, you quarrelled with an old servant.'

'O, no!' she answered. 'I had only had it for a week – since I came here.'

'You have only been here a week?'

'Little more,' she replied. 'I had to move from my old rooms. It is very kind of you to take such an interest in me. Will you tell me what I can do for you?'

My instructions were soon given. The morrow would see them attended to. No, she need not send the copies on. I would myself call for them in the afternoon.

'I hope *this* machine will be more to the purpose,' I said.

'*I* hope so, too,' she answered.

'Well, she seems a lady,' I thought, as I walked home; 'a little anaemic flower of gentility.' But sentiment was not to the point.

That evening, 'over the walnuts and the wine', I tackled Master Jack, my second son. He was a promising youth; was reading for the Bar, and, for all I knew, might have contributed to the 'Gownsman'.

'Jack,' I said, when we were alone, 'I never knew till today that you considered yourself a poet.'

He looked at me coolly and inquiringly, but said nothing.

'Do you consider yourself a marrying man, too?' I asked.

He shook his head, with a little amazed smile.

'Then what the devil do you mean by addressing a copy of love verses to Miss Phillida Gray?'

He was on his feet in a moment, as pale as death.

'If you were not my father—' he began.

'But I am, my boy,' I answered, 'and an indulgent one, I think you'll grant.'

He turned, and stalked out of the room; returned in a minute, and flung down a duplicate draft of *the* poem on the table before me. I put down the crackers, took up the paper, and finished my reading of it.

'Jack,' I said, 'I beg your pardon. It does credit to your heart – you understand the emphasis? You are a young gentleman of some prospects. Miss Gray is a young lady of none.'

He hesitated a moment; then flung himself on his knees before me. He was only a great boy.

'Dad,' he said; 'dear old Dad; you've seen them – you've seen her?'

I admitted the facts. 'But that is not at all an answer to me,' I said.

'Where is she?' he entreated, pawing me.

'You don't know?'

'Not from Adam. I drove her hard, and she ran away from me. She said she would, if I insisted – not to kill those same prospects of mine. My prospects! Good God! What are they without her? She left her old rooms, and no address. How did you get to see her – and my stuff?'

I could satisfy him on these points.

'But it's true,' he said; 'and – and I'm in love, Dad – Dad, I'm in love.' He leaned his arms on the table, and his head on his arms.

'Well,' I said, 'how did *you* get to know her?'

'Business,' he muttered, 'pure business. I just answered her advertisement – took her some of my twaddle. She's an orphan – daughter of a Captain Gray, navy man; and – and she's an angel.'

'I hope he is,' I answered. 'But anyhow, that settles it. There's no marrying and giving in marriage in heaven.'

He looked up. 'You don't mean it? No! you dearest and most indulgent of Dads! Tell me where she is.'

I rose. 'I may be all that; but I'm not such a fool. I shall see her tomorrow. Give me till after then.'

'O, you perfect saint!'

'I promise absolutely nothing.'

'I don't want you to. I leave you to her. She could beguile a Saint Anthony.'

'Hey!'

'I mean as a Christian woman should.'

'O! that explains it.'

The following afternoon I went to West Kensington. The little drab was snuffling when she opened the door. She had a little hat on her head.

'Missus wasn't well,' she said; 'and she hadn't liked to leave her, though by rights she was only engaged for an hour or two in the day.'

'Well,' I said, 'I'm a doctor, and will attend to her. You can go.'

She gladly shut me in and herself out. The clang of the door echoed up the narrow staircase, and was succeeded, as if it had started it, by the quick toing and froing of a footfall in the room above. There was something inexpressibly ghostly in the sound, in the reeling dusk which transmitted it.

I perceived, the moment I set eyes on the girl, that there was something seriously wrong with her. Her face was white as wax, and quivered with an incessant horror of laughter. She tried to rally, to greet me, but broke down at the first attempt, and stood as mute as stone.

I thank my God I can be a sympathetic without being a fanciful man. I went to her at once, and imprisoned her icy hands in the human strength of my own.

'What is it? Have you the papers ready for me?'

She shook her head, and spoke only after a second effort.

'I am very sorry.'

'You haven't done them, then? Never mind. But why not? Didn't the new machine suit either?'

I felt her hands twitch in mine. She made another movement of dissent.

'That's odd,' I said. 'It looks as if it wasn't the fault of the tools, but of the workwoman.'

All in a moment she was clinging to me convulsively, and crying—

'You are a doctor – you'll understand – don't leave me alone – don't let me stop here!'

'Now listen,' I said, 'listen, and control yourself. Do you hear? I have come *prepared* to take you away. I'll explain why presently.'

'I thought at first it was my fault,' she wept distressfully, 'working, perhaps, until I grew light-headed' (Ah, hunger and loneliness and that grinding labour!); 'but when I was sure of myself, still it went on, and I could not do my tasks to earn money. Then I thought – how can God let such things be! – that the instrument itself must be haunted. It took to going at night; and in the morning' – she gripped my hands – 'I burnt them. I tried to think I had done it myself in my sleep, and I always burnt them. But it didn't stop, and at last I made up my mind to take it back and ask for another – another – you remember?'

She pressed closer to me, and looked fearfully over her shoulder.

'It does the same,' she whispered, gulping. 'It wasn't the machine at all. It's the place – itself – that's haunted.'

I confess a tremor ran through me. The room was dusking – hugging itself into secrecy over its own sordid details. Out near the window, the typewriter, like a watchful sentient thing, seemed grinning at us with all its ivory teeth. She had carried it there, that it might be as far from herself as possible.

'First let me light the gas,' I said, gently but resolutely detaching her hands.

'There is none,' she murmured.

None. It was beyond her means. This poor creature kept her deadly vigils with a couple of candles. I lit them – they served but to make the gloom more visible – and went to pull down the blind.

'O, take care of it!' she whispered fearfully, meaning the typewriter. 'It is awful to shut out the daylight so soon.'

God in heaven, what she must have suffered! But I admitted nothing, and took her determinedly in hand.

'Now,' I said, returning to her, 'tell me plainly and distinctly what it is that the machine does.'

She did not answer. I repeated my question.

'It writes things,' she muttered – 'things that don't come from me. Day and night it's the same. The words on the paper aren't the words that come from my fingers.'

'But that is impossible, you know.'

'So *I* should have thought once. Perhaps – what is it to be possessed? There was another typewriter – another girl – lived in these rooms before me.'

'Indeed! And what became of her?'

'She disappeared mysteriously – no one knows why or where. Maria, my little maid, told me about her. Her name was Lucy Rivers, and – she just disappeared. The landlord advertised her effects, to be claimed, or sold to pay the rent; and that was done, and she made no sign. It was about two months ago.'

'Well, will you now practically demonstrate to me this reprehensible eccentricity on the part of your instrument?'

'Don't ask me. I don't dare.'

'I would do it myself, but of course you will understand that a more satisfactory conclusion would be come to by my watching your fingers. Make an effort – you needn't even look at the result – and I will take you away immediately after.'

'You are very good,' she answered pathetically; 'but I don't know that I ought to accept. Where to, please? And – and I don't even know your name.'

'Well, I have my own reasons for withholding it.'

'It is all so horrible,' she said; 'and I am in your hands.'

'They are waiting to transfer you to mamma's,' said I.

The name seemed an instant inspiration and solace to her. She looked at me, without a word, full of wonder and gratitude; then asked me to bring the candles, and she would acquit herself of her task. She showed the best pluck over it, though her face was ashy, and her mouth a line, and her little nostrils pulsing the whole time she was at work.

I had got her down to one of my circulars, and, watching her fingers intently, was as sure as observer could be that she had followed the text verbatim.

'Now,' I said, when she came to a pause, 'give me a hint how to remove this paper, and go you to the other end of the room.'

She flicked up a catch. 'You have only to pull it off the roller,' she said; and rose and obeyed. The moment she was away I followed my instructions, and drew forth the printed sheet and looked at it.

It may have occupied me longer than I intended. But I

was folding it very deliberately, and putting it away in my pocket when I walked across to her with a smile. She gazed at me one intent moment, and dropped her eyes.

'Yes,' she said; and I knew that she had satisfied herself. 'Will you take me away now, at once, please?'

The idea of escape, of liberty once realised, it would have been dangerous to balk her by a moment. I had acquainted mamma that I might possibly bring her a visitor. Well, it simply meant that the suggested visit must be indefinitely prolonged.

Miss Gray accompanied me home, where certain surprises, in addition to the tenderest of ministrations, were awaiting her. All that becomes private history, and outside my story. I am not a man of sentiment; and if people choose to write poems and make general asses of themselves, why – God bless them!

The problem I had set *my*self to unravel was what looked deucedly like a tough psychologic poser. But I was resolute to face it, and had formed my plan. It was no unusual thing for me to be out all night. That night, after dining, I spent in the 'converted' flat in West Kensington.

I had brought with me – I confess to so much weakness – one of your portable electric lamps. The moment I was shut in and established, I pulled out the paper Miss Gray had typed for me, spread it under the glow and stared at it. Was it a copy of my circular? Would a sober 'First Aid Society' Secretary be likely, do you think, to require circulars containing such expressions as '*William! William! Come back to me! 0, William, in God's name! William! William! William!*' – in monstrous iteration – the one cry, or the gist of it, for lines and lines in succession?

I am at the other end from humour in saying this. It is heaven's truth. Line after line, half down the page, went that monotonous, heartbreaking appeal. It was so piercingly moving, my human terror of its unearthliness was all drowned, absorbed in an overflowing pity.

I am not going to record the experiences of that night. That unchanging mood of mine upheld me through consciousnesses and subconsciousnesses which shall be sacred. Sometimes, submerged in these, I seemed to hear the clack of the instrument in the window, but at a vast distance. I may have seen – I may have dreamt – I accepted it all. Awakening in the chill grey of morning, I felt no surprise at seeing some loose sheets of paper lying on the floor. '*William! William!*' their text ran down, '*Come back to me!*' It was all that same wail of a broken heart. I followed Miss Gray's example. I took out my match-box, and reverently, reverently burned them.

An hour or two later I was at Paul's Exchange, privately interviewing my manager.

'Did you ever employ a Miss Lucy Rivers?'

'Certainly we did. Poor Lucy Rivers! She rented a machine from us. In fact—' He paused.

'Well?'

'Well – it is a mere matter of business – she "flitted", and we had to reclaim our instrument. As it happens, it was the very one purchased by the young lady who so interested you here two days ago.'

'The first machine, you mean?'

'The first – *and* the second.' He smiled. 'As a matter of fact, she took away again what she brought.'

'Miss Rivers's?'

He nodded. 'There was absolutely nothing wrong with it – mere fad. Women start these fancies. The click of the thing gets on their nerves, I suppose. We must protect ourselves, you see; and I'll warrant she finds it perfection now.'

'Perhaps she does. What was Miss Rivers's address?'

He gave me, with a positive grin this time, the 'converted' flat.

'But that was only latterly,' he said. 'She had moved from—'

He directed me elsewhere.

'Why,' said I, taking up my hat, 'did you call her "poor Lucy Rivers"?'

'O, I don't know!' he said. 'She was rather an attractive young lady. But we had to discontinue our patronage. She developed the most extraordinary – but it's no business of mine. She was one of the submerged tenth; and she's gone under for good, I suppose.'

I made my way to the *other* address – a little lodging in a shabby-genteel street. A bitter-faced landlady, one of the 'preordained' sort, greeted me with resignation when she thought I came for rooms, and with acerbity when she heard that my sole mission was to inquire about a Miss Lucy Rivers.

'I won't deceive you, sir,' she said. 'When it come to receiving gentlemen privately, I told her she must go.'

'Gentlemen!'

'I won't do Miss Rivers an injustice,' she said. 'It was *a* gentleman.'

'Was that latterly?'

'It was not latterly, sir. But it was the effects of its not being latterly which made her take to things.'

'What things?'

'Well, sir, she grew strange company, and took to the roof.'

'What on earth do you mean?'

'Just precisely what I say, sir; through the trap-door by the steps, and up among the chimney-pots. He'd been there with her before, and perhaps she thought she'd find him hiding among the stacks. He called himself an astronomer; but it's my belief it was another sort of stargazing. I couldn't stand it at last, and I had to give her notice.'

It was falling near a gloomy midday when I again entered the flat, and shut myself in with its ghosts and echoes. I had a set conviction, a set purpose in my mind. There was that which seemed to scuttle, like a little demon of laughter, in my wake, now urging me on, now slipping round and above to trip me as I mounted. I went steadily on and up, past the sitting-room door, to the floor above. And here, for the first time, a thrill in my blood seemed to shock and hold me for a moment. Before my eyes, rising to a skylight, now dark and choked with snow, went a flight of steps. Pulling myself together, I mounted these, and with a huge effort (*the bolt was not shot*) shouldered the trap open. There were a fall and rustle without; daylight entered; and, levering the door over, I emerged upon the roof.

Snow, grim and grimy and knee-deep, was over everything, muffling the contours of the chimneys, the parapets, the irregularities of the leads. The dull thunder of the streets came up to me; a fog of thaw was in the air; a thin drizzle was already falling. I drove my foot forward into a mound, and hitched it on something. In an instant I was down on my knees, scattering the sodden raff right and left, and – my God! – a face!

She lay there as she had been overwhelmed, and frozen, and preserved these two months. She had closed the trap behind her, and nobody had known. Pure as wax – pitiful as hunger – dead! Poor Lucy Rivers!

Who was she, and who the man? We could never learn. She had woven his name, his desertion, her own ruin and despair into the texture of her broken life. Only on the great day of retribution shall he answer to that agonised cry.

THE APOTHECARY'S REVENGE

Prominent, under the shadow of the projecting gable, the little gilded bason and lancet above the door reflected back the light from a single dismal lantern, burning a cotton wick, which hung from a bracket over the archway opposite. It was nearing sundown, and the few pedestrians abroad walked hurriedly and stealthily, keeping in the middle of the street as if they feared some lurking ambush. One of these, a tall, muffled figure of a man, with a drawn, agitated countenance, wheeled suddenly, and, pushing without a pause through the unlocked doorway under the gilded sign, mounted the flight of complaining stairs which rose before him in the gloom beyond. Evidently familiar with the place, the visitor, on reaching the landing, knocked fearfully but resolutely on a dark oblong in the obscurity which betokened where a closed door broke the panelled surface of the wall.

A groan or sigh, some sound indefinite but sufficient, responding, he turned the handle, his long fingers clouding it with a clammy moisture, and, edging round the door, closed it softly behind him and stood looking eagerly towards the end of the room. Its sole occupant, the learned Quinones, that miserly apothecary whose wisdom, nevertheless, served him for a perennial harvest, was, he knew well enough, notoriously chary of speech, grudging it to others as though, like the fairy-gifted maiden's, there were a present of a jewel in every word he let drop. Saturnine, austere, caustic in his few utterances, he was wont to vouchsafe small comment on the catalogues of ills and vapours that were perpetually laid before him; but a phrase with him, so famous was he, took all the force of a prescription. Thus regarded, it was little likely that he would forego the principles of a lifetime for the sake of him who had now broken in upon his solitude.

He was seated at a table in the window opposite the door, his back to the intruder, his left ear turned a little, as if in some listening irascibility over the interruption. The fading alchemy of the sunset, dropping in flakes and dust through the diamond-paned casement, rimmed the hunched silhouette of him with a faint aura, and made an amber mist of the dry thin hair on his scalp, and turned the narrow section of cheek visible from lead to gold. It was to this strangely-crowned and indeterminate shadow that the visitor addressed himself, in hurried, fluttering speech, the true purport of which only gathered form as desperation lent it eloquence:

'You know me, Quinones – yes, you know me, learned master – as I know you. No need to waste a look on recognition. My voice is stored in your memory, with other debts to be liquidated. You do not forget these things.'

He took an impulsive step forward, and the board creaked and jumped under his foot. It seemed as if the figure in the chair started slightly, and then settled again to its listening. The visitor held out his hands with an imploring gesture.

'I did you an ill deed in the past, Quinones, and it is written against me in your books. What is the use to tell you that I have repented it since in sackcloth and ashes? And yet let it be of use. O, in these mortal times, when all the world should be in one brotherhood of help and sympathy, let your resentment sleep – forgive, and prove by that nobility your true title to the greatness that all men allow you. I have bitten the hand, I confess it, that cherished me: let that hand retaliate in the finest spirit by ministering to the wound I inflicted, not first on you, but on my own miserable nature. Be generous to me, Quinones, for I have lived to know and suffer.'

He paused; and in the pause there rose a melancholy cry from the darkening street: 'Bring out your dead; bring out your dead!' The sound seemed to goad him to a frenzy.

'Listen, Quinones; I have learned to know, I say. Love, that in its purity can redeem the worst, has been my teacher. For love I would live – I, who until it transformed me, feared no death, refused no risks. Now, for its sake, I am a coward; I shrink in terror that this mortality may claim me – me, who have learned at last the glory and the fruitfulness of life. O save me, Quinones! You alone among all the Galenical masters can do so, if you will. Fortify my blood; render me immune; give me the secret of your plague-water, the one specific, as all admit, quite certain in its results. Give it to me and mine, and earn for evermore the name of saint, the gratitude of hearts that wait upon your bounty not to break.'

The seated figure seemed, in the uncertain light, to stir and chuckle – or was it a sound of water gurgling in the basement. Still no response came from it; and, hearkening vainly through the thick silence, the mood of the man roared up in a moment from submission to deadly fury:

'Inhuman, unforgiving! Not for you to forget, in your God-feigned aloofness, the least, the most paltry hurt to your vanity. You hear, but you will not answer. Answer to this, then. I came to appeal to the great in you, as other blind fools have certified it; but I came prepared with sharper weapons than entreaty, should, as I foresaw in my heart, the fools prove fools indeed. I am a desperate man, Quinones, and you are alone – quite alone with me, I do believe. It is either the secret yielded, or your life. Make your choice, and quickly. A poor revenge, will you not think it, to lie there in your blood while I am ranging free and unsuspected in this welter!'

He half crouched, peering through the deepening twilight,

a sudden blade in his hand, the tumult in his brain grown rabid – then, with a shriek, 'Let your plague-water save you now!' leapt on the unresponsive figure.

It swayed, swung, and rolled stiffly to the floor, revealing a livid face, blotched and plague-stricken, and fangs – good Lord, they grinned!

Quinones mortal had not half the sinister significance of Quinones dead and rigid. He had sat there, waiting his age-delayed but never-forgotten revenge – sat there a stiffening corpse, long after the rest of his household had fled.

With a scream, the other rushed from the room, into the street – and so in a little for the cart and the plague-pit. Quinones was quits with him at last.

THE GREEN BOTTLE

My knowledge of Sewell was principally of a fox-nosed, weedy, scorbutic youth who wrote four-to-the-pound pars for the *Daily Record*. Further, I bore in mind his flaccid palms, his dropping underjaw, and the way in which in Fleet Street bars he would hang – looking, indeed, rather like a wet towel – on the words of any Captain Bobadil of his craft who would condescend to wipe his boots on him, or, for the matter of that, his foul mouth. He had no principles, I think. He was born lacking the sentiments of pride and decency. If he was kicked into the mud, he would make, before rising, a little conciliatory gift of mud pie for the kicker. On close terms with the petty ailments of his own body, the secret discoveries that delighted him were of similar weaknesses in others. The prescriptively unmentionable was his humour's best inspiration; his belief in the real approval underlying the affected disgust of his hearers quite genuine. He was, in short, a sort of editors' pimp, with all the taste and the instinct to *procure* 'copy', in the detestable sense.

At one time he elected, to my sorrow, to attach himself to me, with this justification (from his point of view) that I then happened to be grinding my literary barrel-organ – always adaptable to the popular need – to the tune of a contemporary interest in the problems of criminology; and the mudlark, being himself of a Newgate complexion of mind, had the assurance in consequence to assume a sympathetic bond between us.

Now, the difficulty being to convince Sewell that decency was ever anything but a diplomatic pose, and that one did not pursue vice, as dogs hunt foxes, because of the mere bestial attraction to an abominable scent, but with the sole purpose to reach and end the offence, I was led, more contemptuously than wisely, into allowing the assumption of claim by default, with the result that for some weeks the unsavoury thing stuck to me like a jigger. Then, at the climax of the annoyance, just when I had resolved, as an anthropological economy, upon dissecting my torment or himself as the closest possible illustration of my meaning, of a sudden the creature vanished – disappeared *sans phrase*; and Fleet Street and the *Daily Record* knew no more.

The fact was that Mr Sewell had been left a competence, and had retired into private life.

I did not see the fellow again for some eighteen months, when, one afternoon, he visited me quite unexpectedly at my lodgings. He accepted, as of old, the finger I committed to his clasp, and which I then – hardly covertly, under my desk – wrenched dry between my knees. He was scarcely altered in appearance. The only accent of difference that I could observe was in his tie, which was a spotted burglarious-looking token, in place of the rusty-black wisp that had been wont to depend, loosely knotted, from his neck. For the rest, he was the slack, unwholesome figure, with the sniggering and inward manner, of my knowledge. And yet, scanned again, there was something unusual about him after all – a suggestion, it might be, of excited nervousness, such as one might imagine in a very fulsome Paul Pry bursting, while fearing, to retail a ticklish piece of scandal.

'Well,' I said, after some indifferent commonplaces, 'so you've got your ticket-of-leave? And aren't your fingers itching, in a vacuous freedom, for oakum and the Fleet Street crank again?'

'Oh, Mr Deering,' says he, tittering and twisting, 'I like that metaphor. I come to report myself to you, Mr Deering.'

'H'mph!' said I. 'Well, when all's said, how *do* you manage to kill time?'

'Why, I kill it,' says he, grinning, 'and I lay it out. It's only necessary to have an object in life, Mr Deering. Mine's killing time, that I may lay it out. You'll never guess what I've become.'

'I'll make one shot. A body-snatcher.'

'Tee-hee! Not so far wrong. A collector, Mr Deering. I wish you'd come and see my museum. Will you have dinner with me tonight?'

'Not to be thought of. See here and here! In fact, I've already given you longer than I can spare. Goodbye, till our next meeting. If I'm on the jury, I'll try to forget the worst I know of you.'

He rose, fidgeted, still lingered.

'I do wish you'd dine with me.'

'I tell you I can't. Besides, I'm particular – it's a fad of mine – about my alimentary atmosphere. An unwholesome one balks my digestion.'

I began to be annoyed that the fellow would not go. Suddenly he turned upon me, with more decision than he had yet shown.

'The fact is something – something very odd has happened; quite impossible, you'd say. I don't know; if you'd only come and look.'

I did look – at him – in surprise.

'Odd – that concerns me? Why not tell me now, then?'

'You'd never believe unless you saw.'

'Saw! Saw what? Why, I'm hanged if, by the jaw of you, you aren't thinking to come the supernatural over me!'

'Yes,' he said, fawningly persistent; 'I want you to see. It's a case of horrors or nothing. You'll be able to judge, as you've made it your line.'

'I've done no such thing. I never raised a banshee yet that would deceive so much as a psychist.'

'Well,' said he, 'that's another inducement. You'd not be predisposed to the infection.'

'Infection!' I shouted. 'What, the devil! You've not been laying-out in earnest!'

He wriggled over a laugh.

'No,' said he. 'I meant the infection of fear.'

'Oh, trust me there!' said I.

This was so far a concession that, under the stimulus of a curiosity the creature had succeeded in arousing in me, I presently accepted, though grudgingly, his invitation. Then he took himself away, and I went on with my work – rather peevishly, for there was a bad taste in my mouth, that I endeavoured unsuccessfully to neutralise with tobacco.

At seven o'clock I packed away and went, depressed, to keep my engagement. It was a July evening of that unsavoury closeness that paints faces with a metallic sweat, and vulgarises out of all picturesqueness the motley concerns of life; an evening when fat women are truculent at omnibus doors; when the brassy twang of piano-organs blends indescribably with the sour stench of the roads; when a dive into a sequestered bar brings no consequence as of virtue refreshed, but rather as of self-indulgence rebuked with an added dyspepsia. And, appropriate to the atmosphere, my goal was in that inferno of dreary unfulfilments, Notting Hill. Thither I made my way, and there in the end house of a stuccoed and lifeless-looking terrace, converted (by a Salvation Army missionary, one might, from its vulgarity, suppose) into flats, came presently to a stop.

There was a bill 'To Let' in the ground-floor window, from which, by inference, my host was engaged to the upper rooms. He himself greeted me at the front door, to which I had mounted by a dozen of ill-laid steps. A second door within, set in a makeshift partition, opened straight upon the stairway that led up to his quarters.

'I hope you won't object to a cold collation, Mr Deering?' said he.

The stairs were so steep, and he looked so down upon me, twisting about from the height at which he led, that his white face seemed to hang like a clammy stone gargoyle from the gloom.

'I wouldn't suggest it's what you're accustomed to,' he said; 'but when one's only slavey goes out with the daylight, and doesn't return till the milk, it can't be helped, you know.'

'It's all right,' I said brusquely, and rudely enough, to be sure. 'I never supposed you kept a retinue. You're the only soul in the house, I conclude?'

We had come to a landing, where the stairs gave a wheel and went up, carpetless, steeper than ever. Looking aloft, it was some unmeaning comfort to me to observe that a skylight, obscured by dirt, took the slope of the ceiling with a wan sheen as of phosphorescence.

Two doorways, a step or so apart, faced us entering upon the landing. Through the nearest of these I caught glimpse of a white tablecloth and our meal set upon it. The second, and further, door, that was opposite the turn of the stairs, was shut.

'Eh!' said Sewell, with a curious intonation. 'The only soul, eh? Well, upon my word, I won't answer for that.'

'What the devil do you mean?' I exclaimed irritably.

'Why,' he answered, propitiatory at once, 'the rooms below are tenantless, if that's what you refer to.'

'What else should I refer to?'

'To be sure, to be sure,' he answered. 'Oh, yes; I'm the only one in possession! I don't mind. Generally speaking – there may be something now and again that makes a difference, you know – but, generally speaking, I think I've got the collector's love of solitude. We sort of hug ourselves over our finds, don't we? and then it isn't nice to have anybody else by, eh? That's my museum – that second door. I'd like you, if you don't mind, just to go cursorily round it now, before we sit down, and see what sort of an impression it makes on you.'

'Is your rotten mystery connected with it?'

'Well, yes, it is.'

'Lead on, then, and let's get it over.'

He obeyed, opening the door gingerly to its full width before entering, as if he half expected something to be there before him. I uttered an instant grunt. A row of unclean faces, their upper prominences so covered with dust as to give one the impression of their posturing over some infernal kind of footlights, leered down upon us from the top of a high bookcase.

'Yes,' said Sewell, though I had not spoken to him, 'they're a pretty lot, aren't they, Mr Deering? I picked 'em up at the Vandal sale – the lunatic specialist, don't you remember, that went mad and cut his own throat in the end? I don't know half their stories; but when I'm in the mood I sit here and try and piece 'em out of their faces. That fellow with the fat wale on his neck, now—'

'Oh, shut your imagination, you anthropophagist! Here, we'll hurry up with this. I see, I see. Absolutely characteristic; and I might have guessed the bent of your virtuosity.'

I found a precursory inspection more than sufficient. The creature had only found himself out of independence. He was become logically an Old Bailey curioso. His collection, disposed about the shelves of that same bookless bookcase and on little tables and whatnots, ranged from housebreakers' tools (miracles of vicious elegance) to a slip from a C.C. open spaces seat, on the branch of a tree above which a suicide had hanged himself. There were murderous revolvers, together with the bullets extracted from their victims. There were knives, lengths of Newgate rope, last confessions, photographs, and bloodstains. And, in inviting me to the discussion of this garbage, Sewell, I believe, was actuated by no inhumanity of malevolence. An unnatural appetite is normal to itself, I suppose.

But all the time his manner was *distrait* – spasmodic – watchful, and not of me, I could have thought.

All at once I felt myself constrained to rise from an examination, and to walk to the window. It looked across to the sordid backs of other converted houses; it looked down into a well of a garden, choked with rank grass, from the jungle of which stiff ears of dockweed stood up, as if picked to the French casement, that I could not see, in the room below. Now the tall buildings so blocked out the sunset that, although day still ruled, the room in which we stood was already appropriated to a livid twilight. I tugged at the window, striving to open it.

'What are you trying?' cried Sewell. 'What are you up to? What's the matter with you?'

He hurried across the room. He looked curiously into my face, as if for confirmation of some hope or fear of his own.

'You can't do it,' he said. 'It's been nailed up. Look here, Mr Deering, we'll feed, shall we?'

'Yes,' I snarled. I was furious with myself. I walked out of the room as still as, and bristling like, a baited cat. For the moment I was exalted above the impulse to put my tail between my legs.

Sewell's cold collation was vile. I swear it, though no sybarite, in some explanation of a subsequent nightmare. Macbeth hadn't supped when he saw the ghost of Banquo. How many ghosts he would have seen after a slice of Sewell's steak pie is conjectural. At the fourth mouthful I put down (I might have, dietetically, with scarce more discomfort to myself) my knife and fork.

'Is that beastly door shut?' I said crossly.

He knew, without my explaining, that I meant the door of the museum.

'Yes,' he answered, impervious to my rudeness, and offered no further remark. But, perhaps from a like sentiment of oppression, he turned up the gas above the table.

I made another effort at the pie, and finally desisted.

'Look here,' I said, falling back in my chair, and streaking down the damp hair on my forehead, 'I'm not a fool. D'you hear? I'm not a fool, I say. I want to know, that's all. What the devil's the matter with that bottle?'

'Ah!' he breathed out, with a curious under-inflexion of relief, of triumph. 'The bottle; yes; I thought you'd come to it.'

'Did you, indeed? So that's your Asian mystery?'

'Yes, that's it,' he said quietly. 'You've found it out, Mr Deering, and I wasn't mistaken, it seems.'

'Mistaken? I don't know. What's the matter with it? What infernal trick have you been planning? Take care!' I said bullyingly.

'Shall we go and look at it again?'

He only answered with the soft question.

I half rose, fought with myself, yielded, and dropped back.

'I'm damned if I do,' I said, 'until you've told me.'

'Very well,' he replied, slinkingly moved to govern and applaud me in a breath. 'I'll tell you at once, Mr Deering.'

He felt in his inner breast-pocket, produced a memorandum-book, withdrew a newspaper cutting from it, rose, and crossing to me, placed the slip in my hand. Accepting it sullenly, and taking my reason by the ears, I forced that to focus itself on the lines. They were headed and ran as follows:

THE LAMBETH TRAGEDY

Mr Hobbins, the south-western district coroner, held an inquest yesterday on the body of Ephraim Ellis, glass-blower, who, as has been stated, fell down dead at the very moment that the officers of justice entered the premises of his employers, Messrs Mackay, to arrest him on suspicion of having caused the death of Francis Riddick, a fellow-workman. Ellis, it will be remembered, was actually engaged in blowing bottles at the moment of his arrest. A verdict of death from syncope, resulting on shock, was returned.

Sewell stood behind me as I read. His long, ropy claw slid over my shoulder, and a finger of it traced along the words 'it will be remembered'.

'Yes,' I muttered, in response to the unspoken query, 'I recollect reading something about it. What then?'

Sewell's finger went on five – six letters, and stopped.

'He was "blowing bottles",' he said. 'He *was*, Mr Deering. I was standing by him at the time, and he was blowing that very green bottle you saw on the table in the next room. Do you know how they do it? They dip the end of their pipe into the melting-pot that sits in the furnace, and then, having rolled the little knob they've fished up tube-shaped on an iron plate, and pinched it for a neck, they take and blow it into a brass mould until it fits out the shape of the thing. Then they open the mould, and the bottle comes free, but stuck to the pipe, until a touch with a cold iron snaps the two apart. That's the way; but this bottle, you'll say, has a neck like a retort. I'll tell you why, Mr Deering. Ellis had just blown the thing complete, when the policeman put a hand on his shoulder. The pipe was at his mouth. He gave a last gasp into it and went down, the soft bottle-neck bending and sealing itself as the falling pipe dragged it over. Very well; I'd known the man and something of his story, and I brought away the green bottle, just as he'd left it, for a memento. But, Mr Deering, I brought away that in it that I hadn't bargained for. Can't you guess what it was?'

'No.'

'Why, Ellis's soul, Mr Deering, that passed into it with that last gasp of his, and was sealed up for anyone that likes to let it out.'

I got to my feet, driven beyond endurance.

'You ass!' I cried. 'Have you drivelled to an end?'

'Oh, dear no!' he whispered, with a little nervous but defiant chuckle. 'Now, you know, don't you, Mr Deering, that there's something uncommon about – about that out there? Perhaps you'll be able to explain it. It was in the hope that I asked you (who've made such a study of psychological phenomena) to endure my company for a night. And, to tell you the truth, there's something more and worse. Wouldn't you like to hear about it, Mr Deering?'

'Oh, go on!' I said, with a groan. 'I've accepted my company, as you say, and—'

'Won't you come further from the door?' he asked, truckling to and hating me, as I believed. 'I can see you aren't comfortable, and no wonder.'

I ground my teeth on a curse, and slouching to the mantelpiece, put my back against it. A blue-bottle, droning heavily in labour, whirled about the room and settled with a buzzing flop on the pie. The cessation of its fulsome chaunt seemed to embolden unseen things to stir and giggle in the dark corners of the room.

'*Aren't* you going on?' I said desperately.

'Yes,' he answered; 'I'm going on. From first to last I'll tell you everything, and then you can form your own conclusions. Mr Deering, I'd got to know, as I said, the man Ephraim Ellis. How, don't particularly matter. I'm fond of prowling about at night. I make acquaintances, and pick up things that interest me. This man did. There was something suggestive about him – something haunted, as I'd like to put it. He kept company at one time with a slavey of mine that died of fits (I've seen her in 'em), and perhaps that led to my following him up to his workplace and getting into talk with him. He was a glass-blower, and on night duty. A queer customer he was, and dark and secret as sin. Sometimes I'd look at him, red and shifty in the glow, and I'd think, "Are you calculating the consequences, my friend, of braining me with a white-hot bottle?" He may have been, more than you'd fancy; for I believe the man took me for an unclean spirit sent to goad him to further desperations. "Further", I say; but, mind you, I only go by report. It would never do, would it, Mr Deering, for you and me to be certain, or they might claim us for accessories?'

I broke into a hoarse, angry exclamation.

'No, no,' he interrupted me hurriedly, 'of course they

couldn't. It was only my fun. But the truth is, Ellis's fellow-workmen were fully persuaded that Ellis had murdered Riddick, who had been found one morning, after he'd relieved Ellis at solitary night duty, with his head melted and run away against the door of a furnace. I don't know; and I don't know what they went upon, seeing the trunk was all right, and that there was no head to examine for trace of injuries. But they made out their suspicions – on technical grounds, I suppose; and, as to the moral – why, Riddick, by their showing, had been a taunting devil, a regular bad lot, who'd made a game of baiting Ellis till he drove the man almost to madness. Anyhow, Ellis was marked down by them, and given the cold shoulder of fear; and so he worked apart (for he was too valuable a hand to be dismissed) – he worked apart – with only me, I really believe, in the wide world to speak to him, until the police, acting upon rumours, or the shadows of 'em, came to lay hands on him.

'But now, I must tell you, before that happened there was something else occurred that was more intimate to the moral, if not to the circumstantial, point. Ellis took to having fits, or seizures, in which he'd rave that Riddick hadn't been got rid of after all, but that he'd all of a sudden be there again, and burrowing into him, and hanging on inside like a bat under ivy, while he'd whisper into his soul blasphemies not fit to be mentioned. He'd not lose his senses – what he'd got of 'em – in these states; but he'd sit down staring, with a face on him as if he'd swallowed a live eel. Sometimes I could have burst with laughter at the sight. And then, once upon a time, Mr Deering, he took me all in a moment into his confidence, as I may say. And it was like a deathbed confession, for that night the police came and finished him.

'I had been standing by, watching him at work, when he broke off for a drink of water. The common tap was in a little yard at the back of the premises, and as he went out to it I fancied he beckoned me to follow him. Anyhow, I did, and faced him there under the starlight. I'm only speaking of three nights ago, so you may believe the whole thing sticks pretty vividly in my memory.

'He glanced up as I stood before him.

'"Why do you follow me?" he says in a low voice. "Why do you come and stand there and look at me? Are you Riddick? My God, I'll melt your head like wax if you are!" says he.

'"Why, Mr Ellis," says I, taken aback, till I jumped to the humour of the thing, "if Riddick grips you, as he has done, while I'm looking on, I can't be Riddick, can I?"

'"No, that's true," he says. "What do you want with me, then?" And, "Oh, my God!" he says, in such a Hamlet's ghost voice as would have set you sniggering, "can you stand by and see a soul raving in the grip of damnation and not offer to help it?"

'"Mr Ellis," I answered, "does Riddick really come to you like that?"

'"He comes and clutches me," he said, "as he clutched me when he was alive. He holds me and claims me to his own wickedness, and I must listen and listen, and can't get away. I want to escape, and he clings on and whispers. And if I strike him down, and melt his bloody battered face into glass, there he is in a little while up and at my soul again, struggling with it in my throat, lest it get away from him and fly free with some last breath I put into my work."

'He looked at me in a death's-head kind of manner, and I had a business, as you may guess, Mr Deering, not to explode in his face.

'Well, after a minute he turns round, with a groan, and goes back to his work. And I followed, as you may suppose.

'Now, he was at his bottles once more, and me standing by him, when all of a sudden he put down his pipe, and his face was like soapy pumice-stone.

'"He's entered into me! He's got me again!" he whispered in a voice like choking.

'"Go on with your work, as if you didn't know," says I,

choking too, though for a different reason. "Then you'll be able to take him off his guard and blow him out into a bottle."

'I thought that was too tall, even for *his* reach. But, Mr Deering – would you believe it? – the mug actually made a run and scramble to do as I told him. Only I suppose Riddick was holding on so tight that, when he blew, the two, himself and the other, came away together. Anyhow, there's the consequences in the next room – sealed and untouched, as it was left from the corpse's mouth; for the police took him while he was near bursting himself over that, the very last bottle he was ever to mould.'

He brought himself to a stop with a feculent chuckle. Then: 'What you'll judge it to be, I can't tell,' he went on. 'It's as funny as fits, whatever it may mean. I know, for myself, I'd sooner sit and watch it – on the right side of the glass – than I would a little fish in an aquarium setting himself to catch, and lose, and catch again, and suck down by fractions a huge, wriggling worm.'

I came away from the mantelpiece. The room seemed a swimming vortex. I have a notion that I cursed Sewell for an unnameable carrion. But, if I did, my loathing and horror hit him without effect. I can only remember that we were in the museum again, that dusk had gathered there heavy and opaque; and then suddenly Sewell had lit a candle, and was holding it behind the thing on the table, while he invited me with a gesture to advance and inspect.

It was an ordinary claret bottle, but distorted at the neck. The light struck into and through it. And I looked, and saw that its milky-greenness was in never-ceasing motion.

'There they are!' whispered Sewell gluttonously. 'Look, Mr Deering, mightn't it be the worm and the fish, now . . .!'

A little palpitating, shuddering blot of terror, human and inhuman; now distended, as if gasping in a momentary respite; now crouching and hugging itself into a shapeless ball, and always steadily, untiringly followed and sprung upon by the thing that had the appearance, through the semi-opaque glass, of a shambling, fat-lidded . . .

Something gave in me, and with a sobbing snarl I caught the bottle up in my hand.

'Mr Deering!' cried Sewell, 'Mr Deering! what are you going to do?'

'Stand back!' I shrieked, 'stand back!'

He ran round at me, with a little nervous gobble of laughter.

'Don't!' he cried. 'Let's take it away and bury it.'

He caught at my arm, but I flung him aside madly, and with all my force dashed the horror to the floor.

A moment's silence succeeded the ringing crash.

'Oh,' whispered Sewell, giggling, 'listen! It's going up the stairs after the other – there's something beating on the skylight!'

I tore on to the landing. There was a sound as if some sprawling, bloated body were climbing the bare treads in a series of scrambling flops. Higher, it might have been a great moth that fluttered frenziedly against the glass.

The cord of the skylight hung down to my hand. I wrenched at it demoniacally, and the glass above swung open with a scream.

A whir, receding into the faint stinging whine of a distant organ, vibrated overhead and was gone. Something on the upper stairs – something unseen and shocking – turned, and began to descend towards me. And at that I wheeled, and rushed staggering for escape and release, leaving Sewell to finish conclusions with what remained.

THE CLOSED DOOR

The Wanderer, the water squelching in his broken boots at every step, splashed his way across the melancholy estate. A drenched moon, seeming to pitch at its moorings as the running clouds lifted it, glazed with a lamentable light the wet roofs and palings of the surrounding houses. Those, scattered loosely over a wide area of swampy ground, illustrated the latest word, in one direction, of suburban expansion. They would close up some day and become part of the city of which they were now only the advanced outposts; at present they stood in their pretentious instability for nothing better than the smart foresight of a speculative builder. So much, in the flying moonshine, was evident to the Wanderer. He marked the little barren, stony gardens, the rows of forlorn saplings, the weedy wastes – dumping-grounds for pots and broken crockery – the unmade roads scarred with their wildernesses of soggy ruts; and his soul yearned for the flare of city slums, whose squalor was still the sweltering over-ripened fruit of exotic ages. A lonely gas-lamp here and there blinked testily, like a light-ship in a waste of waters, whenever the wind smote its solitary eye; for the rest, scarce ten o'clock as it was, drab dejection seemed on all sides to have extinguished its tapers and gone drearily to bed.

The Wanderer, going forward with that stoic, hunch-shouldered aspect which is common to those long familiar with shrunk vitals and the filter of rain into coat-collars, raised his head suddenly and looked about him. A sound of universal running and dripping had succeeded on the passing of the last brief hammering storm.

'The Laurels,' he muttered: 'That was the name the old woman told me – The Laurels! Curse these bally houses! When shall I reach the one I want? Uncle Greg, like all the rest of them, will have gone to bed, if I'm not quick.'

He had not, after all, much to hope of the sinister old man; but anyhow he was Uncle Gregory's own sole sister's child, and any chance was worth risking in this deadly pass to which he had come. If he could only induce Uncle Greg to ship him off somewhere abroad – just to be rid of his intolerable importunities! Surely, for his own sake, he would not drive him to desperation. Uncle Greg was a wicked old Pharisee and humbug, but respectability was the breath of his nostrils. He lived by it and prevailed by it, witness this very estate exploited by him, and on which he himself was established, the crowning expression of its social orthodoxy. It would be ruinous business to have a profligate and pauperised nephew haunting its decent preserves. Yes, his case was strong enough to warrant a descent on Uncle Greg, much as in his heart he feared the malefic old man.

He had come to an abrupt stop in the houses; beyond seemed to stretch a moon-dappled hiatus of broken ground. But, looking intently across this, he perceived distinctly enough a solitary house, standing remote and alone on the limits of the estate. Towards that house, since he had investigated all others, it was necessary for him to make his way. He distinguished a track of some sort, and followed it.

As he approached the building, apprehension stiffened in him to fury. It was dark and lifeless like the others. Not the gleam of a light twinkled anywhere from its windows; the household, to all appearance, was a-bed.

Cursing between his teeth, he came up to the gate, and read without difficulty its inscription. The Laurels, safe enough. He had reached his goal at last, and to what end?

One moment he stood, deliberating the prospect before him; the next, in a rage of decision, he had opened the gate and walked in. A black shrubbery, of the nature to justify the name, appeared to accept him into its yawning arms. There was a gloom of trees about the house, in whose shadow the white shutters in the windows seemed to open and stare at him secretively. Not a sound proceeded from the building anywhere; yet its vulgarity, its raw newness, were enough to allay any sensation of eeriness which its silence, its ghostly isolation in the moonlight, might otherwise have conveyed.

The Wanderer, standing before the hall door, held his breath to consider. His feet had crunched on the gravel path; yet it seemed to him that to breathe were more certainly to betray himself. To betray himself to what?

Yes, to what? Why should he fear or hesitate? Desperate men need dread no ambushes. There was no lower than the bottom of things, and he lay there already, bruised and broken. To turn now were to turn for shelter to the booming wind, the rain-swept waste. There was none other possible to him, save through the door of crime. He might open that yet; Uncle Greg should decide for him. He had one nego-tiable asset – himself. There was a positive value in self-obliteration; it was worth money. The lesson could not be better conveyed than through self-assertion. He lifted his hand to the knocker.

The blow sounded startlingly through the silent house; and yet he had knocked but timidly at the outset – too timidly, it appeared. He raised his hand again; louder this time; and still no one answered.

Then anger grew in him; he refused to be ignored; if he had to wake the whole household he would stay and not desist until he was admitted. The reverberations, violently continued, gave him heart and courage, gave him confidence. Conversely with his own determination must be rising the palpitations of the silent listeners within. It was impossible that they could not hear him. He rained at last a very battery of blows upon the door. Still there followed no response. Then, in a sort of derisive perversity, he took to delivering second taps with the knocker, regular, monotonous, up to fifty or so. That must goad the most resolute inmate to rebellion.

Suddenly, quite suddenly, he paused.

'If you knock too long at a closed door, the devil may open to you.'

Where had he heard that – read that? Superstitious drivel, of course; and yet, the spectral night, the lonely house, and this silence! Pooh! It was Uncle Greg he demanded and was resolute to arouse. Uncle Greg was devil enough for anyone. Let *him* appear, to vindicate the proverb if he liked; he asked nothing better.

He had raised his hand once more, when he fancied he heard the faintest echo of a response within the house. It might have been a faint call or a footstep. 'Ah!' he breathed to himself, 'the old devil at last!'

The sound increased – came on. Unquestionably it was the stealthy tread of a footstep in the hall. A tiny ray of light shot through the keyhole. The Wanderer clutched the rags upon his chest and stood rigid. In the very act of steadying himself, he saw that the hall door was open and Uncle Greg standing motionless on the threshold.

The same heavy, sly figure as of old, beaming hairless self-complacency in its every slab feature. He wore a shawl dressing-gown of a flamboyant pattern, his stumpy feet were encased in gorgeous carpet slippers; in one hand he held a lighted candle, in the other a revolver. He betrayed no astonishment, but only a sort of furtive glee.

'Charlie!' he said, in his whispering chuckle: 'poor Charlie, is it, that has been knocking fit to wake the dead.'

'I was desperate to get in – to make you hear,' muttered the Wanderer. 'Look at my state, Uncle Greg.'

'And you made me hear,' said the old builder. 'What a determined fellow, to be sure. There was nothing for it at last but to get up and come. I have brought my pistol with me, you see.'

'Not to use it on me, I hope, Uncle Greg?' said the Wanderer, with a ghastly jocularity.

'No,' said Uncle Gregory; 'no. It's not the kind of weapon for your sort. I've a better way of retaliating on you.'

The visitor, in this visible presence, was stung to wordy violence on the instant.

'O! a better way, have you?' he said sneeringly. 'We'll see about that. I know where I'm not wanted, and the value to be put on my undesirability. If you wish to hoof me out of this precious dove-cot of yours, you'll have to pay for the privilege, you know, Uncle Greg.'

'Shall I?' said the old man. 'Why, how you go on, Charlie. There are Christian ways of retaliating, ain't there? Suppose in my old age, I have come to that.'

'Come to that!' The Wanderer drew in his breath as if to a sudden pang. Was it conceivable that out of such ineffable slyness and hypocrisy as he remembered of old had blossomed this aftermath of Christian charity and forgiveness? He tried to read the change in the familiar face, but the swaying candlelight distorted it absurdly.

'I can't make out if you're getting at me or not,' he said. 'Anyhow my misery is plain enough. May I come in, Uncle Greg?'

'Why not?' said the old man. 'It's the very thing I want.'

He turned and went silently along the hall. The Wanderer, following half dazed, observed stupidly how the candle-light seemed to have awakened a very phantasmagoria of shadows on the walls and ceiling. They jerked and frolic'd above and around; they tumbled over the stair-rails as if in some fantastic scramble for place and precedence. The effect was so bewildering, that it came as a quick shock to him to notice suddenly, through the thick of their gambolling, the echoing emptiness of the passage he trod. It was without carpet or furniture – bare to its limits.

And so it was with the room into which Uncle Gregory preceded him. From door to shuttered window it was void as death; only a faint, sickly odour pervaded it; only a very little litter of damp straw was scattered about its boards. The Wanderer stopped, petrified, staring before him – staring hither and thither, and then at Uncle Gregory. The old man stood, swaying the candle high, swaying it to and fro so that his own shadow, obeying its motions, danced and leapt and dilated on the walls and floor.

'Damn it!' cried the Wanderer, finding his breath in a gasp; 'stop that – stop it, will you! What is the meaning of this? What trick are you playing on me?'

'Trick, Charlie!' The old builder bent in a soundless chuckle. 'It's all right; it's all right, you know. If I'd known you were coming, I'd have delayed the bankruptcy proceedings.'

'What! Sold up?'

'That's the word, Charlie. Nothing left – only this.'

He held out the revolver, balancing it in his hand.

'A heavy bullet,' he said – 'fit to splash a man's brains all over the shop. What a curse you intended to make of my life, didn't you? A mean, squalid ruffian – you were always that, you know. I hated you, Charlie, my dear; I always hated you, you poisonous prodigal. Now I'm going to have my turn with you at last. You'd come here, would you, to bleed the old man? You shall bleed for him, hang for him, you hound! They'll think you did it, and you shall answer with the red witness on your hands.'

The Wanderer's face was white as drained veal; he had thought for an instant that the other meant to murder him; and then he saw in a flash his more terrific purpose. He gave a scream like a run-over woman, and leapt forward – but it was too late. The pistol crashed, and Uncle Gregory's brains flew all about the room.

Or so they appeared to as, on the moment, darkness rang down. He staggered back, with a sob that was wrenched from him like a hook from a fish's throat. He put his hand to his forehead, and it seemed to adhere there with a little treacly suggestion, and a more overpowering sense of that odour which had already nauseated him. And then he turned and fled. The hall door was still open, revealing a livid oblong of watery moonshine. Into that he fell, rather than plunged, as a man leaps from the side of a burning ship. He had no thought or care for his direction, so long as it bore him from that horror. Once, as he tore along, he stumbled and fell, his hands in a pool of water. That suggesting something to him, frantically, hurriedly, he rinsed his palms and bathed his forehead before he rose again and sped on. He had only one purpose in his mind – to reach the city lights and find shelter from himself in their glare.

Little by little he had come to recognise that the doom imposed upon him was unavoidable and irrevocable. What insidious pressure, intimate and satanic, had persuaded him to that necessity, gradually enveloping his mind until escape from its torture seemed possible in only one direction, he knew well enough, while he was helpless to resist it. There was a limit to the endurance of reason; better the condemned cell and the rope and the pinioned arms than this long drawn-out agony of apprehension. After all, if he were to die, a self-accused though innocent man, perhaps the sacrifice might be accepted by the Unknown in some sort as an atonement, and he might be spared in the hereafter that company which alone he unspeakably dreaded. But a man could not continue for ever with that shadow at his shoulder, which no word of his – he believed it truly – could conceivably dissipate. He might have washed his flesh and his clothes: the stains of blood were indelible. So surely as he confessed his visit to the house on that night of terror, so surely, viewing his antecedents and the purpose for which he had come, would he place the noose about his own neck. He could not resist his impulse the less for that; the diabolical thing which inspired it was more powerful than himself. He was so weary, so nerve-worn in the end, that even the thought of temporising with the truth seemed an intolerable ordeal. Better to confess at once that he was guilty of murder, and get it over. Only that way lay peace from it all.

During all these three days, so haunted, so marked as he was, his immunity from arrest had not ceased to astonish him. It was inconceivable that he had not been observed on his way either to or from the fatal house; it was incredible that that persistent knocking of his had failed to find its echo in some panic heart. He had dared no attempt to leave the place; he had possessed no means to lie hidden in it. On the contrary, some little dawn of luck, which had found him out since that night, had brought him more prominently than usual into the open. Was not that the common irony of Fortune – to bestow her grudging favours at the moment when for all moral purposes they had become valueless? So now, though she was represented by no more than a job to distribute circulars, that respite from starvation was gained at the expense of bitter bread to eat.

On each of the three days he had bought and feverishly perused a halfpenny paper; but never one had contained any mention of the tragedy. No shouting headlines rushed into his ken; no report of discovery or inquest appeared to confirm him in his sickest apprehensions. Was it possible that the police, for their own purposes, were lying low? That were an unusual course, at least in these days of sensational publicity. And then there flashed into his mind another explanation of this silence, and the most hideously plausible of them all. The bankruptcy; the emptied house; its unsuspected inmate. Of course the body was lying there yet, undiscovered; and the crisis, in the prolonged expectation of which he had been lingering out the exquisite torment of these days, were merely postponed.

To the madness of that thought his reason succumbed, and finally. He could endure no more. One morning he walked into the local police station and addressed the inspector on duty.

'I have come to give myself up for the murder at The Laurels.'

The inspector, immovable, grizzle-bearded, with over-hanging eyebrows, betrayed no least hint of emotion; but he just signed to a subordinate to keep the door.

'Yes,' he said evenly. 'What is your name?'

The Wanderer confessed it; as also his relationship to the dead man, the purpose for which he had called upon him and, more excitedly, the measure of his own worthlessness and iniquity.

The inspector stopped him, with official aplomb, in mid-career.

'This occurred three nights ago, you say? I want you to give an account of your movements up to that time.'

'That is easily done,' said the Wanderer, with a little panting laugh, now that the horror was off his mind. 'I had been discharged only a week before from B— Hospital, where I had been an in-patient for two months and more. You won't expect me to tell you for what.'

'No,' said the Inspector; and 'Exactly,' he said. 'Well, I shall have to detain you for inquiries.'

The magistrate, a precise, benevolent man, with a certain soldierly compactness about his attire, ended some remarks he had been making on the advisability of contriving some punishment for those who increasingly took up the time of the Court with unfounded self-accusations, the result commonly of drink.

'Your statement about the hospital,' he said, addressing the prisoner, 'has been confirmed. It is possible that some mental distemper, induced by your recent condition, was responsible for this wild appropriation of a crime which, amounting as it did to an unquestionable case of self-destruction, occurred quite a month ago, when you were lying ill. Not less could excuse you for this wanton imperilling of your own life. What is that you say?'

His words had to be interpreted to the magistrate, so thickly inarticulate they came from his lips.

'I knocked, and knocked, and he opened to me at last. He had a pistol in his hand, and I saw him do it.'

'Come,' said the magistrate kindly; 'you must forget all that. Leave closed doors alone for the future, is my advice. Remember what is said – that the devil lays snares for the importunate; only not being omniscient, he sometimes over-reaches himself on the question of an alibi. Nevertheless, it is not safe to count upon his anachronisms. He has succeeded once or twice, I am afraid, in getting innocent men hanged. The best thing for all of us is to avoid knocking him up when we find him asleep.

'I think, for your own sake, I shall remand you for a week into the hands of the prison doctor.'

THE DARK COMPARTMENT

I remember once, when hunting for a seat in a crowded train, finding unexpectedly an empty compartment, the door of which, when I came to try it, was locked. Holding on to the handle, I looked about for the guard. At that moment another hurrying passenger halted beside me, peered over my shoulder into the carriage, and went quickly away. Something in the man's manner striking me, I also investigated, and saw that the floor of the compartment was sprinkled thick with sawdust. Incontinently I let go the handle, and hastened to find a seat elsewhere.

There cannot be many engines, after all, which do not trail the ghosts of past tragedies in their wake. That was an experience unforeseen enough to give one a sharp little qualm; but I would not willingly exchange it for Manby's. In his case – but let him tell his own story:

'I had been visiting the old Hampshire Abbey town, and a run thence of thirty minutes by rail would take me to the next stopping-place on my itinerary, where there were barracks, and a cathedral, and a public school, and a gaol – not to speak of cosy hotels. It was a dark November evening, and soppingly wet, so that, dawdling over my tea-board comforts at the inn, I came near in the end to missing my train altogether. It was actually starting when I gained the platform, and I had to make a dash for it, and scramble into the first compartment that offered.

'The light in the roof burned so dim that, what with that and the momentary flurry of my entrance, I did not recognise at once whether I were alone or had broken into company. As my eyes, however, accustomed themselves to the obscurity, I saw that there were two men sitting together opposite me at the further end of the compartment.

'The lamp, I say, was so down – a mere night-light in suggestion – that it was difficult to distinguish the character of my travelling companions. Moreover, as one of them seemed thickly bearded, and the other wore a dark felt hat slouched over his eyes, their faces, or the section of each of them visible to me, appeared nothing but featureless white maps, hung up, as it were, in the gloom. The two sat very quiet, close together, but without exchanging the least communication that I could see; and presently, from under cover of my own hat-brim, I took to scrutinising the silent shapes. I was the more emboldened to that inquisition by the utter indifference with which they had accepted my abrupt invasion. They seemed now, even, to be wholly unconscious of my presence.

'The deathliness of that disregard, rigid and motionless; the huddled cohesion of the twin shadows, with those blots of white representing their faces, affected me strangely and uneasily after a while. I wanted one or the other of them to stir, to resolve himself into a detached human entity – and quite suddenly I had my wish. How it happened I don't know; but there came a sort of local shifting of the gloom, a sense of a quick gleam in its midst, and in that moment I understood. The man with the slouched hat had handcuffs on his wrists, and he was travelling in charge of a prison warder.

'And almost as I realised the truth the prisoner began to speak:

'"I'm sick; I want air."

'I say he spoke, and I might say the other answered. A sense of those words, anyhow, throbbed in my brain, and they had their instant corollary in his rising and standing at the window unopposed. I felt the rush of wet air, and saw the wing-like filling of the dark Inverness cape he wore. And then suddenly there was a tiny snap, and he went out of the window like a flying crow. I saw the warder snatch at him, and follow the way he had gone, pulled off his feet by the wrench and jerk. And there was I alone in the dark compartment, with only the window guard, broken and bent askew, to witness to the stunning tragedy which had passed in a moment before my eyes.

'Even as I leapt to my feet I grasped what had happened. Under cover of his cloak, and the roar of wheels and rain, the prisoner, though manacled, had managed rapidly to file through the bar to breaking point.

'I tore at the alarm communication cord, and stood gasping and shaken. Almost against my expectation, the train slowed down within a few seconds and came to a stop. I put my head out of the window on my side, and beckoned frantically to the shape I saw beating towards me along the blown track-side. The guard came below, looking up with the staring, rather combative, expression of the official summoned against his own better faith.

'"What is it?"

'"For God's sake, come here! Two men have just gone out of the window."

'He climbed grudgingly to the footboard, and so into the carriage. "Yes, sir," he said. "Where were they sitting?"

'His cool, incredulous tone maddened me.

'"There, by that open window," I said. "Isn't it plain enough?"

'He crossed the carriage, pressed his hand on the seat, turned to me again. "That won't do. No one's been sitting here. The cushion's cold. Feel for yourself."

'"God in heaven, man!" I cried. "Do you take me to be mad or drunk? They sat there, I tell you – a warder and his charge; and the prisoner stood up on some pretext and went clean out, dragging the other after him. There's the broken window rail to witness."

'"Is there?" He had had his back to it; but moved now, just glancing over his shoulder, so that I might see. And there was the window-rail whole and sound, and the window itself closed.

'Presently, after I don't know what brief interval, I found myself giggling hysterically.

'"Look here," I said, "I think I'll change my carriage."

'"I would," said the guard, "if I were you." Both his tone and his look were odd; but he formally took my name and address, with an intimation that the minimum penalty was five pounds. It was, on the face of it, a serious offence, you will agree. Yet, curiously, I received no summons from the company, or ever heard another word on the matter.'

THE MARBLE HANDS

We left our bicycles by the little lych-gate and entered the old churchyard. Heriot had told me frankly that he did not want to come; but at the last moment, sentiment or curiosity prevailing with him, he had changed his mind. I knew indefinitely that there was something disagreeable to him in the place's associations, though he had always referred with affection to the relative with whom he had stayed here as a boy. Perhaps she lay under one of these greening stones.

We walked round the church, with its squat, shingled spire. It was utterly peaceful, here on the brow of the little town where the flowering fields began. The bones of the hill were the bones of the dead, and its flesh was grass. Suddenly Heriot stopped me. We were standing then to the northwest of the chancel, and a gloom of motionless trees overshadowed us.

'I wish you'd just look in there a moment,' he said, 'and come back and tell me what you see.'

He was pointing towards a little bay made by the low boundary wall, the green floor of which was hidden from our view by the thick branches and a couple of interposing tombs, huge, coffer-shaped, and shut within rails. His voice sounded odd; there was a 'plunging' look in his eyes, to use a gambler's phrase. I stared at him a moment, followed the direction of his hand; then, without a word, stooped under the heavy, brushing boughs, passed round the great tombs, and came upon a solitary grave.

It lay there quite alone in the hidden bay – a strange thing, fantastic and gruesome. There was no headstone, but a bevelled marble curb, without name or epitaph, enclosed a gravelled space from which projected two hands. They were of white marble, very faintly touched with green, and conveyed in that still, lonely spot a most curious sense of reality, as if actually thrust up, deathly and alluring, from the grave beneath. The impression grew upon me as I looked, until I could have thought they moved stealthily, consciously, turning in the soil as if to greet me. It was absurd, but – I turned and went rather hastily back to Heriot.

'All right. I see they are there still,' he said; and that was all. Without another word we left the place and, remounting, continued our way.

Miles from the spot, lying on a sunny downside, with the sheep about us in hundreds cropping the hot grass, he told me the story:

'She and her husband were living in the town at the time of my first visit there, when I was a child of seven. They were known to Aunt Caddie, who disliked the woman. I did not dislike her at all, because, when we met, she made a favourite of me. She was a little pretty thing, frivolous and shallow; but truly, I know now, with an abominable side to her. She was inordinately vain of her hands; and indeed they were the loveliest things, softer and shapelier than a child's. She used to have them photographed, in fifty different positions; and once they were exquisitely done in marble by a sculptor, a friend of hers. Yes, those were the ones you saw. But they were cruel little hands, for all their beauty. There was something wicked and unclean about the way in which she regarded them.

'She died while I was there, and she was commemorated by her own explicit desire after the fashion you saw. The marble hands were to be her sole epitaph, more eloquent than letters. They should preserve her name and the tradition of her most exquisite feature to remoter ages than any crumbling inscription could reach. And so it was done.

'That fancy was not popular with the parishioners, but it gave me no childish qualms. The hands were really beautifully modelled on the originals, and the originals had often caressed me. I was never afraid to go and look at them, sprouting like white celery from the ground.

'I left, and two years later was visiting Aunt Caddie a second time. In the course of conversation I learned that the husband of the woman had married again – a lady belonging to the place – and that the hands, only quite recently, had been removed. The new wife had objected to them – for some reason perhaps not difficult to understand – and they had been uprooted by the husband's order.

'I think I was a little sorry – the hands had always seemed somehow personal to me – and, on the first occasion that offered, I slipped away by myself to see how the grave looked without them. It was a close, lowering day, I remember, and the churchyard was very still. Directly, stooping under the branches, I saw the spot, I understood that Aunt Caddie had spoken prematurely. The hands had not been removed so far, but were extended in their old place and attitude, looking as if held out to welcome me. I was glad; and I ran and knelt, and put my own hands down to touch them. They were soft and cold like dead meat, and they closed caressingly about mine, as if inviting me to pull – to pull.

'I don't know what happened afterwards. Perhaps I had been sickening all the time for the fever which overtook me. There was a period of horror, and blankness – of crawling, worm-threaded immurements and heaving bones – and then at last the blessed daylight.'

Heriot stopped, and sat plucking at the crisp pasture.

'I never learned,' he said suddenly, 'what other experiences synchronised with mine. But the place somehow got an uncanny reputation, and the marble hands were put back. Imagination, to be sure, can play strange tricks with one.'

THE MOON STRICKEN

It so fell that one dark evening in the month of June I was belated in the Bernese Oberland. Dusk overtook me toiling along the great Chamounix Road, and in the heart of a most desolate gorge, whose towering snow-flung walls seemed – as the day sucked inwards to a point secret as a leech's mouth – to close about me like a monstrous amphitheatre of ghosts. The rutted road, dipping and climbing toilfully against the shouldering of great tumbled boulders, or winning for itself but narrow foothold over slippery ridges, was thawed clear of snow; but the cold soft peril yet lay upon its flanks thick enough for a wintry plunge of ten feet, or maybe fifty where the edge of the causeway fell over to the lower furrows of the ravine. It was a matter of policy to go with caution, and a thing of some moment to hear the thud and splintering of little distant icefalls about one in the darkness. Now and again a cold arrow of wind would sing down from the frosty peaks above or jerk with a squiggle of laughter among the fallen slabs in the valley. And these were the only voices to prick me on through a dreariness lonely as death.

I knew the road, but not its night terrors. Passing along it some days before in the glory of sunshine, broad paddocks and islands of green had comforted the shattered white ruin of the place, and I had traversed it merely as a magnificent episode in the indifferent history of my life. Now, as it seemed,

I became one with it – an awful waif of solemnity, a thing apart from mankind and its warm intercourse and ruddy inn doors, a spectral anomaly, whose austere epitaph was once writ upon the snow coating some fallen slab of those glimmering about me. I thought the whole gorge smelt of tombs, like the vault of a cathedral. I thought, in the incomprehensible low moaning sound that ever and again seemed to eddy about me when the wind had swooped and passed, that I recognised the forlorn voices of brother spirits long since dead and forgotten of the world.

Suddenly I felt the sweat cold under the knapsack that swung upon my back; stopped, faced about and became human again. Ridge over ridge to my right the mountain summits fell away against a fathomless sky; and topping the furthermost was a little paring of silver light, the coronet of the rising moon. But the glory of the full orb was in the retrospect; for, closing the savage vista of the ravine, stood up far away a cluster of jagged pinnacles – opal, translucent, lustrous as the peaks of icebergs that are frozen music of the sea.

It was the toothed summit of the Aiguille Verte, now prosaically bathed in the light of the full moon; but to me, looking from that grim and passionless hollow, it stood for the white hand of God lifted in menace to the evil spirits of the glen.

I drank my fill of the good sight, and then turned me to my tramp again with a freshness in my throat as though it had gulped a glass of champagne. Presently I knew myself descending, leaving, as I felt rather than saw, the stark horror of the gorge and its glimmering snow patches above me. Puffs of a warmer air purred past my face with little friendly sighs of welcome, and the hum of a far-off torrent struck like a wedge into the indurated fibre of the night. As I dropped, however, the mountain heads grew up against the moon, and withheld the comfort of her radiance; and it was not until the whimper of the torrent had quickened about me to a plunging roar, and my foot was on the striding bridge that took its waters at a step, that her light broke through a topmost cleft in the hills, and made glory of the leaping thunder that crashed beneath my feet.

Thereafter all was peace. The road led downwards into a broadening valley, where the smell of flowers came about me, and the mountain walls withdrew and were no longer overwhelming. The slope eased off, dipping and rising no more than a ground swell; and by and by I was on a level track that ran straight as a stretched ribbon and was reasonable to my tired feet.

Now the first dusky chalets of the hamlet of Bel-Oiseau straggled towards me, and it was music in my ears to hear the cattle blow and rattle in their stalls under the sleeping lofts as I passed outside in the moonlight. Five minutes more, and the great zinc onion on the spire of the church glistened towards me, and I was in the heart of the silent village.

From the deep green shadow cast by the graveyard wall, heavily buttressed against avalanches, a form wriggled out into the moonlight and fell with a dusty thud at my feet, mowing and chopping at the air with its aimless claws. I started back with a sudden jerk of my pulses. The thing was horrible by reason of its inarticulate voice, which issued from the shapeless folds of its writhings like the wet gutturising of a backbroken horse. Instinct with repulsion, I stood a moment dismayed, when light flashed from an open doorway a dozen yards further down the street, and a woman ran across to the prostrate form.

'Up, graceless one!' she cried; 'and carry thy seven devils within doors!'

The figure gathered itself together at her voice, and stood in an angle of the buttress quaking and shielding its eyes with two gaunt arms.

'Can I not exchange a word with Mère Pettit,' scolded the woman, 'but thou must sneak from behind my back on thy crazed moon-hunting?'

'Pity, pity,' moaned the figure; and then the woman noticed me, and dropped a curtsy.

'Pardon,' she said, 'but he has been affronting Monsieur with his antics?'

'He is stricken, Madame?'

'Ah, yes, Monsieur. Holy Mother, but how stricken!'

'It is sad.'

'Monsieur knows not how sad. It is so always, but most a great deal when the moon is full. He was a good lad once.'

Monsieur puts his hand in his pocket. Madame hears the clink of coin and touches the enclosed fingers with her own delicately. Monsieur withdraws his hand empty.

'Pardon, Madame.'

'Monsieur has the courage of a gentleman. Come, Camille, little fool! a sweet goodnight to Monsieur.'

'Stay, Madame. I have walked far and am weary. Is there an hotel in Bel-Oiseau?'

'Monsieur is jesting. We are but a hundred of poor chalets.'

'An *auberge*, then – a *cabaret* – anything?'

'Les Trois Chèvres. It is not for such as you.'

'Is it, then, that I must toil onwards to Châtelard?'

'Monsieur does not know? The Hôtel Royal was burned to the walls six months since.'

'It follows that I must lie in the fields.'

Madame hesitates, ponders, and makes up her mind.

'I keep Monsieur talking, and the night wind is sharp from the snow. It is ill for a heated skin, and one should be indoors. I have a bedroom that is at Monsieur's disposition, if Monsieur will condescend?'

Monsieur will condescend. Monsieur would condescend to a loft and a truss of straw, in default of the neat little chilly chamber that is allotted him, so sick are his very limbs with long tramping, and so uninviting figures the further stretch in the moonlight to Châtelard, with its burnt-out carcase of an hotel.

This is how I came to quarter myself on Madame Barbière

and her idiot son, and how I ultimately learned from the lips of the latter the strange story of his own immediate fall from reason and the dear light of intellect.

By day Camille Barbière proved to be a young man, some five and twenty years of age, of a handsome and impressive exterior. His dark hair lay close about his well-shaped head; his features were regular and cut bold as an Etruscan cameo; his limbs were elastic and moulded into the supple finish of one whose life has not been set upon level roads. At a speculative distance he appeared a straight specimen of a Burgundian youth – sinewy, clean-formed, and graceful, though slender to gauntness; and it was only on nearer contact that one marvelled to see the soul die out of him, as a face set in the shadow of leafage resolves itself into some accident of twisted branches as one approaches the billowing tree that presented it.

The soul of Camille, the idiot, had warped long after its earthly tabernacle had grown firm and fair to look upon. Cause and effect were not one from birth in him; and the result was a most wistful expression, as though the lost intellect were for ever struggling and failing to recall its ancient mastery. Mostly he was a gentle young man, note-worthy for nothing but the uncomplaining patience with which he daily observed the monotonous routine of simple duties that were now all-sufficient for the poor life that had 'crept so long on a broken wing'. He milked the big, red, barrel-bodied cow, and churned industriously for butter; he kept the little vegetable garden in order and nursed the Savoys into fatness like plumping babies; he drove the goats to pasture on the mountain slopes, and all day sat among the rhodo-dendrons, the forgotten soul behind his eyes conning the dead language of fate, as a foreigner vainly interrogates the abstruse complexity of an idiom.

By-and-by I made it an irregular habit to accompany him on these shepherdings; to join him in his simple midday meal

of sour brown bread and goat-milk cheese; to talk with him
desultorily, and study him the while, inasmuch as he wakened
an interest in me that was full of speculation. For this was
not an imbecility either hereditary or constitutional. From
the first there had appeared to me something abnormal in it
– a suspension of intelligence only, a frost-bite in the brain
that presently some April breath of memory might thaw out.
This was not merely conjectural, of course. I had the story
of his mental collapse from his mother in the early days of
my sojourn in Bel-Oiseau; for it came to pass that a fitful
caprice induced me to prolong my stay in the swart little
village far into the gracious Swiss summer.

The 'story' I have called it; but it was none. He was out
on the hills one moonlit night, and came home in the early
morning mad. That was all.

This had happened some eight years before, when he was
a lad of seventeen – a strong, beautiful lad, his mother told
me; and with a dreamy 'poet's corner' in his brain, she added,
but in her own better way of putting it. She had no shame
that her shepherd should be an Endymion. In Switzerland
they still look upon Nature as a respectable pursuit for a
young man.

Well, they had thought him possessed of a devil; and his
father had at first sought to exorcise it with a chamois-hide
thong, as Munchausen flogged the black fox out of his skin.
But the counter-irritant failed of its purpose. The devil clung
deep, and rent poor Camille with periodic convulsions of
insanity.

It was noted that his derangement waxed and waned with
the monthly moon; that it assumed a virulent character with
the passing of the second quarter, and culminated, as the orb
reached its fulness, in a species of delirium, during which it
was necessary to watch him carefully; that it diminished with
the lessening crescent until it fell away into a quiet abeyance
of faculties that was but a step apart from the normal intelligence of his kind. At his worst he was a stricken madman

acutely sensitive to impressions; at his best an inoffensive peasant who said nothing foolish and nothing wise.

When he was twenty, his father died, and Camille and his mother had to make out existence in company.

Now, the veil, in my knowledge of him, was never rent; yet occasionally it seemed to me to gape in a manner that let a little momentary finger of light through, in the flashing of which a soul kindled and shut in his eyes, like a hard-dying spark in ashes. I wished to know what gave life to the spark, and I set to pondering the problem.

'He was not always thus?' I would say to Madame Barbière.

'But no, Monsieur, truly. This place – bah! we are here imbeciles all to the great world, without doubt; but Camille – *he* was by nature of those who make the history of cities – a rose in the wilderness. Monsieur smiles?'

'By no means. A scholar, Madame?'

'A scholar of nature, Monsieur; a dreamer of dreams such as they become who walk much with the spirits on the lonely mountains.'

'Torrents, and avalanches, and the good material forces of nature, Madame means.'

'Ah! Monsieur may talk, but he knows. He has heard the *föhn* sweep down from the hills and spin the great stones off the house-roofs. And one may look and see nothing, yet the stones go. It is the wind that runs before the avalanche that snaps the pine trees; and the wind is the spirit that calls down the great snow-slips.'

'But how may Madame who sees nothing, know then a spirit to be abroad?'

'My faith; one may know one's foot is on the wild mint without shifting one's sole to look.'

'Madame will pardon me. No doubt also one may know a spirit by the smell of sulphur?'

'Monsieur is a sceptic. It comes with the knowledge of cities. There are even such in little Bel-Oiseau, since the evil time, when they took to engrossing the contracts of good citizens on the skins of the poor jew-beards that give us flesh and milk. It is horrible as the Tannery of Meudon. In my young days, Monsieur, such agreements were inscribed upon wood.'

'Quite so, Madame, and entirely to the point. Also one may see from whom Camille inherited his wandering propensities. But for his fall – it was always unaccountable?'

'Monsieur, as one trips on the edge of a crevasse and disappears. His soul dropped into the frozen cleft that one cannot fathom.'

'Madame will forgive my curiosity.'

'But surely. There was no dark secret in my Camille's life. If the little head held pictures beyond the ken of us simple women, the angels painted them of a certainty. Moreover, it is that I willingly recount this grief to the wise friend that may know a solution.'

'At least the little-wise can seek for one.'

'Ah, if Monsieur would only find the remedy!'

'It is in the hands of fate.'

Madame crossed herself.

'Of the *Bon Dieu*, Monsieur.'

At another time Madame Barbière said:

'It was in such a parched summer as this threatens to be that my Camille came home in the mists of the morning possessed. He was often out on the sweet hills all night – that was nothing. It had been a full moon, and the whiteness of it was on his face like leprosy, but his hands were hot with fever. Ah, the dreadful summer! The milk turned sour in the cows udders and the tufts of the stone pines on the mountains fell into ashes like Dead Sea fruit. The springs were dried, and the great cascade of Buet fell to half its volume.'

'This cascade; I have never seen it. It is in the neighbourhood?'

'Of a surety. Monsieur must have passed the rocky ravine that vomits the torrent, on his way hither.'

'I remember. I will explore it. Camille shall be my guide.'

'Never.'

'And why?'

Madame shrugged her plump shoulders.

'Who may say? The ways of the afflicted are not our ways. Only I know that Camille will never drive his flock to pasture near the lip of that dark valley.'

'That is strange. Can the place have associations for him connected with his malady?'

'It is possible. Only the good God knows.'

But *I* was to know later on, with a little reeling of the reason also.

'Camille, I want to see the Cascade de Buet.'

The hunted eyes of the stricken looked into mine with a piercing glance of fear.

'Monsieur must not,' he said, in a low voice.

'And why not?'

'The waters are bad – bad – haunted!'

'I fear no ghosts. Wilt thou show me the way, Camille?'

'I!' The idiot fell upon the grass with a sort of gobbling cry. I thought it the prelude to a fit of some sort, and was stepping towards him, when he rose to his feet, waved me off and hurried away down the slope homewards.

Here was food for reflection, which I mumbled in secret.

A day or two afterwards I joined Camille at midday on the heights where he was pasturing his flocks. He had shifted his ground a little distance westwards, and I could not find him at once. At last I spied him, his back to a rock, his hand dabbled for coolness in a little runnel that trickled at his side. He looked up and greeted me with a smile. He had conceived an affection for me, this poor lost soul.

'It will go soon,' he said, referring to the miniature streamlet. 'It is safe in the woods; but tomorrow or next day the sun will lap it up ere it can reach the skirt of the shadow above there. A farewell kiss to you, little stream!'

He bent and sipped a mouthful of the clear water. He was

in a more reasonable state than he had shown for long, though it was now close on the moon's final quarter, a period that should have marked a more general tenor of placidity in him. The summer solstice, was, however, at hand, and the weather sultry to a degree – as it had been, I did not fail to remember, the year of his seizure.

'Camille,' I said, 'why today hast thou shifted thy ground a little in the direction of the Buet ravine?'

He sat up at once, with a curious, eager look in his face.

'Monsieur has asked it,' he said. 'It was to impel Monsieur to ask it that I moved. Does Monsieur seek a guide?'

'Wilt thou lead me, Camille?'

'Monsieur, last night I dreamed and one came to me. Was it my father? I know not, I know not. But he put my forehead to his breast, and the evil left it, and I remembered without terror. "Reveal the secret to the stranger," he said; "that he may share thy burden and comfort thee; for he is strong where thou art weak, and the vision shall not scare him." Monsieur, wilt thou come?'

He leapt to his feet, and I to mine.

'Lead on, Camille. I follow.'

He called to the leader of his flock: 'Petitjean! stray not, my little one. I shall be back sooner than the daisies close.' Then he turned to me again. I noticed a pallid, desperate look in his face, as though he were strung to great effort; but it was the face of a mindless one still.

'Do you not fear?' he said, in a whisper; and the apple in his throat seemed all choking core.

'I fear nothing,' I answered with a smile; yet the still sombreness of the woods found a little tremor in my breast.

'It is good,' he answered, regarding me. 'The angel spoke truth. Follow, Monsieur.'

He went off through the trees of a sudden, and I had much ado to keep pace with him. He ran as one urged on by a sure sense of doom, looking neither to right nor left. His mountain instincts had remained with him when memory itself had closed around like a fog, leaving him face to face and isolated with his one unconfessed point of terror. Swiftly we made our way, ever slightly climbing, along the rugged hillside, and soon broke into country very wild and dismal. The pastoral character of the scene lessened and altogether disappeared. The trees grew matted and grotesquely gnarled, huddling together in menacing battalions – save where some plunging rock had burst like a shell, forcing a clearing and strewing the black moss with a jagged wreck of splinters. Here no flowers crept for warmth, no sentinel marmot turned his little scut with a whistle of alarm to vanish like a red shadow. All was melancholy and silence and the massed defiance of ever-impending ruin. Storm, and avalanche, and the bitter snap of frost had wrought their havoc year by year, till an uncrippled branch was a rare distinction. The very saplings, of stunted growth, bore the air of thieves reared in a rookery of crime.

We strode with difficulty in an inhuman twilight through this great dark quickset of Nature, and had paused a moment where the thronging trunks thinned somewhat, when a little mouthing moan came towards us on the crest of a ripple of wind. My companion stopped on the instant, and clutched my arm, his face twisting with panic.

'The Cascade, Monsieur!' he shook out in a terrified whisper.

'Courage, my friend! It is that we come to seek.'

'Ah! My God, yes – it is that! I dare not – I dare not!'

He drew back livid with fear, but I urged him on.

'Remember the dream, Camille!' I cried.

'Yes, yes – it was good. Help me, Monsieur, and I will try – yes, I will try!'

I drew his arm within mine, and together we stumbled on. The undergrowth grew denser and more fantastic; the murmur filled out, increased and resolved itself into a sound of falling water that ever took shape, and volume, and depth, till its crash shook the ground at our feet. Then in a moment a white blaze of sky came at us through the trunks, and we burst through the fringe of the wood to find ourselves facing the opposite side of a long cleft in the mountain and the blade's edge of a roaring cataract.

It shot out over the lip of the fall, twenty feet above us, in a curve like a scimitar, passed in one sheet the spot where we stood, and dived into a sunless pool thirty feet below with a thunderous boom. What it may have been in full phases of the stream, I know not; yet even now it was sufficiently magnificent to give pause to a dying soul eager to shake off the restless horror of the world. The flat of its broad blade divided the lofty black walls of a deep and savage ravine, on whose jagged shelves some starved clumps of rhododendron shook in the wind of the torrent. Far down the narrow gully we could see the passion of water tossing, champed white with the ravening of its jaws, until it took a bend of the cliffs at a leap and rushed from sight.

We stood upon a little platform of coarse grass and bramble, whose fringe dipped and nodded fitfully as the sprinkle caught it. Beyond, the sliding sheet of water looked like a great strap of steel, reeled ceaselessly off a whirling drum pivoted between the hills. The midday sun shot like a piston down the shaft of the valley, painting purple spears and angles behind its abutting rocks, and hitting full upon the upper curve of the fall; but halfway down the cataract slipped into shadow.

My brain sickened with the endless gliding and turmoil of descent, and I turned aside to speak to my companion. He was kneeling upon the grass, his eyes fixed and staring, his white lips mumbling some crippled memory of a prayer. He started and cowered down as I touched him on the shoulder.

'I cannot go, Monsieur; I shall die!'

'What next, Camille? I will go alone.'

'My God, Monsieur! the cave under the fall! It is there the horror is.'

He pointed to a little gap in the fringing bushes with

shaking finger. I stole gingerly in the direction he indicated. With every step I took the awful fascination of the descending water increased upon me. It seemed hideous and abnormal to stand mid-way against a perpendicularly rushing torrent. Above or below the effect would have been different; but here, to look up was to feel one's feet dragging towards the unseen – to look down and pass from vision of the lip of the fall was to become the waif of a force that was unaccountable.

I had a battle with my nerves, and triumphed. As I approached the opening in the brambles I became conscious of a certain relief. At a little distance the cataract had seemed to actually wash in its descent the edge of the platform. Now I found it to be further away than I had imagined, the ground dropping in a sharp slope to a sort of rocky buttress which lay obliquely on the slant of the ravine, and was the true margin of the torrent. Before I essayed the descent, I glanced back at my companion. He was kneeling where I had left him, his hands pressed to his face, his features hidden; but looking back once again, when I had with infinite caution accomplished the downward climb, I saw that he had crept to the edge of the slope, and was watching me with wide, terrified eyes. I waved my hand to him and turned to the wonderful vision of water that now passed almost within reach of my arm. I stood near the point where the whole glassy breadth glided at once from sunlight into shadow. It fell silently, without a break, for only its feet far below trod the thunder.

Now, as I peered about, I noticed a little cleft in the rocky margin, a minute's climb above me. I was attracted to this by an appearance of smoke or steam that incessantly emerged from it, as though some witch's cauldron were simmering alongside the fall. Spray it might be, or the condensing of water splashed on the granite; but of this I might not be sure. Therefore I determined to investigate, and straightway began climbing the rocks – with my heart in my mouth, it must be confessed, for the foothold was undesirable and the way perilous. And all the time I was conscious that the white face of Camille watched me from above. As I reached the cleft I fancied I heard a queer sort of gasping sob issue from his lips, but to this I could give no heed in the sudden wonder that broke upon me. For, lo! it appeared that the cleft led straight to a narrow platform or ledge or rock right underneath the fall itself, but extending how far I could not see, by reason of the steam that filled the passage, and for which I was unable to account. Footing it carefully and groping my way, I set step in the little water-curtained chamber and advanced a pace or two. Suddenly, light grew about me, and a beautiful rose of fire appeared on the wall of the passage in the midst of what seemed a vitrified scoop in the rock.

Marvelling, I put out my hand to touch it, and fell back on the narrow floor with a scream of anguish. An inch farther, and these lines had not been written. As it was, the fall caught me by the fingers with the suck of a catfish, and it was only a gigantic wrench that saved me from slipping off the ledge. The jerk brought my head against the rock with a stunning blow, and for some moments I lay dizzy and confused, daring hardly to breathe, and conscious only of a burning and blistering agony in my right hand.

At length I summoned courage to gather my limbs together and crawl out the way I had entered. The distance was but a few paces, yet to traverse these seemed an interminable nightmare of swaying and stumbling. I know only one other occasion upon which the liberal atmosphere of the open earth seemed sweeter to my senses when I reached it than it did on this.

I tumbled somehow through the cleft, and sat down, shaking, upon the grass of the slope beyond; but, happening to throw myself backwards in the reeling faintness induced by my fright and the pain of my head, my eyes encountered a sight that woke me at once to full activity.

Balanced upon the very verge of the slope, his face and neck craned forward, his jaw dropped, a sick, tranced look upon his features, stood Camille. I saw him topple, and shouted to him; but before my voice was well out, he swayed, collapsed, and came down with a running thud that shook the ground. Once he wheeled over, like a shot rabbit, and, bounding thwack with his head against a flat boulder not a dozen yards from me, lay stunned and motionless.

I scrambled to him, quaking all over. His breath came quick, and a spurt of blood jerked from a sliced cut in his forehead at every pump of his heart.

I kicked out a wad of cool moist turf, and clapped it in a pad over the wound, my handkerchief under. For his body, he was shaken and bruised, but otherwise not seriously hurt.

Presently he came to himself; to himself in the best sense of the word – for Camille was sane.

I have no explanation to offer. Only I know that, as a fall will set a long-stopped watch pulsing again, the blow here seemed to have restored the misplaced intellect to its normal balance.

When he woke, there was a new soft light of sanity in his eyes that was pathetic in the extreme.

'Monsieur,' he whispered, 'the terror has passed.'

'God be thanked! Camille,' I answered, much moved.

He jerked his poor battered head in reverence.

'A little while,' he said, 'and I shall know. The punishment was just.'

'What punishment, my poor Camille?'

'Hush! The cloud has rolled away. I stand naked before *le bon Dieu*. Monsieur, lift me up; I am strong.'

I winced as I complied. The palm of my hand was scorched and blistered in a dozen places. He noticed at once, and kissed and fondled the wounded limb as softly as a woman might.

'Ah, the poor hand!' he murmured. 'Monsieur has touched the disc of fire.'

'Camille,' I whispered, 'what is it?'

'Monsieur shall know – ah! yes, he shall know; but not now. Monsieur, my mother.'

'Thou art right, good son.'

I bound up his bruised forehead and my own burnt hand as well as I was able, and helped him to his feet. He stood upon them staggering; but in a minute could essay to stumble on the homeward journey with assistance. It was a long and toilsome progress; but in time we accomplished it. Often we had to sit down in the blasted woods and rest awhile; often moisten our parched mouths at the runnels of snow-water that threaded the undergrowth. The shadows were slanting eastwards as we reached the clearing we had quitted some hours earlier, and the goats had disappeared. Petitjean was leading his charges homewards in default of a human commander, and presently we overtook them browsingly loitering and desirous of definite instructions.

I pass over Camille's meeting with his mother, and the wonder, and fear, and pity of it all. Our hurts were attended to, and the battery of questions met with the best armour of tact at command. For myself, I said that I had scorched my hand against a red-hot rock, which was strictly true; for Camille, that it were wisest to take no early advantage of the reason that God had restored to him. She was voluble, tearful, half-hysterical with joy and the ecstasy of gratitude.

'That a blow should effect the marvel! Monsieur, but it passes comprehension.'

All night long I heard her stirring and sobbing softly outside his door, for I slept little, owing to pain and the wonder in my mind. But towards morning I dozed, and my dreams were feverish and full of terror.

The next day Camille kept his bed and I my room. By this I at least escaped the first onset of local curiosity, for the villagers naturally made of Camille's restoration a nine-days' wonder. But towards the evening Madame Barbière brought a message from him that he would like to see Monsieur alone, if Monsieur would condescend to visit him in his room. I went at once, and found him, as Haydon found Keats, lying

in a white bed, hectic, and on his back. He greeted me with
a smile peculiarly sweet and restful.

'Does Monsieur wish to know?' he said in a low voice.

'If it will not hurt thee, Camille.'

'Not now – not now; the good God has made me sound.
I remember, and am not terrified.'

I closed the door and took a seat by his bedside. There,
with my hand shading my eyes from the level glory of sunset
that flamed into the room, I listened to the strange tale of
Camille's seizure.

'Once, Monsieur, I lived in myself and was exultant with a
loneliness of fancied knowledge. My youth was my excuse; but
God could not pardon me all. I read where I could find books,
and chance put an evil choice in my way, for I learned to sneer
at His name, His heaven, His hell. Each man has his god in
self-will, I thought in my pride, and through it alone he accepts
the responsibility of life and death. He is his own curse or
blessing here and hereafter, inheriting no sin and earning no
doom but such as he himself inflicts upon himself. I interpret
this from the world about me, and knowing it, I have no fear
and own no tyrant but my own passions. Monsieur, it was
through fear the most terrible that God asserted Himself to me.'

The light was fading in the west, and a lance of shadow
fell upon the white bed, as though the hushed day were
putting a finger to its lips as it withdrew.

'I was no coward then, Monsieur – that at least I may say.
I lived among the mountains, and on their ledges the feet of
my own goats were not surer. Often, in summer, I spent the
night among the woods and hills, reading in them the story
of the ages, and exploring, exploring till my feet were wearier
than my brain. Strangers came from far to see the great
cascade; but none but I – and you, too, Monsieur, now –
know the track through the thicket that leads to the cave
under the waters. I found it by chance, and, like you, was
scorched by the fire, though not badly.'

'Camille – the cause?'

'Monsieur, I will tell you a wonderful thing. The falling waters there make a monstrous burning glass, when the hot sun is upon them, which has melted the rock behind like wax.'

'Can that be so?'

'It is true – dear Jesus, I have fearful reason to know it.'

He half rose on his elbow, his face, crossed by the bandage, grey as stone in the gathering dusk. Hereafter he spoke in an awed whisper.

'When the knowledge broke upon me, I grew great to myself in the possession of a wonderful secret. Day after day I visited the cave and examined this phenomenon – and yet another more marvellous in its connection with the first. The huge lens was a simple accident of curved rocks and convex water, planed smooth as crystal. In other than a droughty summer it would probably not exist; the spouting torrent would overwhelm it – but I know not. Was not this astonishing enough? Yet Nature had worked a second miracle to mock in anticipation the self-sufficient plagiarism of little man. I noticed that the rays of the sun concentrated in the lens only during the half-hour of the orb's apparent crossing of the ravine. Then the light smote upon a strange little fan of water, that spouted from a high crevice at the mouth of the shallow vitrified tunnel, and devoured it, and played upon the rocks behind, that hissed and spluttered like pitch, and the place was blind with steam. But when the tooth of fire was withdrawn, that tiny inner cascade fell again and wrought coolness with its sprinkling.

'I did not discover this all at once, for at first fright took me, and it was enough to watch for the moment of the light's appearance and then flee with a little laughter. But one day I ventured back into the cave after the sun had crossed the valley, and the steam had died away, and the rock cooled behind the miniature cascade.

'I looked through the lens, and it seemed full of a great white light that blazed into my eyes, so that I fell back through the inner fan of water and was well soused by it; but my sight presently recovering, I stood forward in the scoop of rock admiring the dainty hollow curve the fan took in its fall. By and by I became aware that I was looking out through a smaller lens upon the great one, and that strange whirling mists seemed to be sweeping across a huge disc, within touch of my hand almost.

'It was long before I grasped the meaning of this; but, in a flash, it came upon me. The great lens formed the object glass, the small, the eyeglass, of a natural telescope of tremendous power, that drew the high summer clouds down within seeming touch and opened out the heavens before my staring eyes.

'Monsieur, when this dawned upon me I was wild. That so astonishing a discovery should have been reserved for a poor ignorant Swiss peasant filled me with pride wicked in proportion with its absence of gratitude to the mighty dispenser of good. I came even to think my individuality part of the wonder and necessary to its existence. "Were it not for my courage and enterprise," I cried, "this phenomenon would have remained a secret of the Nature that gave birth to it. She yields her treasures to such only as fear not."

'I had read in a book of Huyghens, Guinand, Newton, Herschel – the great high-priests of science who had striven through patient years to read the hieroglyphics of the heavens. "The wise imbeciles," I thought. "They toiled and died, and Nature held no mirror up to them. For me, the poor Camille, she has worked in secret while they grew old and passed unsatisfied."

'Brilliant projects of astronomy whirled in my brain. The evening of my last discovery I remained out on the hills, and entered the cave as it grew dusk. A feeling of awe surged in me as dark fell over the valley, and the first stars glistened

faintly. I dipped under the fan of water and took my stand
in the hollow behind it. There was no moon, but my telescope
was inclined, as it were, at a generous angle, and a section
of the firmament was open before me. My heart beat fast as
I looked through the lens.

'Shall I tell you what I saw then and many nights after?
Rings and crosses in the heavens of golden mist, spangled,
as it seemed, with jewels; stars as big as cartwheels, twinkling
points no longer, but round, like great bosses of molten fire;
things shadowy, luminous, of strange colours and stranger
forms, that seemed to brush the waters as they passed, but
were in reality vast distances away.

'Sometimes the thrust of wind up the ravine would produce
a tremulous motion in the image at the focus of the mirror;
but this was seldom. For the most part the wonderful lenses
presented a steady curvature, not flawless, but of magnificent
capacity.

'Now it flashed upon me that, when the moon was at the
full, she would top the valley in the direct path of my telescope's range of view. At the thought I grew exultant. I – I,
little Camille, should first read aright the history of this strange
satellite. The instrument that could give shape to the stars
would interpret to me the composition of that lonely orb as
clearly as though I stood upon her surface.

'As the time of her fulness drew near I grew feverish with
excitement. I was sickening, as it were, to my madness, for
never more should I look upon her willingly, with eyes either
speculative or insane.'

At this point Camille broke off for a little space, and lay
back on his pillow. When he spoke again it was out of the
darkness, with his face turned to the wall.

'Monsieur, I cannot dwell upon it – I must hasten. We
have no right to peer beyond the boundary God has drawn
for us. I saw His hell – I saw His hell, I tell you. It is peopled
with the damned – silent, horrible, distorted in the midst of
ashes and desolation. It was a memory that, like the snake

of Aaron, devoured all others till yesterday – till yesterday, by Christ's mercy.'

It seemed to me, as the days wore on, that Camille had but recovered his reason at the expense of his life; that the long rest deemed necessary for him after his bitter period of brain exhaustion might in the end prove an everlasting one. Possibly the blow to his head had, in expelling the seven devils, wounded beyond cure the vital function that had fostered them. He lay white, patient, and sweet-tempered to all, but moved by no inclination to rise and re-assume the many-coloured garment of life.

His description of the dreadful desert in the sky I looked upon, merely, as an abiding memory of the brain phantasm that had finally overthrown a reason, already tottering under the tremendous excitement induced by his discovery of the lenses, and the magnified images they had presented to him. That there was truth in the asserted fact of the existence of these, my own experience convinced me; and curiosity as to this alone impelled me to the determination of investigating further, when my hand should be sufficiently recovered to act as no hindrance to me in forcing my way once more through the dense woods that bounded the waterfall. Moreover, the dispassionate enquiry of a mind less sensitive to impressions might, in the result, do more towards restoring the warped imagination of my friend to its normal state than any amount of spoken scepticism.

To Camille I said nothing of my resolve; but waited on, chafing at the slow healing of my wounds. In the meantime the period of the full moon approached, and I decided, at whatever cost, to make the venture on the evening she topped her orbit, if circumstances at the worst should prevent my doing so sooner – and thus it turned out.

On the eve of my enterprise, the first fair spring of rain in a drought of two months fell, to my disappointment, among the hills; for I feared an increase of the torrent and the effacement of the mighty lens. I set off, however, on the afternoon of the following day, in hot sunshine, mentally prognosticating a favourable termination to my expedition, and telling Madame Barbière not to expect me back till late.

In leisurely fashion I made my way along the track we had previously traversed, risking no divergence through over-haste, and carefully examining all landmarks before deciding on any direction. Thus slowly proceeding, I had the good fortune to come within sound of the cataract as the sun was sinking behind the mountain ridges to my front; and presently emerged from the woods at the very spot we had struck in our former journey together.

A chilly twilight reigned in the ravine, and the noise that came up from the ruin of the torrent seemed doubly accented by reason of it. The sound of water moving in darkness has always conveyed to me an impression of something horrible and deadly, be it nothing of more moment than the drip and hollow tinkle of a gutter pipe. But the crash in this echoing gorge was appalling indeed.

For some moments I stood on the brink of the slope, looking across at the great knife of the fall, with a little shiver of fear. Then I shook myself, laughed, and without further ado took my courage in hand, and scrambled down the declivity and up again towards the cleft in the rocks.

Here the chill of heart gripped me again – the watery sliding tunnel looked so evil in the contracting gloom. A false step in that humid chamber, and my bones would pound and crackle on the rocks forty feet below. It must be gone through with now, however; and, taking a long breath, I set foot in the passage under the curving downpour that seemed taut as an arched muscle.

Reaching the burnt recess, a few moments sufficed to restore my self-confidence; and without further hesitation I dived under the inner little fan-shaped fall – which was there, indeed, as Camille had described it – and recovered my balance with pulses drumming thicker than I could have desired.

In a moment I became conscious that some great power was before me. Across a vast, irregular disc filled with the ashy whiteness of the outer twilight, strange, unaccountable forms misty and undefined, passed, and repassed, and vanished. Cirrus they might have been, or the shadows flung by homing flights of birds; but of this I could not be certain. As the dusk deepened they showed no more, and presently I gazed only into a violet fathomless darkness.

My own excitement now was great; and I found some difficulty in keeping it under control. But for the moment, it seemed to me, I pined greatly for free commune with the liberal atmosphere of earth. Therefore, I dipped under the little fall and made my cautious way to the margin of the cataract.

I was surprised to find for how long a time the phenomenon had absorbed me. The moon was already high in the heavens, and making towards the ravine with rapid steps. Far below, the tumbling waters flashed in her rays, and on all sides great tiers of solemn trees stood up at attention to salute her.

When her disc silvered the inner rim of the slope I had descended, I returned to my post of observation with tingling nerves. The field of the great object lens was already suffused with the radiance of her approach.

Suddenly my pupils shrank before the apparition of a ghastly grey light, and all in a moment I was face to face with a segment of desolation more horrible than any desert. Monstrous growths of leprosy that had bubbled up and stiffened; fields of ashen slime – the sloughing of a world of corruption; hills of demon fungus swollen with the fatness of putrefaction; and, in the midst of all, dim, convulsed shapes wallowing, protruding, or stumbling aimlessly onwards, till they sank and disappeared.

Madame Barbière threw up her hands when she let me in at the door. My appearance, no doubt, was ghastly. I knew not the hour nor the lapse of time covered by my wanderings about the hills, my face hidden in my palms, a drawn feeling about my heart, my lips muttering – muttering fragments of prayers, and my throat jerking with horrible laughter.

For hours I lay face downwards on my bed.

'Monsieur has seen it?'

'I have seen it.'

'I heard the rain on the hills. The lens will have been blurred. Monsieur has been spared much.'

'God, in His mercy, pity thee! And me – oh, Camille, and me too!'

'He has held out His white hand to me. I go, when I go, with a safe conduct.'

He went before the week was out. The drought had broken and for five days the thunder crashed and the wild rain swept the mountains. On the morning of the sixth a drenched shepherd reported in the village that a landslip had choked the fall of Buet, and completely altered its shape. Madame Barbière broke into the room where I was sitting with Camille, big with the news. She little guessed how it affected her listeners.

'The *bon Dieu*,' said Camille, when she had gone, 'has thundered His curse on Nature for revealing His secrets. I, who have penetrated into the forbidden, must perish.'

'And I, Camille?'

He turned to me with a melancholy sweet smile, and answered, paraphrasing the dying words of certain noble lips—

'Be good, Monsieur; be good.'

THE QUEER PICTURE

It was standing with its face to the wall in a dark corner of
the dingy old shop in Beak Street, whose miscellaneous litter
had peered at me through a window so dirty as to make its
owner appear rather to wish to baffle custom than to court
it. Nor in that respect was its owner's manner reassuring. His
eyes peered dimly out of an unwashed face, like the pale
blue oriental saucers through the window. He seemed to
regard me with indifference and a little weariness, as if the
profit of chaffering were hardly worth its trouble. 'O, yes!'
he said, in a weak, hoarse voice, to my appreciations of
this or that, as I edged my way through the labyrinth of
Chippendale chairs, bureaux, coffin-stools, and gate-legged
tables piled with Staffordshire figures, brass door-knockers,
candlesticks, and 'genuine antiques' of every sort, description
and plausibility.

A little nettled by the creature's apathy, I stooped, somewhat truculently, and turned the picture round for myself.
It showed a landscape, pretty dark and mellow in tone, of,
I fancied, the Crome or Nasmyth period. A woodland road,
receding from the middle foreground of the canvas, presently
took a curve round some palings to the left, and disappeared
into greenery. Prominent over the near palings towered a
huge oak; on the other side was a close medley of foliage
gradually dimming into blue distances. The whole was feel-
ingly painted and composed, the large oak tree, quite superbly

rendered, forming its predominant feature. It all only suffered slightly to my mind as a composition from the white empti- ness of the road and the absence of figures. I said so to the dealer. 'O, yes!' he answered, with a dry cough, and I shrugged my shoulders.

I have had one or two 'finds' in my time – enough to stimulate my adventurous nerve. This thing seemed to me good: there was power in it, and knowledge. The time was evidently near twilight, still and darkling – a lonely, solemn place. The atmosphere was unmistakably suggested. Its canvas measurement was some 34 by 28 inches, and it possessed a frame, a little dingy and battered, but of the right sort. 'Whom is it by?' I said.

The dealer made as if to bend, cleared his thin old throat and stood up again. 'It's unsigned,' he said.

'But don't you know?'

'If you were to ask me,' he answered, 'I should say – no more than that, mind you – that it was Urquhart's work.' Then, in response to my mute inquiry, 'He was a follower of John Constable, you know.'

I didn't know; I knew nothing about the man; but, whoever he was, his capacity was plain. I decided to risk it. 'Well, how much?' I said.

'Twenty pounds,' said the dealer.

As a matter of principle I protested – 'Unsigned; of disput- able origin; preposterous!' 'O, yes!' he said, in his indifferent way. 'Twenty pounds is the price. It's a greatly admired piece. If you change your mind, I will take it back any time within a week, less ten per cent.'

That seemed a fair offer, and I ended by carrying the picture home with me in a cab. Alone, I cleared the mantelpiece of my sitting-room, and stood the treasure up on it. I thought it distinctly an admirable piece of work, and so far rejoiced in my bargain. It seemed to reflect the very spirit of the twilight which was even now creeping over my room, to assimilate and conform to it. As I gazed I grew penetrated, possessed, by what I gazed on. I was on the wide, white road, standing or crouching somewhere down here out of the picture, and staring into its diminishing distances. The great oak was motionlessly alive; there seemed 'a listening fear in its regard'. An expectation, an indescribable awe, held me amazedly entranced. And then my breath caught in a quick gasp. Round by the bend of the road, far away, there occurred a minute stirring, and something came into the picture that was not there before. The thing came on, increasing in regular progression as it advanced – and it was the figure of a young man, in a bygone costume, swinging airily towards me. I sat petrified, dumbstricken; and all in an instant there arose between me and the illusion, blotting it out, a vague, shadowy shape. That receded quickly, shrinking as it withdrew, until it also was the figure of a man going away from me along the road to meet the other. The two encountered, and had passed, when the second wheeled suddenly in his tracks, and struck the first on the neck, so that the young man fell into the road. I saw something – a running stain of red, and simultaneously broke, with a cry, from my stupefaction and, leaping to the mantelpiece, turned the horror with its face to the wall. As I did so I saw that the canvas was empty of figures.

The old dealer made no demur whatever about my returning the picture. 'It always comes back,' he said impassively, as he paid me in cash eighteen pounds out of the twenty I had given for it. 'It stands me in well, you see, as an investment. It's a fine work. I dare say you'll be the dozenth or more who's been struck by it, and carried it away with the same result. Twilight's the time, they say.'

'Don't you know it is?' I responded warmly. 'Haven't you seen it yourself?'

'No,' he said, with a thin cough, 'no.' (He had returned the picture to its former place and position.) 'I don't bother to look. It wouldn't be policy, and it wouldn't be fair, you know, for me to sell it if I had. I'm not bound to go upon hearsay; and it doesn't trouble me where it stands.'

'But' – I turned on my heel indignantly, and came back – 'you said it was an Urquhart.'

'On its intrinsic evidences,' he responded; 'not in the least because it happens that Urquhart was hanged for the murder of his wife's paramour on a country road he was engaged in painting at the time. He stuck him in the neck with a palette-knife. That *may* have been the very picture – or it may not – before the figures were filled in. Urquhart generally used sheep and countrymen. But all that's no concern of mine. I say it's an Urquhart because of the style. No one but him, in my opinion, could have painted that oak.'

DARK DIGNUM

'I'd not go nigher, sir,' said my landlady's father.

I made out his warning through the shrill piping of the wind; and stopped and took in the plunging seascape from where I stood. The boom of the waves came up from a vast distance beneath; sky and the horizon of running water seemed hurrying upon us over the lip of the rearing cliff.

'It crumbles!' he cried. 'It crumbles near the edge like as frosted mortar. I've seen a noble sheep, sir, eighty pound of mutton, browsing here one moment, and seen it go down the next in a puff of white dust. Hark to that! Do you hear it?'

Through the tumult of the wind in that high place came a liquid vibrant sound, like the muffled stroke of iron on an anvil. I thought it the gobble of water in clanging caves deep down below.

'It might be a bell,' I said.

The old man chuckled joyously. He was my cicerone for the nonce; had come out of his chair by the inglenook to taste a little the salt of life. The north-easter flashed in the white cataracts of his eyes and woke a feeble activity in his scrannel limbs. When the wind blew loud, his daughter had told me, he was always restless, like an imprisoned sea-gull. He would be up and out. He would rise and flap his old draggled pinions, as if the great air fanned an expiring spark into flame.

'It *is* a bell!' he cried – 'the bell of old St Dunstan's, that was swallowed by the waters in the dark times.'

'Ah,' I said. 'That is the legend hereabouts.'

'No legend, sir – no legend. Where be the tombstones of drownded mariners to prove it such? Not one to forty that they has in other sea-board parishes. For why? Dunstan bell sounds its warning, and not a craft will put out.'

'There is the storm cone,' I suggested.

He did not hear me. He was punching with his staff at one of a number of little green mounds that lay about us.

'I could tell you a story of these,' he said. 'Do you know where we stand?'

'On the site of the old churchyard?'

'Ay, sir; though it still bore the name of the *new* yard in my first memory of it.'

'Is that so? And what is the story?'

He dwelt a minute, dense with introspection. Suddenly he sat himself down upon a mossy bulge in the turf, and waved me imperiously to a place beside him.

'The old order changeth,' he said. 'The only lasting foundations of men's works shall be godliness and law-biding. Long ago they builded a new church – here, high up on the cliffs, where the waters could not reach; and, lo! the waters wrought beneath and sapped the foundations, and the church fell into the sea.'

'So I understand,' I said.

'The godless are fools,' he chattered knowingly. 'Look here at these bents – thirty of 'em, may be. Tombstones, sir; perished like man his works, and the decayed stumps of them coated with salt grass.'

He pointed to the ragged edge of the cliff a score paces away.

'They raised it out there,' he said, 'and further – a temple of bonded stone. They thought to bribe the Lord to a partnership in their corruption, and He answered by casting down the fair mansion into the waves.'

I said, 'Who – who, my friend?'

'They that builded the church,' he answered.

'Well,' I said. 'It seems a certain foolishness to set the edifice so close to the margin.'

Again he chuckled.

'It was close, close, as you say; yet none so close as you might think nowadays. Time hath gnawed here like a rat in a cheese. But the foolishness appeared in setting the brave mansion between the winds and its own graveyard. Let the dead lie seawards, one had thought, and the church inland where we stand. So had the bell rung to this day; and only the charnel bones flaked piecemeal into the sea.'

'Certainly, to have done so would show the better providence.'

'Sir, I said the foolishness *appeared*. But, I tell you, there was foresight in the disposition – in neighbouring the building to the cliff path. *For so they could the easier enter unobserved, and store their kegs of Nantes brandy in the belly of the organ.*'

'They? Who were they?'

'Why, who – but two-thirds of all Dunburgh?'

'Smugglers?'

'It was a nest of 'em – traffickers in the eternal fire o' weekdays, and on the Sabbath, who so sanctimonious? But honesty comes not from the washing, like a clean shirt, nor can the piety of one day purge the evil of six. They built their church anigh the margin, forasmuch as it was handy, and that they thought, "Surely the Lord will not undermine His own?" A rare community o' blasphemers, fro' the parson that took his regular toll of the organ-loft, to him that sounded the keys and pulled out the joyous stops as if they was so many spigots to what lay behind.'

'Of when do you speak?'

'I speak of nigh a century and a half ago. I speak of the time o' the Seven Years' War and of Exciseman Jones, that, twenty year after he were buried, took his revenge on the cliff side of the man that done him to death.'

'And who was that?'

'They called him Dark Dignum, sir – a great feat smuggler, and as wicked as he was bold.'

'Is your story about him?'

'Ay, it is; and of my grandfather, that were a boy when they laid, and was glad to lay, the exciseman deep as they could dig; for the sight of his sooty face in his coffin was worse than a bad dream.'

'Why was that?'

The old man edged closer to me, and spoke in a sibilant voice.

'He were murdered, sir, foully and horribly, for all they could never bring it home to the culprit.'

'Will you tell me about it?'

He was nothing loth. The wind, the place of perished tombs, the very wild-blown locks of this 'withered apple-john', were eerie accompaniments to the tale he piped in my ear:

'When my grandfather were a boy,' he said, 'there lighted in Dunburgh Exciseman Jones. P'r'aps the village had gained an ill reputation. P'r'aps Exciseman Jones's predecessor had failed to secure the confidence o' the exekitive. At any rate, the new man was little to the fancy o' the village. He was a grim, sour-looking, brass-bound galloot; and incorruptible – which was the worst. The keg o' brandy left on his doorstep o' New Year's Eve had been better unspiled and run into the gutter; for it led him somehow to the identification of the innocent that done it, and he had him by the heels in a twinkling. The squire snorted at the man, and the parson looked askance; but Dark Dignum, he swore he'd be even with him, if he swung for it. They were hurt and surprised, that was the truth, over the scrupulosity of certain people; and feelin' ran high against Exciseman Jones.

'At that time Dark Dignum was a young man with a reputation above his years for profaneness and audacity. Ugly things were said about him; and amongst many wicked he was feared for his wickedness. Exciseman Jones had his eye on him; and that was bad for Exciseman Jones.

'Now one murky December night Exciseman Jones staggered home with a bloody long slice down his scalp, and the red drip from it spotting the cobblestones.

'"Summut fell on him from a winder," said Dark Dignum, a little later, as he were drinkin' hisself hoarse in the Black Boy. "Summut fell on him retributive, as you might call it. For, would you believe it, the man had at the moment been threatenin' me? He did. He said, 'I know damn well about you, Dignum; and for all your damn ingenuity, I'll bring you with a crack to the ground yet!'"

'What had happened? Nobody knew, sir. But Exciseman Jones was in his bed for a fortnight; and when he got on his legs again, it was pretty evident there was a hate between the two men that only blood-spillin' could satisfy.

'So far as is known, they never spoke to one another again. They played their game of death in silence – the lawful, cold and unfathomable; the unlawful, swaggerin' and crool – and twenty year separated the first move and the last.

'This were the first, sir – as Dark Dignum leaked it out long after in his cups. This were the first; and it brought Exciseman Jones to his grave on the cliff here.

'It were a deep soft summer night; and the young smuggler sat by hisself in the long room of the Black Boy. Now, I tell you he were a fox-ship intriguer – grand, I should call him, in the aloneness of his villainy. He would play his dark games out of his own hand; and sure, of all his wickedness, this game must have seemed the sum.

'I say he sat by hisself; and I hear the listening ghost of him call me a liar. For there were another body present, though invisible to mortal eye; and that second party were Exciseman Jones, who was hidden up the chimney.

'How had he inveigled him there? Ah, they've met and worried that point out since. No other will ever know the truth this side the grave. But reports come to be whispered;

and reports said as how Dignum had made an appointment
with a bodiless master of a smack as never floated, to meet
him in the Black Boy and arrange for to run a cargo as would
never be shipped; and that somehow he managed to acquent
Exciseman Jones o' this dissembling appointment, and to
secure his presence in hidin' to witness it.

'That's conjecture; for Dignum never let on so far. But
what *is* known for certain is that Exciseman Jones, who were
as daring and determined as his enemy – p'r'aps more so –
for some reason was in the chimney, on to a grating in which
he had managed to lower hisself from the roof; and that he
could, if given time, have scrambled up again with difficulty,
but was debarred from going lower. And, further, this is
known – that, as Dignum sat on, pretendin' to yawn and
huggin' his black intent, a little soot plopped down the
chimney and scattered on the coals of the laid fire beneath.

'At that – "Curse this waitin'!" said he. "The room's as
chill as a belfry", and he got to his feet, with a secret grin,
and strolled to the hearthstone.

'"I wonder," said he, "will the landlord object if I ventur'
upon a glint of fire for comfort's sake?" and he pulled out
his flint and steel, struck a spark, and with no more feeling
than he'd express in lighting a pipe, set the flame to the
sticks.

'The trapt rat above never stirred or give tongue. My God!
what a man! Sich a nature could afford to bide and bide – ay,
for twenty year, if need be.

'Dignum would have enjoyed the sound of a cry; but he
never got it. He listened with the grin fixed on his face; and
of a sudden he heard a scrambling struggle, like as a dog
with the colic jumping at a wall; and presently, as the sticks
blazed and the smoke rose denser, a thick coughin', as of a
consumptive man under bed-clothes. Still no cry, or any
appeal for mercy; no, not from the time he lit the fire till a
horrible rattle come down, which was the last twitches of
somethin' that choked and died on the sooty gratin' above.

'When all was quiet, Dignum he knocks with his foot on the floor and sits hisself down before the hearth, with a face like a pillow for innocence.

'"I were chilled and lit it," says he to the landlord. "You don't mind?"

'Mind? Who would have ventur'd to cross Dark Dignum's fancies?

'He give a boisterous laugh, and ordered in a double noggin of humming stuff.

'"Here," he says, when it comes, "is to the health of Exciseman Jones, that swore to bring me to the ground."

'"To the ground," mutters a thick voice from the chimney.

'"My God!" says the landlord – "there's something up there!"

'Something there was; and terrible to look upon when they brought it to light. The creature's struggles had ground the soot into its face, and its nails were black below the quick.

'Were those words the last of its death-throe, or an echo from beyond? Ah! we may question; but they were heard by two men.

'Dignum went free. What could they prove agen him? Not that he knew there was aught in the chimney when he lit the fire. The other would scarcely have acquent him of his plans. And Exciseman Jones was hurried into his grave alongside the church up here.

'And therein he lay for twenty year, despite that, not a twelve-month after his coming, the sacrilegious house itself sunk roaring into the waters. For the Lord would have none of it, and, biding His time, struck through a fortnight of deluge, and hurled church and cliff into ruin. But the yard remained, and, nighest the seaward edge of it, Exciseman Jones slept in his fearful winding sheet and bided *his* time.

'It came when my grandfather were a young man of thirty, and mighty close and confidential with Dark Dignum. God forgive him! Doubtless he were led away by the older smuggler, that had a grace of villainy about him, 'tis said, and used Lord Chesterfield's printed letters for wadding to his bullets.

'By then he was a ramping, roaring devil; but, for all his bold hands were stained with crime, the memory of Exciseman Jones and of his promise dwelled with him and darkened him ever more and more, and never left him. So those that knew him said.

'Now all these years the cliff edge agen the graveyard, where it was broke off, was scabbing into the sea below. But still they used this way of ascent for their ungodly traffic; and over the ruin of the cliff they drove a new path for to carry up their kegs.

'It was a cloudy night in March, with scud and a fitful moon, and there was a sloop in the offing, and under the shore a loaded boat that had just pulled in with muffled rowlocks. Out of this Dark Dignum was the first to sling hisself a brace of rundlets; and my grandfather followed with two more. They made softly for the cliff path – began the ascent – was half-way up.

'Whiz! – a stone of chalk went by them with a skirl, and slapped into the rubble below.

'"Some more of St Dunstan's gravel!" cried Dignum, pantin' out a reckless laugh under his load; and on they went again.

'Hwish! – a bigger lump came like a thunderbolt, and the wind of it took the bloody smuggler's hat and sent it swooping into the darkness like a bird.

'"Thunder!" said Dignum; "the cliff's breaking away!"

'The words was hardly out of his mouth, when there flew such a volley of chalk stones as made my grandfather, though none had touched him, fall upon the path where he stood, and begin to gabble out what he could call to mind of the prayers for the dying. He was in the midst of it, when he heard a scream come from his companion as froze the very marrow in his bones. He looked up, thinkin' his hour had come.

'My God! What a sight he saw! The moon had shone out of a sudden, and the light of it struck down on Dignum's face, and that was the colour of dirty parchment. And he looked higher, and give a sort of sob.

'For there, stickin' out of the cliff side, was half the body of Exciseman Jones, with its arms stretched abroad, *and it was clawin' out lumps of chalk and hurling them down at Dignum*!

'And even as he took this in through his terror, a great ball of white came hurtling, and went full on to Dignum's face with a splash – and he were spun down into the deep night below, a nameless thing.'

The old creature came to a stop, his eyes glinting with a febrile excitement.

'And so,' I said, 'Exciseman Jones was true to his word?'

The tension of memory was giving – the spring slowly uncoiling itself.

'Ay,' he said doubtfully. 'The cliff had flaked away by degrees to his very grave. They found his skelington stickin' out of the chalk.'

'His *skeleton*?' said I, with the emphasis of disappointment.

'The first, sir, the first. Ay, his was the first. There've been a many exposed since. The work of decay goes on, and the bones they fall into the sea. Sometimes, sailing off shore, you may see a shank or an arm protrudin' like a pigeon's leg from a pie. But the wind or the weather takes it and it goes. There's more to follow yet. Look at 'em! look at these bents! Every one a grave, with a skelington in it. The wear and tear from the edge will reach each one in turn, and then the last of the ungodly will have ceased from the earth.'

'And what became of your grandfather?'

'My grandfather? There were something happened made him renounce the devil. He died one of the elect. His youth were heedless and unregenerate; but, 'tis said, after he were turned thirty he never smiled agen. There was a reason. Did I ever tell you the story of Dark Dignum and Exciseman Jones?'

THE MASK

Le masque tombe, l'homme reste.

There are mental modes as there are sartorial, and, commercially, the successful publisher is like the successful tailor, a man who knows how timely to exploit the fashion. Is it for the moment realism, romance, the psychic, the analytic, the homely – he makes, with Rabelais, his soup according to his bread, and feeds the multitude, as it asks, either on turtle or pease-porridge.

It was on the crest of a big psychic wave that Hands and Cumberbatch launched their *Haunted Houses* – a commonplace but quite effective title. It was all projected and floated within the compass of a few months, and it proved a first success. The idea was, of course, authentic possessions, or manifestations, and the thing was to be done in convincing style, with photogravure illustrations. The letterpress was entrusted to Penn-Howard, and the camera business to an old college friend of his selection, J.B. Lamont. The two worked in double harness, and collected between them more material than could be used. But the cream of it was in the book, though not that particular skimming I am here to present, and for whose suppression at the time there were reasons.

I knew Penn-Howard pretty intimately, and should not have thought him an ideal hand for the task. He was a younger son of Lord Staveley, and carried an Honourable to his name. A brilliant fellow, cool, practical, modern, with infinite humour and aplomb, he would yet to my mind have lacked the first essential of an evangelist, a faith in the gospel he preached. He did not, in short, believe in spooks, and his dealings with the supernatural must all have been in the nature of an urbane pyrrhonism. But he was a fine, imaginative writer, who could raise terrors he did not feel; and that, no doubt, explained in part his publishers' choice. What chiefly influenced them, however, was unquestionably his social popularity; he was known and liked everywhere, and could count most countable people among his friends, actual or potential. Where he wanted to go he went, and where he went he was welcome – an invaluable factor in this somewhat delicate business of ghost-hunting. But fashion affects even spirits, and, when the supernatural is *en vogue*, doors long jealously shut upon family secrets will be found to open themselves in a quite wonderful way. Hence, the time and the man agreeing, the success of the book.

I met Penn-Howard at Lady Caroon's during the time he was collecting his material. There were a few other guests at Hawkesbury, among them, just arrived, a tall, serious young fellow called Howick. Mr Howick, I understood, had lately succeeded, from a collateral branch, to the Howick estates in Hampshire. His sister was to have come with him, but had excused herself at the last moment – or rather, had been excused by him. She was indefinitely 'ailing', it appeared, and unfit for society. He used the word, in my hearing, with a certain hard decisiveness, in which there seemed a hint of something painful. Others may have felt it too, for the subject of the absentee was at once and discreetly waived.

Hawkesbury has its ghost – a nebulous radiance with a face that floats before one in the gloom of corridors – and naturally at some time during the evening the talk turned upon visitations. Penn-Howard was very picturesque, but, to me, unconvincing on the subject. There was no feeling behind his imagination; and, when put to it, he admitted as much. Someone had complimented him on the gruesome originality of a story of his which had recently appeared in one of the sixpenny magazines, and, quite good-humouredly, he had repudiated the term.

'No mortal being,' he said, 'may claim originality for his productions. There are the three primary colours, blue, red and yellow, and the three dimensions, length, breadth and thickness. They are original; it would be original to make a fourth; only we can't do it. We can only exploit creation ready-made as we find it. Everything for us is comprised within those limits – even Lady Caroon's ghost. It is a question of selection and chemical affinities, that is all. There is no such thing here as a supernature.'

He was cried out on for his heresy to his own art – for his confession of its soullessness.

'Soul,' he contended at that, 'is not wanted in art, nor is religion; but only the five unperturbed and explorative senses. Pan, I think, would have made the ideal artist.'

I saw Howick, who was sitting silently apart, suddenly hug himself at these words, bending forward and stiffening his lips, as a man does who mutely traverses a sentiment he is too shy or too superior to discuss. I did not know which it was with him; but inclined to the latter. There was something bonily professorial in his aspect.

While we were talking Lamont came in. He had not appeared at dinner, and I had not yet seen him. He was a compact, stubby man, in astigmatic glasses, and very dark, with a cleft chin, and a resolute mouth under a moustache in keeping with his strong, thick eyebrows. He gave me somehow in the connection a feeling of much greater fitness than did Penn-Howard. There was no expression of the *esprit-fort* about *him*, and I got an idea that, though only the technical collaborator, the right atmosphere of the book, if and when it appeared, would be due more to him than to the other. He spoke little, but authoritatively; and I remember he told us that night some queer things about photography – such, for instance, as its mysterious relation to *something* in light-rays, which was not heat and was not light, and yet like light could reveal the hidden, as a mirror reveals to one the objects out of sight behind one's back. Thence, touching upon astral charts and composite portraits by the way, he came to his illustration, which was creepy enough. He had once for some reason, it appeared, taken a post-mortem photograph. The man, the subject, had cut in life a considerable figure in the parliamentary world as an advanced advocate of social and moral reform, and had died in the odour of political sanctity. In securing the negative, circumstances had necessitated a long exposure; but accident had contrived a longer and a deadlier, in the double sense. The searchlight of the lens, being left concentrated an undue time on the lifeless face, had discovered things hitherto impenetrable and unguessed-at. The nature of the real horror had been drawn through the superimposing veil, and the revelation of what had been existing all the time under the surface was not pleasant. The photograph had not appeared in the illustrated paper for which it was intended, and Lamont had destroyed the negative.

So he told us, in a forcible, economic way which was more effective than much verbal adornment; and again my attention was caught by Howick, who seemed dwelling upon the speaker's words with an expression quite arresting in its ungainly intensity. Later on I saw the two in earnest conversation together.

That was in October, and I left Hawkesbury on the following day. Full ten months passed before I saw Penn-Howard again; and then one hot evening towards dusk he walked into my chambers in Brick Court and asked for a cigarette.

He seemed distraught, withdrawn, like a man who, having something on his mind, was pondering an uncompromising way of relief from it. Quite undesignedly and inevitably I gave him his cue by asking how the book progressed. He heaved out a great, smoke-laden sigh at once, stirred, drew up and dropped his shoulders, and looked at the fiery point of his cigarette before replacing the butt between his lips.

'O, the book!' he said. 'It's ready for the press, so far as I'm concerned.'

'And Lamont?'

'Yes, and J.B.'

He got up, paced the width of the room and back, and stood before me, alternately drawing at and withdrawing his cigarette.

'There's one thing that won't go into it,' he said, his eyes suggesting a rather forced evasion of mine.

'O! What's that?'

Again, as if doubtful of himself, he turned to tramp out his restlessness or agitation; thought better of it, and sat resolutely down in a chair against the dark end of the book-case.

'Would you care to know?' he said. 'Truth is, I came to tell you – if I could; to ask your opinion on the thing. There's the comfort of the judicial brain about you: I can imagine, like a client, that simply to confide one's case to such is to feel relieved of a load of responsibility. It won't go into the book, I say; but I want it to go out of me. I'm too full of it for comfort.'

'Of *it*? Of what?'

'What?' he said, as if in a sudden spasm of violence. 'I wish to God you'd tell me.'

He sat moodily silent for some minutes, and I did nothing to help him out. A hot, sour air came in by the open window, and the heavy red curtains shrank and dilated languidly in it, as if they were the lungs of the stifling room. Outside the dusty roar of the traffic went on unceasingly, with a noise like that of overhead machinery. I was feeling stale and tired, and wished, in the Rooseveltian phrase, that Penn-Howard would either get on or get out.

'It's a queer thing, isn't it,' he said suddenly, with an obvious effort, 'that of all the stuff collected for that book you were speaking of, the only authentic instance for which

I can personally vouch is the only instance to be excluded? All the rest was on hearsay.'

'Well, you surprise me,' I said, quietly, after a pause. 'Not because any authentic instance, about which I know nothing, is excluded, but because, by your own confession, there is one to exclude.'

'I know what you mean, of course,' he answered; and quoted: '"But, spite of all the criticising elves, those who would make us feel must feel themselves." Quite right. I never really believed in supernatural influences. Do I now? That is what I want you to decide for me.'

He laughed slightly; sighed again, and seemed rather to shrink into his dusky corner.

'I'm going to tell you at a run,' he said. 'Bear with me, like an angelic fellow. You remember that man Howick at Lady Caroon's?'

'Yes, quite well.'

'It seemed, when he learnt our business, Lamont's and mine, that there was something he wished to tell us. He pitched upon J.B. as the more responsible partner; and I'm not sure he wasn't right.'

'Nor am I.'

'O! you aren't, are you? Well, Jemmy was my choice, anyhow, and for the sake of the qualities you think I lack. He has a way of getting behind things – always had, even at Oxford. Some men seem to know the trick by instinct. He is a very queer sort, and the featest with the camera of any one I've ever seen or heard of. It was for that reason I asked him to come – to get the ghostliest possible out of ghostly buildings and haunted rooms. You remember what he told us that night? I've seen some of his spirit photographs, though without feeling convinced. But his description of that dead face! My God! I thought at the time he was just improvising to suit the occasion; but—'

He stopped abruptly. There was something odd here. It was evident that, for an unknown reason, the thought of *that* time was not the thought of this. I detected an obvious emotion, quite strange to it, in Penn-Howard's voice. His face, from our positions and the dusk, was almost hidden from me. I made no comment; and thenceforth he spoke on uninterruptedly, while the room slowly darkened about us as we sat.

'Howick wanted us, at the end of our visit, to go with him to his house. Something was happening there, he said, for which he was unable to account. We could not, however, consent, owing to our engagements; but we undertook to include him sooner or later in our ghostly itinerary. He was obliged; but, being so put off, would give us no clue to the nature of the mystery which was disturbing him. As it turned out, we had no choice but to take Haggarts the very last on our list.'

'That is the name of his place?'

'Yes. It sounds a bit thin and eerie, doesn't it? but in point of fact, I believe, haggart is a local word for hawthorn. We went there last of all, and we went there intending to stay a night, and we stayed seven. It was a queer business; and I come to you fresh from it.

'The estate lies slap in the middle of Hampshire. To reach it you alight at a country station which might serve roughly on the map for the hub of the county wheel. The train slides from a tunnel into a ravine of chalk, deep and dazzling, and you have to get on a level with the top of that ravine; and there at once you find immeasurable silence and loneliness. Nothing in my home peregrinations has struck me more forcibly than the real insignificance of urban expansion in its relation to the country as a whole. Towns, however they grow and multiply, remain but inconsiderable freckles on that vast open countenance. Outside the City man's possible radius, and excepting the great manufacturing centres, two miles, one mile beyond the boundary of ninety-nine towns out of a hundred will find you in pastoral solitudes apparently limitless. Here, with Winchester lying but eight miles southward, it was so. From the top of the tunnel we had just penetrated came into view, first a wilderness of thorn-scattered downs, dipping steeply and ruggedly into the railway cutting, then an endlessly extended panorama of wood and waste and field, seemingly houseless and hamletless, and broken only by the white scars of roads, mounting few and far like the crests of waves on a desert sea. Howick had sent a car to meet us, and we switch-backed on monotonously, by unrailed pastures, by woody bottoms, by old hedges grey with dust and draggled with straw. We saw the house long before we headed for it – a strange, ill-designed structure standing out by itself in the fields. It was an antique moat-house, disproportionately tall for its area, and its front flanked by a couple of brick towers, one squat, one lofty. One wound about the lanes to reach it, having it now at this side, now at that, now fairly at one's back, until suddenly it came into close view, a building far more grandiose and imposing than one had surmised. There was the ancient moat surrounding it, and much water channelling the flats about. But there was evidence too, at close quarters, of what one had not guessed – rich, quiet gardens, substantial outbuildings, and a general atmosphere of prosperity.

'An odd, remote place, but in itself distinctly attractive. And Howick did us well. You remember him? A tall stick of a fellow, without a laugh to his whole anatomy, and the hair gone from his temples at thirty; but with the grand manner in enter-taining. We had some '47 port that night – a treat – one of a few remaining bottles laid down by his granduncle, Roger Howick, of whom more in a little. And everything was in mellow keeping – pictures, furniture, old crusted anecdote. Only our host was, for all his gracious unbending, somehow out of tone with his environments – in that connection of fruitiness, like the dry nodule on a juicy apple. Constitutionally reserved, I should think, circumstance at that time had drained him of the last capacity for spontaneity. The little fits of abstrac-tion and the wincing starts from them; the forced conversation; the atmosphere of brooding trouble felt through his most hospitable efforts – all pointed to a state of mind which he could neither conceal nor as yet indulge. Often I detected him looking furtively at J.B., often, still more secretively, at his sister, who was the only other one present at the dinner-table.'

For a moment Penn-Howard ceased speaking; and I heard him shift his position, as if suddenly cramped, and slightly clear his throat.

'I mention her now for the first time,' he went on presently. 'She came in after we were seated, and there was the briefest formal introduction, of which she took no notice. She was a slender, unprepossessing woman – her brother's senior by some ten years, I judged – with a strange, unnatural complexion, rather long, pale eyes in red rims, and a sullen manner. Responding only after the curtest fashion to any commonplaces addressed to her, she left us, much to my relief, before dessert, and we saw her no more that evening.

'"Unfit for society"? Most assuredly she was. I remembered her brother's words spoken ten months before, and concluded that nothing had occurred, since then to qualify his verdict. A most disagreeable person; unless, perhaps—

'It came to me all at once: was she connected with the mystery, or the mystery with her? A ghost seer, perhaps – neurotic – a victim to hallucinations? Well, Howick had not spoken so far, and it was no good speculating. I turned to the pious discussion of the '47.

'After dinner we went into the gardens where, the night being hot and still, we lingered until the stars came out. During the whole time Howick spoke no word of our mission; but, about the hour the household turned in, he took us back to the hall – a spacious, panelled lounge between the towers – where we settled for a pipe and nightcap. And there silence, like a ghostly overture to the impending, entered our brains and we sat, as it were, listening to it.

'Presently Howick got up. The strained look on his face was succeeded all at once by a sort of sombre light, odd and revealing. All sound in the house had long since ceased.

'"I want you to come with me," he said quietly.

'We rose at once; and he went before, but a few paces, and opened a door.

'"Yes, here," he said, in answer to a look of J.B.'s, "quite close, quite domestic; no bogey of rat-infested corridors or tumble-down attics – no bogey at all, perhaps. It lies under the east tower, this room. When we first came here I *thought* to make it my study."

'He seemed to me then, and always, like a man whose strait concepts of decency had suffered some startling offence, as it might be with one into whose perfectly planned tenement had crept the insidious poison of sewer-gas. Sliding his hand along the wall, he switched on the electric light (Haggarts had its own power station), and the room leapt into being. We entered, I leading a little. You must remember I was by then a hardened witchfinder, and inured to atmospheres concocted of the imagination.

'It was not a large room, and it was quite comfortable. There was a heavily clothed table in the middle, a few brass-nailed, leather-backed and seated Jacobean chairs, a high white Adams mantelpiece surmounted by a portrait, a full Chippendale bookcase to either side of it, and on the walls three or four pictures, including a second portrait, of a woman, half-length in an oval frame, which hung opposite the other.

'"Miss Howick, I see," I murmured, turning with a nod to our host. He heard me, as his eyes denoted: but he gave no answer. And then the portrait over the mantelpiece drew my attention. It was in a very poor style of art; yet somehow, one felt, crudely truthful in an amateurish way. There is a class of peripatetic painters, a sort of pedlars in portraiture among country folk, which, having a gift for likenesses, often succeeds photographically in delineating what a higher art inclines to idealise – the obvious in character. Such a one, I concluded, had worked here, painting just what he saw, and only too faithfully. For the obvious was not pleasant – a dark, pitiless face, with a brutal underlip and challenging green eyes, that seemed for ever fixed on the face on the wall opposite. It was that of a middle-aged man, lean and thin-haired, and must have dated, by the cut of its black, brass-buttoned coat, from the late Georgian era.

'I turned again questioningly to Howick. This time he enlightened me. "Roger Howick," he said, "my great-uncle. It is said he painted that himself, looking in the glass. He had a small gift. Most of the pictures in this room are by him."

'Instinctively I glanced once more towards the oval frame, and thought: "Most – but not that one." Unmistakably it was a portrait of our host's sister – the odd complexion, the sullen, fixed expression, the very dress and coiffure, they were all the same. I wondered how the living subject could endure the thought of that day-long, night-long stare focused for ever on her painted presentment.

'And then silence ensued. We were all in the room, and not a word was spoken. I don't know how long it lasted; but suddenly Lamont addressed me, in a quick, sharp voice:

'"What's the matter, Penn-Howard?"

'The shock of the question took me like a blow out of sleep. I answered at once: "Something's shut up here. Why don't you let it out?"

Howick pushed us from the room, and closed the door. "That's it," he said, and that was all. I felt dazed and amazed. I wanted to explain, to protest. A most extraordinary sensation like suppressed tears kept me dumb. I felt humiliated to a degree, and inclined to ease all my conflict of emotions in hysterical laughter. Curse the thing now! It makes me go hot to think of it.

'Howick showed me up to my bedroom. "We'll talk of it tomorrow," he said, and he left me. I was glad to be alone, to get, after a few moments, resolute command of myself. I had a good night after all, and awoke, refreshed and sane, in the clear morning.

'I learned, when I came downstairs, that J.B. and our host were gone out together for an early stroll in the cool. Pending their return, I came to a resolution. I would go and face the room alone, in the bright daylight. Both my pride and my principles were at stake, and I owed the effort to myself. There was nothing to prevent me. I found the door unlocked, and I went in.

'There was some sunlight in the room, penetrating through a thickish shrubbery outside the two windows. I thought the place peculiarly quiet, with an atmosphere of suspense in it which suggested the inaudible whisperings of some infernal inquisition. Nothing was watching me: the green eyes of the man were fixed eternally on the face opposite; and yet I was being watched by everything. It was indescribable, maddening. Determined not to succumb to what I still insisted to myself was a mere trick of the nerves, I walked manfully up to the oval portrait to examine it at close hand. A name and date near the lower margin caught my eye – *T. Lawrence, 1828*. I fairly gasped, reading it. A "Lawrence", and of that remoteness? Then it was not our host's sister! I turned sharply, hearing light breathing – and there she was behind me.

'"What are you doing here?" she said, in a small, cold voice. "Don't you know it is my room?"

'How can I convey the impression she made upon me by daylight? I can think only of one fantastic image to describe her complexion – the hands of a young laundress, puffed and mottled and mealily wrinkled after many hours work at the tub. So in this face was somehow spoilt and slandered youth, subdued, like the dyer's hand, to "what it worked in". And yet it was the face of the portrait, even to the dusty gold of the hair.

'I made some lame apology. She stamped her foot to end it and dismiss me. But as I passed her to go, she spoke again: "*You* will never find it. It is only faith that can move such mountains."

'I encountered J.B. in the morning-room, and we breakfasted alone together. Howick did not appear – purposely, I think. I felt somehow depressed and uneasy, but resolved to hold fast to myself without too many words. Once I enlightened Lamont: "That portrait," I said, "is not Howick's sister."

J.B. lifted his eyebrows. "O!" said he, "you have been paying it a morning visit, have you? No, it is a portrait of Maud Howick, daughter to Roger, the man who hangs opposite her." It was my turn to stare. "Howick has been giving you his family history?" I asked. J.B. did not answer for a minute; then he said: "I hope you won't take it in bad part, Penn-Howard; but – yes, he has been talking to me. I know, I think, all there is to know." I had some right to be offended; and he admitted it. "Howick *would* put it to me," he said. "He was struck, it seemed, by something I said that night at Lady Caroon's; and he thinks you at heart a polite sceptic." "Well," I said, "have *you* solved the mystery, whatever it is?" He answered no, but that he had a theory; and asked me if I had formed any. "Not a ghost of one," I replied; "and so Howick was certainly right in confiding first in you – first and last, indeed, if I am to be kept in the dark." "On the contrary," said J.B.; "I am going to repeat every word of Howick's story to you – only in a quiet place."

'We found one presently, out in the fields in the shadow of a ruined byre. It stood up bare and lonely, like a tattered baldachin, and far away under the stoop of its roof we could see the walls of the moathouse rising lean and brown into a cloudless sky. Lamont began his narration with a question: "How old would you suppose this Miss Ruth Howick, the sister, to be?" I was about to answer promptly, recalled my perplexity, and hesitated. "Tell me, without more ado," I responded. "Nineteen," he said, and shut his lips like a trap. Something caught at me, and I at myself. "Go on," I said; "anything after that." And J.B. responded, speaking in his abrupt, incisive way:

'"This James Howick came into his own here some year and a half ago. There were only himself and his sister – to whom he was and is devoted – the sole survivors of a once considerable family. Their father, Gilbert Howick – son of Paul, who was younger brother to the Roger of the portrait – married one Margaret (a beautiful ward of Paul's, and brought up by him as a member of his own family) about whose origin attached some mystery, which was only made clear to her husband on the occasion of their marriage. Margaret, in brief, was then revealed to Gilbert for his own first cousin once removed, being the natural daughter of his cousin Maud, one of the two children of Roger. I know nothing about the liaison which necessitated this explanation, nor do we need to know. Its results are what concern us. Roger, it is certain, took his daughter's dereliction in a truly devilish spirit. He was an evil, dark man, it was said, pledged to the world and its pride, and once a notorious liver. There is none so extreme in fanaticism as a convert from irreligion; none so damnably righteous as a rake reformed. Having committed the fruits of her sin to the merciful custody of his younger brother – a very different soul, of a humane and pious disposition – Roger turned his attention to the moral and physical ruin of the sinner. He swore that she should forfeit the youth she had abused; and he was as good as his word. No one knows how it happened; no one knows what passed in that dark and haunted house. But Maud grew old in youth. She had been spoiled and petted for her beauty; now the spirit broke in her, and she seemed to shrink and disappear behind the wrinkled, crumbling veil of what had been – like a snake, Penn-Howard, that struggles and cannot cast its dead skin. She grew old in youth. That portrait of her was painted when she was nineteen."

'I cried out. "It was impossible!" "It would seem so," said Lamont. "By what infernal arts he held her to his will – holds her now – it is sickening to conjecture." I turned to look at him. "Holds her now!" I repeated. "Then you mean—" "Yes," he said; "it is imprisoned youth that is for ever trying to escape, to emerge, like the snake, from its dead self. That is the secret of the room. At least, such is my theory."

'I sat as in a dream, awed by, yet struggling to reject, a conclusion so fantastic. "Well, grant your theory," I said at length, with a deep breath; "how does it affect this woman – or girl – this Ruth?"

'"Think," said Lamont. "She is actually that erring child's granddaughter. It seems wonderfully pitiful to me. Her own mother died in that house, during a visit, in giving birth to her. At the time, the son, Roger's son, was master of Haggarts. He was a poor-witted creature, Howick tells me; but he lived, as the imbecile often will, to a ripe old age. Ruth was born prematurely. Her mother, it was said, fell under the cursed influence of the place, and withered in her prime. Maud herself, according to the story, had already died in that very room – was found dead there, little more than a child still in years, a poor, worn ghost of womanhood in seeming. Since then, the room has always had an evil reputation – with what justice Howick never knew or regarded, until the death of his uncle put him, a year and a half ago, in possession of the place."

'"But this Ruth—"

'"It came upon her, it seems, gradually at first, then more rapidly. She lost her health and vivacity; she was for ever haunting the room. When we first met Howick, she was already horribly changed. Ten months have passed since then. He has tried to hide it from the world; has made practically a hermit of himself. The servants of that date have been changed for others, and changed again. She feels, it must be supposed, what we felt – a ceaseless anguish to release something – nothing – a mere pent shadow of horror. And more than that: the sin of the mother is being visited on the child of the child – and through the same diabolical agency." Lamont paused a moment, staring before him, and knotting his fingers together till they cracked. "Penn-Howard," he said, "I believe – I do believe, on my soul, that the secret, whatever it is, lies at the hands of that devil portrait."

'"Then why, in God's name, not remove and burn the thing?"

'"He has offered to. It had a dreadful effect upon her. She cried that so the clue would be lost for ever. And so it affects her to be excluded from the room. He has had to give it all up as hopeless."

'He rose, and I rose with him, not in truth convinced, but oddly agitated.

'"Well," I said, "what do you propose doing?"

'He seemed deep in thought, and did not answer me. At the door we parted. Entering alone, I met Howick in the hall. He looked at me searchingly in his lank, haggard way, then suddenly took my hand. "You know?" he said. "He has told you? Mr Penn-Howard, she was such a bright and pretty child." I saw tears in his eyes, and understood him better from that moment.

'Lamont was absent all day, and returned late from a prolonged tramp over the hills. The poignant subject was tacitly shelved that night, and we went to bed early.

'The next morning, after breakfast, J.B. turned upon our host. "I want," he said, "that room to myself, possibly for the whole morning, possibly for longer. Can you secure it to me?" Howick nodded. I could detect in his eyes some faint reflection of the strong spirit which faced him. Somehow one never despairs in J.B.'s presence. "I will say you are looking for it," he said. "She will not disturb you then." "There is a closet," said Lamont, "in my bedroom which will do very well for a dark-room."

'He disappeared soon after with his camera. It was his business, and I seldom disturbed him at it. We left him alone, and tried to forget him, though I could see all the morning that Howick was in a state of painful nervous tension. Not till after lunch did we hear or see anything of my colleague, and then he came in, descending from his improvised dark-room. He held a negative in his hand, and he shut the door behind him like a man who had something to reveal. "Mr Howick," he said, straight out and at once, "I am going to ask you to let me destroy that portrait of your great-uncle."

'The words took us like a smack; and, as we stood gaping, J.B. held out his negative. "Look at this," he said, and beckoning us to the window, let the light slant upon the thing so as to disclose its subject. "The secret stands revealed, does it not?" said he, quiet and low. "A long, a very long exposure, and the devil is betrayed. O, a wonderful detective is the camera."

'I heard Howick breathing fast over my shoulder. For myself, I was as much perplexed as astonished. "It is the portrait," I muttered, "and yet it is not. There is the ghost of something revealing itself through it." "Exactly," said J.B. drily – and went and put the negative behind the clock on the mantelpiece. "Well, shall we do it?" he asked, turning to our host. Howick's face was ghastly. He could hardly get out the words, "In God's name, do what you will! Better to dare and end it all than live on like this." J.B. stood looking at him earnestly. "No," he said. "You go to *her*. Penn-Howard and I will manage the business."

'We left him, and went to the room and locked ourselves in. I confess my blood was tingling. So shut in with it, the unspeakable atmosphere of that place seemed to intensify to a degree quite infernal. I seemed to realise in it a battle of two wills, Lamont's and another's. My friend's face was a little pale; but the set of its every feature spoke of an inexorable purpose. As we handled the portrait to lower it, it fell heavily and unaccountably forward, an edge of the massive frame just missing J.B.'s skull by an inch. "That miscarriage does for *you*, my friend," he said, showing his teeth a little, like a dog. Portrait and frame lay apart on the floor; the shock had disunited them. Lamont knelt, and went over the former unflinchingly. The green eyes, caught from their age-long inquisition of the face on the wall opposite, seemed to glare up into his in hate and fury. "Get out your knife," I cried irresistibly, "and slash the cursed thing to pieces." "No," he answered; "that is not at all my purpose."

'What was his purpose? I knew in a moment. He fetched out his knife indeed, and, hunting over the surface of the thing, found a blister in the paint, cut into it, seized an edge between thumb and finger, and, flaying away a long strip, uttered a loud, jubilant exclamation. "Look at this, Penn-Howard." I bent over

– and then I understood in a flash. It was but a strip exposed; but it was like a chink of dazzling daylight let through. There was another portrait underneath.

'Artists tell me that when one oil-painting is superimposed on another within a few years of the production of the first, only exceptional circumstances can render their successful separation possible. I know nothing about the technical difficulties; I know only that in this case we were able to remove the overlying skin, strip by strip, almost without a hitch, until the whole of the upper portrait lay in flakes of rubbish upon the floor – to be delivered within a few minutes to consuming fire. And the thing revealed! I cannot describe the beauty of that vision, bursting into flower out of its age-long cimmerian darkness. It was the personification of youth – a young girl (she might have been sixteen), laughing and lovely, the most wilful, bewitching face you could imagine – Maud Howick.'

Once more Penn-Howard fell silent. The room by now was dark; his figure was indistinguishable, and his voice, when he spoke again, seemed a shadow borne out of the shadows:

'While we gazed, fascinated, there came a knock on the door. It was Howick. His face was transfigured – his eyes glowed. "She has fallen asleep," he said; "and that is not all. My God, what has happened?" We took him in and showed him the portrait. He broke down before it. "The little grandmother!" he said, "the poor, erring child! And it was of that, and by that damnable method, that that fiend incarnate robbed her! To imprison her youth within his wicked soul, drawn by him out of the mirror to stand for ever at sentry over her lest she escape. And she pined and withered in that hideous bondage, until he could show her, in that other, what his hate had wrought of her. But she is free at last – her soul is free to fly for ever this dark house of its captivity."

'J.B. looked at him searchingly. "And your sister?" he said. Howick did not answer; but he beckoned us to follow him, and he led us into the drawing-room where she lay. Fast in dreamless slumber as the sleeping beauty. But the change! God in heaven; she was already a child again!'

The speaker halted for the last time. It was minutes before he took up the tale, in a constrained and hesitating way:

'I saw all this, I tell you – saw it with these eyes. We stayed there yet a week longer; and I left her in the end a radiant, laughing child, a joyous, captivating little soul, who remembered, or seemed to remember, nothing of the fearful months preceding. And yet, now I am away, I doubt. It is the curse of my disposition. What, for instance, if one were to yield her one's soul and discover, too late, that one had succumbed to some unreal glamour, to the arts of a veritable and most feminine Lamia. I believe it is not so; I know it is not so – and yet, the incredible—'

His voice died out. I saw how it was, and answered, I am afraid, brutally:

'You aren't really in love with her, of course. That is as clear as print.'

He rose at once. 'That decides it,' he said. 'I shall go back and ask her to be my wife.'

But he did not do so. Two days later I met him in the street. His manner was quite breezy and insouciant. 'O, by the by!' he said, in a break of our conversation, 'did I tell you that I had heard from J.B.? He and Miss Howick are engaged.'

THE STRENGTH OF THE ROPE

Si finis bonus est, totum bonum erit.

There were notices, of varying dates, posted in prominent places about the cliffs to warn the public not to go near them – unless, indeed, it were to read the notices themselves, which were printed in a very unobtrusive type. Of late, however, this Dogberrian *caveat* had been supplemented by a statement in the local gazette that the cliffs, owing to the recent rains succeeding prolonged frost, were in so ill a constitution that to approach them at all, even to decipher the warnings not to, was – well, to take your life out of the municipal into your own hands.

Now, had the Regius Professor a bee in his bonnet? Absurd. He knew the risks of foolhardiness as well as any pickpocket could have told him. Yet, neither general nor particular caution availed to abate his determination to examine, as soon as we had lunched, the interior formation of a cave or two, out of those black and innumerable, with which the undercliff was punctured like a warren.

I did not remonstrate, after having once discovered, folded down under his nose on the table, the printed admonition, and heard the little dry, professorial click of tongue on palate which was wont to dismiss, declining discussion of it, any idle or superfluous proposition. I knew my man – or

automaton. He inclined to the Providence of the unimagina-
tive; his only fetish was science. He was one of those who,
if unfortunately buried alive, would turn what opportunity
remained to them to a study of geological deposits. My
'nerves', when we were on a jaunt (fond word!) together,
were always a subject of sardonic amusement with him.

Now, utterly unmoved by the prospect before him, he ate
an enormous lunch (confiding it, incidentally, to an unerring
digestion), rose, brushed some crumbs out of his beard, and
said, 'Well, shall we be off?'

In twenty minutes we had reached the caves. They lay in
a very secluded little bay – just a crescent of sombre sand,
littered along all its inner edge with debris from the towering
cliffs which contained it.

'Are you coming with me?' said the Regius Professor.

Judged by his anxious eyes, the question might have been
an invitation, almost a shamefaced entreaty. But the anxiety,
never more than apparent, was delusive product of the
preposterous magnifying-glasses which he wore. Did he ever
remove those glasses, one was startled to discover, in the
seemingly aghast orbs which they misinterpreted, quite mean
little attic windows to an unemotional soul.

'Not by any means,' I said. 'I will sit here, and think out
your epitaph.'

He stared at me a moment with a puzzled expression,
grinned slightly, turned, strode off towards the cliffs, and
disappeared, without a moment's hesitation, into the first
accessible burrow. I was moved on the instant to observe
that it was the most sinister-looking of them all. The tilted
stratification, under which it yawned oblique, seemed on the
very poise to close down upon it.

Now I set to pacing to and fro, essaying a sort of mechanical
preoccupation in default of the philosophy I lacked. I was
really in a state of clammy anxiety about the Professor. I
poked in stony pools for little crabs, as if his life depended
on my success. I made it a point of honour with myself not

to leave off until I had found one. I tried, like a very amateur pickpocket, to abstract my mind from the atmosphere which contained it, only to find that I had brought mind and atmosphere away together. I bent down, with my back to the sea, and looking between my legs sought to regard life from a new point of view. Yet, even in that position, my eyes and ears were conscious, only in less degree, of the spectres which were always moving and rustling in the melancholy little bay.

Tekel upharsin. The hand never left off writing upon the rocks, nor the dust of its scoring to fall and whisper. That came away in flakes, or slid down in tiny avalanches – here, there, in so many places at once, that the whole face of the cliffs seemed to crawl like a maggoty cheese. The sound was like a vast conspiracy of voices – busy, ominous – aloft on the seats of an amphitheatre. They were talking of the Regius Professor, and his consideration in making them a Roman holiday.

Here, on no warrant but that of my senses, I knew the gazette's warning to be something more than justified. It made no difference that my nerves were at the stretch. One could not hear a silence thus sown with grain of horror, and believe it barren of significance. Then, all in a moment, as it seemed to me, the resolution was taken, the voices hushed, and the whole bay poised on tiptoe of a suspense which preluded something terrific.

I stood staring at the black mouth which had engulfed the Regius Professor. I felt that a disaster was imminent; but to rush to warn him would be to embarrass the issues of his Providence – that only. For the instant a fierce resentment of his foolhardiness fired me – and was as immediately gone. I turned sick and half blind. I thought I saw the rock-face shrug and wrinkle; a blot of gall was expelled from it – and the blot was the Professor himself issued forth, and coming composedly towards me.

As he advanced, I turned my back on him. By the time he reached me I had made some small success of a struggle for self-mastery.

'Well,' he said. 'I left myself none too much of a margin, did I?'

With an effort I faced about again. The base of the cliff was yet scarred with holes, many and irregular; but now some of those which had stared at me like dilated eyes were, I could have sworn it, over-lidded – the eyes of drowsing reptiles. *And the Professor's particular cave was gone.*

I gave quite an absurd little giggle. This man was soulless – a monstrosity.

'Look here,' he said, conning my face with a certain concern, 'it's no good tormenting yourself with what might have happened. Here I am, you know. Supposing we go and sit down yonder, against that drift, till you're better.'

He led the way, and, dropping upon the sand, lolled easily, talking to himself, by way of me, for some minutes. It was the kindest thing he could have done. His confident voice made scorn of the never-ceasing rustling and falling sounds to our rear. The gulls skated before my eyes, drawing wide arcs and figures of freedom in the air. Presently I topped the crisis, and drew a deep breath.

'Tell me,' I said – 'have you ever in all your life known fear?'

The Regius Professor sat to consider.

'Well,' he answered presently, rubbing his chin, 'I was certainly once near losing hold of my will, if that's what you mean. Of course, if I *had* let go—'

'But you didn't.'

'No,' he said thoughtfully. 'No – luckily.'

'You're not taking credit for it?'

'Credit!' he exclaimed, surprised. 'Why should I take credit for my freedom from a constitutional infirmity? In one way, indeed, I am only regretful that I am debarred that side of self-analysis.'

I could laugh lovelily, for the first time.

'Well,' I said, 'will you tell me the story?'

'I never considered it in the light of a story,' answered the

Regius Professor. 'But, if it will amuse and distract you, I will make it one with pleasure. My memory of it, as an only experience in that direction, is quite vivid, I think I may say—' and he settled his spectacles, and began:

'It was during the period of my first appointment as Science Demonstrator to the Park Lane Polytechnic, a post which my little pamphlet on the Reef-building *Serpulæ* was instrumental in procuring me. I was a young man at the time, with a wide field of interests, but with few friends to help me in exploring it. My holidays I generally devoted to long, lonely tramps, knapsack on back, about the country.

'It was on one of these occasions that you must picture me entered into a solitary valley among the Shropshire hills. The season was winter; it was bitterly cold, and the prospect was of the dreariest. The interesting conformations of the land – the bone-structure, as I might say – were blunted under a thick pelt of snow, which made walking a labour. One never recognises under such conditions the extent of one's efforts, as inequalities of ground are without the contrast of surroundings to emphasise them, and one may be conscious of the strain of a gradient, and not know if it is of one foot in fifty or in five hundred.

'The scene was desolate to a degree; houseless, almost treeless – just white wastes and leaden sky, and the eternal fusing of the two in an indefinite horizon. I was wondering, without feeling actually dispirited, how long it was to last, when, turning the shoulder of a hill which had seemed to hump itself in my path, I came straight upon a tiny hamlet scattered over a widish area. There were some cottages, and a slated school building; and, showing above a lower hump a quarter of a mile beyond, the roofs and tall chimney of a factory.

'It was a stark little oasis, sure enough – the most grudging of moral respites from depression. Only from one place, it seemed, broke a green shoot. Not a moving figure was abroad; not a face looked from a window. Deathlily the little stony buildings stood apart from one another, incurious, sullen, and self-contained.

'There was, however, the green shoot; and the stock from which it proceeded was the school building. That in itself was unlovely enough – a bleak little stone box in an arid enclosure. It looked hunched and grey with cold; and the sooty line of thaw at the foot of its wall only underscored its frostiness. But as if that one green shoot were the earnest of life lingering within, there suddenly broke through its walls the voices of young children singing; and, in the sound, the atmosphere of petrifaction lifted somewhat.

'Yes? What is it? Does anything amuse you? I am glad you are so far recovered, at least. Well—

'I like, I must confess, neither children nor music. At the same time, I am free to admit that those young voices, though they dismissed me promptly on my way, dismissed me pleased, and to a certain degree, as it were, reinvigorated. I passed through that little frigid camp of outer silence, and swung down the road towards the factory. As I advanced towards what I should have thought to be the one busy nucleus of an isolated colony, the aspect of desolation intensified to my surprise, rather than diminished. But I soon saw the reason for this. The great forge in the hills was nothing but a wrecked and abandoned ruin, its fires long quenched, its ribs long laid bare. Seeing which, it only appeared to me a strange thing that any of the human part of its affairs should yet cling to its neighbourhood; and stranger still I thought it when I came to learn, as I did by-and-by, that its devastation was at that date an ancient story.

'What a squalid carcass it did look, to be sure; gaunt, and unclean, and ravaged by fire from crown to basement. The great flue of it stood up alone, a blackened monument to its black memory.

'Approaching and entering, I saw some writhed and tortured guts of machinery, relics of its old vital organs, fallen, withered, from its ribs. The floor, clammy to the tread, was littered with tumbled masonry; the sheet iron of the roof was shattered in a hundred places under the merciless bombardment of the weather; and, here and there, a scale of this was corroded so thin that it fluttered and buzzed in the draught like a ventilator. Bats of grimy cobweb hung from the beams; and the dead breath of all the dead place was acrid with cold soot.

'It was all ugly and sordid enough, in truth, and I had no reason to be exacting in my inspection of it. Turning, in a vaulting silence, I was about to make my way out, when my attention was drawn to the black opening of what looked like a shed or annex to the main factory. Something, some shaft or plant, revealing itself from the dim obscurity of this place, attracted my curiosity. I walked thither, and, with all due precaution because of the littered ground, entered. I was some moments in adapting my vision to the gloom, and then I discovered that I was in the mill well-house. It was a little deadlocked chamber, its details only partly decipherable in the reflected light which came in by the doorway. The well itself was sunk in the very middle of the floor, and the projecting wall of it rose scarce higher than my knees. The windlass, pivoted in a massive yoke, crossed the twilight at a height a little above my own: and I could easily understand, by the apparent diameter of its barrel, that the well was of a considerable depth.

'Now, as my eyes grew a little accustomed to the obscurity, I could see how a tooth of fire had cut even into this fastness. For the rope, which was fully reeled up upon the windlass, was scorched to one side, as though some exploded fragment of wood or brickwork had alighted there. It was an insignificant fact in itself, but my chance observation of it has its importance in the context; as has also the fact that the bight of the rope (from which the bucket had been removed), hung down a yard or so below the big drum.

'You have always considered me a sapient, or at least a rational creature, have you not? Well, listen to this. Bending over to plumb with my eyes the depth of the pit (an absurdity, to begin with, in that vortex of gloom), I caught with my left hand (wisdom number two) at the hanging end of rope in order to steady myself. On the instant the barrel made one swift revolution, and stuck. The movement, however, had thrown me forward and down, so that my head and shoulders, hanging over, and actually into, the well, pulled me, without possibility of recovery, from my centre of gravity. With a convulsive wrench of my body, I succeeded in bringing my right hand to the support of my left. I was then secure of the rope; but the violence of the act dragged my feet and knees from their last desperate hold, and my legs came whipping helpless over the well-rim. The weight of them in falling near jerked me from my clutch – a bad shock, to begin with. But a worse was in store for me. For I perceived, in the next instant, that the rusty, long-disused windlass was beginning slowly to revolve, *and was letting me down into the abyss*.

'I broke out in a sweat, I confess – a mere diaphoresis of nature; a sort of lubricant to the jammed mechanism of the nerves. I don't think we are justified in attributing my first sensations to fear. I was exalted, rather – promoted to the analysis of a very exquisite, scarce mortal, problem. My will, as I hung by a hair over the abysm, was called upon to vindicate itself under an utmost stress of apprehension. I felt, ridiculous as it may appear, as if the surrounding dark were peopled with an invisible auditory, waiting, curious, to test the value of my philosophy.

'Here, then, were the practical problems I had to combat. The windlass, as I have said, revolved slowly, but it revolved persistently. If I would remain with my head above the well-rim – which, I freely admit, I had an unphilosophic desire to do – I must swarm as persistently up the rope. That was an eerie and airy sort of treadmill. To climb, and climb, and always climb, paying out the cord beneath me, that I might remain in one place! It was to repudiate gravitation, which I spurned from beneath my feet into the depths. But when, momentarily exhausted, I ventured to pause, some nightmare revolt against the sense of sinking which seized me, would always send me struggling and wriggling, like a drowning body, up to the surface again. Fortunately, I was slightly built and active; yet I knew that wind and muscle were bound sometime to give out in this swarming competition against death. I measured their chances against the length of the rope. There was a desperate coil yet unwound. Moreover, in proportion as I grew the feebler, grew the need for my greater activity. For there were already signs that the great groaning windlass was casting its rust of ages, and was beginning to turn quicker in its sockets. If it had only stuck, paused one minute in its eternal round, I might have set myself oscillating, gradually and cautiously, until I was able to seize with one hand, then another, upon the brick rim, which was otherwise beyond my reach. But now, did I cease climbing for an instant and attempt a frantic clutch at it, down I sank like a clock weight, my fingers trailed a yard in cold slime, and there I was at my mad swarming once more – the madder that I must now make up for lost ground.

'At last, faint with fatigue, I was driven to face an alternative resource, very disagreeable from the first in prospect. This was no less than to resign temporarily my possession of the upper, and sink to the under world; in other words, to let myself go with the rope, and, when it was all reeled out, to climb it again. To this course there were two objections: one, that I knew nothing of the depth of the water beneath me, or of how soon I should come to it; the other, that I was grown physically incapable of any further great effort in the way of climbing. My reluctance to forgo the useless solace of the upper twilight I dismiss as sentimental. But to drop into that sooty pit, and then, perhaps, to find myself unable to reascend it! to feel a gradual paralysis of heart and muscle committing me to a lingering and quite unspeakable death – that was an unnerving thought indeed!

'Nevertheless, I had actually resolved upon the venture, and was on the point of ceasing all effort, and permitting myself to sink, when – I thought of the burnt place in the rope.

'Do you grasp what that sudden thought meant to me? Death, sir, in any case; death, if, with benumbed and aching hands and blistered knees, I continued to work my air-mill; death, no earlier and no later, no less and no more certainly, if I ceased of the useless struggle and went down into the depths. So soon as the strain of my hanging should tell direct upon that scorched strand, that strand must part.

'Then, I think, I knew fear – fear as demoralising, perhaps, as it may be, short of the will-surrender. And, indeed, I'm not sure but that the will which survives fear may not be a worse last condition than fear itself, which, when exquisite, becomes oblivion. Consciousness *in extremis* has never seemed to me the desirable thing which some hold it.

'Still, if I suffered for retaining my will power, there is no doubt that its loss, on the flash of that deadly reflection, would have meant an immediate syncope of nerve and an instant downfall; whereas – well, anyhow, here I am.

'I was fast draining of all capacity for further effort. I climbed painfully, spasmodically; but still I climbed, half hoping I should die of the toll of it before I fell. Ever and again I would glance faintly up at the snarling, slowly-revolving barrel above me, and mark how death, as figured in that scorched strand, was approaching me nearer at every turn. It was only a few coils away, when suddenly I set to doing what, goodness knows, I should have done earlier. I screamed – screamed until the dead marrow must have crawled in the very bones of the place.

'Nothing human answered – not a voice, not the sound of a footfall. Only the echoes laughed and chattered like monkeys up in the broken roof of the factory. For the rest, my too-late outburst had but served to sap what little energy yet remained to me.

'The end was come. Looking up, I saw the burnt strand reeling round, a couple of turns away, to the test; and, with a final gulp of horror, I threw up the sponge, and sank.

'I had not descended a yard or two, when my feet touched something.'

The Regius Professor paused dramatically.

'Oh, go on!' I snapped.

'That something,' he said, 'yielded a little – settled – and there all at once was I, standing as firmly as if I were in a pulpit.

'For the moment, I assure you, I was so benumbed, physically and mentally, that I was conscious of nothing in myself but a small weak impatience at finding the awful ecstasy of my descent checked. Then reason returned, like blood to the veins of a person half drowned; and I had never before realised that reason could make a man ache so.

'With the cessation of my strain upon it, the windlass had ceased to revolve. Now, with a sudden desperation, I was tugging at the rope once more – pulling it down hand over hand. At the fifth haul there came a little quick report, and I staggered and near fell. The rope had snapped; and the upper slack of it came whipping down upon my shoulders.

'I rose, dimly aware of what had happened. I was standing on the piled-up fathoms of rope which I had paid out beneath me. Above, though still beyond my effective winning, glimmered the moonlike disc of light which was the well mouth. I dared not, uncertain of the nature of my tenure, risk a spring for it. But, very cautiously, I found the end of the rope that had come away, made a bend in it well clear of the injured part, and, after many vain attempts, slung it clean over the yoke above, coaxed down the slack, spliced it to the other, and so made myself a fixed ladder to climb by. Up this, after a short interval for rest, I swarmed, set myself swinging, grasped the brick rim, first with one hand, then with both, and in another instant had flung myself upon the ground prostrate, and for the moment quite prostrated. Then presently I got up, struck some matches, and investigated.'

The Regius Professor stopped, laughing a little over the memory.

'*Do* go on!' I said.

'Why,' he responded, chuckling, 'generations of school children had been pitching litter into that well, until it was filled up to within a couple yards of the top – just that. The rope, heaping up under me, did the rest. It was a testimony to the limited resources of the valley. What the little natives of today do with their odd time, goodness knows. But it was comical, wasn't it?'

'Oh, most!' said I. 'And particularly from the point of view of the children's return to you for your dislike of them.'

'Well, as to that,' said the Regius Professor, rather shame-facedly, 'I wasn't beyond acknowledging a certain indebtedness.'

'Acknowledging? How?'

'Why, I happened to have in my knapsack one of my pamphlets on the Reef-building *Serpulæ*; so I went back to the school, and gave it to the mistress to include in her curriculum.'

THE WHITE HARE

You know the Mendips or you don't know them – their
beauty, their savagery, their wide-flung loneliness sweeping
miles down into the haunted valley called the moors, where,
in the moonlit nights, strange craft come floating from
Glastonbury on mystic waters long since sunk and lost.
There may be trippers in this place and that to vulgarise
the brooding hours, and if you see with their eyes you see
nothing; but they are local, after all – mere profaners of
places already profaned to show. One may leave them
behind, to resettle like flies disturbed from carrion, and,
entering into the fastnesses of the hills, forget them in a
moment.

The place belongs to legend and the past; it murmurs with
inarticulate voices, drums and rustles under visionary footfalls. Once, long ago there stood a little ruined church,
difficult to strangers to find, among the high, far thickets,
and there the dead lay tumbled and neglected, because the
building had been desecrated of old, and never since recon-
secrated; so that it was avoided by the people, and the fence
surrounding the graveyard rotted piecemeal and grew choked
with fungus and brier.

There was an evening when young Modred, abroad with
his gun, found himself benighted, a little cold, but curious,
near that thicket – and suddenly a white hare slipped from
the palings, and ran before him like a jumping snowball. He

fired on the instant, and could have sworn his unerring eye had not failed him; but the hare ran on and melted, verily like snow, into the glooms. He was startled, awed, but not to be browbeaten by puss or devil. Another evening he sought the place, sighted his quarry, and again failed inexplicably to bring her down. Then he remembered – white hare, white witch – silver alone could prevail against the cursed thing. On the third evening therefore he loaded with a silver button from his coat, a keepsake from his maiden love, and, biding his time, let fly at the loping succuba. There was a scream like a woman's – and the hare sped on and vanished. But she was hit at last.

The next day Modred learned that his love was dead. She had taken down her father's gun, not knowing it was loaded, to clean, and by some means the charge had been exploded into her breast.

Hideous the tragedy; hideous the moral to be drawn from it. From that time the man went like a mad thing, his heart broken, his soul an alien from earth and heaven. That it should have been she, and her gift to him her death! But most he raved against the cynic God, who might have ordered things differently, but would have them thus and thus to make sport for himself.

And then the dead girl's mother came to die; but she could not die; and she screamed and stormed on life to let her go; but life held her still fast in her agony. Then one day she sent for Modred.

'Cut the cursed thing from my shoulder,' she said, 'and let me pass.'

'What thing?' he asked stupefied.

'Your silver button,' she said, 'that mauled, but could not end me. It has lain there ever since, keeping me from the churchyard and my friends the outlawed dead. I killed the innocent girl myself to mislead you, and I bore the pain of this, until now I cannot bear it. Cut it out.'

Her shoulder was bare, and the button stood under the

skin of it like a little blue plum. Modred, with a howl of fury, took it in his fingers and tore it away.

At that the woman screeched and fell, and out of the window leapt a white hare and vanished up the hill.

AN EDDY ON THE FLOOR

I had the pleasure of an invitation to one of those reunions or seances at the house, in a fashionable quarter, of my distant connection, Lady Barbara Grille, whereat it was my hostess's humour to gather together those many birds of alien feather and incongruous habit that will flock from the hedgerows to the least little flattering crumb of attention. And scarce one of them but thinks the simple feast is spread for him alone. And with so cheap a bait may a title lure.

That reference to so charming a personality should be in this place is a digression. She affects my narrative only inasmuch as I happened to meet at her house a gentleman who for a time exerted a considerable influence over my fortunes.

The next morning after the séance, my landlady entered with a card, which she presented to my consideration:

MAJOR JAMES SHRIKE,
H.M. PRISON, D—

All astonishment, I bade my visitor up.

He entered briskly, fur-collared, hat in hand, and bowed as he stood on the threshold. He was a very short man – snub-nosed; rusty-whiskered; indubitably and unimpressively a cockney in appearance. He might have walked out of a Cruikshank etching.

I was beginning, 'May I inquire—' when the other took

me up with a vehement frankness that I found engaging at once.

'This is a great intrusion. Will you pardon me? I heard some remarks of yours last night that deeply interested me. I obtained your name and address from our hostess, and took the liberty of—'

'Oh! pray be seated. Say no more. My kinswoman's introduction is all-sufficient. I am happy in having caught your attention in so motley a crowd.'

'She doesn't – forgive the impertinence – take herself seriously enough.'

'Lady Barbara? Then you've found her out?'

'Ah! – you're not offended?'

'Not in the least.'

'Good. It was a motley assemblage, as you say. Yet I'm inclined to think I found my pearl in the oyster. I'm afraid I interrupted – eh?'

'No, no, not at all. Only some idle scribbling. I'd finished.'

'You are a poet?'

'Only a lunatic. I haven't taken my degree.'

'Ah! it's a noble gift – the gift of song; precious through its rarity.'

I caught a note of emotion in my visitor's voice, and glanced at him curiously.

'Surely,' I thought, 'that vulgar, ruddy little face is transfigured.'

'But,' said the stranger, coming to earth, 'I am lingering beside the mark. I must try to justify my solecism in manners by a straight reference to the object of my visit. That is, in the first instance, a matter of business.'

'Business!'

'I am a man with a purpose, seeking the hopefullest means to an end. Plainly: if I could procure you the post of resident doctor at D— gaol, would you be disposed to accept it?'

I looked my utter astonishment.

'I can affect no surprise at yours,' said the visitor. 'It is perfectly natural. Let me forestall some unnecessary expression of it. My offer seems unaccountable to you, seeing that we never met until last night. But I don't move entirely in the dark. I have ventured in the interval to inform myself as to the details of your career. I was entirely one with much of your expression of opinion as to the treatment of criminals, in which you controverted the crude and unpleasant scepticism of the lady you talked with. Combining the two, I come to the immediate conclusion that you are the man for my purpose.'

'You have dumbfounded me. I don't know what to answer. You have views, I know, as to prison treatment. Will you sketch them? Will you talk on, while I try to bring my scattered wits to a focus?'

'Certainly I will. Let me, in the first instance, recall to you a few words of your own. They ran somewhat in this fashion: Is not the man of practical genius the man who is most apt at solving the little problems of resourcefulness in life? Do you remember them?'

'Perhaps I do, in a cruder form.'

'They attracted me at once. It is upon such a postulate I base my practice. Their moral is this: To know the antidote the moment the snake bites. That is to have the intuition of divinity. We shall rise to it some day, no doubt, and climb the hither side of the new Olympus. Who knows? Over the crest the spirit of creation may be ours.'

I nodded, still at sea, and the other went on with a smile:

'I once knew a world-famous engineer with whom I used to breakfast occasionally. He had a patent egg-boiler on the table, with a little double-sided ladle underneath to hold the spirit. He complained that his egg was always undercooked. I said, "Why not reverse the ladle so as to bring the deeper cut uppermost?" He was charmed with my perspicacity. The solution had never occurred to him. You remember, too, no doubt, the story of Coleridge and the horse collar. We aim too much at great developments. If we cultivate resourcefulness, the rest will follow. Shall I state my system *in nuce*? It is to encourage this spirit of resourcefulness.'

'Surely the habitual criminal has it in a marked degree?'

'Yes; but abnormally developed in a single direction. His one object is to out-manoeuvre in a game of desperate and immoral chances. The tactical spirit in him has none of the higher ambition. It has felt itself in the degree only that stops at defiance.'

'That is perfectly true.'

'It is half self-conscious of an individuality that instinctively assumes the hopelessness of a recognition by duller intellects. Leaning to resentment through misguided vanity, it falls "all oblique". What is the cure for this? I answer, the teaching of a divine egotism. The subject must be led to a pure devotion to self. What he wishes to respect he must be taught to make beautiful and interesting. The policy of sacrifice to others has so long stunted his moral nature because it is an hypocritical policy. We are responsible to ourselves in the first instance; and to argue an eternal system of blind self-sacrifice is to undervalue the fine gift of individuality. In such he sees but an indefensible policy of force applied to the advantage of the community. He is told to be good – not that he may morally profit, but that others may not suffer inconvenience.'

I was beginning to grasp, through my confusion, a certain clue of meaning in my visitor's rapid utterance. The stranger spoke fluently, but in the dry, positive voice that characterises men of will.

'Pray go on,' I said; 'I am digesting in silence.'

'We must endeavour to lead him to respect of self by showing him what his mind is capable of. I argue on no sectarian, no religious grounds even. Is it possible to make a man's self his most precious possession? Anyhow, I work to that end. A doctor purges before building up with a tonic. I eliminate cant and hypocrisy, and then introduce self-respect. It isn't enough to employ a man's hands only. Initiation in some labour that should prove wholesome and remunerative is a redeeming factor, but it isn't all. His mind must work also, and awaken to its capacities. If it rusts, the body reverts to inhuman instincts.'

'May I ask how you—?'

'By intercourse – in my own person or through my officials. I wish to have only those about me who are willing to contribute to my designs, and with whom I can work in absolute harmony. All my officers are chosen to that end. No doubt a dash of constitutional sentimentalism gives colour to my theories. I get it from a human trait in me that circumstances have obliged me to put a hoarding round.'

'I begin to gather daylight.'

'Quite so. My patients are invited to exchange views with their guardians in a spirit of perfect friendliness; to solve little problems of practical moment; to acquire the pride of self-reliance. We have competitions, such as certain newspapers open to their readers, in a simpler form. I draw up the questions myself. The answers give me insight into the mental conditions of the competitors. Upon insight I proceed. I am fortunate in private means, and I am in a position to offer modest prizes to the winners. Whenever such a one is discharged, he finds awaiting him the tools most handy to his vocation. I bid him go forth in no pharisaical spirit, and invite him to communicate with me. I wish the shadow of the gaol to extend no further than the road whereon it lies. Henceforth, we are acquaintances with a common interest at heart. Isn't it monstrous that a state-fixed degree of misconduct should earn a man social ostracism? Parents are generally inclined to rule extra tenderness towards a child whose peccadilloes have brought him a whipping. For myself, I have no faith in police supervision. Give a culprit his term and have done with it. I find the majority who come back to me are ticket-of-leave men.

'Have I said enough? I offer you the reversion of the post. The present holder of it leaves in a month's time. Please to determine here and at once.'

'Very good. I have decided.'
'You will accept?'
'Yes.'

With my unexpected appointment as doctor to D— gaol, I seemed to have put on the seven-league boots of success. No doubt it was an extraordinary degree of good fortune, even to one who had looked forward with a broad view of confidence; yet, I think, perhaps on account of the very casual nature of my promotion, I never took the post entirely seriously.

At the same time I was fully bent on justifying my little cockney patron's choice by a resolute subscription to his theories of prison management.

Major James Shrike inspired me with a curious conceit of impertinent respect. In person the very embodiment of that insignificant vulgarity, without extenuating circumstances, which is the type in caricature of the ultimate cockney, he possessed a force of mind and an earnestness of purpose that absolutely redeemed him on close acquaintanceship. I found him all he had stated himself to be, and something more.

He had a noble object always in view – the employment of sane and humanitarian methods in the treatment of redeemable criminals, and he strove towards it with completely untiring devotion. He was of those who never insist beyond the limits of their own understanding, clear-sighted in discipline, frank in relaxation, an altruist in the larger sense.

His undaunted persistence, as I learned, received ample illustration some few years prior to my acquaintance with him, when – his system being experimental rather than mature – a devastating epidemic of typhoid in the prison had for the time stultified his efforts. He stuck to his post; but so virulent was the outbreak that the prison commissioners judged a complete evacuation of the building and overhauling of the drainage to be necessary. As a consequence, for some eighteen months – during thirteen of which the Governor and his household remained sole inmates of the solitary pile (so sluggishly do we redeem our condemned social bog-lands) – the 'system' stood still for lack of material to mould. At the end of over a year of stagnation, a contract was accepted and workmen put in, and another five months saw the prison reordered for practical purposes.

The interval of forced inactivity must have sorely tried the patience of the Governor. Practical theorists condemned to rust too often eat out their own hearts. Major Shrike never referred to this period, and, indeed, laboriously snubbed any allusion to it.

He was, I have a shrewd notion, something of an officially petted reformer. Anyhow, to his abolition of the insensate barbarism of crank and treadmill in favour of civilising methods no opposition was offered. Solitary confinement – a punishment outside all nature to a gregarious race – found no advocate in him. 'A man's own suffering mind,' he argued, 'must be, of all moral food, the most poisonous for him to feed on. Surround a scorpion with fire and he stings himself to death, they say. Throw a diseased soul entirely upon its own resources and moral suicide results.'

To sum up: his nature embodied humanity without sentimentalism, firmness without obstinacy, individuality without selfishness; his activity was boundless, his devotion to his system so real as to admit no utilitarian sophistries into his scheme of personal benevolence. Before I had been with him a week, I respected him as I had never respected man before.

One evening (it was during the second month of my appointment) we were sitting in his private study – a dark, comfortable room lined with books. It was an occasion on which a new characteristic of the man was offered to my inspection.

A prisoner of a somewhat unusual type had come in that day – a spiritualistic medium, convicted of imposture. To this person I casually referred.

'May I ask how you propose dealing with the newcomer?'

'On the familiar lines.'

'But, surely – here we have a man of superior education, of imagination even?'

'No, no, no! A hawker's opportuneness; that describes it. These fellows would make death itself a vulgarity.'

'You've no faith in their—'

'Not a tittle. Heaven forfend! A sheet and a turnip are poetry to their manifestations. It's as crude and sour soil for us to work on as any I know. We'll cart it wholesale.'

'I take you – excuse my saying so – for a supremely sceptical man.'

'As to what?'

'The supernatural.'

There was no answer during a considerable interval. Presently it came, with deliberate insistence:

'It is a principle with me to oppose bullying. We are here for a definite purpose – his duty plain to any man who *wills* to read it. There may be disembodied spirits who seek to distress or annoy where they can no longer control. If there are, mine, which is not yet divorced from its means to material action, declines to be influenced by any irresponsible whimsey, emanating from a place whose denizens appear to be actuated by a mere frivolous antagonism to all human order and progress.'

'But supposing you, a murderer, to be haunted by the presentment of your victim?'

'I will imagine that to be my case. Well, it makes no difference. My interest is with the great human system, in one of whose veins I am a circulating drop. It is my business to help to keep the system sound, to do my duty without fear or favour. If disease – say a fouled conscience – contaminates me, it is for me to throw off the incubus, not accept it, and transmit the poison. Whatever my lapses of nature, I owe it to the entire system to work for purity in my allotted sphere, and not to allow any microbe bugbear to ride me roughshod, to the detriment of my fellow drops.'

I laughed.

'It should be for you,' I said, 'to learn to shiver, like the boy in the fairy-tale.'

'I cannot,' he answered, with a peculiar quiet smile; 'and yet prisons, above all places, should be haunted.'

Very shortly after his arrival I was called to the cell of the medium, F—. He suffered, by his own statement, from severe pains in the head.

I found the man to be nervous, anaemic; his manner characterised by a sort of hysterical effrontery.

'Send me to the infirmary,' he begged. 'This isn't punishment, but torture.'

'What are your symptoms?'

'I see things; my case has no comparison with others. To a man of my super-sensitiveness close confinement is mere cruelty.'

I made a short examination. He was restless under my hands.

'You'll stay where you are,' I said.

He broke out into violent abuse, and I left him.

Later in the day I visited him again. He was then white and sullen; but under his mood I could read real excitement of some sort.

'Now, confess to me, my man,' I said, 'what do you see?'

He eyed me narrowly, with his lips a little shaky.

'Will you have me moved if I tell you?'

'I can give no promise till I know.'

He made up his mind after an interval of silence.

'There's something uncanny in my neighbourhood. Who's confined in the next cell – there, to the left?'

'To my knowledge it's empty.'

He shook his head incredulously.

'Very well,' I said, 'I don't mean to bandy words with you'; and I turned to go.

At that he came after me with a frightened choke.

'Doctor, your mission's a merciful one. I'm not trying to sauce you. For God's sake have me moved! I can see further than most, I tell you!'

The fellow's manner gave me pause. He was patently and beyond the pride of concealment terrified.

'What do you see?' I repeated stubbornly.

'It isn't that I see, but I know. The cell's *not* empty!'

I stared at him in considerable wonderment.

'I will make inquiries,' I said. 'You may take that for a promise. If the cell proves empty, you stop where you are.'

I noticed that he dropped his hands with a lost gesture as I left him. I was sufficiently moved to accost the warder who awaited me on the spot.

'Johnson,' I said, 'is that cell—'

'Empty, sir,' answered the man sharply and at once.

Before I could respond, F— came suddenly to the door, which I still held open.

'You lying cur!' he shouted. 'You damned lying cur!'

The warder thrust the man back with violence.

'Now you, 49,' he said, 'dry up, and none of your sauce!' and he banged to the door with a sounding slap, and turned to me with a lowering face. The prisoner inside yelped and stormed at the studded panels.

'That cell's empty, sir,' repeated Johnson.

'Will you, as a matter of conscience, let me convince myself? I promised the man.'

'No, I can't.'

'You can't?'

'No, sir.'

'This is a piece of stupid discourtesy. You can have no reason, of course?'

'I can't open it – that's all.'

'Oh, Johnson! Then I must go to the fountainhead.'

'Very well, sir.'

Quite baffled by the man's obstinacy, I said no more, but

walked off. If my anger was roused, my curiosity was piqued in proportion.

I had no opportunity of interviewing the Governor all day, but at night I visited him by invitation to play a game of piquet.

He was a man without 'incumbrances' – as a severe conservatism designates the *lares* of the cottage – and, at home, lived at his ease and indulged his amusements without comment.

I found him 'tasting' his books, with which the room was well lined, and drawing with relish at an excellent cigar in the intervals of the courses.

He nodded to me, and held out an open volume in his left hand.

'Listen to this fellow,' he said, tapping the page with his fingers:

The most tolerable sort of Revenge, is for those wrongs which there is no Law to remedy. But then, let a man take heed, the Revenge be such, as there is no law to punish. Else, a man's Enemy, is still before hand, and it is two for one. Some, when they take Revenge, are Desirous the party should know, whence it cometh. This is the more Generous. For the Delight seemeth to be, not so much in doing the Hurt, as in making the Party repent: But Base and Crafty Cowards, are like the Arrow that flyeth in the Dark. Cosmus, Duke of Florence, had a Desperate Saying against Perfidious or Neglecting Friends, as if these wrongs were unpardonable. You shall read (saith he) that we are commanded to forgive our Enemies: But you never read, that we are commanded to forgive our Friends.

'Is he not a rare fellow?'
'Who?' said I.

'Francis Bacon, who screwed his wit to his philosophy, like a hammer-head to its handle, and knocked a nail in at every blow. How many of our friends round about here would be picking oakum now if they had made a gospel of that quotation?'

'You mean they take no heed that the Law may punish for that for which it gives no remedy?'

'Precisely; and specifically as to revenge. The criminal, from the murderer to the petty pilferer, is actuated solely by the spirit of vengeance – vengeance blind and speechless – towards a system that forces him into a position quite outside his natural instincts.'

'As to that, we have left Nature in the thicket. It is hopeless hunting for her now.'

'We hear her breathing sometimes, my friend. Otherwise Her Majesty's prison locks would rust. But, I grant you, we have grown so unfamiliar with her that we call her simplest manifestations *super*natural nowadays.'

'That reminds me. I visited F— this afternoon. The man was in a queer way – not foxing, in my opinion. Hysteria, probably.'

'Oh! What was the matter with him?'

'The form it took was some absurd prejudice about the next cell – number 47. He swore it was not empty – was quite upset about it – said there was some infernal influence at work in his neighbourhood. Nerves, he finds, I suppose, may revenge themselves on one who has made a habit of playing tricks with them. To satisfy him, I asked Johnson to open the door of the next cell—'

'Well?'

'He refused.'

'It is closed by my orders.'

'That settles it, of course. The manner of Johnson's refusal was a bit uncivil, but—'

He had been looking at me intently all this time – so intently that I was conscious of a little embarrassment and confusion. His mouth was set like a dash between brackets, and his eyes glistened. Now his features relaxed, and he gave a short high neigh of a laugh.

'My dear fellow, you must make allowances for the rough old lurcher. He was a soldier. He is all cut and measured out to the regimental pattern. With him Major Shrike, like the king, can do no wrong. Did I ever tell you he served under me in India? He did; and, moreover, I saved his life there.'

'In an engagement?'

'Worse – from the bite of a snake. It was a mere question of will. I told him to wake and walk, and he did. They had thought him already in *rigor mortis*; and, as for him – well, his devotion to me since has been single to the last degree.'

'That's as it should be.'

'To be sure. And he's quite in my confidence. You must pass over the old beggar's churlishness.'

I laughed an assent. And then an odd thing happened. As I spoke, I had walked over to a bookcase on the opposite side of the room to that on which my host stood. Near this bookcase hung a mirror – an oblong affair, set in brass *repoussé* work – on the wall; and, happening to glance into it as I approached, I caught sight of the Major's reflection as he turned his face to follow my movement.

I say 'turned his face' – a formal description only. What met my startled gaze was an image of some nameless horror – of features grooved, and battered, and shapeless, as if they had been torn by a wild beast.

I gave a little indrawn gasp and turned about. There stood the Major, plainly himself, with a pleasant smile on his face.

'What's up?' said he.

He spoke abstractedly, pulling at his cigar; and I answered rudely, 'That's a damned bad looking-glass of yours!'

'I didn't know there was anything wrong with it,' he said, still abstracted and apart. And, indeed, when by sheer mental effort I forced myself to look again, there stood my companion as he stood in the room.

I gave a tremulous laugh, muttered something or nothing, and fell to examining the books in the case. But my fingers shook a trifle as I aimlessly pulled out one volume after another.

'Am *I* getting fanciful?' I thought – 'I whose business it is to give practical account of every bugbear of the nerves. Bah! My liver must be out of order. A speck of bile in one's eye may look a flying dragon.'

I dismissed the folly from my mind, and set myself resolutely to inspecting the books marshalled before me. Roving amongst them, I pulled out, entirely at random, a thin, worn duodecimo, that was thrust well back at a shelf end, as if it shrank from comparison with its prosperous and portly neighbours. Nothing but chance impelled me to the choice; and I don't know to this day what the ragged volume was about. It opened naturally at a marker that lay in it – a folded slip of paper, yellow with age; and glancing at this, a printed name caught my eye.

With some stir of curiosity, I spread the slip out. It was a title-page to a volume, of poems, presumably; and the author was James Shrike.

I uttered an exclamation, and turned, book in hand.

'An author!' I said. '*You* an author, Major Shrike!'

To my surprise, he snapped round upon me with something like a glare of fury on his face. This the more startled me as I believed I had reason to regard him as a man whose principles of conduct had long disciplined a temper that was naturally hasty enough.

Before I could speak to explain, he had come hurriedly across the room and had rudely snatched the paper out of my hand.

'How did this get—' he began; then in a moment came to himself, and apologised for his ill manners.

'I thought every scrap of the stuff had been destroyed,' he said, and tore the page into fragments. 'It is an ancient effusion, doctor – perhaps the greatest folly of my life; but it's something of a sore subject with me, and I shall be obliged if you'll not refer to it again.'

He courted my forgiveness so frankly that the matter passed without embarrassment; and we had our game and spent a genial evening together. But memory of the queer little scene stuck in my mind, and I could not forbear pondering it fitfully.

Surely here was a new side-light that played upon my friend and superior a little fantastically.

Conscious of a certain vague wonder in my mind, I was traversing the prison, lost in thought, after my sociable evening with the Governor, when the fact that dim light was issuing from the open door of cell number 49 brought me to myself and to a pause in the corridor outside.

Then I saw that something was wrong with the cell's inmate, and that my services were required.

The medium was struggling on the floor, in what looked like an epileptic fit, and Johnson and another warder were holding him from doing an injury to himself.

The younger man welcomed my appearance with relief.

'Heard him guggling,' he said, 'and thought as something were up. You come timely, sir.'

More assistance was procured, and I ordered the prisoner's removal to the infirmary. For a minute, before following him, I was left alone with Johnson.

'It came to a climax, then?' I said, looking the man steadily in the face.

'He may be subject to 'em, sir,' he replied evasively.

I walked deliberately up to the closed door of the adjoining cell, which was the last on that side of the corridor. Huddled against the massive end wall, and half embedded in it, as it seemed, it lay in a certain shadow, and bore every sign of dust and disuse. Looking closely, I saw that the trap in the door was not only firmly bolted, but *screwed into its socket*.

I turned and said to the warder quietly—

'Is it long since this cell was in use?'

'You're very fond of asking questions,' he answered doggedly.

It was evident he would baffle me by impertinence rather than yield a confidence. A queer insistence had seized me – a strange desire to know more about this mysterious chamber. But, for all my curiosity, I flushed at the man's tone.

'You have your orders,' I said sternly, 'and do well to hold by them. I doubt, nevertheless, if they include impertinence to your superiors.'

'I look straight on my duty, sir,' he said, a little abashed. 'I don't wish to give offence.'

He did not, I feel sure. He followed his instinct to throw me off the scent, that was all.

I strode off in a fume, and after attending F— in the infirmary, went promptly to my own quarters.

I was in an odd frame of mind, and for long tramped my sitting-room to and fro, too restless to go to bed, or, as an alternative, to settle down to a book. There was a welling up in my heart of some emotion that I could neither trace nor define. It seemed neighbour to terror, neighbour to an intense fainting pity, yet was not distinctly either of these. Indeed, where was cause for one, or the subject of the other? F— might have endured mental sufferings which it was only human to help to end, yet F— was a swindling rogue, who, once relieved, merited no further consideration.

It was not on him my sentiments were wasted. Who, then, was responsible for them?

There was a very plain line of demarcation between the legitimate spirit of inquiry and mere apish curiosity. I could recognise it, I have no doubt, as a rule, yet in my then mood, under the influence of a kind of morbid seizure, inquisitiveness took me by the throat. I could not whistle my mind from the chase of a certain graveyard will-o'-wisp; and on it went stumbling and floundering through bog and mire, until it fell into a state of collapse, and was useful for nothing else.

I went to bed and to sleep without difficulty, but I was conscious of myself all the time, and of a shadowless horror that seemed to come stealthily out of corners and to bend over and look at me, and to be nothing but a curtain or a hanging coat when I started and stared.

Over and over again this happened, and my temperature rose by leaps, and suddenly I saw that if I failed to assert myself, and promptly, fever would lap me in a consuming fire. Then in a moment I broke into a profuse perspiration, and sank exhausted into delicious unconsciousness.

Morning found me restored to vigour, but still with the maggot of curiosity in my brain. It worked there all day, and for many subsequent days, and at last it seemed as if my every faculty were honeycombed with its ramifications. Then 'this will not do', I thought, but still the tunnelling process went on.

At first I would not acknowledge to myself what all this mental to-do was about. I was ashamed of my new development, in fact, and nervous, too, in a degree of what it might reveal in the matter of moral degeneration; but gradually, as the curious devil mastered me, I grew into such harmony with it that I could shut my eyes no longer to the true purpose of its insistence. It was the *closed cell* about which my thoughts hovered like crows circling round carrion.

'In the dead waste and middle' of a certain night I awoke with a strange, quick recovery of consciousness. There was the passing of a single expiration, and I had been asleep and was awake. I had gone to bed with no sense of premonition or of resolve in a particular direction; I sat up a monomaniac. It was as if, swelling in the silent hours, the tumour of curiosity had come to a head, and in a moment it was necessary to operate upon it.

I make no excuse for my then condition. I am convinced I was the victim of some undistinguishable force, that I was an agent under the control of the supernatural, if you like.

Some thought had been in my mind of late that in my position it was my duty to unriddle the mystery of the closed cell. This was a sop timidly held out to and rejected by my better reason. I sought – and I knew it in my heart – solution of the puzzle, because it was a puzzle with an atmosphere that vitiated my moral fibre. Now, suddenly, I knew I must act, or, by forcing self-control, imperil my mind's stability.

All strung to a sort of exaltation, I rose noiselessly and dressed myself with rapid, nervous hands. My every faculty was focused upon a solitary point. Without and around there was nothing but shadow and uncertainty. I seemed conscious only of a shaft of light, as it were, traversing the darkness and globing itself in a steady disc of radiance on a lonely door.

Slipping out into the great echoing vault of the prison in stockinged feet, I sped with no hesitation of purpose in the direction of the corridor that was my goal. Surely some resolute Providence guided and encompassed me, for no meeting with the night patrol occurred at any point to embarrass or deter me. Like a ghost myself, I flitted along the stone flags of the passages, hardly waking a murmur from them in my progress.

Without, I knew, a wild and stormy wind thundered on the walls of the prison. Within, where the very atmosphere was self-contained, a cold and solemn peace held like an irrevocable judgement.

I found myself as if in a dream before the sealed door that had for days harassed my waking thoughts. Dim light from a distant gas jet made a patch of yellow upon one of its panels; the rest was buttressed with shadow.

A sense of fear and constriction was upon me as I drew softly from my pocket a screwdriver I had brought with me. It never occurred to me, I swear, that the quest was no business of mine, and that even now I could withdraw from it, and no one be the wiser. But I was afraid – I was afraid. And there was not even the negative comfort of knowing that the neighbouring cell was tenanted. It gaped like a ghostly garret next door to a deserted house.

What reason had I to be there at all, or, being there, to fear? I can no more explain than tell how it was that I, an impartial follower of my vocation, had allowed myself to be tricked by that in the nerves I had made it my interest to study and combat in others.

My hand that held the tool was cold and wet. The stiff little shriek of the first screw, as it turned at first uneasily in its socket, sent a jarring thrill through me. But I persevered, and it came out readily by and by, as did the four or five others that held the trap secure.

Then I paused a moment; and, I confess, the quick pant of fear seemed to come grey from my lips. There were sounds about me – the deep breathing of imprisoned men; and I envied the sleepers their hard-wrung repose.

At last, in one access of determination, I put out my hand, and sliding back the bolt, hurriedly flung open the trap. An acrid whiff of dust assailed my nostrils as I stepped back a pace and stood expectant of anything – or nothing. What did I wish, or dread, or foresee? The complete absurdity of my behaviour was revealed to me in a moment. I could shake off the incubus here and now, and be a sane man again.

I giggled, with an actual ring of self-contempt in my voice, as I made a forward movement to close the aperture. I advanced my face to it, and inhaled the sluggish air that stole forth, and – God in heaven!

I had staggered back with that cry in my throat, when I felt fingers like iron clamps close on my arm and hold it. The grip, more than the face I turned to look upon in my surging terror, was forcibly human.

It was the warder Johnson who had seized me, and my heart bounded as I met the cold fury of his eyes.

'Prying!' he said, in a hoarse, savage whisper. 'So you will, will you? And now let the devil help you!'

It was not this fellow I feared, though his white face was

set like a demon's; and in the thick of my terror I made a feeble attempt to assert my authority.

'Let me go!' I muttered. 'What! you dare?'

In his frenzy he shook my arm as a terrier shakes a rat, and, like a dog, he held on, daring me to release myself.

For the moment an instinct half-murderous leapt in me. It sank and was overwhelmed in a slough of some more secret emotion.

'Oh!' I whispered, collapsing, as it were, to the man's fury, even pitifully deprecating it. 'What is it? What's there? It drew me – something unnameable.'

He gave a snapping laugh like a cough. His rage waxed second by second. There was a maniacal suggestiveness in it; and not much longer, it was evident, could he have it under control. I saw it run and congest in his eyes; and, on the instant of its accumulation, he tore at me with a sudden wild strength, and drove me up against the very door of the secret cell.

The action, the necessity of self-defence, restored me to some measure of dignity and sanity.

'Let me go, you ruffian!' I cried, struggling to free myself from his grasp.

It was useless. He held me madly. There was no beating him off: and, so holding me, he managed to produce a single key from one of his pockets, and to slip it with a rusty clang into the lock of the door.

'You dirty, prying civilian!' he panted at me, as he swayed this way and that with the pull of my body. 'You shall have your wish, by G—! You want to see inside, do you? Look, then!'

He dashed open the door as he spoke, and pulled me violently into the opening. A great waft of the cold, dank air came at us, and with it – what?

The warder had jerked his dark lantern from his belt, and now – an arm of his still clasped about one of mine – snapped the slide open.

'Where is it?' he muttered, directing the disc of light round and about the floor of the cell. I ceased struggling. Some counter influence was raising an odd curiosity in me.

'Ah!' he cried, in a stifled voice, 'there you are, my friend!'

He was setting the light slowly travelling along the stone flags close by the wall over against us, and now, so guiding it, looked askance at me with a small, greedy smile.

'Follow the light, sir,' he whispered jeeringly.

I looked, and saw twirling on the floor, in the patch of radiance cast by the lamp, *a little eddy of dust*, it seemed. This eddy was never still, but went circling in that stagnant place without apparent cause or influence; and, as it circled, it moved slowly on by wall and corner, so that presently in its progress it must reach us where we stood.

Now, draughts will play queer freaks in quiet places, and of this trifling phenomenon I should have taken little note ordinarily. But, I must say at once, that as I gazed upon the odd moving thing my heart seemed to fall in upon itself like a drained artery.

'Johnson!' I cried, 'I must get out of this. I don't know what's the matter, or— Why do you hold me? D— it! man, let me go; let me go, I say!'

As I grappled with him he dropped the lantern with a crash and flung his arms violently about me.

'You don't!' he panted, the muscles of his bent and rigid neck seeming actually to cut into my shoulder-blade. 'You don't, by G—! You came of your own accord, and now you shall take your bellyful!'

It was a struggle for life or death, or, worse, for life and reason. But I was young and wiry, and held my own, if I could do little more. Yet there was something to combat beyond the mere brute strength of the man I struggled with, for I fought in an atmosphere of horror unexplainable, and I knew that inch by inch the *thing* on the floor was circling round in our direction.

Suddenly in the breathing darkness I felt it close upon us,

gave one mortal yell of fear, and, with a last despairing fury, tore myself from the encircling arms, and sprang into the corridor without. As I plunged and leapt, the warder clutched at me, missed, caught a foot on the edge of the door, and, as the latter whirled to with a clap, fell heavily at my feet in a fit. Then, as I stood staring down upon him, steps sounded along the corridor and the voices of scared men hurrying up.

Ill and shaken, and, for the time, little in love with life, yet fearing death as I had never dreaded it before, I spent the rest of that horrible night huddled between my crumpled sheets, fearing to look forth, fearing to think, wild only to be far away, to be housed in some green and innocent hamlet, where I might forget the madness and the terror in learning to walk the unvext paths of placid souls. That unction I could lay to my heart, at least. I had done the manly part by the stricken warder, whom I had attended to his own home, in a row of little tenements that stood south of the prison walls. I had replied to all inquiries with some dignity and spirit, attributing my ruffled condition to an assault on the part of Johnson, when he was already under the shadow of his seizure. I had directed his removal, and grudged him no professional attention that it was in my power to bestow. But afterwards, locked into my room, my whole nervous system broke up like a trodden ant-hill, leaving me conscious of nothing but an aimless scurrying terror and the black swarm of thoughts, so that I verily fancied my reason would give under the strain.

Yet I had more to endure and to triumph over.

Near morning I fell into a troubled sleep, throughout which the drawn twitch of muscle seemed an accent on every word of ill-omen I had ever spelt out of the alphabet of fear. If my body rested, my brain was an open chamber for any toad of ugliness that listed to 'sit at squat' in.

Suddenly I woke to the fact that there was a knocking at my door – that there had been for some little time.

I cried, 'Come in!' finding a weak restorative in the mere sound of my own human voice; then, remembering the key was turned, bade the visitor wait until I could come to him.

Scrambling, feeling dazed and white-livered, out of bed, I opened the door, and met one of the warders on the threshold. The man looked scared, and his lips, I noticed, were set in a somewhat boding fashion.

'Can you come at once, sir?' he said. 'There's summat wrong with the Governor.'

'Wrong? What's the matter with him?'

'Why' – he looked down, rubbed an imaginary protuberance smooth with his foot, and glanced up at me again with a quick, furtive expression – 'he's got his face set in the grating of 47, and danged if a man Jack of us can get him to move or speak.'

I turned away, feeling sick. I hurriedly pulled on coat and trousers, and hurriedly went off with my summoner. Reason was all absorbed in a wildest phantasy of apprehension.

'Who found him?' I muttered, as we sped on.

'Vokins see him go down the corridor about half after eight, sir, and see him give a start like when he noticed the trap open. It's never been so before in my time. Johnson must ha' done it last night, before he were took.'

'Yes, yes.'

'The man said the Governor went to shut it, it seemed, and to draw his face to'ards the bars in so doin'. Then he see him a-lookin' through, as he thought; but nat'rally it weren't no business of his'n, and he went off about his work. But when he come anigh agen, fifteen minutes later, there were the Governor in the same position; and he got scared over it, and called out to one or two of us.'

'Why didn't one of you ask the Major if anything was wrong?'

'Bless you! we did; and no answer. And we pulled him, compatible with discipline, but—'

'But what?'

'He's stuck.'

'Stuck!'

'See for yourself, sir. That's all I ask.'

I did, a moment later. A little group was collected about the door of cell 47, and the members of it spoke together in whispers, as if they were frightened men. One young fellow, with a face white in patches, as if it had been floured, slid from them as I approached, and accosted me tremulously.

'Don't go anigh, sir. There's something wrong about the place.'

I pulled myself together, forcibly beating down the excitement reawakened by the associations of the spot. In the discomfiture of others' nerves I found my own restoration.

'Don't be an ass!' I said, in a determined voice. 'There's nothing here that can't be explained. Make way for me, please!'

They parted and let me through, and I saw him. He stood, spruce, frock-coated, dapper, as he always was, with his face pressed against and into the grill, and either hand raised and clenched tightly round a bar of the trap. His posture was as of one caught and striving frantically to release himself; yet the narrowness of the interval between the rails precluded so extravagant an idea. He stood quite motionless – taut and on the strain, as it were – and nothing of his face was visible but the back ridges of his jawbones, showing white through a bush of red whiskers.

'Major Shrike!' I rapped out, and, allowing myself no hesitation, reached forth my hand and grasped his shoulder. The body vibrated under my touch, but he neither answered nor made sign of hearing me. Then I pulled at him forcibly, and ever with increasing strength. His fingers held like steel braces. He seemed glued to the trap, like Theseus to the rock.

Hastily I peered round, to see if I could get a glimpse of his face. I noticed enough to send me back with a little stagger.

'Has none of you got a key to this door?' I asked, reviewing the scared faces about me, than which my own was no less troubled, I feel sure.

'Only the Governor, sir,' said the warder who had fetched me. 'There's not a man but him amongst us that ever seen this opened.'

He was wrong there, I could have told him; but held my tongue, for obvious reasons.

'I want it opened. Will one of you feel in his pockets?'

Not a soul stirred. Even had not sense of discipline precluded, that of a certain inhuman atmosphere made fearful creatures of them all.

'Then,' said I, 'I must do it myself.'

I turned once more to the stiff-strung figure, had actually put hand on it, when an exclamation from Vokins arrested me.

'There's a key – there, sir!' he said – 'stickin' out yonder between his feet.'

Sure enough there was – Johnson's, no doubt, that had been shot from its socket by the clapping to of the door, and afterwards kicked aside by the warder in his convulsive struggles.

I stooped, only too thankful for the respite, and drew it forth. I had seen it but once before, yet I recognised it at a glance.

Now, I confess, my heart felt ill as I slipped the key into the wards, and a sickness of resentment at the tyranny of Fate in making me its helpless minister surged up in my veins. Once, with my fingers on the iron loop, I paused, and ventured a fearful side glance at the figure whose crooked elbow almost touched my face; then, strung to the high pitch of inevitability, I shot the lock, pushed at the door, and in the act, made a back leap into the corridor.

Scarcely, in doing so, did I look for the totter and collapse outwards of the rigid form. I had expected to see it fall away, face down, into the cell, as its support swung from it. Yet it was, I swear, as if *something* from within had relaxed its grasp and given the fearful dead man a swingeing push outwards as the door opened.

It went on its back, with a dusty slap on the stone flags, and from all its spectators – me included – came a sudden drawn sound, like a wind in a keyhole.

What can I say, or how describe it? A dead thing it was – but the face!

Barred with livid scars where the grating rails had crossed it, the rest seemed to have been worked and kneaded into a mere featureless plate of yellow and expressionless flesh.

And it was this I had seen in the glass!

There was an interval following the experience above narrated, during which a certain personality that had once been mine was effaced or suspended, and I seemed a passive creature, innocent of the least desire of independence. It was not that I was actually ill or actually insane. A merciful Providence set my finer wits slumbering, that was all, leaving me a sufficiency of the grosser faculties that were necessary to the right ordering of my behaviour.

I kept to my room, it is true, and even lay a good deal in bed; but this was more to satisfy the busy scruples of a *locum tenens* – a practitioner of the neighbourhood, who came daily to the prison to officiate in my absence – than to cosset a complaint that in its inactivity was purely negative. I could review what had happened with a calmness as profound as if I had read of it in a book. I could have wished to continue my duties, indeed, had the power of insistence remained to me. But the saner medicus was acute where I had gone blunt, and bade me to the restful course. He was right. I was mentally stunned, and had I not slept off my lethargy, I should have gone mad in an hour – leapt at a bound, probably, from inertia to flaming lunacy.

I remembered everything, but through a fluffy atmosphere, so to speak. It was as if I looked on bygone pictures through ground glass that softened the ugly outlines.

Sometimes I referred to these to my substitute, who was wise to answer me according to my mood; for the truth left me unruffled, whereas an obvious evasion of it would have distressed me.

'Hammond,' I said one day, 'I have never yet asked you. How did I give my evidence at the inquest?'

'Like a doctor and a sane man.'

'That's good. But it was a difficult course to steer. You conducted the postmortem. Did any peculiarity in the dead man's face strike you?'

'Nothing but this: that the excessive contraction of the bicipital muscles had brought the features into such forcible contact with the bars as to cause bruising and actual abrasion. He must have been dead some little time when you found him.'

'And nothing else? You noticed nothing else in his face – a sort of obliteration of what makes one human, I mean?'

'Oh, dear, no! nothing but the painful constriction that marks any ordinary fatal attack of angina pectoris.— There's a rum breach of promise case in the paper today. You should read it; it'll make you laugh.'

I had no more inclination to laugh than to sigh; but I accepted the change of subject with an equanimity now habitual to me.

One morning I sat up in bed, and knew that consciousness was wide awake in me once more. It had slept, and now rose refreshed, but trembling. Looking back, all in a flutter of new responsibility, along the misty path by way of which I had recently loitered, I shook with an awful thankfulness at sight of the pitfalls I had skirted and escaped – of the demons my witlessness had baffled.

The joy of life was in my heart again, but chastened and made pitiful by experience.

Hammond noticed the change in me directly he entered, and congratulated me upon it.

'Go slow at first, old man,' he said. 'You've fairly sloughed the old skin; but give the sun time to toughen the new one. Walk in it at present, and be content.'

I was, in great measure, and I followed his advice. I got leave of absence, and ran down for a month in the country to a certain house we wot of, where kindly ministration to my convalescence was only one of the many blisses to be put to an account of rosy days.

> 'Then did my love awake,
>   Most like a lily-flower,
> And as the lovely queene of heaven,
>   So shone shee in her bower.'

Ah, me! ah, me! when was it? A year ago, or two-thirds of a lifetime? Alas! 'Age with stealing steps hath clawde me with his crowch'. And will the yews root in *my* heart, I wonder?

I was well, sane, recovered, when one morning, towards the end of my visit, I received a letter from Hammond, enclosing a packet addressed to me, and jealously sealed and fastened. My friend's communication ran as follows:

'There died here yesterday afternoon a warder, Johnson – he who had that apoplectic seizure, you will remember, the night before poor Shrike's exit. I attended him to the end, and, being alone with him an hour before the finish, he took the enclosed from under his pillow, and a solemn oath from me that I would forward it direct to you sealed as you will find it, and permit no other soul to examine or even touch it. I acquit myself of the charge, but, my dear fellow, with an uneasy sense of the responsibility I incur in thus possibly suggesting to you a retrospect of events which you had much best consign to the limbo of the – not inexplainable, but not worth trying to explain. It was patent from what I have gathered that you were in an overstrung and excitable condition at that time, and that your temporary collapse was purely nervous in its character. It seems there was some nonsense abroad in the prison about a certain cell, and that there were fools who thought fit to associate Johnson's attack and the

other's death with the opening of that cell's door. I have
given the new Governor a tip, and he has stopped all that.
We have examined the cell in company, and found it, as one
might suppose, a very ordinary chamber. The two men died
perfectly natural deaths, and there is the last to be said on
the subject. I mention it only from the fear that the enclosed
may contain some allusion to the rubbish, a perusal of which
might check the wholesome convalescence of your thoughts.
If you take my advice, you will throw the packet into the
fire unread. At least, if you *do* examine it, postpone the duty
till you feel yourself absolutely impervious to any mental
trickery, and – bear in mind that you are a worthy member
of a particularly matter-of-fact and unemotional profession.'

I smiled at the last clause, for I was now in a condition to
feel a rather warm shame over my erst weak-knee'd collapse
before a sheet and an illuminated turnip. I took the packet
to my bedroom, shut the door, and sat myself down by the
open window. The garden lay below me, and the dewy
meadows beyond. In the one, bees were busy ruffling the
ruddy gillyflowers and April stocks; in the other, the hedge
twigs were all frosted with Mary buds, as if Spring had brushed
them with the fleece of her wings in passing.

I fetched a sigh of content as I broke the seal of the packet
and brought out the enclosure. Somewhere in the garden a
little sardonic laugh was clipt to silence. It came from groom
or maid, no doubt; yet it thrilled me with an odd feeling of
uncanniness, and I shivered slightly.

'Bah!' I said to myself determinedly. 'There is a shrewd
nip in the wind, for all the show of sunlight'; and I rose,
pulled down the window, and resumed my seat.

Then in the closed room, that had become deathly quiet
by contrast, I opened and read the dead man's letter.

'SIR, – I hope you will read what I here put down. I lay it
on you as a solemn injunction, for I am a dying man, and

I know it. And to who is my death due, and the Governor's death, if not to you, for your pryin' and curiosity, as surely as if you had drove a nife through our harts? Therefore, I say, Read this, and take my burden from me, for it has been a burden; and now it is right that you that interfered should have it on your own mortal shoulders. The Major is dead and I am dying, and in the first of my fit it went on in my head like cimbells that the trap was left open, and that if he passed he would look in and it would get him. For he knew not fear, neither would he submit to bullying by God or devil.

'Now I will tell you the truth, and Heaven quit you of your responsibility in our destruction.

'There wasn't another man to me like the Governor in all the countries of the world. Once he brought me to life after doctors had given me up for dead; but he willed it, and I lived; and ever afterwards I loved him as a dog loves its master. That was in the Punjab; and I came home to England with him, and was his servant when he got his appointment to the jail here. I tell you he was a proud and fierce man, but under control and tender to those he favoured; and I will tell you also a strange thing about him. Though he was a soldier and an officer, and strict in discipline as made men fear and admire him, his hart at bottom was all for books, and literature, and such-like gentle crafts. I had his confidence, as a man gives his confidence to his dog, and before others. In this way I learnt the bitter sorrow of his life. He had once hoped to be a poet, acknowledged as such before the world. He was by natur' an idelist, as they call it, and God knows what it meant to him to come out of the woods, so to speak, and swet in the dust of cities; but he did it, for his will was of tempered steel. He buried his dreams in the clouds and came down to earth greatly resolved, but with one undying hate. It is not good to hate as he could, and worse to be hated by such as him; and I will tell you the story, and what it led to.

'It was when he was a subaltern that he made up his mind to the plunge. For years he had placed all his hopes and confidents in a book of verses he had wrote, and added to, and improved during that time. A little encouragement, a little word of praise, was all he looked for, and then he was redy to buckle to again, profitin' by advice, and do better. He put all the love and beauty of his hart into that book, and at last, after doubt, and anguish, and much diffidents, he published it, and give it to the world. Sir, it fell what they call still-born from the press. It was like a green leaf flutterin' down in a dead wood. To a proud and hopeful man, bubblin' with music, the pain of neglect, when he come to relise it, was terrible. But nothing was said, and there was nothing to say. In silence he had to endure and suffer.

'But one day, during manoovers, there came to the camp a grey-faced man, a newspaper correspondent, and young Shrike nocked up a friendship with him. Now how it come about I cannot tell, but so it did that this skip-kennel wormed the lad's sorrow out of him, and his confidents, swore he'd been damnabilly used, and that when he got back he'd crack up the book himself in his own paper. He was a fool for his pains, and a serpent in his croolty. The notice come out as promised, and, my God! the author was laughed and mocked at from beginning to end. Even confidentses he had given to the creature was twisted to his ridicule, and his very appearance joked over. And the mess got wind of it, and made a rare story for the dog days.

'He bore it like a soldier and that he became hart and liver from the moment. But he put something to the account of the grey-faced man and locked it up in his breast.

'He come across him again years afterwards in India, and told him very politely that he hadn't forgotten him, and didn't intend to. But he was anigh losin' sight of him there for ever and a day, for the creature took cholera, or what looked like it, and rubbed shoulders with death and the devil before he pulled through. And he come across him again over here, and that was the last of him, as you shall see presently.

'Once, after I knew the Major (he were Captain then), I was a-brushin' his coat, and he stood a long while before the glass. Then he twisted upon me, with a smile on his mouth, and says he—

'"The dog was right, Johnson: this isn't the face of a poet. I was a presumtious ass, and born to cast up figgers with a pen behind my ear."

'"Captain," I says, "if you was skinned, you'd look like any other man without his. The quality of a soul isn't expressed by a coat."

'"Well," he answers, "my soul's pretty clean-swept, I think, save for one Bluebeard chamber in it that's been kep' locked ever so many years. It's nice and dirty by this time, I expect," he says. Then the grin comes on his mouth again. "I'll open it some day," he says, "and look. There's something in it about comparing me to a dancing dervish, with the wind in my petticuts. Perhaps I'll get the chance to set somebody else dancing by-and-by."

'He did, and took it, and the Bluebeard chamber come to be opened in this very jail.

'It was when the system was lying fallow, so to speak, and the prison was deserted. Nobody was there but him and me and the echoes from the empty courts. The contract for restoration hadn't been signed, and for months, and more than a year, we lay idle, nothing bein' done.

'Near the beginnin' of this period, one day comes, for the third time of the Major's seein' him, the grey-faced man. "Let bygones be bygones," he says. "I was a good friend to you, though you didn't know it; and now, I expect, you're in the way to thank me."

'"I am," says the Major.

'"Of course," he answers. "Where would be your fame and reputation as one of the leadin' prison reformers of the day if you had kep' on in that riming nonsense?"

'"Have you come for my thanks?" says the Governor.

'"I've come," says the grey-faced man, "to examine and report upon your system."

'"For your paper?"

'"Possibly; but to satisfy myself of its efficacy, in the first instance."

'"You aren't commissioned, then?"

'"No; I come on my own responsibility."

'"Without consultation with anyone?"

'"Absolutely without. I haven't even a wife to advise me," he says, with a yellow grin. What once passed for cholera had set the bile on his skin like paint, and he had caught a manner of coughing behind his hand like a toast-master.

'"I know," says the Major, looking him steady in the face, "that what you say about me and my affairs is sure to be actuated by conscientious motives."

'"Ah," he answers. "You're sore about that review still, I see."

'"Not at all," says the Major; "and, in proof, I invite you to be my guest for the night, and tomorrow I'll show you over the prison and explain my system."

'The creature cried, "Done!" and they set to and discussed jail matters in great earnestness. I couldn't guess the Governor's intentions, but, somehow, his manner troubled me. And yet I can remember only one point of his talk. He were always dead against making public show of his birds. "They're there for reformation, not ignominy," he'd say. Prisons in the old days were often, with the asylum and the work'us, made the holiday show-places of towns. I've heard of one Justice of the Peace, up North, who, to save himself trouble, used to sign a lot of blank orders for leave to view, so that applicants needn't bother him when they wanted to go over. They've changed all that, and the Governor were instrumental in the change.

'"It's against my rule," he said that night, "to exhibit to a stranger without a Government permit; but, seein' the place is empty, and for old remembrance' sake, I'll make an exception in your favour, and you shall learn all I can show you of the inside of a prison."

'Now this was natural enough; but I was uneasy.

'He treated his guest royly; so much that when we assembled the next mornin' for the inspection, the grey-faced man were shaky as a wet dog. But the Major were all set prim and dry, like the soldier he was.

'We went straightaway down corridor B, and at cell 47 we stopped.

'"We will begin our inspection here," said the Governor. "Johnson, open the door."

'I had the keys of the row; fitted in the right one, and pushed open the door.

'"After you, sir," said the Major; and the creature walked in, and he shut the door on him.

'I think he smelt a rat at once, for he began beating on the wood and calling out to us. But the Major only turned round to me with his face like a stone.

'"Take that key from the bunch," he said, "and give it to me." I obeyed, all in a tremble, and he took and put it in his pocket.

'"My God, Major!" I whispered, "what are you going to do with him?"

'"Silence, sir!" he said; "How dare you question your superior officer!"

'And the noise inside grew louder.

'The Governor, he listened to it a moment like music; then he unbolted and flung open the trap, and the creature's face came at it like a wild beast's.

'"Sir," said the Major to it, "you can't better understand my system than by experiencing it. What an article for your paper you could write already – almost as pungint a one as that in which you ruined the hopes and prospects of a young cockney poet."

'The man mouthed at the bars. He was half-mad, I think, in that one minute.

'"Let me out!" he screamed. "This is a hidius joke! Let me out!"

'"When you are quite quiet – deathly quiet," said the Major, "you shall come out. Not before"; and he shut the trap in its face very softly.

'"Come, Johnson, march!" he said, and took the lead, and we walked out of the prison.

'I was like to faint, but I dared not disobey, and the man's screeching followed us all down the empty corridors and halls, until we shut the first great door on it.

'It may have gone on for hours, alone in that awful emptiness. The creature was a reptile, but the thought sickened my heart.

'And from that hour till his death, five months later, he rotted and maddened in his dreadful tomb.'

There was more, but I pushed the ghastly confession from me at this point in uncontrollable loathing and terror. Was it possible – possible, that injured vanity could so falsify its victim's every tradition of decency?

'Oh!' I muttered, 'what a disease is ambition! Who takes one step towards it puts his foot on Alsirat!'

It was minutes before my shocked nerves were equal to a resumption of the task; but at last I took it up again, with a groan.

'I don't think at first I realised the full mischief the Governor intended to do. At least, I hoped he only meant to give the man a good fright and then let him go. I might have known better. How could he ever release him without ruining himself?

'The next morning he summoned me to attend him. There was a strange new look of triumph in his face, and in his hand he held a heavy hunting-crop. I pray to God he acted in madness, but my duty and obedience was to him.

'"There is sport towards, Johnson," he said. "My dervish has got to dance."

'I followed him quiet. We listened when I opened the jail door, but the place was silent as the grave. But from the cell, when we reached it, came a low, whispering sound.

'The Governor slipped the trap and looked through.

'"All right," he said, and put the key in the door and flung it open.

'He were sittin' crouched on the ground, and he looked up at us vacant-like. His face were all fallen down, as it were, and his mouth never ceased to shake and whisper.

'The Major shut the door and posted me in a corner. Then he moved to the creature with his whip.

'"Up!" he cried. "Up, you dervish, and dance to us!" and he brought the thong with a smack across his shoulders.

'The creature leapt under the blow, and then to his feet with a cry, and the Major whipped him till he danced. All round the cell he drove him, lashing and cutting – and again, and many times again, until the poor thing rolled on the floor whimpering and sobbing. I shall have to give an account of this some day. I shall have to whip my master with a red-hot serpent round the blazing furnace of the pit, and I shall do it with agony, because here my love and my obedience was to him.

'When it was finished, he bade me put down food and drink that I had brought with me, and come away with him; and we went, leaving him rolling on the floor of the cell, and shut him alone in the empty prison until we should come again at the same time tomorrow.

'So day by day this went on, and the dancing three or four times a week, until at last the whip could be left behind, for the man would scream and begin to dance at the mere turning of the key in the lock. And he danced for four months, but not the fifth.

'Nobody official came near us all this time. The prison stood lonely as a deserted ruin where dark things have been done.

'Once, with fear and trembling, I asked my master how

he would account for the inmate of 47 if he was suddenly called upon by authority to open the cell; and he answered, smiling—

'"I should say it was my mad brother. By his own account, he showed me a brother's love, you know. It would be thought a liberty; but the authorities, I think, would stretch a point for me. But if I got sufficient notice, I should clear out the cell."

'I asked him how, with my eyes rather than my lips, and he answered me only with a look.

'And all this time he was, outside the prison, living the life of a good man – helping the needy, ministering to the poor. He even entertained occasionally, and had more than one noisy party in his house.

'But the fifth month the creature danced no more. He was a dumb, silent animal then, with matted hair and beard; and when one entered he would only look up at one pitifully, as if he said, "My long punishment is nearly ended." How it came that no inquiry was ever made about him I know not, but none ever was. Perhaps he was one of the wandering gentry that nobody ever knows where they are next. He was unmarried, and had apparently not told of his intended journey to a soul.

'And at the last he died in the night. We found him lying stiff and stark in the morning, and scratched with a piece of black crust on a stone of the wall these strange words: "An Eddy on the Floor". Just that – nothing else.

'Then the Governor came and looked down, and was silent. Suddenly he caught me by the shoulder.

'"Johnson," he cried, "if it was to do again, I would do it! I repent of nothing. But he has paid the penalty, and we call quits. May he rest in peace!"

'"Amen!" I answered low. Yet I knew our turn must come for this.

'We buried him in quicklime under the wall where the murderers lie, and I made the cell trim and rubbed out the writing, and the Governor locked all up and took away the key. But he locked in more than he bargained for.

'For months the place was left to itself, and neither of us went anigh 47. Then one day the workmen was to be put in, and the Major he took me round with him for a last examination of the place before they come.

'He hesitated a bit outside a particular cell; but at last he drove in the key and kicked open the door.

'"My God!" he says, "he's dancing still!"

'My heart was thumpin', I tell you, as I looked over his shoulder. What did we see? What you well understand, sir; but, for all it was no more than that, we knew as well as if it was shouted in our ears that it was him, dancin'. It went round by the walls and drew towards us, and as it stole near I screamed out, "An Eddy on the Floor!" and seized and dragged the Major out and clapped to the door behind us.

'"Oh!" I said, "in another moment it would have had us."

'He looked at me gloomily.

'"Johnson," he said, "I'm not to be frightened or coerced. He may dance, but he shall dance alone. Get a screwdriver and some screws and fasten up this trap. No one from this time looks into this cell."

'I did as he bid me, swetin'; and I swear all the time I wrought I dreaded a hand would come through the trap and clutch mine.

'On one pretex' or another, from that day till the night you meddled with it, he kep' that cell as close shut as a tomb. And he went his ways, discardin' the past from that time forth. Now and again a over-sensitive prisoner in the next cell would complain of feelin' uncomfortable. If possible, he would be removed to another; if not, he was dam'd for his fancies. And so it might be goin' on to now, if you hadn't pried and interfered. I don't blame you at this moment, sir. Likely you were an instrument in the hands of Providence; only, as the instrument, you must now take the burden of the truth on your own shoulders. I am a dying man, but I cannot die till I have confessed. Per'aps you may find it in your hart some day to give up a prayer for me – but it must be for the Major as well.

'Your obedient servant,
J. JOHNSON'

What comment of my own can I append to this wild narrative? Professionally, and apart from personal experiences, I should rule it the composition of an epileptic. That a noted journalist, nameless as he was and is to me, however nomadic in habit, could disappear from human ken, and his fellows rest content to leave him unaccounted for, seems a tax upon credulity so stupendous that I cannot seriously endorse the statement.

Yet, also – there *is* that little matter of my personal experience.

ACKNOWLEDGEMENTS

At the eleventh hour, the 1998 edition of *The Black Reaper* was transformed from simply an enlarged version to something quite different, thanks to a chance letter from Capes's grandson, Ian Burns. A friend had sent him my introduction to the first edition, and Ian wrote to me from Melbourne with no more to go on than my name and the town I live in. Not only that, he wrote scant weeks before the book was due to be typeset. A month or so later and it would all have been in vain.

So my first acknowledgements and thanks go to the Capes family, for supplying the kind of material you cannot get other than from an author's relatives: Ian Burns, for making contact, supplying pictures of Bernard Capes and the Winchester plaque, for writing his splendid foreword, and for revealing the existence of Bevis Cane; Brion Burns, Nerine's elder son, for supplying a much appreciated copy of *The Hampshire Observer*'s report of Bernard's memorial service in 1919, where his plaque was unveiled; the late Helen Capes, Renalt's widow, who turned out to live near me, and kindly supplied much valuable background on the Capes household and the subsequent history of Bernard's children; Harriet Capes, Helen's daughter, who sent me a copy of Renalt's unpublished memoir, full of invaluable Capes family history; and Elissa, Ian Burns's daughter, who paid me a surprise visit with her husband Geoff on 29 May 1998 while on a trip to

England. I hope they approve of this new edition of tales by their distinguished ancestor.

The Black Reaper goes back some years, of course, and my grateful thanks are due to the late Michael Cox, who was responsible for publishing the first edition in 1989, as part of his splendid but short-lived Chillers series for Equation/Thorsons.

That fine researcher, the late Richard Dalby, supplied what biographical details we had of Bernard Capes for the first edition, and without his priceless work the book would have been pretty thin. Thanks also to the staff of Sutton Public Library, who tracked down all but one of Capes's books of short stories.

And finally, my friend Mike Ashley, who drove the pair of us to Winchester on 10 May 2000, to look for Bernard Capes' grave. We didn't find it (discovering later he had been cremated) but we did find two houses where he had lived. The kindly owners of the last one he occupied invited us in. When we explained our search for Bernard Capes, the husband popped upstairs for a while and came back with a bundle of old papers and deeds that had been in the house when they bought it. Among them were several letters and deeds signed by Rosalie herself. A memorable day – thanks, Mike.

BIBLIOGRAPHY

As explained in the introduction, Bernard Capes gathered together at various intervals those stories he had published in magazines, and tied them up into very enjoyable books of short stories. It is those books I have consulted, not the magazines.

The stories in this edition of *The Black Reaper* are taken from the following sources:

At a Winter's Fire (Pearson, 1899)
'The Black Reaper'
'Dark Dignum'
'An Eddy on the Floor'
'The Moon Stricken'
'The Vanishing House'
'William Tyrwhitt's "Copy"'

From Door to Door (Blackwoods, 1900)
'The Sword of Corporal Lacoste'

Plots (Methuen, 1902)
'The Accursed Cordonnier'
'The Green Bottle'

Loaves and Fishes (Methuen, 1906)
'A Gallows-bird'
'Poor Lucy Rivers'
'The Strength of the Rope'

The Fabulists (Mills and Boon, 1915)
'The Apothecary's Revenge'
'The Closed Door'
'The Dark Compartment'
'The Glass Ball'
'The Marble Hands'
'The Mask'
'A Queer Cicerone'
'The Queer Picture'
'The Shadow-Dance'
'The Thing in the Forest'
'The White Hare'

All Capes's books of stories are well worth finding. Another volume, *Historical Vignettes* (T. Fisher Unwin, 1910; revised and enlarged version, Sidgwick & Jackson, 1912) contains no tales of terror but is an interesting collection of stories based on historical figures, ranging from Beau Brummel to Cleopatra.

There is another collection of stories, *Bag and Baggage* (Constable, 1913) worth tracking down, although it is very rare. It is not Bernard Capes at full strength, but is still of interest.